THE LAST OF THE MAGI

THE LAST OF THE MAGI

The Devouring

Book I

Story by G.S. Eli

G. S. ELI AND PATRICK WILEY

ISBN: 979-8-2180523-3-1

This novel is dedicated to the countless Roma who lost their lives at the hands of the Nazis in the Porajmos.

May we never forget those who were maliciously targeted in one of the darkest periods in history.
Te aven yerto

(Rest in peace)

Dear Reader,

Growing up a Romani boy in America, my parents kept me out of school, as is tradition, so I never formally learned how to read and write or about history for that matter. I did attend some school, but too little to be considered fully literate by anybody's standards.

My only true education came from sitting in front of the television, watching movies, sitcoms, and the occasional newsreel, and that's where I would see old black and white footage of Adolf Hitler and Nazis. Although I was too young to know what the Holocaust meant or to understand the Roma involvement, the images would deeply frighten me.

As I grew up, always absorbing what was being projected on the screen, I learned more. I was taught that Hitler and the Nazi movement murdered some six million Jews and countless Roma, because he wanted a pure Aryan race, and believed in white superiority. Even as a child, this did not sit right with me. To better explain, being Romani, I was taught to be more religious than analytical...and I always felt that this deep-seeded hatred that the Nazis felt toward non-Aryan groups was more spiritual than the academics and historians would believe.

For years, I kept this "feeling" to myself, mainly because I did not have any religious or historical evidence to back this up, nor did I have any clear understanding of the Third Reich. All I knew were two things, that this was not solely about racial purity, and white supremacy, I was sure about that.

One day I was more fed up than usual, and skimming through the TV, watching teenagers glorifying vampire cults and Vlad Dracula, this also disgusted me deep to my core. I remember saying to a friend, "*This is crazy, Vlad Dracula was a real evil man who murdered many Roma just like Hitler,*" and that was the moment my feeling turned from just a simple feeling, to a real spiritual awakening.

I could not overcome the overwhelming sensation to put this into writing... However, I had no writing experience, nor could I even read very well... Nevertheless, I sat in front of my laptop and began to type. I had no idea where I would start or what would wind up on the page, all I knew was to type! Forty days later, I had the first draft of the novel that you are about to read. I would very much love to take credit for the story and all its theories, however, I truly believe I became a vessel for a higher power. Believe me if you will, either way, I know that as you read, you will agree that this is eerily close to the truth.

G. S. Eli

MUNICH, GERMANY, 1919

The young German corporal breathed in the sweet, exotic smell of incense as the Gypsy guided him into her parlor. She drew back a thick, red velvet curtain and gestured for him to pass through a narrow doorway into a small, dimly lit back room.

Seating herself on the far side of a tiny round table, she gestured for him to take the chair opposite her. As he sat down, he could feel the heat from the half dozen candles that flickered eerily in ruby glass jars, like something in a church or shrine.

"Give me your hand," the Gypsy said.

The soldier was suddenly filled with an indescribable fear. Ancient and frail as she was, this woman surely couldn't hurt him. Yet he found himself terrified. He could hear his mother's voice from long ago, telling the innocent child he had once been, "My son, beware of the Gypsies! Satan himself created them. He put Gypsies on the Earth to steal from good German people."

The soldier had never forgotten his mother's warning. Nervously slicking his dark hair to the side and stuttering a bit, he told the old woman, "I ... I didn't come here for a palm reading."

"Yes, I see. You are here because you want something. You are a seeker," she said with a piercing stare. "And what is it that you seek from me, an old Gypsy woman?"

The corporal stared back at her. Taking a moment to survey her feeble frame, he reminded himself that she posed no danger to him at all. He made a manful effort to summon his strength and tell her why he'd come, what he sought. He looked down at his chest, glancing at the black metal cross he'd been awarded when wounded in battle. The medallion seemed to give him the courage to answer the crone.

Adjusting his posture, he replied in his sternest voice, "I was badly hurt in the war. I nearly died. Then somehow, in almost no time, I was mysteriously healed. A woman in the hospital told me something I never forgot. She said, 'Ask the Gypsies. The Gypsies carry special gifts within that provide the answers to many questions, the solutions to many mysteries, the keys to many conundrums.' It is for this reason I am here."

The Gypsy paused a moment, sizing up the soldier. He had a strong jaw but a slight frame, and his eyes flickered with a sinister gleam that filled her with deep foreboding. She kept her expression guarded, not wanting to give herself away. "Whoever that woman was, she spoke the truth," the Gypsy replied. "I can tell you how you were wounded in battle. I can tell you why you were mysteriously healed. But the consultation will cost you. Do you have money to pay?"

"Not much. But if you answer my questions, I'll pay you—*after* the consultation. Not before. After all, how can I trust a Gypsy woman to tell me the truth?"

The old woman didn't like to be tested by her clients, nor did she care to be called a thief. She'd heard many such insults in her long life, and now she tired of them easily. She glanced toward the door, then back at her would-be customer.

"Young man, you are wasting my time," she said curtly.

She stood up with finality.

Not wanting to be outdone, the soldier rose, too. He was taller than the diminutive woman, but not by much. He felt small. Trying to get the most from his thin frame, he puffed his chest and stood perfectly straight. Still, he felt small. He was desperate for the knowledge that this woman secreted within her soul, knowledge that should rightfully belong to him, not some thieving Gypsy. He looked into her searching eyes and knew she could sense his desperation. It enraged him. But it was from his rage that the soldier drew strength. Emboldened, he pulled out all the money he had and rebelliously tossed it onto the little table.

"Here's all I have. Take it or leave it."

The Gypsy's practiced eye quickly counted five German marks on her tabletop. If she could just bring herself to answer his invasive silly questions, she could feed her family for two weeks or more. Yet the thought of communing with his spirit troubled her. There was something vile about the man, a darkness in which she did not want to partake.

"I do not want your money. You have offended me. Leave my house," she commanded, regally drawing herself up to her full height.

"No! It is *you* who have offended *me!*" the soldier angrily shouted. "You and your hordes of *zigeuner* have infected our land for centuries!" he went on, using the insulting German word for the people who called themselves the Rom. "Yet we allow you to exist here among our pure race, like bloodsucking fleas infesting a thoroughbred stallion."

Mortified and livid, the woman glared at him. She had faced this kind of racism, as well as persecution, all her life. She thought she had grown used to it. But something about this soldier deeply angered her. *So, he seeks answers, does he?* She thought. *Very well! I will give him the knowledge he seeks, and much more. I will give him the future!* The Gypsy sat down in the semidarkness behind the flickering candles.

"The wounds you suffered in battle were much like those inflicted on Longinus, the Roman soldier who pierced the side of our Lord Jesus Christ. Longinus, too, was blinded, but he was healed by the grace of God," she said. "But you were not healed by God. During the war, when you were digging your trench, you stumbled on an unmarked grave, and from that grave you stole something. That is what healed you."

The soldier was shocked at the woman's magical powers. How could she know about his past and the exact wounds he'd suffered in battle? What's more, how could she know about the artifact, the treasure he'd found lying among the bones, wrapped in a rotted red cloth?

Though he was amazed by what he heard, the corporal realized that he was no better off than when he'd first walked into the Gypsy's parlor. It was no help to him that the woman knew these things. What he wanted was to look behind the curtain into the other world, the world of the secret knowledge of the Gypsies, with their mysterious, perhaps Satanic, power. Where did this power come from? How had this withered old crone used it to divine things that should be out of her reach?

Before he could ask these questions, she continued. "As for you, you are no Longinus, brave-hearted and filled with the love of God. No, your destiny is very different. Your heart is full of hate. The hate will blind you. Until you release that hatred, you will suffer from total blindness. And soon enough, you will surely die." She stood up once more. "Now, leave my house!" she said, pointing a bony finger at the door.

As the young man turned to leave, in a final display of her power, she called out his name, which he had never told her.

"Never return here, Corporal Hitler."

I

THE MAGICIAN

The past is never truly lost. Landscapes and ruins leave tales that can still be told. Visible reminders of what has transpired survive as scars on the land. Nowhere is this more true than in Berlin: a city haunted by its past. For a time, many Berliners were all too happy to see the last century end. Their evil part in three wars—two hot and one cold—had left them ashamed.

But the citizens of Berlin felt different now. After all, they were seven years into a new millennium—and an innovative one at that. Hope was in the air. Berlin was now at the forefront of liberty, freedom, and equality. The only reminders of the evil, racism, and inequality of the past were relegated to museums and historical sites, relics wholly apart from this modern city and its denizens' way of life.

Or so they liked to believe.

In truth, just four train stops from the city's center lay not a museum or memorial but a living reminder, a scar on the land.

Each morning, the first thing west-bound commuters would see as they passed on trains from their comfortable suburbs was filthy black smoke rising from the Strauss Rubber Company. Then, as the train continued, two run-down concrete buildings would gradually emerge from the smog. The abandoned, decrepit highrises, known simply as Building A and Building B, once served as administration offices for communist government workers. The gray towers stood like tombstones of the old regime.

Nestled between the two towering structures lay a shantytown of sorts. The slum was reminiscent of a time when the nation bowed down to acts of pure evil. It should have been a national embarrassment, but those who passed by barely gave it a thought. They cared as little for this place as they did for its inhabitants, for the slum was home to the most hated people in all of Europe. Most called them Gypsies, but they called themselves Rom.

The nameless lot between Building A and Building B was a modern ghetto for the Rom. The slum was tightly packed with threadbare tents and shacks built from scrap wood. If the inhabitants were lucky, they'd have a rusted piece of corrugated metal for a roof, but more often than not, the Rom had only garbage bags to keep out the rain. Though abandoned, the buildings were far from empty. Each of the old apartments and offices could be home to as many as twenty people. Entire extended families lived packed into little concrete boxes.

Outside of Building A, on a windy summer afternoon, a young Roma boy called Mila knelt before his rebuilt BMW motorcycle and finished installing the cables that had arrived in the post earlier that morning. The hulking ramshackle high-rises loomed over him like giant stonework shadows. The installation had taken two long, painstaking hours. Finally, it was done.

He jumped up and folded his tiny pliers back into the base of his BMW key fob. The clever device looked like an ordinary key chain, but it contained everything from screwdrivers to Mila's favorite toy, the lock pick.

He took a seat on the bike, put the key in the ignition, and turned it slowly. He stepped on the kick-starter of the old motorbike and closed his eyes to pray.

"Come on, baby."

He stepped down hard.

Click

Nothing.

He took a deep breath and stepped down again.

Click

"Seriously!" he cried out. He stepped down a few more times. Still nothing.

Mila chided himself for trying to do the job by instinct, instead of using the repair manual. *If I believed in curses, I'd swear this was fate trying to trap me in these damn buildings,* he thought.

He climbed off the bike and looked it over, trying to figure out where his installation job had gone astray.

The motorcycle was a '71 he found in the city dump while searching for scrap metal to barter. Since then, the bike had become his purpose in life. He had put every euro he earned singing on the metro line into restoring it.

Its original color was dark blue. But with some spray paint, it was now a shiny black, which made the chrome seem to glisten even more by contrast. There was no doubt the bike was cool. The sleek, curved frame gave it a vintage look. The chrome tailpipes looked as if flames could spring from them instead of petrol fumes, even if they did need a little polish. And the BMW nameplate told the world that Mila mattered. This was his way of feeling less like a Gypsy, less like a captive of Buildings A and B. He was proud for that one moment when he hopped on the bike and thought, *I matter.* Now he just needed to get it running.

Mila turned away and rummaged through the mess of tools and parts, looking for his repair manual. It was nowhere to be found. Suddenly, his instinct kicked in. He knew where it was, and who took it.

Intent on finding his manual, he ran into Building A, weaved through the piles of rubbish crowding the ground floor, hurtled up the graffiti-spattered stairwell, and disappeared into a squalid labyrinth of hallways in the building's upper reaches. He made his way to a small room and frantically ransacked every drawer and hunted under every piece of furniture, with no luck.

His instinct convinced him that his mischievous 11-year-old twin cousins stole the manual. Not to read, of course. Mila knew that the twins could not read or write. Education had never been a priority to his community. They believed school was something for the *gadje,* the outsiders. Most certainly, the boys stole it to make paper airplanes, or perhaps to ignite a fire in the rusted barrel next to the football field.

Just as hope was fading away, Mila remembered the old wooden chest that served as the family's coffee table. Something about the chest roused his intuition. *I bet the twins stash their bounty in there,* he thought. He threw it open and dug through old pictures, knickknacks, and countless unopened eviction notices sent by the rubber factory that owned Buildings A and B. Sure enough, he came across some of the old comic books he once used to teach himself to read, along with his latest copy of the American comic *Whistleblower,* which he'd been looking for all week. "So, the twins took that, too," he said to himself, annoyed. Finally, he reached the bottom of the black hole of useless junk. No repair manual. By now, Mila had made a pretty decent mess in the already cluttered room.

Suddenly, darkness filled the concrete room as the ambient hum of electricity died.

"Damn it!" Mila shouted, fumbling through the dark room for the light switch. At last, he found the little plastic tab and flipped it. Nothing. *The factory must have found our wire tie-in again*, he guessed.

"Jesus! Could this day get any worse?" Mila shouted.

"Thou shalt not take the Lord's name in vain," his great-aunt Nasta replied from behind the closed door of a tiny side room. "And yes, it can get worse. You're still a Gypsy," she reminded him, both scolding and teasing her nephew.

"Sorry!" he quickly apologized, realizing he should not disturb her while she was in her sanctuary. Mila figured the small nook must have been a walk-in closet for office supplies back in the days of communism. Nasta had converted it to a religious space, and as such it was the only place in the buildings that was peaceful.

The old mystic emerged from the shrine and stepped into the darkened room dressed in her usual hand-sewn outfit. A long skirt brushed the tops of her worn-out house slippers, and she wore a long-sleeved blouse that kept her arms covered even in the heat of the summer. She had a smile on her wrinkled, eighty-year-old face and at least a dozen candles in her frail hands. She stood on her toes and kissed Mila's cheek.

Mila turned and slid open the drapes of the tiny rectangular windows, letting in some sun from the blustery summer day. *I need to find that manual! Where could they have put it?* he asked himself.

"Don't worry about the lights," Nasta said. "I'll send one of the twins to reconnect the cords later. Are you hungry?"

"No," Mila said. "I'm in a rush. I need my motorcycle manual. Have you seen it?"

Nasta ignored his question. She headed to the kitchen and lit a few of the candles, placing them around a makeshift table. She dipped a large spoon into a stew of lumpy white gravy with a bit of meat, ladled it into a bowl, then placed the dish on the table next to the newly-lit candles.

"Come, Mila. Come sit down and have some *himoco* stew," Nasta said.

Mila ignored her request and continued his hunt for the lost manual, now in the dark.

"The stew is getting cold! What are you looking for anyway?" she asked again.

"I told you! I need my motorcycle manual!" he yelled with frustration.

"Mila," Nasta said with a subtle tone of accusation in her voice.

Mila immediately felt ashamed for yelling at the old woman. After all, she had been looking after him since he was an infant. He was an orphan, and Nasta was the only mother figure he had ever known. *Don't be a jerk,* Mila chided himself.

7

"OK," he said with a guilty sigh, "I'm coming."

Taking a seat at the family table, Mila stirred his stew with a spoon. It had the appearance of white glue, but the rich, savory vapors filled his nostrils and made his stomach growl.

Nasta moved to sit next to her great-nephew, smiling broadly again. She noticed how handsome he was getting. He looked older now, more serious than his seventeen years. The gentle flame from candles enhanced his olive complexion, thick sheen black hair, and sharp jawline. She could see the flames dancing in his dark, almond-shaped eyes.

"You have become so handsome, Mila," she said with pride.

Mila ignored the compliment and took a bite out of the traditional stew, which turned out to be pretty good, despite its appearance.

The old woman's smile faded as she turned to a more serious subject. "You had another dream," she said.

Mila had almost forgotten. But now, the terror of his recurring nightmare returned in full force. He'd had it again the night before.

"Mila, we must do a tarot reading to find out what is going on," Nasta warned.

No way, was his first thought. *I'm not getting pulled into that nonsense again. It was fine when I was a kid. But now I just want to fix my bike and get the hell out of here!*

Mila was starting to believe that there was no future for him in Buildings A and B. It was becoming more obvious to him that he was different. He just did not fit in. At the same time, he didn't think he would do much better in *gadjo* school, either. *Anyway, I just need to find that damn manual and I'm out of here!* Mila told himself, though he hadn't yet given much thought as to where he would go.

"Maybe another time," he said sternly.

"Mila, listen to me. I told you that if you had another dream, then that would make three of the same dream in nine days. It's no coincidence that the evil painting was put up in the train station the same day you had the first dream and—"

"Jesus! It's just a painting!" he abruptly interrupted. Everyone in the camp knew the painting's history. It had been the main topic of conversation for weeks. But Nasta insisted it actually possessed evil powers. *No way!* he thought. *Save your spooky fairy tales for the twins!*

For a moment, neither of them said a word.

"May I finish my sentence, please?" Nasta asked, breaking the silence. Mila motioned her to continue. "As I was saying, if you had the same dream on the very same day the painting was put up in the station, then that is the first omen... And if the dream was repeated on the third day, that is the second ome—"

"I know," Mila said, interrupting again. "And if the third dream comes on the ninth day, then it must mean something. Yeah, I got it."

"That's correct!" Nasta said with a gleam in her eyes. "You're not like the rest of us in the buildings, Mila," she reminded him.

"That's for sure," he replied, ironically.

"You are special, Mila," she said.

"If I'm so special, and being a Rom is so great, then how come we gotta live in Building A and Building B like rats? Not to mention stealing power from the factory," he said in frustration.

"Mila, you offend me," she answered. "You think to be a Rom is a curse? It's a gift! We carry the purpose of God in our blood!" she proclaimed.

"It doesn't feel like a gift," he whispered underneath his breath.

Nasta sighed and gazed at Mila softly. "Tell me what you saw in your dream," she pressed.

"Later. I have to find my manual. I'm not spending the rest of my day wasting time with superstition," he said, rising from the table.

Suddenly, with surprising force, Nasta gripped his shoulder and pushed him back down into his seat. Her shocking strength paralyzed him.

A gust of air seemed to come out of nowhere. It blew out the candles.

"There was a woman in a black-hooded cloak. She held a large book," Nasta said, her voice deepening.

Shaken, the bewildered boy simply nodded.

"She directed you. She told you to go up, up to the roof of the building?"

Mila watched as Nasta's eyes drifted to the ceiling, as if she were connecting with the place she called the *Medi*: the mystical realm between heaven and earth, a place one could visit in dreams or in deep meditation, where the ancient mystics could commune with the angels, speak to long-departed loved ones, and conjure powerful magic.

She went on: "The woman, she faded away. Her dust spun into a flock of white birds." Mila nodded once more. "You arrived at the top. There were dark clouds that seemed angry. Did you see an Anubis?"

Mila shrugged, but Nasta didn't see it. She was still gazing up. "I saw a man," he said, "maybe a soldier, only with the head of a dog, like something out of ancient Egypt."

"Yes," Nasta replied. "Yes, the Anubis, he was there. He was leading the family into a church. Only there was water coming out of the church, like it was flooding from the inside." Nasta paused. "Then what?"

Mila just sat in silence, still reluctant. *This is just going to get worse. I need to go!*

Nasta got up and grabbed her deck of tarot cards from the desk. "There is evil coming. Rain is bad in a dream."

"Water is bad?" Mila knew he shouldn't have asked. It would only encourage her and prolong things. But, despite himself, he was curious, and a little spooked. *How could she know what I saw in my dream? And what was that with the candles? The wind, perhaps?* "I read that water meant purity," he said.

"Purity? Where did you read that?" Nasta asked while rifling through her cards.

"I don't know. One of my comics, I think."

"Trust me, Mila. Water is negative, evil even. You're reading the wrong books. Try the Bible and see what water did to Noah." She slammed the tarot deck down next to Mila. "Clear the table! We must make room for the reading of the cards!"

Nasta stood up and walked over to the stove. She lit a piece of paper with the flame of the burner and used it to relight the candles. She then pointed at the tarot deck. "Shuffle them well," she said, wiping the table clean.

Nasta sat back down in silence. Mila shuffled the cards and placed the stack back on the table. She picked them up and cut the deck.

"Choose one," she said, placing the two stacks next to each other.

Mila hesitated a moment, then pointed to the right. Nasta took the right-hand cards and laid them out side by side. The star card came up first.

"Darkness is all around you. It is in your near future," she said with certainty.

The Emperor card came next. "Power?" she said, sounding confused. Then came The Lovers. "A union," she went on, with more confidence this time.

And finally came a card that had no words, no name, just a depiction of a woman wrapped in a shawl, sitting in a small boat. A man stood behind her, pushing the boat on its way with a long staff. "A journey of purpose," Nasta said.

Mila sat still, staring at the cards in silence.

"This is the final omen, Mila. You must not ignore this omen," Nasta warned.

Mila sensed the truth of his dear aunt's words. He felt danger creeping in around him.

This is crazy! I need to get out of here!

Mila tried to stand, but Nasta again caught his arm in her vice-like grip.

How can such a frail old woman be so strong? He wondered, amazed.

Nasta's superhuman strength only added to Mila's sense of confusion and dread. He couldn't deny what was happening, yet he would not allow himself to believe. *There must be a rational explanation*, he thought, trying to get a hold of himself. *A storm is coming tonight, and the wind must have blown the cords we use to steal electricity from the factory. That's why the lights went out. As for the candles ... this old drafty building is practically a wind tunnel!*

He tried to pull away, to rise from the table. But Nasta wouldn't let go. She pulled Mila close, reached into her pocket, and produced a little piece of foil. She took Mila's hand and gently placed the little package in his palm.

"Take this," she said. "It is *chukrayi.*"

"Eww," said Mila, remembering that *chukrayi* was tree sap mixed with bird dung, a powerful potion in Romani tradition, which required a timely ritual.

"You must take this," Nasta instructed. "Find a strong, tall tree, one that looks full of life. Then, write down this dream in detail. Burn the paper while mixing the potion with the ash, and bury the ash at the base of the tree. You must do this to ward off the dream."

"Come on, Aunt Nasta! That seems like a lot to do!" Mila said, now burdened with a superstitious task.

She squeezed his hand tighter. "Mila, my precious boy, you must take this seriously and do it soon, or the omens will start to come true." Her face was somber, almost mournful. "Do not ignore this omen. If you do, it will cease to be a mere omen. It will become a prophecy. Do you understand?"

Nasta's grip was still like a vice, crushing Mila's hand. "Ow! That hurts!" he said. But the old woman only gazed deeper into his eyes, searching, imploring.

"OK, Auntie. I won't ignore it. I'll ward off the dream. I promise." Only then did she finally let go.

Mila stared at her a minute, searching her eyes as she had searched his. He could see her age, her wisdom—and her sorrows.

Mila felt cold fingers twisting his guts. He hadn't told Nasta everything about his dream. There was something more. Something that chilled him to the bone. He was afraid to tell her. Yet he was also afraid not to tell her. *Anyway, this is all complete nonsense,* he told himself. *I should just leave.*

"There was one more thing in the dream," Mila said after a long pause.

Nasta moved closer, listening carefully.

"When I looked down from the roof of Building A and saw that man with the head of a dog, guiding the family into the flooding church, I turned around because I heard a girl crying."

"A girl? Did you recognize her?" Nasta asked.

"No, she was very pretty, but she was a *gadje* girl. She was with a young boy, and there was a dead man lying on the ground next to them. The girl was wearing a string of gold coins, like you wore on your wedding day in the photo you showed me," Mila said. He remembered the photo well. There were so many coins on his aunt's traditional wedding necklace that the long strand of gold nearly touched the floor.

Nasta sat as still as a stone. Her eyes seemed to be looking at something or someplace far away again.

"Ah ... you think this girl was a bride?" she asked. "When one sees gold in a dream, it often means the guarding of something evil. This is why brides wear gold on their wedding day. Gold wards off evil, or it can be used to seal evil."

"OK, if she was not a bride, who was she?"

"There were two, correct? They will take you on a journey of purpose or darkness and power, as the cards read. The star is darkness, or evil, and the emperor is power. The dead man was ..."

Nasta paused, then turned over another card. It showed a tall man in red princely robes. With his right hand, he lifted a scepter up to the sky. His left hand pointed down while he made a strange symbol with his fingers. The bottom of the card read, *The Magician.*

"The dead man is a Rom. A special one," Nasta said. Her ancient eyes stared into Mila's, her expression severe.

Mila was amazed. According to the reading, the dead man was a Rom?

This has gone too far, he thought. He didn't want to scare himself anymore. He knew he couldn't tell Nasta the most terrifying part of the dream: the beautiful girl was holding some sort of weapon, a crude-looking object made of decaying wood, dripping with blood. It was not clear if she was the murderer of the dead man.

When Mila moved closer, he realized that the dead man was he himself.

The horrifying image flashed in Mila's mind: his own body lying lifeless on the ground.

Again, the candles blew out.

Nasta started relighting them, using another piece of torn paper that she lit from the stove. This time, Mila noticed a picture of a BMW logo on the edge of the burning paper.

"My manual!"

II

THE PICKPOCKET

"*Prikaza!*" Mila shouted. *I must be cursed!* he thought. There was no other explanation. He had spent two hours meticulously going over every plug, wire, and fuse that the slightly burned manual directed him to, but he had no luck starting the classic ride. The sun was already starting to set, and the winds were picking up as the storm clouds moved in.

Defeated, Mila tossed his manual into his toolbox and sat next to his lifeless motorcycle. He gazed at the beautiful machine. *It's never going to run. Who was I kidding, spending all that time learning how to read this gadjo manual,* he asked himself, desperately trying to accept reality. Fighting his deep passion, he slammed the toolbox shut.

Just then, Mila's cousins Petre and Kore marched up, pulling a rusty wagon full of junk, no doubt from the garbage dumps near the factory. The boys were identical twins, and it was always a challenge to know who was who, especially since they dressed alike. The mischievous twins looked so similar that even their parents could not always tell them apart. Mila often wondered why Uncle Lolo and Aunt Margaret put so much effort into dressing them the same, which was definitely a challenge, since all of their clothes came out of the Holy Cross Church donation box.

"Hey, Mila, why are you so sad?" Petre asked.

"Yeah, don't worry. We'll have the lights back on before the storm," Kore said.

"I'm still upset with you guys. How many times do I have to tell you to stay out of my stuff?" Mila said, scolding the boys.

"We didn't take your comics," Korey insisted.

"Is that right?" Mila asked. "Well then how do you know I'm talking about comics?"

"Well ... well, we ... Petre made me, Mila!" Kore said, pointing at his brother. The twins began to bicker, yelling at one another at the tops of their little lungs. Mila just smiled at the boys. He loved them dearly and was enjoying teasing them. Mila grabbed Petre in a playful headlock and began punishing him.

"It was you! You took it!" Mila said as his scolding turned to merciless tickling.

Petre pulled away from Mila's feeble attempt at torture. "What did you guys get from the dump?" Mila asked.

"We didn't go to the dump. We got some more wire cords from the toolshed," Petre said. Mila observed the wagon. Sure enough, there were wire cables, some masking tape, and a small, bright-red petrol tank. Something about the red tank grabbed Mila's attention. He gazed at it, then looked at his bike.

"No, it can't be," he said.

"What?" the boys asked.

"It can't be that simple," he repeated.

"What can't?" Kore asked again.

"Hey, is there any petrol in that tank?" Mila asked.

"No, but there's a little left in the barrel in the toolshed," Kore said. "Why?"

Mila knocked on the bike's fuel tank. Sure enough, the damn thing was empty. "I'm such an idiot!" he shouted with glee. "Let me borrow this tank." Mila grabbed the tank and gave each of the boys a quick kiss on the cheek. He popped the kickstand and started lugging the heavy bike through the mucky grass, toward the only space between Buildings A and B that wasn't crowded with tents, shacks, and broken-down trailers—a muddy football field. He looked back at the twins and saw them pointing to their heads and twirling their fingers, motioning to each other that he had lost his mind.

Mila pushed on, hoping there would be enough petrol in the barrel to get to the station up the road.

It was getting dark, yet Rom both young and old lined either side of the well-trodden open field, cheering for their side in a football match between Buildings A and B. The biggest crowds were to Mila's left, so he skirted the field and crossed over behind the goal posts on the right. As he did, an errant football rolled toward him. With expert skill, he hooked his foot around the ball and intercepted it. It bounced a bit, so Mila stomped down on it, all the while never letting go of the bike. With the ball at a dead stop, he looked up to locate its owner. Jogging toward him was his cousin and best friend, Stephan, a gangly boy with bushy eyebrows that came dangerously close to joining. He had a long, protruding nose and a pockmarked face that was always shadowed by a ratty old New York Yankees cap.

"Hey, Mila, come play! We're a man short," Stephan called.

"Um, I can't. I gotta get to the shed," Mila said.

Stephan rolled his eyes at the hasty excuse. "Yeah, maybe you don't play so good anymore," he mocked, hoping to goad Mila into joining.

"I told you, I can't!" Mila teased back. "I've got grown-up things to do! By the way, shouldn't you be preparing for your wedding ceremony next week instead of playing games?"

"Yeah, listen to your cousin!" Rosa, Stephan's soon-to-be wife, shouted from the crowd of spectators, making Stephan blush with embarrassment.

"Fine!" Stephan snapped. "If you can't play, then give me the ball back."

Mila extended his foot, rolled the ball up over his toes to the top of his arch, and gave it an agile flick into the air. With his knee, he bounced it up to his head, then threw a head-butt and sent the ball flying toward Stephan. His cousin had to duck to keep the ball from slamming into his face. He glared at Mila with annoyance. Mila shot back a sly smile, then continued on his way.

Mila reached the far side of the field and navigated the bike through the throng of tents and shacks. Screaming with glee, a group of little children dressed in rags rushed past him as they chased one another between the ramshackle dwellings. A narrow walkway crossed his path, and he stopped to let a group of older boys pass. Mila didn't recognize them. They had a mean look and their conversation was laced with every curse word he knew, and a few he didn't.

As they turned a corner, he heard them mutter, "Where's Simon? We've gotta divide up the cash."

Their accent was different from the German Rom. They were Romanian, from different families with very different ways of doing things. For a week now, they had been guests in Mila's camp. They were starting to wear out their welcome, but there was little the leaders of the camp could do. They had to show hospitality to their fellow Rom.

At last, Mila reached Building B. Just outside, a group of older Rom sat in a circle with an air of dignity and importance. Mila respectfully nodded to the men as he went by. He noticed his uncle Lolo sitting with the older men. "Hey, Uncle Lolo," Mila said.

"Mila, I need you to guard that painting tomorrow," his uncle replied.

Yoy dale, not this again, Mila thought. By "guard" the painting, Uncle Lolo meant, "wait for a chance to vandalize it."

"I might have some things to do tomorrow," Mila said, trying to think of an excuse. "Aunt Nasta told me to ward off a dream, and as you know that takes a lot of time."

"You need to stop encouraging my dear Mamo with that superstitious magic! She's old and not well! Going senile! Now, what was I saying again?"

Mila tried not to roll his eyes. "The painting," he reminded his uncle.

"Oh yes! Mila, that ugly painting is an insult!" Lolo exclaimed. "They know what it means, but they still put it right in the main train station where we do business!"

"Is it really that important? I mean, it was painted a long time ago," Mila said.

Lolo looked left and right, then leaned in and whispered, "What that painting shows being done to our people ... Well, it's too horrible to say! And that's not all! Father Leichman told me about the original version of the painting, not the copy in the train station, but the one they've got in the museum. It was in the personal collection of Hitler!"

"You mean the Unholy One," snapped Merikano, Rosa's grandfather and a respected elder. The remark was meant to remind Lolo of proper etiquette, for the failed dictator's name was never to be uttered around the Romani people. Merikano never passed up an opportunity to scold another Rom, a trait Rosa seemed to have inherited.

"Uncle Lolo, the German politicians don't care what we Rom think. They won't take it down," Mila argued.

"Now you listen here, Mila," Lolo said. "Ever since your father disappeared and your mother passed, God rest her soul, my family has looked out for you. We love you, Mila, but lately, every time I ask you to do something for the camp, all I get from you are excuses!"

That stung. Mila didn't like being reminded that he was an orphan.

"Fine, I'll go," Mila relented. He could always fake sick tomorrow to get out of it.

Mila nodded farewell to his uncle, then walked over to the rusted old toolshed and pulled open the makeshift metal door. The shed was just big enough to fit a small collection of tired and battered tools, several barrels of clean water, some broken machinery, and a small gas barrel. Mila held the door with his arm as he pulled the bike into the tiny space. He tapped on the barrel to see if it had any petrol. The sound was hollow. If there was any at all, it was probably just a few drops, just like the twins had warned. *Probably not even enough to get it started*, thought Mila, *assuming lack of petrol is actually the problem.* Figuring there was no harm in trying, he used the tube next to the barrel to suck out the last of the fuel. Then, he poured it from his cousins' red container into the bike's fuel tank.

Just as he was finishing, he heard violent shouting from outside the shed. *That's not cheering from the football match*, he thought, alarmed. He peered out of the cracked window to see what was going on.

"Psst!" came a whispered voice from somewhere inside the shed. "Don't tell anyone I'm here!"

Mila spun around. It was his friend, Simon, one of the Romanian Rom, squatting behind a stack of water barrels.

The twenty-something-year-old boy was shivering in his ragged brown jacket.

"What's the matter?" Mila asked.

"The *gendarya* are coming for me."

"The police?" asked Mila. "Why?"

"I don't know! I was working at the Metro station, and they freaked out!"

Mila heard police sirens coming from the front of the camp. He glanced out the window again and saw an officer approach Uncle Lolo. Mila could hear their voices from inside the shed.

"What can I do for you tonight, Officer Belz?" Lolo asked the officer, whom he knew far too well.

"Lolo, I don't want any Gypsy games," Belz snapped. He spoke in a loud, authoritative voice. Mila figured he was in charge. "There is a criminal delinquent hiding here. We know this! He assaulted and robbed an elderly woman, hit her so hard she needed to go to the hospital!" The rest of the Rom soon crowded around to see what the panic was all about.

"You attacked a woman? Put her in the hospital?" Mila asked Simon, shocked by what the officer was saying.

"No!" Simon insisted. "He's lying. I just did some pickpocketing. And I stole a few of the new iPhones and a little cash. I didn't hurt anybody. I swear!" Simon said frantically.

"Oh man, Simon, this is not Romania. You got the whole camp in trouble," Mila said. He peeked out the window again. About a dozen police were marching through the camp.

"Are you in charge here?" another officer said to Uncle Lolo in German. "We know he is here. His name is Simon."

"There is no Simon here," Uncle Lolo said to the officer. "And these people don't speak German. You're wasting your time." Uncle Lolo turned away from the officers. "Pretend you don't speak German!" he shouted to the Rom, speaking in Romanes, so the police couldn't understand.

"OK, that's it! Search the entire camp!" ordered the lead officer.

The police charged through the camp. They knocked on roofs with their batons and kicked in doors as Roma, mostly women and children, scampered about in fear and confusion. A few tried to distract the rampaging cops, shouting nonsense and waving their arms frantically.

"Stephan! Find Father Leichman!" shouted Uncle Lolo.

The ruckus in the camp was in full force. Mila knew it was only a matter of time before they found Simon hiding in the shed.

"What are we going to do?" implored Simon.

Mila didn't know what to say. He looked out the window again. The officer in charge was staring straight back at him.

"Who's that hiding over there?" he shouted, pointing with his baton. He pulled out a whistle and blew. An ear-piercing screech filled the air, signaling the other policemen to come. That was Uncle Lolo's cue to try his last resort. He gripped his chest, groaned in pain, and collapsed to the ground. The officer panicked, thinking he'd given the man a heart attack.

With the camp in a state of chaos and confusion, Mila hopped on the bike. "Get on!" he urged Simon. He put the key in the ignition and turned it slowly. He stepped on the kick-starter of the old motorbike and closed his eyes to pray again. This time, the prayer had to work. "I believe," he confessed.

He stepped down hard, and the engine sputtered to life. He revved it to keep it from dying.

Mila was thrilled that his bike was finally running, but there was no time for him to appreciate the moment. An officer was opening the shed door. "Hold on!" Mila warned. He let go of the brake, and the bike peeled out, breaking the door and knocking over the police officer.

Mila raced across the football field, trying desperately not to hit any of the Rom that were in his way. By the time he made it off the field, he heard a siren close at his back. One of the police cars was in pursuit.

Mila could feel the car gaining on him quickly. It pulled up on his left to block him from escaping toward the dirt lot in front of Building A, which led to the road. If he veered left to try for the lot, he was afraid the car might ram him. He jammed the throttle, trying to get out ahead of the cop car.

It was no use. The car's engine was too powerful. He couldn't outrun it. Mila looked down at his fuel gauge. It was pegged on EMPTY, and a red light was flashing.

Just as he was about to give up, Mila spotted a huge dirt pile in the far-right corner of the camp. At the top of the pile was the road.

Mila yanked the bike right and opened the throttle. He wove through tents and horrified onlookers toward the mountain of dirt. It was way too steep. He probably wasn't going to make it. He knew that. But he had to try. He wasn't going to let those dirty cops have their way with Simon. Not without a fight, anyway.

The pile loomed over him as the bike's front tires hit its base. The impact rocked the bike, throwing Mila and Simon from the seat. Mila held tight to the handlebars, and Simon held on to Mila. The two of them hung in the air for what seemed like an eternity. Mila heard the sirens racing up behind. The cop car would slam into them any second.

Then, Mila found himself back on the seat, Simon still holding on as the bike fishtailed wildly, spinning out in the dirt. Finally, the wheels found traction, and they rocketed up the pile. The police car tried to follow, but the slope was too steep. The car slammed into the dirt, spitting great clouds of dust back at the stunned Rom.

Mila and Simon hadn't made it more than a mile down the road before the engine started to sputter. Soon after, it died. Mila hopped off and began to push as Simon walked cheerfully beside.

"Woo! We made it!" Simon cheered. "That was a rush! Can't wait to tell the guys about this one!"

"You're welcome," Mila snapped.

"Yeah, yeah," Simon replied.

Thick clouds began to gather overhead, and the wind picked up. The damp, chill air meant only one thing: a storm was coming.

A few minutes later, they arrived at the gas station. It sat adjacent to a bar. Mila smiled at the familiar sign: a huge, foaming mug of beer, outlined in bright neon with the word *Schmidt's* below. The owner had worked out a deal with the Rom. They were welcome in the bar as long as they didn't bother the other customers. No stealing, no begging, and no fortune-telling. On Friday nights, Schmidt's would even pay a few Rom to sing, dance, and play Gypsy music for the customers. Mila's singing was always a hit, especially with the girls.

He snapped back to the present as he dragged the bike up to the pump. He reached into his pockets and turned them inside out, looking for even a euro or two. All he found was the little foil package Nasta had given him.

"Goddammit!" Mila shouted, staring at the useless charm.

"Here," said Simon. He opened his coat and pulled out an ugly tan purse, the kind only an old lady would carry. He reached inside and pulled out a wad of euros and offered them to Mila. As he did, Mila spotted blood on the boy's knuckles.

"Wait, you're bleeding," Mila pointed out, bewildered. Simon said nothing, using his jacket sleeve to wipe the blood clean. "You really did beat up an old lady?" Mila asked, puzzled.

"Yeah. So what? The stupid old *gadji* wouldn't let go of the purse," Simon said.

"It's wrong! It's … it's a sin!" Mila said, upset and filled with guilt for having helped Simon escape.

"Is that what Father Leichman's been teaching you?" Simon asked. "Open your eyes, Mila! That priest is no saint, trust me. It's not a sin for Rom to steal. Don't you know the legend of the Fourth Nail?"

Of course, Mila knew. Every Gypsy knew the legend. It had been told and retold among the Rom since before anyone could remember. As the story goes, when Christ was crucified, the Romans had a Gypsy blacksmith forge four nails, one for each palm, one for his feet, and a fourth to pierce his heart. The Gypsy had mercy on Jesus and stole the fourth nail. So, even as he suffered on the cross, Jesus blessed the Gypsies forever, giving them the right to steal from the *gadje* for all time.

"That story's bullshit," Mila said. "It's not in the Bible or nothing."

"How do you know? You ain't never read it," Simon countered.

Mila glared at Simon's outstretched hand, filled with crumpled bills.

"How could you do that? How could you hit an old woman? And on top of that, you're bringing heat on the camp when you steal. See what happened tonight? They've been trying to evict us for years, you know!"

"I like you, Mila. That's why I'm sharing my earnings with you."

"Get outta here, Simon. I don't want that blood money." Mila dismissed Simon with a wave of the hand and grabbed hold of his bike.

"You think you're better than me? You're still a Gypsy," Simon pointed out. "Don't ever forget that."

"Just because being a Gypsy sucks doesn't mean you have to be a jerk!" Mila retorted.

"What!?" Simon shouted. "Being a Gypsy doesn't suck. It's the best thing ever! We're free to do what we want, and we've always got family around to get us out of trouble."

Mila paused to ponder Simon's philosophy.

"Mila, listen, the *gazhe* will always treat us like thieves," Simon put in. "It don't matter if you steal or not. As long as you're Gypsy, they'll treat you like dirt. You might as well just steal and enjoy the easy money."

With that, he dropped a 20-euro bill at Mila's feet and headed off toward the bar.

Great, Mila thought, *he'll probably get us all banned from Schmidt's on top of everything else!*

Mila glanced at the money on the ground, then at his bike. He thought of the long road he'd have to walk, pushing his bike the entire way, if he didn't fuel it up.

The *chukrayi* was still in his hands. He looked down at the small bundle of shiny foil wrapped with a red ribbon and stared at it for a minute. Words echoed in his head—first, Simon's declaration: *We're free to do what we want.* Then came Nasta's words: *You're special, Mila. Gypsies are special.*

They sounded like insults now, mockery, a big, sick joke. *What's so special about being a Gypsy?* Mila wondered. *I'm a Gypsy, and I have nothing. I don't even have parents. I'm not special. I'm alone, and instead of money to fill up my bike, all I've got is some ridiculous voodoo trinket. Simon was right. This is preposterous!*

He reluctantly picked up the money and stared at it. Then he looked at the *chukrayi* in his other hand. The wind blew harder. In the distance, storm clouds gathered over Berlin. Finally, Mila tossed the *chukrayi* over the field of tangled brush beside the gas station. To his surprise, the wind caught the little packet. It flew high into the air.

Lightning flashed. For an instant, the foil shined bright as a star. Then, thunder rumbled as it disappeared into the shadows.

III

THE PROPHECY

"We're all going to die!" a cowardly teenage boy screamed as the jumbo jet violently plummeted toward Earth. A few seconds earlier, lightning had struck. Now the plane was dropping in a terrifying nosedive.

A highlight reel of Casey Richards' short seventeen years of life flashed before her eyes. All she could hear above the ringing in her ears was the eerie wail of the plane's engine and the screams of her fellow passengers, confirming that she was not imagining things. It was all very real and happening too fast. One minute, she had been sitting in her first-class window seat, quietly drawing in a leather sketchbook, and the next minute both her sketchbook and glasses went flying as a deafening *BOOM!* rocked the cabin. She shut her eyes tight and clutched the armrests of her seat, praying for her life.

Just as all hope felt lost, the plane began to level out, the powerful jet fighting through the wind and clouds and rain like it was in a battle. Casey felt every bump and thud as the pilot struggled for control of the huge airplane. She felt hard pressure on her head and gut as the craft worked desperately to regain altitude. Before she got a chance to process what had happened, the pilot's voice came over the intercom.

"Ladies and gentlemen, please remain calm. The lighting storm caused an electrical surge, which disabled the autopilot. Our apologies for the inconvenience. There is no harm to the airplane, and we are now in full control. We just received permission to climb above the storm for the rest of the flight to Austria." He repeated the message in German.

Casey realized she had been holding her breath throughout the horrifying ordeal. She exhaled with relief and glanced over at her classmates from Charlton Heights Preparatory School, most of whom were now cheering for joy. Many of the students were hugging each other, grateful for the pilot's expert skill. A few others were upset, angry with the pilot and crew for allowing such a frightening incident to occur.

"My dad is going to sue this airline," said Vivian Levine, the school's self-proclaimed mean girl.

Once the dust settled, the teenagers turned rowdy, amped up from their near-death experience. They teased one another, making a game out of who had been the most terrified. The fresh-faced Tyler Murphy leaned across the aisle toward Vivian, waving his brand-new iPhone in her face.

"I got the whole thing on video," Tyler bragged. "Your pop could use it in a lawsuit." He raised his eyebrows in a pathetic attempt to look seductive and added, "For a price."

Without even looking, Vivian slapped the phone out of his hand. Then she turned to look out the window.

Casey didn't join in the fun. She was still too shaken up. Trying to calm herself, she took a deep breath. It caught in her throat. She thought she detected the faint smell of something. Her blood ran cold, her eyes darting around the cabin and out the window, scanning for signs of a fire. But without her glasses, she could hardly see a thing. None of the other students seemed concerned. In fact, now that the plane was flying smoothly again, they were all having a blast. So maybe she was imagining things, after all. Still, Casey couldn't shake the feeling that something was wrong. Fire or no, she was beginning to think that perhaps this was not going to be the trip of a lifetime, as she had hoped.

Maybe Uncle John and mom were right, Casey thought. Her uncle and mother warned her that it was too dangerous for her to travel unaccompanied. She had never traveled alone before, but at the last minute she convinced them to let her go without Deborah to chaperone her. Now, she was starting to regret it. Deborah wouldn't have been able to stop the plane from almost crashing, but at least Casey would have had someone to cling to, someone to make her feel safe.

Casey tried to shake her dark mood and convince herself that the harrowing incident was just a bump in the road. These sorts of things happen all the time. The bad part was already over with. The rest of the trip would go smoothly, and she would have the trip of her life, just as wonderful as she had dreamed it would be. Casey had even prepared for it with a new hairstyle. Her dark locks, cut to chin length, were easier to manage than her long hair had been. She had been worried it wouldn't come out right, but to her joy, the new style was totally badass. With her creamy skin and enchanting blue eyes, she looked like a cooler, teenage version of Snow White. To highlight her baby blues, she normally wore contacts. But she'd decided not to wear them today, fearing that the recycled air on the plane would dry them out. She didn't want to show up in Austria with her eyes bleary and bloodshot.

The plane climbed out of the clouds, then leveled off above the storm. Feeling better, Casey searched the floor for her sketchbook and eyeglasses.

"Are you guys OK?" asked a voice from the aisle.

Out of the corner of her eye, Casey spotted her classmate Jack Riley. He stood just shy of six feet tall, with sandy-brown hair and gorgeous green eyes. His years of fencing had given him a lean physique and legs ripped with muscle. Casey had admired his calves more than once during PE class.

He wore his usual battered, oversized camouflage jacket. He practically lived in that thing. The look might have worked in public school, but not at Charlton Prep. The girls called him a "Double H" or "Hidden Hottie" behind his back. They said things like, "I would love to just pry him out of that stupid GI Joe getup and put him in some Abercrombie and Fitch." That wasn't going to happen, of course. Jack didn't concern himself with anything as shallow as fashion. He was more interested in burying his nose in a book or getting into debates with Charlton's best teachers. It wasn't unusual to see him hanging around after class to discuss the finer points of comparative religion or military history.

Jack noticed a sketchbook lying in the aisle. He picked it up, but before he could open it, Casey snatched it from his hands.

"That's mine," she said. "Thanks."

Jack smiled. "I thought we had a full flight?" he said, gesturing to the empty seat next to Casey.

"It was a last-minute cancellation from one of the chaperones," she said, with a bit of regret in her voice. Casey found her glasses on the floor. She put them on and looked up at Jack.

"I didn't know you wore glasses," Jack said.

"I normally don't, but it's a long flight," chuckled Casey. "Thanks again for finding my notebook."

"Oh, no worries," Jack answered. He glanced at her cover drawing, instantly recognizing the character's teased blonde hair, black tights, and trench coat. "Hey, is that Liza Carver?" he asked with enthusiasm. "That's really good."

Normally, someone admiring her drawings would have embarrassed Casey, but she was too surprised that Jack knew who Liza Carver was. The anti-heroine protagonist of the cult hit *Whistleblower* was the result of illegal drug experimentation, which left her with superhuman intelligence, heightened senses, and incessant hallucinations. She was particularly popular among female readers, many of whom didn't like to admit that they even read comic books.

"Yes ... it is," Casey answered simply.

"I started reading the *Whistleblower* series this year," Jack explained as he sat down next to her. "Carver is easily in my top ten comic characters. I'm up to Volume Three. How about you?"

"Umm ... I have all twelve volumes ... and the Twentieth Anniversary Edition," she replied, keeping her voice low. "Also, the unproduced movie script."

Jack's eyes widened. "Wow. Can I borrow those sometime?" he asked.

"I guess," Casey replied.

Jack settled in the luxurious first-class leather seat and tucked a green backpack underneath. One of the teachers on the trip, Mr. Garson, was sitting just a few rows behind Casey and Jack. With her head now bent over her drawing, Casey heard: "Mr. G! Mr. G!" The voice emanated from the next seat over. "I don't think Mr. Riley is in first class." It was Vivian. She was never ashamed to point out what class she was in, and, more importantly to her, what class others were not in. There was a rumor that Jack could only afford to attend Charlton Prep because his mother was the school nurse, a rumor Vivian loved to spread.

Mr. Garson, who was sitting just a few rows toward the back, answered, "OK, Miss Levine, leave the seating to the flight crew, all right?" The quintessential history teacher had arranged the whole trip, which was bound first for Vienna, Austria. From there, the class would tour much of Europe, traveling by train to Italy, then France, and of course ending with a stop in Amsterdam to see the famous Rembrandts.

"Hey, Jack, maybe you should head back to your seat before we land, what do you say, Soldier?" Mr. Garson kindly asked Jack. The nickname "Soldier" referred not to his jacket but to their ongoing conversation about the great wars and battles of history.

"It's an empty seat, Mr. Garson. The chaperone canceled last-minute," Casey pointed out to the teacher.

Before Mr. Garson could answer, a voice came over the loudspeaker: "Sorry, folks, but we're heading into some more bad weather. Please fasten your seat belts.

There might be turbulence," the pilot said. Again, he repeated the warning in German.

Just then, the huge plane hit an air pocket, violently dropping a great many feet. Casey's heart sunk into her belly once again. Grabbing the armrest for balance, she felt Jack's hand holding on as well.

"Don't worry. It's just a little turbulence. We're above the storm now," he said in a soothing tone.

"Wow, that was intense," Casey whispered to herself. She took a look at the students. They all seemed as startled as she was—all except for Tyler, who had fallen into a dead sleep and was drooling with his mouth open.

"So, are you going to art school after graduation?" Jack asked.

"No. I'm not really an artist. I'm not really sure what I am," Casey told him, clutching her sketchbook tightly in her lap. She added with a hint of sadness, "I guess it's just a hobby for now."

"Well, how about you show me the rest of your work?" Jack reached toward the book but stopped short of grabbing it. Almost instinctively, Casey slapped his hand away.

"Ow! What was that for?"

"Oh, shoot, sorry! I didn't mean ... I mean, I didn't mean to hit you so hard. S-sorry," Casey stammered.

"I'll say," Jack responded, rubbing his hand. "That was practically a karate chop."

"Sorry," Casey repeated, sounding more embarrassed than sympathetic.

"So … let me see your drawings?" Jack asked again.

She paused for a moment, thinking about the request. "Mmm, I don't know," she said slowly.

"Come on," Jack pleaded. "It's the least you could do. After all, I'm pretty sure you broke my hand." He stared at her with big puppy dog eyes.

"All right, since I hurt you, I'll show you. But you better not laugh," she warned, reluctantly starting to turn the pages of the sketchbook.

"I might," Jack said with a grin.

Casey slowly opened the cover of the sketchbook. She flipped through several pages that had only a few lines, sketches she'd started and quickly abandoned. At last, she stopped at her first finished drawing. It showed a young girl at the top of a large castle. A dragon hovered over her, its leathery wings threatening to envelop her. The girl stood with fists raised, her look defiant.

"Wow, that's cool," Jack said.

"It's a nightmare I had as a kid," Casey explained.

"You draw dreams?"

"Not just dreams. Memories, mostly, and some stuff from my imagination."

He noticed a strip of tape with little raised bumps. The tape was attached to the bottom of the sketch. "What's this for? It looks like Braille."

"It is Braille. I learned it when I was a kid. It describes the images."

"That's cool. Why?" Jack asked.

"For my mom. She's blind," Casey replied tersely.

Jack paused. "Oh … I'm sorry," he said.

As if thinking the same thing, they both reached to turn the page at the same time. Their hands touched. They looked into each other's eyes for a moment.

The plane began to shake.

Jack and Casey grabbed their armrests a second time as the plane dipped in midair once again. A swooshing sound filled the cabin as wind buffeted the fuselage. The 'Fasten Seat Belt' sign came on with a ding! ding! Students screamed as they were thrown back in their seats.

Tyler abruptly woke from his stupor. He sat up straight and glanced out the window. "Oh my God!" he screamed, "We're going down!"

"Shut up! You're gonna scare people!" Jack yelled back at him.

Casey smelled smoke again. Stronger this time. She was sure of it. The bad feeling came back, only worse. In her mind's eye, she saw that horrible, blinding flash of lightning that had struck just before the plane lost control. She was overcome with an unshakable sense that something had gone terribly wrong.

She heard a low clacking sound from outside. She looked out the window, saw a thin wisp of smoke seeping from the wing. *Isn't that the engine?*

A giant plume of flames burst from the wing.

"Oh my God! The engine's on fire!" Casey screamed.

The aircraft angled sharply. It arched to the left, and the resulting G-force pushed everyone to the right. Casey felt Jack take her hand. She instinctively grabbed his arm with her other hand and held on tight.

The plane thrashed back and forth wildly throwing the book and Jack's backpack into the air as it tried desperately to stabilize. The pitch and roll of the aircraft were disorienting. Casey's stomach did somersaults. All around them people were screaming, their cries clashing with the sickening death rattle of the engine.

Oxygen masks dropped. Casey let go of Jack and tried to snatch hers, but she was too dizzy to get a hold of it. Jack grabbed it for her and helped her put it on. She noticed that he already had his mask on.

"Passengers and crew: we are making an emergency landing," a voice announced over the intercom. "Passengers and crew, assume crash position."

This cannot be happening, Casey thought in total panic. Once more, she saw scenes from her life, saw her uncle and mother waving goodbye as she boarded the plane, saw their anxious expressions, as if deep down they had known. She froze, unable to think or move. Then she felt a strong arm across her shoulders.

"Like this!" Jack shouted over the other passengers' screams. He put his head against the seat in front of them and gently guided Casey to do the same. He protectively placed his arms over his head, showing Casey the position for bracing against a crash.

Casey wrapped her arms around her head as he had done. *Please, God! Please, God!* she silently prayed, over and over.

The plane pitched forward, then dipped. For a moment, Casey felt herself floating, lighter than air.

Her weight returned as the aircraft leveled off.

"Ladies and gentlemen, we have clearance to make an emergency landing at Tegel Airport. Please remain calm. We will be on the ground shortly," the voice on the intercom said. The plane started to descend toward the Earth, the red overhead light still ringing. "Please remain seated with your seat belts on."

Terrified and confused, Casey turned to Jack. "Where the hell is Tegel Airport?" she asked.

"Berlin," Jack answered.

IV

THE
PROCLAMATION

"Whoa! Slow down, Mila!" Rosa yelled, holding his waist tight as he throttled his motorcycle. Mila could barely hear her over the awesome roar of his bike's powerful engine. It was a cloudy morning in the heart of Berlin. The two teens were racing toward the city's central train station. Mila had a promise to fulfill. He had vowed to his Uncle Lolo that he would "guard" the hated painting called *The Proclamation*. Mila and Rosa planned to team up with their friends to get that job done. Mila was also flat broke. He needed to make some money, and singing on the subway lines was the best way he and Stephan knew how.

"Hold on loosely, and lean into the turns!" Mila yelled back at Rosa just before taking another curve in the road at high speed. Rosa screamed again, her olive-toned skin turning pale, the bright scarf that tied her dark hair back nearly flying off her head.

A few exhilarating minutes later, Mila pulled the bike to a stop outside the bustling main entrance of the Hauptbahnhof, Berlin's main railroad station. Rosa jumped from her seat before Mila had even turned off the engine.

"I am never getting on that thing again! Are you trying to kill me before my wedding?" she said, her face red with anger.

"Of course not, Rosa," Mila said with a big smile. "Then I'd need to help Stephan find a new fiancée, and with his big nose that wouldn't be easy," he joked.

"Shut up!" Rosa snapped.

Mila still couldn't believe that Rosa and Stephan were getting married. It seemed like only yesterday they were just little kids playing together. He wondered what would happen after the wedding. Would Stephan and Rosa even have time for him anymore?

Just then, a group of rowdy teenagers walked past Mila and Rosa, then stopped in front of the train station's entrance. The teenagers in the group huddled together, and a man in a tweed jacket started lecturing them in English.

"Now please try and stay together. Berlin was not on our schedule until next week. However, we've tried to put together an itinerary on short notice," the man in the tweed jacket told the group. Many paid no attention to him; they were too busy talking to one another and concentrating on looking at their shiny new iPhones.

It was a busy summer day, and people were everywhere. For Mila and Rosa, it was not unusual to see American students in the train station. Mila began chaining his bike to the metal rack in front of the massive glass entrance of the Hauptbahnhof.

One of the American students in designer jeans approached Mila. The boy did a slight wave of his hand and said, "I am Tyler, A-mer-ic-an," speaking loudly with exaggerated slowness as if somehow that would translate better. Tyler then put two fingers to his lips in a V, as if smoking. Mila stared back at him blankly.

"Smoky-smoky? Ganja? Mary Jane?" Tyler asked. "Where. Can. Buy?"

But before Mila or Rosa could tell him they didn't know, Mr. Garson snatched Tyler from behind and pulled him back toward the rest of the class. As he pulled Tyler away, he spoke to Mila and Rosa. *"Kein geld! Kein geld!"*—No money! No money!" Mr. Garson said, relying on the few words of German he knew.

Ignoring them, Mila finished locking up his bike. Rosa smiled at the American, then turned to her fiancé's cousin. "Like we are the criminals?" Mila complained, "We're not the ones looking to buy drugs."

"Forget about them," Rosa said as they approached the entrance of the train station, which was now blocked by the group of students. As Mila and Rosa moved to the side to try and go around them, they couldn't help overhearing the teacher's warnings.

"Before you all go, Tyler just reminded me of something you all have to know while traveling in Europe. I need to warn you about the Gypsies," Mr. Garson began.

A few students cocked their heads. To them, the word "Gypsies" was something out of a fairy tale, not real life. The racist tone of the speaker grabbed Mila's and Rosa's attention. They slowed their steps in order to hear him.

"You all probably think that Gypsies just steal chickens from farmers—" Mr. Garson said.

"But really ... they turn people into vampires!" Tyler interrupted. Everyone rolled their eyes at the stoner's stupid joke, including Mila and Rosa.

"Tyler, that's enough," the teacher snapped.

"Sorry, Mr. Garson," the fresh-faced teenager said.

"Now, you may have seen a few rather odd-looking people wandering on the streets on our way in," Mr. Garson continued. "Those are Gypsies. You can generally recognize them by their costumes. The women wear bright headscarves, and they all wear bright colors. They travel in packs, usually with lots of small, unkempt children. They don't go to school; their only education is practicing thievery and petty theft. The kids may look cute, but beware. These people will try to steal from you. Some might try to lure you into alleys. Kidnappings by Gypsies are very common. The bottom line is to stay away as best you can. If they approach you, walk away. If they get close, keep a firm hand on your bags. Never look them in the eye. I cannot stress enough that these are dangerous people. I want you all to stay safe."

"Jack, is any of that true?" a voice asked.

Mila scanned the group and spotted a young, beautiful American student standing beside a tall boy in a camouflage jacket. Mila found himself drawn in by her dark shiny locks, cut to chin length, and her enchanting blue eyes, which were both dazzling and gentle. He stopped and listened a moment more even as Rosa tried to pull him into the station.

"I don't think so," Jack replied.

Mr. Garson gestured toward Mila and Rosa. "There are two of them just behind us. They were trying to deal drugs to Tyler," he said. Half the class turned back to gawk at Mila and Rosa.

"Gee, I really hope those people don't speak English," she said to her friend Jack.

"We do!" Rosa blurted out loudly. Mila noticed the *gadji* girl's cheeks turn red with embarrassment. She put up her hand to cover her mouth. Her friend Jack had an equally regretful look on his face.

Mila and Rosa kept on walking and entered the station with the group of American students close behind.

"I thought it was legal over here?" they heard Tyler mutter.

"That's Amsterdam, dumbass," Jack replied.

As he and Rosa stepped onto an escalator that led to the subway line below, Mila felt compelled to glance back at the girl with the kind blue eyes and the pretty white summer shorts. He didn't know why he had to look back at her: perhaps it was her sympathy, or maybe just because she was beautiful. He turned and spotted her as the escalator carried him down.

To his surprise the girl was staring right at him with a pitiful frown. She mouthed the words "I'm sorry." Again, Mila was taken by the gentleness in her beautiful blue eyes. Normally, tourist girls didn't appeal to him at all, but in this case her gesture felt right. When he and Rosa reached the bottom of the escalator, he looked back again, but the girl had disappeared from view.

Rosa was mumbling something, but he wasn't paying any attention. His thoughts were still with the blue-eyed girl. Mila was torn as he had never been before: happy and hopeless, both at the same time. This girl drew a totally different reaction from him than the girls at Schmidt's could ever evoke. He felt something deep within his belly—a pain that wasn't hunger.

"Mila!" Rosa yelled, waving her hand in front of his face and pulling him out of his thoughts.

"What?" he yelled back, startled.

"Look over at the painting! There are no police guarding it," Rosa pointed out.

Mila looked over and saw *The Proclamation*. It was massive, a full-sized reproduction of the famous painting, made to advertise an art exhibition coming in summer, 2007, to the Berlinische Galerie art museum.

The artwork was protected by a Plexiglass shield, which was now marred with graffiti. Despite the shroud of vandalism, the basic scene could still be made out. It depicted a regal-looking woman bedecked with jewels and wearing an elegant gown. The woman wore a crown, but in one of her pale, delicate hands she held a curious-looking royal scepter. Her other hand was extended to offer a rolled-up scroll to a kneeling soldier. Behind the two figures stood a cluster of simply dressed, olive-skinned women, all with frightened expressions on their faces and fear in their dark eyes. The dark women were clearly Gypsy slaves. That is what offended many of the local Rom, especially considering what they knew about the history of the event the painting portrayed, what was written on the scroll, and what it had meant to their people.

Mila knew what was written on that scroll. He'd heard it whispered in the camp, for the older Rom said it was a proclamation too wicked to speak of aloud. And Nasta? She would go even further. Nasta insisted that the words of the proclamation were pure evil. Naturally the scroll itself was a popular target for the Rom's vandalism, but the woman's unusually shaped scepter received equal attention.

THE MOON

"That's weird," said Mila. The Rom had been vandalizing the painting, so the police had started guarding it day and night. "I wonder what's going on," Mila said, puzzled about why the painting wasn't being guarded.

"They might be taking it down," whispered Rosa. "Here's our chance!" She took Mila's arm. "Come on. Let's go find Stephan and the twins."

Mila and Rosa hurried through the underground station. The historic nature of this part of the building was a stark contrast to the hyper-modern glass structure above. It was a grand and nostalgic place; some might say it exuded the essence of Old Europe. The ornate light fixtures were solid brass, and in the center of the palatial main hall stood a huge clock that appeared to be made entirely of gold. Four large pillars held up the hall's arched ceiling. For the Roma, the corners where the pillars stood held a secret purpose. The acoustics in the grand hall were the work of an architectural genius. From the center of the hall, the echo of a shout could be heard throughout the space. But if you stood in any of the four corners right next to one of the pillars and whispered, your words would travel perfectly up the arch and back down again, all the way to the opposite corner. The Roma frequently used their knowledge of this acoustical marvel to warn each other about police or point out where the most generous tourists were headed. They could even listen while staying relatively hidden, thanks to the large garbage and recycling bins the station had placed right in front of the pillars.

Mila spotted Stephan and his twin cousins, Korey and Petre, next to the pillar in the far-right corner. Another of his cousins was with them, a boy Stephan's age named Jolly. They looked like they were having an intense conversation.

"Hey guys! What's going on?" asked Mila.

Stephen, Jolly, and the twins cut their conversation abruptly. They just stared at Mila in silence.

"Did you guys see?" Rosa asked. "There are no police at the painting! Are they taking it down?"

She didn't get any response, either. Stephan gave them both an awkward look. Jolly studied his shoes.

"OK," said Mila. "What's going on?"

"All the police are in the metro looking for you, Mila!" Petre shouted.

Mila was shocked. "What? Me? Why?" he asked.

"Because of Simon," Stephan answered.

Mila stood in silence for a moment, trying to figure out what exactly was happening.

"Simon has had the whole Berlin police department in an uproar since he and his gang arrived from Romania," Jolly put in.

"Simon is in trouble with the police? What else is new?" Mila replied in a sarcastic tone. "But what does that have to do with me?"

"They think you helped him rob that poor old woman," Korey said.

"What?" Rosa and Mila shouted in unison.

"That's crazy! I did not help him!" Mila said. "I was at camp the whole day, working on my bike! I would never do something like that!"

"We know that, Mila," said Stephan. "But the police saw you help Simon escape, Now the police are out for blood. They know you come here to work, to sing on the trains for tips. They're looking all over the metro for you and Simon. They're looking on the trains, too."

"This is terrible!" said Rosa. "Mila, you'd better get out of here, now."

"That's not all," said Stephan. "There is a *kris* tonight at the camp."

Mila's heart sank. A *kris* was bad news. It was like a tribunal, a gathering of Rom elders to investigate wrongdoing and hand out punishment to the guilty parties.

"The elders are gathering to tell Simon and his family that they must leave or we will get evicted for sure," said Jolly. "The elders also want to talk to you about your involvement. They are very unhappy with the situation, and they're demanding answers. They don't want any more trouble with the police, so they gave strict orders that you are not allowed to return to camp until after dark, when it's time for the *kris*."

Mila was paralyzed with fear and overcome with regret. He stood in stunned silence, trying to wrap his head around the fact that he was being hunted by the police and, worst of all, that he had caused trouble for the camp.

"I am really sorry, Mila," said Stephan. "We all know you were just trying to help Simon."

"I'm flat broke, and I only have enough gas in my tank to get back to camp. If I can't go until tonight, what am I supposed to do until then?" Mila asked the group.

"Don't worry, Mila" said Stephan.

"Yeah, Mila, don't worry!" Korey and Petre chimed in.

"And until then?" asked Mila.

"Come read palms with me," said Rosa. "Everyone knows you sing on the trains to earn money, so that's where the police will be looking for you. They won't be looking for a palm reader."

"No way! That's for girls!" said Mila.

"Relax," said Rosa. "You don't have to actually do any readings. Just help me scope out the best prospects."

"And if the police show up?" asked Mila, exasperated. He knew Rosa's plan wasn't very good, but he couldn't think of anything better.

"If the police show up, just head to the nearest exit!" Rosa said.

"Oh yeah? And where would that be? The subway tunnel?" Mila asked sarcastically.

The two groups split up. Stephan, Jolly, Korey, and Petre headed for the trains to sing, and Mila and Rosa walked back to *The Proclamation*. Rosa picked out a spot near the painting to do palm readings.

"Lay low, Mila. I have an idea that will guarantee you will not be caught," Rosa said. Mila felt alone and vulnerable. His stomach was sick from nerves. *I need to leave the station*, he thought. *Staying here is too much of a risk.*

As he stood up to leave, Mila saw the American girl, the one with the dark hair and beautiful blue eyes. She was standing alone in front of the painting. She seemed fixated on the vandalized advertisement. *Maybe she's thinking about visiting that museum today*, Mila thought.

Suddenly, the girl opened her bag and pulled out an expensive-looking leather book and a pencil. She started to write in it, or at least that's what it looked like to Mila.

Mila didn't know why, but he felt intrigued as to what she was writing. Slowly, Mila began to walk toward the beautiful girl. *Why is she alone? Where is the rest of the group?* Mila thought as he approached, feeling a bit unnerved by her interest in the painting. As he got closer, he could see that she was sketching the painting. She had started with the scepter, quickly penciling its likeness in great detail. Mila was impressed, even more drawn to her than before. He found himself a foot or two behind her, watching her work. But she was too engrossed in her artistry to notice him. In no time, she had skillfully sketched out an exact depiction of the intricate scepter, except for a few markings hidden beneath the black spray-paint graffiti.

"It's called The Proclamation," Mila heard himself say. The girl jumped back, startled by his sudden intrusion, and dropped her sketchbook. It fell to the ground, pages face down on the dirty floor. They both knelt to pick it up.

"Now I'm sorry," Mila said, grabbing the book and rising. "I didn't mean to startle you."

The book was still open to the page the girl had been working on. Mila looked down and saw a skillful sketch of the scepter and, holding it, was one of his favorite comic book characters: Liza Carver, from *Whistleblower.*

"Liza from *Whistleblower!* That's really good!" Mila said.

"Thank you. So I have been told," she said with a shy smile.

Mila took a second look at the young girl's skillful drawing. Something about the image felt familiar to him, but he didn't know why.

She held out her hand. "Would you mind giving me my book back?"

"Oh! Sorry!" said Mila, breaking his gaze. "Of course!" He handed the book back to her.

"You speak English?" she asked.

"Yes, I learned mostly from American music and movies, and comics." There was a moment of awkward silence. Mila didn't want the conversation to end. "So ... why do you like this painting? No one else does."

"I see that," the girl replied, looking up at *The Proclamation*. "It's all covered in graffiti. Are those rotten eggs on her face?" she asked.

"Yes. My friends are spending a lot of time making sure it gets messed up real good."

"Why?" the girl asked with a shocked expression.

"It's complicated," Mila answered. For a moment, they both stared at the painting. Mila peeked from the corner of his eye to steal another glance at her. He was surprised to see that she was doing the same thing. He could not help but smile. The girl giggled in embarrassment.

"I'm really sorry about what our teacher said earlier," the girl said, still embarrassed. "I want you to know that not all Americans are jerks."

"Of course not," said Mila. "And not all Gypsies are thieves." He gave her a wry smile and shot her a quick wink. She giggled at that, too.

"Hi. Is everything OK?"

Mila turned to see the girl's companion.

"Oh! Yeah!" answered the girl. "Jack, this is my new friend ..."

"Mila."

The boy held his hand out to Mila. "Nice to meet you, Mila."

Mila shook Jack's hand. It was a firm grip, maybe a bit too firm. And though there was an undeniable kindness in Jack's eyes, Mila also detected coldness, a warning perhaps. *This guy is definitely her boyfriend,* thought Mila. *Or at least he wants to be.*

"And this is Casey," Jack said.

Mila turned to Casey. "Nice to meet you, Casey," Mila said.

"Likewise," Casey said. She smiled again. "Mila—isn't that a girl's name?"

"No ... I mean, kind of, but not really ... it's also complicated," Mila finally said.

Casey laughed again and smiled at Mila sweetly.

"I got the tickets," Jack said to Casey. "The next train's only a few minutes away. Nice meeting you, Mila."

Mila just nodded. Casey waved to him, and she and Jack turned away.

Suddenly, Casey pulled Jack back. "Jack, wait a sec!" She then opened her bag and pulled out one of the new iPhones the world was raving about. She pointed it at the painting and snapped a few photos. For some reason, fear filled Mila's chest.

"What did you do that for?" Mila asked.

"Oh, I want to finish sketching this painting, especially the scepter," Casey said.

Jack and Casey turned and walked toward the subway platform. Something about what she had said worried him, or perhaps he feared he would never see her again. He watched them standing on the platform, hoping she would turn around to look at him again. But she didn't. Instead, the train pulled up and Jack gently grabbed Casey's hand, kissed her on the cheek, and pulled her into the subway car, verifying Mila's fear that the beautiful girl was taken.

"She is rich," a voice said from behind his shoulder. Mila knew the voice.

"You're a real Sherlock Holmes, Simon," Mila answered, without turning around to look at the guy who was the cause of all his troubles.

"A regular who?" Simon asked.

"Never mind," Mila said. "What do you want?"

Simon walked around to face Mila. "Well, for starters, that girl you are scoping. She is a good one. Not your typical rich girl."

Mila watched as Jack and Casey walked to the platform. They stood close together, forty feet down from Simon and Mila, waiting for their train to arrive. It was getting late. There was no one else nearby except a bum passed out in a corner and a couple of teenagers making out on a bench near the far wall.

"What the hell are you talking about, Simon?" Mila asked.

"I mean she's not just rich, Mila. She is what they call wealthy. You see her bag? You see her clothes?"

"Yes. She's wearing clothes. She has a bag. So?"

Simon laughed and rolled his eyes. "You see, but you don't really see, Mila. So, let me explain. Everything about that girl is top shelf: her clothes, her bag, her jewelry. But you wouldn't know it unless you understood exactly what to look for. You see, rich girls flash their money with popular designer handbags and luxury brand logos stamped on their clothes and luggage for all the world to see. Not this girl. No Louis V for her. She is trying to *hide* her wealth. And that's how you know she's really rich!" Simon explained.

"I don't have time for this, Simon," Mila said, trying to contain his anger. "The cops are out looking for me, and you, too."

"They don't scare me. I know how to handle them. Besides, I've got a little more work to do. Then I'm going to the park to fence the goodies I got today. Maybe you could help me out? Give me a lift on your bike?"

Mila tried to walk away, but Simon grabbed his arm.

"That girl is a good score, Mila!" Simon whispered in his ear. "Did you find out where she's staying?"

Mila yanked his arm away from Simon. "You stay away from her!" he said, trying to keep his voice down. He could feel the heat rising in his neck and face. "And stay away from me, too, Simon!"

"Fine. Have it your way." Simon stomped away, then headed up the escalators.

"Here you go!" It was Rosa, back from her trip upstairs. She held out a ridiculous baseball cap, a pair of sunglasses, and an over-sized backpack that read *Berlin is for Lovers.*

"What the hell is this, Rosa?" Mila asked.

"Your tourist disguise! You will blend in, and the police won't even give you a second look!" She explained, clearly proud of herself.

Mila took a moment to think about it. He decided she was right. At the train station, tourists blended in like chameleons on tree branches. He grabbed the loot and put it on as Rosa called a tourist over for a palm reading. "Wait, did you steal this?" he asked. But Rosa was already busy telling some woman that she saw something interesting in her future.

The day passed slowly. Mila wished he could be on the subway lines. He actually liked to sing, and he was the best in the group. On a good day, he could belt out a few show tunes, a Motown classic, and a Disney song and come home with his pockets full of tips. Instead, he just sat in the whisper corner while Rosa did what he felt was a cheap trick. She'd come over to the corner, listen to someone's conversation until she learned a few choice things about them, then walk over and pretend she'd read the tourist's mind. She usually got at least a euro or two.

"Don't look at me like that," Rosa said, knowing Mila didn't approve. "Think of it as a magic trick. *Gadje* pay hundreds to see some magician pull a bird out of his butt. Trust me. They're going to go back to America and tell all their friends how they met a real Gypsy witch in Europe."

"Yeah, well I just don't like hustling people like that," Mila said.

"Oh really? Is that why you made me teach you how to pick a lock?" Rosa asked.

"We were just kids, and you're just jealous because I'm better than you now," Mila snapped.

"Oh yeah? Well, unlike you I don't need a key fob. I can pick a lock with a simple hair pin," Rosa retorted.

Mila rolled his eyes. "Why don't you learn to tell fortunes by using your intuition, like Nasta?" Mila asked.

"You really believe in that?" said Rosa.

"Sometimes."

"I dunno," Rosa said. "Maybe some of our people have 'the gifts' as Nasta calls them. But I sure don't, and I've gotta make a living somehow."

Finally, night had fallen on Berlin. The train station was nearly deserted, and all of the shops had been closed for at least two hours. Fortunately, no police had bothered Mila. The money Rosa gave to him, the most they had ever made in a day at the station, was enough to last a week, maybe more. Turns out Mila's intuition helped him pick out the most generous tourists in Berlin. He had hardly used the whisper corner.

Maybe things aren't so bad, Mila thought. "You sure you're okay being on the metro alone?" he asked Rosa as she stepped aboard the U5 line.

"I told you I wasn't getting back on that bike," Rosa answered. "Look, you know I can't attend the *kris*, so don't let my grandfather be too harsh on you tonight."

"Uncle Merikano? Ah don't worry about him. He's a pussy cat," joked Mila as the doors to the U5 closed.

Mila headed toward the escalators to the main exit, where his bike was chained outside. As he stepped on the escalator, he turned and spotted Jack and Casey exiting a newly arrived train, looking exhausted but still holding hands. Halfway up the escalator, Mila noticed Simon, with five of his friends from Romania, coming down the opposite side, eyeing Jack and Casey. Instinctively, Mila knew what Simon was going to do, and now he had his gang to help him.

"Simon! No! Stop!" Mila yelled. He jumped the divide between the escalators and ran after Simon and his friends. The gang hurtled to the bottom of the escalators, then peeled left, toward Jack and Casey.

By the time Mila caught up with them, Simon and his gang already had Jack and Casey surrounded. He tried to reach Simon, but two of the others grabbed him and restrained him. He struggled with all his might to get loose, but he couldn't.

"Give me your bag, your coat, and your jewelry," Simon demanded, leering at Casey.

The Americans stood near the entrance to the subway tunnel, with their backs to the edge of the platform. The train tracks were seven feet below.

Jack stepped in front of Casey. "No," he said firmly.

"Do as I say, and I promise you won't get hurt," growled Simon. "Make things hard for me, and I'll make things hard for you. Either way, I get your stuff."

"Leave her alone," said Jack, holding his ground.

Simon punched him in the stomach. Jack moaned and bent forward, knocking Casey backward. One of her feet slipped over the edge of the platform. She screamed and grabbed hold of Jack's jacket to regain her footing.

"Simon! Please! Stop!" yelled Mila as he fought to get free of the two gang members holding him back.

Jack was bent over in front of Simon, clutching his stomach. Simon had knocked the wind out of him, and he was struggling to breathe.

"Move away from the girl!" Simon yelled. Jack just gasped for air and shook his head.

Simon took another swing. Jack dodged it, but in doing so he stumbled backward into Casey.

Casey fell from the platform.

"No!" yelled Mila. The two guys holding him, surprised by Casey's fall, loosened their grip. Mila took advantage of the moment and broke free. He jumped down onto the train tracks to help Casey.

She was on the ground, grabbing her ankle.

"Casey! Are you OK?" Mila asked. Above them on the platform, he could hear Simon and his gang shouting at Jack, demanding that he turn over his wallet.

Casey looked up at Mila and nodded. "I landed on my feet," she said. "My ankle hurts bad, but I don't think it's broken."

Jack jumped down onto the tracks.

Simon jumped down after him, followed by one of his gang. Simon pulled a switchblade and lunged at them.

"Simon! Are you crazy?" Mila said, stepping between Simon and the Americans.

"Come on!" Jack said to Casey. "I need to get you out of here!" He lifted her to her feet, put her arm around his shoulders to support her weight, and walked her away from the two Gypsies, into the dark tunnel.

"Put the knife away," Mila said, keeping himself between Simon and the tunnel entrance.

"Why are you siding with those rich *gadje?*" asked Simon. "You're a Gypsy, Mila. They hate Gypsies!"

Three of Simon's gang were standing at the edge of the platform, yelling at him. "Let's go, Simon! It's not worth it!"

Mila heard a whistle start to blow.

At the sound, one of the gang members turned his head behind him, then turned back. "Cops are coming, Simon!" he shouted. He laid down on the platform and reached out his arm. "Come on! I'll pull you up!"

Simon turned and took hold of his hand, then scrambled up the side.

The whistle continued to blow, getting closer and closer. Mila heard the police shouting. He couldn't let the cops see him, especially with Simon. He needed to get out of sight until the situation blew over. He turned and looked into the tunnel, barely able to make out Jack and Casey standing in the shadows twenty feet down. He ran toward them.

"Stay away from her!" yelled Jack, raising his fists as Mila approached.

"Jack, stop!" yelled Casey. "That's Mila, the one who was trying to help us."

Jack put his hands down. A moment later, Mila caught up with them.

"You guys OK?" asked Mila.

Casey was leaning against the wall for support. She nodded. "My ankle hurts like hell, but otherwise, yes, I'm fine."

"I'm really sorry about what happened back there," said Mila.

"Not your fault," said Jack. "Thanks for the help."

Mila nodded.

"Is it safe to go back?" Casey asked.

Mila hesitated. "Yeah, you guys go ahead. I'm going to stay here for a while."

"Why?" asked Jack.

Beeeep! The tunnel was filled with the sound of a loud whistle.

They looked toward the station. Two pinpoints of light shone out from the tunnel on the other side of the platform. It was an approaching train.

"That train is going to stop at the platform, right?" asked Casey, looking at Mila with wide eyes.

"Probably," said Mila, nervously.

"Probably?" asked Jack.

"I mean … unless it's not a local," answered Mila. To his horror, the two bright beams became larger and larger, brighter and brighter. The tracks at his feet began to shake. The train wasn't slowing down.

"Run!" he yelled.

"We have to help her!" Jack shouted.

"To hell with my ankle, Jack!" Casey yelled. "Run!" She turned and ran into the darkness. Mila and Jack immediately followed.

The train came up on them fast. The lights bored into their backs and illuminated the path ahead. *Beeeep! Beeeep!* Mila heard the terrifying sound of the horn as the train came speeding up behind them, gaining quickly.

Beeeeep!

"Just run!" Jack shouted. "Don't look back! Run!"

Mila scanned the concrete walls for some kind of escape: a maintenance hatch, a sewer grate, anything to get them out of the path of the oncoming train, now almost at their heels. He spotted some sort of alcove—just a slight widening of the tunnel. No more than two feet deep, the space extended for perhaps two yards along the side of the tunnel.

"There!" he shouted. He grabbed Jack's arm and pulled them all toward the alcove.

Bammm! The three of them slammed into the space and flattened their bodies against the rough stone. A heartbeat, maybe two, then *woosh!* The subway train flew past, just inches from their backs. The wind kicked up by the train pressed them against the wall. The entire space shook. The train's rear lights made a disorienting strobe effect as it receded into the distance.

As the three huddled together in the tiny space, Mila felt a shift beneath his feet. He glanced down and saw that they were standing not on the dirt and gravel that covered the rest of the tracks, but rather on a sheet of badly cracked concrete. To his horror, he realized the cracks were widening. A large chunk fell away beneath his feet, revealing blackness beneath. There was some sort of pit under them. In the darkness, it was impossible to tell how deep it went: it could have been as little as three feet down or as much as thirty.

"Help!" Casey yelled. "I'm going to fall through!"

Suddenly, the floor gave way, crumbling to nothing under their feet and sending them tumbling into the shadowy abyss below.

V

~~~

THE BUNKER

lick! A flame sprang to life from the lighter tool on Mila's ingenious key fob. He held it up and tried to get his bearings. He could just barely make out the hole they'd fallen through. It was ten, maybe twelve feet above their heads.

"Ow," Casey groaned. Mila turned, holding out the flame. In the flickering yellow light, he could see Casey grimacing in pain as she lay amid the chunks of concrete and steel rebar that littered the floor. Jack moved to help her up. She slowly rose, struggling not to put pressure on her injured ankle, clinging to his arm, and cringing with each movement.

"Is anything broken?" Mila asked.

"I don't think so."

"You're bleeding!" Jack exclaimed, staring at her right arm.

Mila stepped toward them and held his lighter tool closer. Casey's delicate sleeveless blouse revealed a deep, four-inch gash down the back of her upper arm. Blood had gushed out of the wound and was splashed all the way to her elbow.

"I-I didn't even feel it..." Casey stammered.

"Hold this," Mila said, passing the flickering light to Jack.

Mila pulled off his shirt and pressed it against the wound for a few tense moments. The bleeding seemed to stop. In the camps, he'd seen milder cuts turn gangrenous, so he did his best to wipe away the dirt and dust that had mixed with Casey's blood to form a sticky paste around the edges of the nasty gash. Finally, he bound the wound with his shirt, tying it as tightly as possible.

Then, his hands still on her arm, Mila paused. He looked—really looked—at Casey. The light of the flame danced across her face, outlining every delicate curve. Her eyes reflected a bit of the light. To Mila, their deep blue seemed to shine like the eyes of an angel and yet he could sense some inner pain behind them.

He slowly let go of her arm. Her brilliant eyes scanned downward. Was she admiring his now-naked torso? Years of football games had given him a lean, sculpted chest and firm washboard abs. But Casey was looking at something else entirely. "You're hurt, too," she told him gently.

She pointed to Mila's stomach. Glancing down, he realized he had a scrape of his own. But it was superficial: a shallow cut with hardly any blood.

"I'll be fine," he assured her, looking straight into her deep, shining blue eyes. "It's nothing."

"Um...where are we, do you think?" Jack awkwardly interrupted.

"I dunno. A sewer, maybe? Or an old subway tunnel," Mila guessed.

"Let's get some more light down here," Casey suggested. She checked her pockets front and back, then repeated the check. "Are you kidding me?" she said with frustration. "I lost my phone."

Jack scanned the ground with the lighter tool, pushing chunks of concrete around with his foot. He bent over and poked at the rubble. "Whoa," he said, his right hand closing around whatever he had spotted. He pulled the object toward him.

"Did you find my phone?" Casey asked.

"No. But look." He stood up, and in his closed fist she saw a large metal spike. Nearly a foot long, it was caked with layers of filth. Years' worth of oil, grease, dirt, and rust gave the object a mottled brown color. One end was flat, while the other came to a sharp point. Fresh blood covered the pointed end.

"Jesus. This thing is dangerous," Jack said. "I think we know what cut you. Is this a railroad spike?"

"Who knows," Mila said. "Just put it someplace where we won't step on it."

Ignoring Mila, Jack examined the object under the lighter tool's flame. The foot-long spike was oddly crafted. It had one pointed end and one flat end, shaped like a heptagon. Jack could just barely make out a swastika engraved on the seven-sided surface. He picked at the grimy coating of the spike with his fingernail, trying to see what was underneath. His efforts revealed a glimpse of something shiny.

"I think this might be important," Jack said. "It looks like an artifact."

"Whatever," Mila said. "Put it away before it cuts somebody else."

Jack shot Mila an angry glance and laid the artifact up against the wall. He returned the lighter to Mila. Together, they resumed their search for the phone by feeling around the mud-covered concrete floor. Casey joined in, not straying too far thanks to her twisted ankle.

In the mess on the ground, Mila found a stack of old newspapers. He'd started enough fires in the rusty barrels at camp to know what they were good for. He picked out three and rolled them up, then held one end to the lighter tool's flame, creating a torch. "Here," Mila said, offering the brightly burning torch to Casey. They looked into each other's eyes across the flame.

"Um," Jack said, "let me get one?"

Mila came out of his trance. "Sure, but they won't last long," he warned.

The three held up the torches, and the pale-yellow light reached all corners of the space. The left side appeared to be caved in. A pile of large concrete blocks formed a crude slope running up to the ceiling. Mila noticed a couple of old desks and chairs lining the back wall. They looked sturdy. *Maybe,* Mila thought, *they could be stacked to make a ladder...*

"Holy shit!" Jack clutched his head with one hand and stared at the far wall.

Mila swiveled to see what was wrong. What he saw put a knot in his stomach. Emblazoned on the far-right wall was a giant Nazi flag. Even in semidarkness among chipped and peeling paint, the blood-red background and black swastika inside a glowing white circle vividly stood out.

"That can't be good," Casey said.

"Could this be ..." Jack trailed off.

"What?" Casey asked.

"Could it be *Hitler's bunker?*" Jack asked excitedly. "You know—his secret hideout during the siege of Berlin. Hitler hid there and eventually killed himself. My uncle told me all about it when I was a kid."

"Weird story to tell a kid," said Casey curiously.

"Not if your whole family served in the military," said Jack. "My uncle was special ops. He was stationed here in Berlin during the Cold War. He told me the Russians tried to blow the bunker up, but the concrete was too thick, so they just built over it."

"Why didn't they make it a museum?" Mila pried.

"The Allies kept the location secret for years afterward," responded Jack. "They didn't want neo-Nazis turning it into a shrine."

"Whatever," Mila said tersely. "Your imagination's working overtime. Who cares about that shit? Help me move these desks."

Jack gave him another scowl. "So, you don't care about the Nazis? Don't you know they exterminated more than *six million* Jews? Women and little kids included?"

Mila limped over and grabbed a corner of the desk. "Are you Jewish?" he asked Jack.

Reluctantly, Jack grabbed the other corner. "No, I'm not, but that's not the point," he retorted.

The two of them half lugged, half dragged the heavy desk to line up directly under the gap in the ceiling. Casey stood behind them, standing on one foot and listening.

"The point is, those evil persecutors murdered millions of Roma—'Gypsies' to you—as well," Mila said. "Did they teach you that in your American school? That we're real people, not just a bunch of thieves? The Nazis weren't the first you know! *Gadje* have been trying to wipe us out for a thousand years! Spain, Austria, they all tried to get rid of us! Not to mention that we were slaves in Romania for five hundred years! So, don't you try to lecture me about extermination—my people lived it!" The words tumbled out of Mila till he stopped, out of breath.

"Really...? That's horrible," Casey said gently.

Mila looked at her. "Yeah, sure, but we haven't got time for a history lesson right now. If we can't get out of here, Hitler's gonna be responsible for one more dead Rom. Let's get to work."

Before they could get another piece of furniture, Casey's head spun and her knees buckled. She gripped the far corner of the desk to keep from falling over. It took a moment for Jack and Mila to notice.

"What happened? Are you OK?" Jack asked.

"I just got really dizzy," Casey said.

"Take it easy. We'll get out of here soon," Jack assured her.

Casey limped over to the nearest wall to move away from the desk.

He and Mila started for the second desk that fortunately was smaller than the first. They dragged it over, lined it up next to the first, and braced themselves.

"On three," Mila said.

They counted together: "One ... two ... *three!*"

With a groan, they heaved the second desk up and onto the worn surface of the first. The stacked desks reached about five feet into the air.

Mila headed to the far wall and grabbed a worm-eaten wooden chair. "All right, this should be easy," he said, placing the chair on top of the stack. Confidently, he climbed onto the first desk, then the second, then onto the chair. He went into a crouch. "Maybe I can jump on this, then help you two—"

With a loud snap, the chair seat split in two. Mila fell flat on his backside, then tumbled onto the dusty concrete floor. He choked back an "ouch" and rose silently to his feet.

"Well done," Jack said, clapping his hands sarcastically.

"Shut up," Mila snapped.

"Hey, it's your fault we're down here," Jack retorted.

"My fault? I was trying to help you! You ran into the tunnel."

"That's because your *friends* attacked us!" Jack shouted.

Mila shouted back, "He is not my friend! Just because he is a Gypsy doesn't mean he's my friend! I only followed you into the tunnel to get away from the police."

"Why would you run from the police?" Jack asked.

"'Cause they would have arrested me!"

"Why? What did you do?" asked Jack.

"Why do you think I did anything? You don't have to be guilty of a crime to be arrested when you're a Gypsy!" said Mila angrily.

Suddenly, the bunker began to violently shake, breaking the escalating argument. Frightened, they scrambled for something stationary to hold on to, then realized that the tremors must have been caused by an approaching train. It soon passed.

"Looks like the trains are still running," said Jack.

"Yeah," said Mila. "That means our problems are not over once we climb out."

"What do we do?" Casey asked.

The three teens stopped to rack their brains for a solution.

"I got it!" Jack said. "We'll have to time it just right to beat the trains."

"You're right," Casey agreed. "We've been in here what, maybe fifteen minutes? We'll have to climb out the second after the train passes. Then it's anybody's guess if we'll have enough time to escape from the tunnel before the next train!"

"It's worth a try. When the next train comes, I'll start counting to see how much time we have," Jack said.

"Good idea," Mila said. "Why don't we get busy and look for something to raise us up to the opening, so we can climb out?"

The teens got to searching. A few moments later, Casey stumbled upon some old radio wire and took it to Mila. "Will this work?" she asked, holding out the coil of thin metal.

Mila grabbed the rusty wire. It was only about four feet long: not strong enough to hold either one of them. As he handed it back to her, he noticed she was flushed and sweating. "Are you OK?" he asked.

"I'm not sure. It's really hot in here," she said as she mopped her forehead, which was beaded with sweat.

"I got something!" Jack yelled from across the bunker.

Mila and Casey walked over to see that Jack had found a tall bookshelf that they could easily place over the desks and climb up like a ladder. "That should work great!" Mila said.

"Hey, are you OK?" Jack asked Casey, noticing her pale face and weakened state. Something was clearly wrong.

"It's nothing. I'll be fine," she reassured him.

Wrapping an arm around Casey's back, Jack helped her over to a pile of collapsed concrete and supported her as she sat down against it. "Your eyes look really bloodshot, too," he said with concern.

"It's all the dust in here. My contacts are killing me."

"Ouch, that's no fun. Just wait here and rest those eyes while I move the bookshelf," Jack said confidently, as if he could do it alone.

Together, he and Mila shoved the heavy piece of furniture toward the desk, then heaved it up on top. Another train passed in what seemed like another quarter hour or so. The boys agreed to position themselves at the stack of furniture just after the next train went by, hoping that would give them time to climb out and run for the exit. Once they were reasonably certain their makeshift ladder and escape plan could work, they turned their attention back to Casey's condition. "You think she's OK?" Mila asked.

"I'm not sure," Jack answered. "If this really is Hitler's bunker, there could be poison down here or something."

Just then, another train rumbled through the tunnel. Jack began to count the seconds. "One, one thousand. Two, one thousand—" as he reached sixty, he'd yell out how many minutes had passed, then start again from one.

Mila hopped off the desk and walked over to where Casey was sitting quietly with her eyes closed. "Hey, we'll be out of here soon," he said, softly wiping the sweat from her face.

She turned to face him and opened her eyes. "I'll be fine," she said unconvincingly, her voice weak. Mila saw that the whites of her beautiful blue eyes were now covered with a blood-red web. "I have to take my contacts out as soon as we're out of here...if we get out," she said, looking at him uncertainly. "Mila...right?"

"Yeah, and you're Casey," he stated.

"So, you really learned how to speak English from comic books like *Whistleblower*?" Casey asked.

"Well … not exactly. I learned English from movies and music mostly. I learned American slang from *Whistleblower*, like 'cool, man' and 'badass,'" he answered, awkwardly leaning against a pile of broken concrete next to her.

"You're right. Lisa Carver is a badass," Casey chuckled.

Mila smiled with embarrassment. "I should go check on your boyfriend."

"He's not my boyfriend," Casey said brusquely.

Mila raised an eyebrow in doubt.

"What?" she asked. "He's not!"

"OK," Mila said as he turned away.

Clearly annoyed, Casey went on. "Why do you think he's my boyfriend?"

Mila stopped and turned back. "I saw you kiss him when you left the painting earlier."

"So? That doesn't mean anything!" said Casey.

"Well, in my world a kiss means everything!" said Mila calmly.

Casey paused to consider his statement. "It's complicated … you know, like your painting," she said, clearly annoyed and wanting to change the subject.

"Five!" Jack shouted. "One, one thousand, two, one thousand,"

Mila chuckled. He realized the mention of the kiss ticked Casey off.

"Oh, real nice," she complained. "My ankle is killing me, my eyes hurt, I'm probably riddled with tetanus, and now you're laughing at me."

"Sorry," Mila replied, trying not to laugh again at Casey's rant.

"What was with that painting, anyway?" she asked.

"If you really want to know, we were just trying to wreck the damn thing. We figured once it was ruined, they would have to take it down."

"But, why? It's just a print of an old painting," she replied, confused and frustrated. "What am I missing?"

Mila paused. It was too much to get into, but he knew if he didn't say something, she would think the Rom were a bunch of thieving vandals. He couldn't stand the thought of her feeling that way about him, especially after what Simon did. "You see, the painting is just like the Holocaust: they're trying to eliminate us from the face of the earth," he explained. "The painting shows the empress of Austria holding a scroll. The scroll is a proclamation that ordered her soldiers to rape Gypsy women. The plan was to eliminate our race by diluting our Romani bloodline. And what's worse, the story is true. It's a historical fact."

"That's disgusting! Who would paint something like that?" Casey asked.

"I dunno. Some Austrian asshole," Mila joked.

"Are you messing with me?" Casey asked. "I've aced AP history every year in school, and I never heard of anything like that."

"I swear it's all true," Mila assured her. "The painting tells the story. It was long ago, but we have not forgotten. As a matter of fact, my superstitious Aunt Nasta claims the scepter the empress holds embodies the story's deepest evil and that it is possibly even cursed. It's the symbol of her power to give such an order."

"Is that why you freaked out when I snapped the picture?" Casey asked.

Mila took a moment to think back. *Why did I freak out?* He struggled with his own thoughts. "I don't know. Maybe," he said.

"Why don't people talk about this?" Casey asked. "Why is it left out of the history books?"

"We Rom are always left out. If no one talks about the Nazis trying to exterminate us, why would they care about some Austrian doing the same thing hundreds of years ago?"

"Yeah ... I mean, I took a Holocaust studies class, and my teacher never said anything about gyp-I mean, the Romani people."

"We don't call it the Holocaust. We call it *Porajmos*, which means 'the devouring,'" Mila said.

"I didn't realize ..." Casey whispered.

They paused a moment, just listening to Jack count.

"Fifty-nine, one thousand. Sixty, one thousand. Ten!"

"Well if it means anything, I think this was all my fault," Casey confessed. "It was my idea to ditch the class today and go off on our own. We weren't even supposed be in Berlin for that matter," she said regretfully.

"Why is that?"

"Our trip got all screwed up from a flight problem. We were kinda forced to be here for the whole day. We leave for Austria tomorrow afternoon."

"Mmm, I see," Mila said. *Could this have something to do with what I saw in the dream?* he wondered.

"I didn't believe her," he whispered to himself.

"What was that? Casey asked.

"Oh nothing—was something stupid my superstitious aunt told me."

"Get into position!" Jack called before resuming his count. He dashed across the space to help Mila get Casey over to the makeshift ladder. She was now squinting even more.

"Hey! Up here!"

All three of them looked up. A shadowy face stared down at them from the hole in the ceiling.

"Who's there …?" Jack asked, losing his count.

"Deborah!" Casey exclaimed.

"If you can reach me, I can pull you up," the woman said, extending a well-muscled arm in their direction.

"Deborah?" Jack said to Casey.

"The empty seat, remember? Oh my God! I knew Uncle John would never trust me on my own. Thank God for that!"

"Never mind that! Hurry!" Mila insisted.

"He's right. We've got less than five minutes!" Jack added.

Working on pure adrenaline, Casey climbed up the bookshelf, her legs a little wobbly. "I'm the shortest. If I can make it, so can you guys."

She stood on the top shelf and reached up. Deborah's hand was inches away.

Casey stretched her arm as far as her muscles would allow, barely grazing Deborah's fingertips.

"I can't reach!" Casey panicked.

"Hurry, we are running out of time!" Jack pleaded, not helping the cause.

Without a second thought, Deborah reached for her satchel that was drooped over her shoulder. "Grab hold of this!" Deborah demanded, fashioning the strap into a tiny noose, and lowering it into the bunker.

Casey rose onto her tiptoes. She was so close. At last, she bent at the knees, leaped up, and grabbed Deborah's strap with both hands. Deborah pulled Casey up with no trouble.

Jack climbed on top of the desk next, then clambered up the bookshelf. He, too, needed to jump a bit but managed to grab hold of Deborah's makeshift noose.

As the tallest, Mila didn't need to jump. The woman's strength amazed him: Deborah pulled him up with one arm, letting out just a slight sigh as she did. Once free from the bunker, Mila stood stunned a minute as he got a better look at Deborah. She stood a good two or three inches taller than him, making her over six feet tall. The flashlight she carried cast menacing shadows over her already stern face. She wore her hair in a close-cut bob, almost military-looking, which clashed with her more feminine pearl earrings. If he had to guess her age, he'd say forty years, forty very harsh years.

Free from the bunker, the three teens collapsed on the loose gravel that lined the subway tracks. But their rest was short-lived. In a moment, they spotted lights advancing down the tunnel.

"Not again," Mila groaned.

"Come on, the station's close," Deborah said. "We can make it."

She picked up Casey and broke into a sprint. The other three followed, and the light of the nearest platform soon came into view. It was only about a hundred feet away, but the train was closing in on them fast. "Keep moving!" Deborah shouted, "and get ready to jump!"

They reached the platform and vaulted over the ledge to safety. Mere seconds later, the train flew through the tunnel and a gust of wind blew through the station. They all lay sprawled on the tile for a moment, then clambered to their feet as the train pulled to a stop.

"Everyone all right?" Deborah asked.

"I guess," Jack muttered.

Mila nodded.

"I'm fine," Casey replied.

"No, you're not," Deborah argued. She pointed to Casey's bleeding arm. "That needs to be looked at." The blood had soaked right through Mila's makeshift bandage.

Casey shot her a sardonic look but didn't argue. The subway doors hissed open behind her.

Jack turned to Deborah. "How'd you find us?" he asked.

"She can track my phone," Casey replied with annoyance.

"She can what? How? But we lost your phone!" Jack exclaimed.

"It must have been close by," Deborah said.

"No way! We searched everywhere. Unless..." Jack trailed off and looked around the platform. "Where's Mila?"

The three of them looked around. Mila had vanished. Then, as if with the same thought, they all turned to the subway train just as its doors slid shut. There was Mila, inside the nearest car. They watched him pull the phone from his pocket as the train began to move, gathered speed, and sped away.

VI

⌒⌇⌒

THE CHAPERONE?

B undestag Station was nearly empty, except for a few derelicts who were rushing in to seek refuge from an unexpected thunderstorm that had suddenly appeared over Berlin. The winds reverberated through the building, echoing all the way down to the subway platform. Deborah rushed a dreary Casey over to the vacant steel benches that lined platform 3.

"I can't believe he stole your phone!" Jack said while pacing behind them, still shocked by the apparent betrayal Mila had committed just moments ago.

Deborah immediately took a knee beside Casey and began to fumble through her satchel.

"That phone has to be at least $600. I guess Mr. G was right about the Gypsies," Jack continued.

The chaperone pulled out what looked like a first-aid kit and a small pen.

"Whoa!" Jack gasped at the *flick!* of a sharp blade as it emerged from the butt end of the pen. He was awe-struck as he watched Deborah use the gadget to cut the makeshift bandage that Mila had applied earlier in the bunker. She then cleaned the wound with antibiotic ointment.

"I think it had something to do with the picture I took of the painting," Casey said in a weak voice.

"Picture of the painting?" Jack asked, flabbergast-ed over the chaperone's precise work, not to mention her pen-knife that seemed to come straight out of a spy novel.

"The picture ... the picture!" Casey said, desperately out of breath but trying to shake Jack out of his mini-trance. "The one I took on my phone, of the painting. I noticed it freaked Mila out when I snapped those pictures." It was obvious that Casey was rapidly growing weaker.

"You mean the painting in the ad for the museum?" Jack asked. "Why would he freak out about that?"

"Are you lightheaded?" Deborah interrupted as she pulled out some Steri-Strips and OD green gauze. Her voice bore just the hint of an accent, but Jack couldn't place it.

"I'm fine, it's just ... my eyes are burning ..."

Deborah retracted the blade, flipped the pen around, then shined a beam of light into Casey's eyes.

"Damn. That's like a Swiss army pen," Jack joked. "I bet it's got a toothpick and a magnifying glass, too."

"Remove your contacts. Right now. Do it!" Deborah said, revealing a slight panic that the teens had yet to witness from the stern chaperone.

Casey complied, bringing her finger against the edge of her contacts and gently removing them. Deborah shined the beam into each eye, making Casey blink and wince in pain.

"Pupil response isn't good and they're bloodshot," she said to herself as she turned her attention back to Casey's wound.

"Sooooo ... this is your chaperone?" Jack asked Casey, his eyes glued to Deborah's imposing figure.

"Well, I ... she's more than that," Casey stammered.

Jack raised an eyebrow.

"I'm a personal assistant for the family," Deborah said. "That sometimes entails keeping an eye on the primary benefactor of the estate."

"Primary benefactor? Huh?" Jack asked.

"I told you it's complicated," Casey replied.

"And she's a 'personal assistant,'" Jack added with skepticism.

"OK, all done," Deborah announced as she finished wrapping the wound. "This will do until we get you to the hospital."

"Hospital?" Casey asked, her voice quavering in fear.

"Wow, that's ... pretty good," Jack said, examining the expert work that Deborah had done on Casey's wound. "That dressing would impress my mom, and she's a nurse. Where'd you learn that?" he pried.

Deborah gave him a quick glance and went back to examining Casey. She put the back of her hand to Casey's sweat-soaked forehead. "You're running a fever. We need to get you to a doctor," she said.

Just then, the last train pulled in to the station and the doors opened.

"Jack, I need you to get back to the hotel and tell Mr. Garson that I'm taking Ms. Richards to the hospital. Tell him to send Casey's luggage over, and don't forget her glasses! Also, let him know that she won't be accompanying the class to Vienna."

"What?" Casey asked. "No. I'm fine. Let's just go back to the hotel. I'll be better by... morning."

"Jack, you need to get going," Deborah insisted.

Deborah helped Casey to her feet, pulled out a flip phone, and dialed three keys. "Zulu Romeo Tango. This is Musef. Blackbird is secure but has suffered lacerations and a possible concussion and infection. Requesting a CASEVAC at Bundestag Station. Repeat, Bundestag ... Yes, the next station after Hauptbahnhof," she yelled into the phone. "Yes, I'll stay on the line. Tell me when transport is en route."

"You use radio codes?" Jack continued to pry.

Deborah ignored the question and supported Casey against her shoulder, rushing her toward the exit.

"Ow!" Casey yelled as she put pressure on her injured ankle.

Jack was clearly upset about the proposed separation, and even more worried about Casey's condition. He let the last train leave the station without him, ignoring Deborah's wishes. He tip-toed behind his new friends. "Wait up! Maybe I can help!" His voice echoed down the hall.

"Go back, Jack. You're in enough trouble as it is," Deborah barked.

"I could be another set of eyes, or hands, ya know?" Jack insisted. He ran to the other side of Casey and propped her up with his shoulder in an attempt to assist Deborah.

"Fine, I'll drop you on the way, but we have to hurry!" Deborah reluctantly agreed, avoiding an argument with the stubborn teen.

"Sooo ... what agency were you with before the personal assistant gig?" Jack pried in a condescending voice. "Special ops? You know, my uncle was a SEAL."

It was clear that Casey was not feeling well, and that her condition was worsening.

"Please, Deborah," Casey said. "I don't want to make this a thing. I just need some rest. I'm really tired, and my head is pounding. Plus, you know how Uncle John gets."

"Do you have a gun? Licensed to kill, maybe?" Jack jokingly inquired.

"Jack, you're not helping!" Casey yelled.

"I'm sorry, Casey. I'm just not buying this chaperone crap," Jack continued as they made their way to the street exit. "It's got to be some sort of cover story—"

"Oh, for God's sake!" Casey interrupted. "Deborah is an ex-Israeli spy. My uncle brags about it all the time! Happy now?!"

"I knew it! Israeli Intelligence? As in Mossad!" Jack said, impressed.

"Casey!" Deborah scolded, "save your strength. You're only getting worse. And Jack, cut it out. Let's go!"

Finally, they burst through the street exit. The thunderstorm was now in full force, immediately drenching the group. A grid of green spaces crisscrossed by roads surrounded the station. They could see for a quarter mile, but the car was nowhere in sight. The bodyguard shifted Casey's weight over Jack's shoulder, stepped away, and gazed down the street, searching for their ride. She pulled her phone out again and hit redial, then yelled over the pouring rain: "ETA!"

"Deborah! Deborah! Deborah! Something's wrong!" Jack yelled through the tumultuous downpour.

Still on her call, Deborah turned around to find Casey violently convulsing in Jack's arms.

Before anyone could react, a black SUV pulled up right beside them.

VII

ROMANI KRIS

Dense clouds the color of charcoal rolled in from the German countryside, blacking out the skies above Berlin. A chilly wind whipped through the streets and rain fell in heavy torrents. The city soon began to echo with the howls of roving packs of wild dogs. A grim omen cast its shadow.

With all his strength, Mila shoved open the door into the small space he called home. He was soaking wet from the ride back, and he shook with chills caused by something more than his soggy clothing. The dense smoky clouds over the city were heavy, strange, and ominous. An inexplicable fear rising in his throat, he had gunned the bike to go as fast as it could. Even so, he barely escaped the slavering wild dogs that chased him through the dark, smoky streets, baring their fangs as they eerily howled.

He stood in the doorway for a moment, catching his breath. Ever since he'd left the train, the rain had been relentless. He opened the door of the cinder block room which he shared with no one. The decrepit door read "Maintenance Quarters." He'd found the room years ago. For a Gypsy like Mila, the bleak cubicle was a palace. He found the dingy cinder block walls—covered in layer upon layer of graffiti—familiar, even comforting. He began to empty his pockets, putting everything onto the floor: keys, a large stack of dollars and euro notes from his share of the palm readings, his key fob, and Casey's cracked iPhone. He didn't like to pickpocket. All through the ride home, he couldn't stop himself from feeling guilty. But the enormous urge to prevent Casey from duplicating *The Proclamation* had been too strong to overcome. He remembered all three of them had been pressed together against the subway tunnel's hard wall as the train roared by. Who'd have noticed the gentle fingers reaching in and slipping something out of an unprotected pocket? It couldn't have been easier. "I must be going out of my mind," Mila mumbled to himself. "Nasta's superstitions are really getting to me."

For a moment, Mila thought back to the woman who'd rescued them. *Who was she? Was she one of their mothers? They'd called her by her first name. Are gadje that disrespectful of their parents?* he wondered. *Maybe she was an aunt or something like that. But God, she was strong! And the way she talked! Like a police officer or a soldier.*

Mila let go of the thought and began to peel off his wet clothes. *Whatever. Just crazy Americans,* he thought to himself. His wet jeans felt as heavy as lead as he laid them over the steam pipe to dry.

He pulled a bin from under his bed. The top portion of the contents was a stack of old American comic books, mostly from the early 1990s: the cheapest ones you could buy. He grinned at the sight of the topmost issue: *Whistleblower.* It reminded him of Casey, and he smiled. Then he put the comics aside and pulled out an old, moth-eaten towel. Using it to dry off, he went to the mirror. The gash across his muscular ribs had already scabbed over: nothing serious. Prodding it with his finger, he felt a twinge of pain, one of many little aches and pains all over his body. He'd been through a lot, it seemed.

After changing into dry boxers and a fresh T-shirt with a BMW logo on it, Mila collapsed onto his cot. He turned onto his left side. It was slightly less sore than his back. Before he could shut his eyes, he saw the cracked iPhone light up. He grabbed it, and took a look. The time read 11:11 p.m. *The kris is starting soon,* he recalled. A text message had just come in: "Mr. Garson is flipping out. Where are you? With that Jack guy? He's not even that cute! You're going to get us in trouble." The sender: Vivian.

Shrugging at the message, Mila flipped back to the home screen and scrolled through the apps. At last he found the Photos app. He opened it and started looking through the pictures. He passed a few images of some famous Berlin tourist spots, pausing when he came across a picture of Casey holding the phone while snapping a photo of Jack kissing her in front of a chunk of the Berlin wall. "Complicated, my ass," Mila muttered. He finally reached what he was looking for: several photos of The *Proclamation*. One was a close-up of the scepter. Mila stared at it a moment. He gazed deeper at the gilded object, trying to see what was so special about it. The hairs on his neck began to rise. Vulnerability mixed with passion tingled throughout his body as his ears began to ring louder and louder until it became deafening, paralyzing him. Summoning all his strength, Mila used his thumb to erase the photo. Instantaneously, he regained control of his body and the ringing ceased. *What the hell was that?* Mila thought as he wiped his brow, which was now drenched in sweat.

Bang, bang, bang! "Mila! Are you in there? Open the door!"

Is that Korey? Mila wondered, snapping back to reality. The twins' voices could be hard to tell apart, but Korey's was usually the louder and more exuberant of the two. With a groan, Mila quickly shoved the cash and phone into the pocket of his black denim jacket and then sleepily trudged to the door. Sure enough, there was Korey on the other side. "They're ready for you now,

Mila. Everyone has assembled. The priest is there, too," Korey announced, looking up at Mila.

Mila had never been called to a *kris* before, but he understood why he was being summoned now. Even without ever attending a *kris*, Mila knew its importance and necessity. *We do things our own way*, Mila thought. It was one of the things he respected about his community. *We have our own traditions, our own language, our own laws, and we have our own way of enforcing those laws; things the rest of the world would never understand.*

"Come on," Korey said, seizing Mila's hand and pulling him into the hallway.

"Hold on, little man!" Mila exclaimed. "Let me get some pants on!"

Mila yanked his jeans from the steam pipe. They were still quite damp, but they'd have to do. He tugged them on, threw on his jacket, then followed Korey out the door.

They made their way down the first-floor corridor by the dim streetlight peering through its cracked, dusty windows. Turning to look outside, Mila nearly jumped out of his skin. Outlined by the window's shabby frame was the wide face of a snarling dog, its teeth bared and its fur bristling. Its huge forepaws rested on the sill outside as it growled through the glass at the two boys. Many people in the camp took in stray dogs for company and protection. But this was no pet. A mangy mongrel, it was lean, fierce, and hungry-looking: more like a wolf than a dog.

"Come on, they want to see you *now!*" Korey insisted, giving Mila's arm a tug. This was no time to worry about a dog. The elders did not like to be kept waiting.

Together, they hurried to Lolo's apartment, now filled with Rom. The living room sofas had been moved to stiffly line one wall of the room. Half a dozen men sat talking on them. Young Romani boys sat cross-legged on the floor in front of the couches, facing the opposite side of the room. Korey found his twin and joined him. The women were gathered nearby in the kitchen, except for Nasta, who stood in the doorway listening quietly.

A row of teenage boys stood with their backs against a sidewall. Mila scouted the room for Simon or any of his gang, but they were nowhere to be found. Father Leichman was there too, sitting in a battered armchair (the best seat in the house, Lolo would say). Father Leichman was a wiry old man with a few strands of thin white hair clinging to his head. He wore the long black cassock and white clerical collar of a Catholic priest. He also had on soft black gloves. Rumor had it that they covered burn injuries. His trusted dog, Drago, lay curled up at his feet. It was very unusual for the priest to be there, but Mila felt protected by his presence. Father Leichman was always kind to him. The German holy man was responsible for bringing the entire community to Berlin for a better life. Since then, he had been watching over the camp like they were his own people.

Stephan picked up a simple wooden chair and carried it to the center of the room, where he set it down so it faced the men on the couches. He looked at Mila, who stepped forward and sat down in the solitary chair. As he looked into the severe eyes of the assembled men, he felt for the first time the seriousness of the situation. He sat up straighter, tall, and strong even when sitting down. *I am on trial,* he thought. *But I am guilty of nothing.*

The first person to speak was Merikano. He stood up, revealing his towering height, his mustachioed lips in a stern frown. Like Mila's Uncle Lolo, Rosa's grandfather was a *baro*. Literally, the word meant "a big man," and big Merikano surely was. But in reality, the title stood for much more. It commanded the ultimate in respect and authority as well as bringing with it great responsibility. The most important duty of the powerful group of *baré* was to solve any problem that arose in the camp—or outside the camp, among the outsiders, the *gadje*. Merikano had a fierce reputation, and Mila couldn't help flinching at the accusation coming from the old man's eyes. The *baro* spoke in formal, old-fashioned Romani, which Mila knew was reserved for serious occasions such as this.

"First, I would like to thank Father Leichman for staying up at this ungodly hour and for his assistance in calming the police so that we may have our own tribunal before turning anybody over to the authorities." Father Leichman nodded with gratitude at Merikano.

Merikano then turned to Mila. "Mila, *chava*," he said, using the Roma word for 'son',

"it is of great importance that you speak honestly to us today. There are many accusations against your character. The police are asking that we turn you over along with Simon and his gang. They are suggesting that you have been committing crimes all over Berlin."

"Mila didn't do nothing!" Nasta interrupted from the doorway.

The room of men shushed her. Everyone knew it was forbidden for women to speak at the *kris*. Merikano continued his questioning.

"Mila, listen to me. Father Leichman managed to convince the police not to arrest anyone. As you know, he's been protecting us, may God bless him, for years." Merikano paused to make the sign of the cross. "However, in order for us to stay in the camp in peace, they are demanding that the guilty parties be deported back to Romania. What do you have to say for yourself?"

Mila looked over at Nasta for guidance but found none. The thought of him being sent away from the only family he'd ever known frightened him deeply. He managed to summon some words to offer to the tribunal. "Uncle Merikano, it is true that I helped Simon escape the police, but I had nothing to do with him hurting that old lady or any other crimes."

"How do you know it is an old lady that was injured?" asked Father Leichman.

Mila stumbled for an answer.

"This *kris* is foolish," Nasta yelled. "The whole camp has been talking about it! That's how he knows!"

Merikano turned to Lolo and glared. "Your old lady is insulting the *kris*," Merikano said accusingly.

"Shut your mouth, Merikano. I have been coming to the *kris* since before you were born," she told him harshly.

"Enough," said Uncle Lolo. "Mila, how do you answer this charge?"

"I barely know Simon," Mila explained. "I assure you, I have not helped him to steal. He tricked me into helping him escape from the *gendarya*. He told me he was innocent. My only mistake was believing his lies. That's it."

The whole room went still for a moment. Father Leichman broke the silence. "Mila, I have known you since you were a baby. Can you swear in front of almighty God that you did not help Simon or any of his gang commit any crimes?"

"I assure it!" Mila responded quickly.

"Bring out the witness!" belted Merikano.

Everyone's eyes moved toward the door. To Mila's joy, he recognized his distant cousin Jolly. *For sure Jolly will vouch for me*, Mila thought.

Stephan brought another chair and put it next to Mila. Jolly took a seat. Mila nodded respectfully at Jolly, and his cousin returned the gesture.

"Jolly," Uncle Merikano said, "Are you friends with Mila?"

"Yes, Uncle Merikano, very good friends," Jolly replied. "We grew up here in the camp, and as everybody knows we are distant cousins." His genial remarks gave Mila more assurance that things would turn out all right.

"Is there any reason for you to falsely accuse Mila or lie about his character?" asked Uncle Merikano.

"No, sir! I would not lie to the *kris* or make up stories about anyone, especially my cousin and friend!" Jolly assured him.

"Okay, good. Then why don't you share with the *kris* what you shared with me earlier today."

Again, the room fell silent. Suddenly Mila's joy turned into fear as the hairs on his neck rose again.

"I ran into Simon and his gang in the train station earlier today. Simon told me that Mila has been helping them commit crimes all over Berlin," Jolly said.

"This is a lie! What is your evidence?" Uncle Lolo asked.

"I have no evidence, only this," said Jolly. "I saw Simon and Mila earlier today, next to the painting, looking at two Americans. When I asked Simon what they were doing, he told me Simon and Mila planned to rob the Americans later that day."

The statement drew grumbles and whispers from around the room.

"This is nonsense," yelled Uncle Lolo. "Mila, is there any truth to this? What is Jolly talking about?"

Mila paused, racking his brain. Romani rules and traditions were complicated, and at age seventeen, he was no expert. But one thing he knew very well: above all, he must show respect. "If you will permit me to speak freely, Uncle Merikano?" Mila asked, following the custom that all *baro* were to be addressed as "uncle" even if they were unrelated.

The *baro* extended an arm, the hand toward Mila with its palm up, in a gesture which meant, "You are not worthy of even a word of permission from me. But go ahead if you must."

Mila took a deep breath, knowing that his whole life might very well depend on what he said next.

"Uncle Lolo, Uncle Merikano, everyone: Jolly is a good and honest person, but he is mistaken. Simon wanted me to work for him. That is why Jolly saw us talking and that is why Simon lied about me, because it's what he wanted to be true, but I never stole with him, nor would I." He looked into Merikano's eyes. "*Dao so-lakh kow dell*," he said, the words meaning that he was giving a solemn oath before God. "I will never become a thief like Simon!"

The whole room seemed impressed. Nasta nodded with approval from the kitchen. Then, as everyone considered Mila's words a *Bzzzt! Bzzzt!* sound disturbed the quiet. Mila looked down at his jacket pocket as everyone else stared on. He reached inside and pulled out the iPhone. As he did, a wad of cash fell out, scattering on the floor. He saw a new text on the screen from "Uncle John" reading "Please stop trying to ditch Deborah. She is there for your protection. and her services do not come cheap."

For a moment, everyone was silent. Then they began to whisper and murmur, until at last Merikano cried out, "He lies! That's one of those new American phones!"

The crowd gasped.

"Where did you get all that money?" asked Uncle Lolo.

Mila's cheeks grew hot, and his stomach churned. He rushed to explain. "Well ... 1 ... she was taking a picture of the painting. Um... you see, we got trapped in a tunnel. Simon and his gang were coming. We had to run!" Mila said nervously trying to explain the whole evening in one breath. He realized that everything he said made him sound more guilty.

"Wait, Mila. Who had to run? What tunnel?" asked Uncle Lolo.

Feeling scared and overwhelmed, Mila scanned the room. He could see the disappointment in the eyes of Aunt Nasta, Stephan, and the rest of his family.

"I realize this looks bad, but I'm innocent. I swear!" Mila pleaded.

Uncle Lolo replied, "Yes, Mila, this looks really bad. I think Jolly is the only one telling the truth here."

"He gave a false oath before God!" Merikano yelled.

Mila again looked over at Aunt Nasta for guidance. She gave him a nod as if to say, "Be strong."

Father Leichman noticed the exchange. "Mila, calm down for a moment, and tell us what happened," Father Leichman said. "Start with the painting."

"I think we've heard enough," Merikano said. "We've brought enough trouble to the camp. We should decide whether we are going to send Mila back to Romania with Simon and his gang." Merikano's statement brought an immediate uproar from the entire room. Half the *kris* was advocating for Mila, and the other half for the safety of the camp, but all Mila could hear was the pounding of his heart.

Suddenly, Father Leichman took the tip of his cane and banged it on the table in front of him as if it were a gavel. "Silence. SILENCE!" he exclaimed. The room went quiet.

"Before I give my counsel, I would like to remind you that decisions made in fear are seldom good ones," Father Leichman proclaimed, turning toward Merikano. "Brother Merikano, I realize that you are fearful for the camp's safety, and I must admit, we are wearing out our welcome with the authorities. Not to mention the greedy owners of the rubber factory who desperately want possession of these buildings. I truly believe that the inspector will only grant me this last favor. Any more malicious activity from this camp will surely get the community evicted."

He then turned to face Mila. "Mila, I realize that your lack of having parents has steered you in the wrong direction. I'm hearing that you have been disobedient to Uncle Lolo, spending all your time dilly-dallying with a toy motorbike instead of helping out at the camp. And now you're accused of bringing havoc to the entire community." Leichman paused, as if to let the words sink in. "However, I also know that you are a pious boy and would never take the Lord's name in vain by swearing a false oath. Mila, my son, please explain."

Mila took another deep breath. "The American girl took pictures of the painting so she could make a copy of it. I didn't want her to do that, so I took the phone," Mila explained. "But it wasn't for Simon or anything, I even protected her and her friend from Simon."

The *kris* looked skeptical.

"Please go on," said Father Leichman. "How is it that you *protected* them?"

Mila took a deep breath and began explaining what had transpired earlier that day. As he recounted the unusual turn of events, he found it difficult to believe his own words. Still, he continued, despite knowing that it would be impossible for anyone to believe this ridiculous story. Still, Father Leichman seemed to be listening with great interest, even asking questions that would allude to Mila's innocence, which gave Mila some comfort and confidence.

"May we see these pictures?" asked Father Leichman

"Umm, I deleted them ..." Mila explained.

Merikano got ready to shout something, but Father Leichman, without even looking, held up a finger for him to be patient.

"Mila, when you saw her taking these pictures, what did you feel?" the priest asked.

Everyone in the room seemed confused by this question. They looked at each other, whispering about what it could mean. All except for Nasta, she locked eyes with Mila, shaking her head frantically. Mila could not understand why.

"I felt ... the presence of evil," he explained. "And later when I looked at the pictures, it was even worse. There was one of the scepter in the queen's hand. It almost hurt to look at it."

Aunt Nasta covered her mouth with her hands as if Mila had made a grave mistake. Everyone else just seemed confused.

Again, the room was silent. Awaiting his sentence, Mila felt his body trembling in fear.

"I believe him," the holy man replied. "It is obvious that he has been infected with old superstitions. Someone has been teaching this poor boy divinations.

The Bible warns not to practice divination or seek omens. Many in this community have embraced this wisdom, but it seems a few still cling to ancient madness. As we see, this devilry has tricked Mila into committing a sin."

People cast furtive glances around the room. Aunt Nasta scowled at the priest. Merikano moved to take a vote, but again was interrupted by Father Leichman. At this point, Mila figured it could go either way.

"I suggest Mila perform a penance," Father Leichman said. "If Mila promises that he can return the phone to the rightful owners, donate the money, sell his bike to help pay for the repairs to the camp, and come to church every Sunday to help me with the sermons, then perhaps we can put this mess behind us. Mila, would you agree to these terms?"

Mila thought about his precious bike and all the time he spent rebuilding it, but the prospect of being deported to Romania was too frightening to bear. Reluctantly, he agreed.

Merikano immediately chimed in. "Great. Let's all vote on whether Mila should be punished or deported. Those in favor for deporting Mila to Romania say aye." A few scattered voices said "aye." Merikano continued. "All those in favor of Mila being punished and staying with the camp say aye." Simultaneously, the rest of the room said "Aye." Mila let out his breath in relief.

"Mila, you have been judged by the *kris*," Father Leichman said. "You must serve your penance. We will start by returning the phone to its owner. Do you have any idea where these American tourists are staying?"

"I have no idea where they are staying, and I believe they are leaving for Austria tomorrow afternoon."

"Then you have until tomorrow to find them and return the phone, or there will be further consequences," Father Leichman ordered.

VIII

HOLY CROSS

Lightning crackled in the sky above the chapel of Holy Cross Church, revealing storm clouds gathering around the building's Gothic steeple. Inside, all was dark but for a handful of newly-lit candles on the main altar, their dim light reaching just to the first few pews. Above the altar and down the sides of the sanctuary shined the deep colors of spectacular stained-glass windows.

The east window was supposed to be the most beautiful of all. Stretching sixty feet from floor to ceiling, it depicted a number of well-known biblical scenes in jewel-like tones. The topmost arch was a massive image of Christ dragging the cross through the crowds in Jerusalem on his final journey to the crucifixion.

The east wall was famous for having miraculously survived the war. Bombs had leveled the rest of the church, but the east wall had remained intact, with only minor damage to the stained glass. To many Catholic Berliners, this was as a true act of God. Now bathed in the feeble candlelight, otherwise cloaked in shadow, the wall looked menacing rather than uplifting.

Father Leichman lit the last of a host of candles on the massive altar. His beloved German shepherd, Drago, wandered the aisles. Normally pets weren't allowed in the church, but the priest could do as he wished.

At the first pew, the dog sniffed the sleeve of a kneeling visitor. The stern figure spoke to him in greeting, and Drago cautiously wagged his tail once or twice. The man was dressed in a black trench coat, opened to reveal a dark-blue suit with gray pinstripes. Perhaps in his late seventies, he wore his gray hair pulled back into a short ponytail. Two men in matching black trench coats stood still as statues, one at each end of the pew, with their feet shoulder-width apart and their hands clasped behind their backs: they were clearly bodyguards.

The guard on the inner aisle moved as little as possible to let Leichman pass. The cleric gave his dog a quick scratch behind the ears and stood before his visitor. "Victor Strauss," the priest said. "It's been a long time."

"Eighteen years," Victor Strauss replied.

Leichman reached into his pocket and drew out a ring. It was engraved with a strange symbol: something like a swastika, but with the bars curved inward on themselves, creating a circular pattern. He placed the ring on his finger. He offered his hand to Strauss, who kissed the ring quickly, automatically. It was a ritual he'd performed many times before, albeit not in recent years.

Strauss slid across the pew's dark, polished wood, making room for Father Leichman. The priest's feeble bones seemed to grind together as he slowly took a seat. His visitor didn't look at him but instead stared straight ahead at the huge stained-glass window. Lightning flashed outside, illuminating the windows' many colors in a bright array. The rain's pitter-patter increased to a downpour. Sheets of water began to run down the colored glass.

"Why am I here?" Strauss queried Leichman.

"I think you know," the priest replied. "There is but a single reason for me to call you after almost twenty years and insist you come directly to Berlin."

Strauss took a deep breath. "I flew here from Brussels in a storm. I thought someone was dying!" He checked his watch as if to remind himself of the unbelievably early hour. "Are you telling me this is about the talisman? It's not here. It's probably gone for good, destroyed in the bombing or melted down for scrap by some ignorant Gypsy!"

"No, it is here," the priest insisted.

Strauss sighed. "I feel sorry for you, old man. Your mind is starting to go."

Leichman scowled with rage. He seized Strauss by the collar, forcing his attention. "Do not mock me,

Strauss!" he shouted, his voice surprisingly strong for someone so frail.

The security guards immediately assumed an aggressive stance. They moved closer, but Strauss raised a hand and shooed them away. His demeanor calm and sympathetic, Strauss stood up. He put his hands on the cleric's shoulders and gently held him at arm's length. He looked into Leichman's eyes. "Father, my friends in the Communist government searched high and low. We had unlimited access to the bunker. Don't you think we would have found it?"

"I know why it is you failed. It doesn't matter. Listen to that rain outside—it's a deluge! And can't you hear how the wind howls? Like an enraged beast! It's almost a hurricane!" Leichman said fearfully.

"Oh, Father! Big storms like this happen all the time. It's just global warming. Don't you read the papers?" Strauss joked.

The priest raised his index finger. "I warned you not to mock me," he scolded.

The clergyman's statement changed Strauss's demeanor. He adjusted his suit, nervously smoothing out imaginary wrinkles.

"That is no earthly weather out there. It is more," Leichman insisted. "I know it. I feel it in my heart. The talisman has been found, and its power has been unleashed."

"And the painting...*The Proclamation*...I read that it has been recently recovered by Munich Police," Strauss said uneasily.

"Yes, it has ... along with a fortune in artworks that the Nazis stole from the Jews. And they will soon be displaying *The Proclamation* this week at the Berlinische Galerie. I suppose that's a coincidence as well?"

"Even if you're right, we're too late," Strauss replied. Pushing past the priest and the security guards, he walked to the front of the church.

Leichman used the pew to pull himself upright. Once on his feet he followed Strauss. "Victor, Victor—what has happened to you? You used to be the most ambitious of all of us. You were so certain of your destiny! You knew you were fated to be the next Master."

Strauss paused and made a show of admiring the enormous stained-glass window. He watched as the rain outside cascaded down the glass, then spoke forcefully, his back still turned to the priest. "I realized I don't need it! I own factories in Romania, Hungary, and Germany. I flew here on a private jet, for Christ's sake! *I have real power.* Why waste my time playing with ancient mysticism?"

"Be careful how you mock the name of Christ," Leichman admonished him. "You were always a fool. One of us was meant to be the next Master. It is our destiny! I'm far too old for this. It's a curse that I've lived this long."

Strauss raised an eyebrow at the old man's absurdity. He continued to pretend to study the ornate glass. "And what of Paul? Why don't you ask him to find it?" he suggested.

"I've tried every manner of divination and augury to find him: scrying, the cards, the stones, even bibliomancy. Nothing! He is surely dead."

"How tragic," Strauss said mockingly, without a hint of remorse.

"Surely you're not satisfied with a bit of money and some influence," Leichman argued.

"I'd like more of both," Strauss admitted, "but I don't need to rely on some relic to get it."

"You're running for office, correct?"

Strauss turned back to the priest. "Yes," he said. "I'm running for the EU Parliament, and I'm sure to win."

Leichman looked unimpressed. "I suppose you'll hold that position for a few years, and if your party wins enough seats in Parliament, you'll come into some real power just in time for your eighty-fifth birthday."

Strauss frowned at the man's sarcasm. He turned once again to the awe-inspiring stained glass, his eyes drifting to an arresting detail of the crucifixion scene. The figures of a man and three young boys could be seen just faintly in the background. The man pushed a wheelbarrow up a hill as the three little ones trailed behind. Victor wondered who they were supposed to be.

There was something conspicuous about their olive skin and jet-black hair.

"Our previous master had no money—and no influence, either. Not at first. We both know what the talisman gave him. If you had it, you could run for chancellor of Germany tomorrow—and win! You could walk into the European Union and have everyone eating out of your hand. It will be much easier now. Today's politicians are as corrupt as ever, but their minds are so much weaker—" before he could go on, Leichman broke down in a fit of coughing.

Strauss walked back to the pew. Noticing a trail of saliva shining from the priest's chin, he offered the old man a handkerchief. The priest wiped his face. Like stones, the raindrops continued to pound the chapel's tiled roof. From nearby came an earsplitting crack of thunder. The wild, distant howls of dogs that sounded like hungry wolves grew louder.

"Do you hear them?" Leichman asked. "The dogs—they were summoned! They are seeking the one who stole our destiny."

The priest handed back the now-soiled handkerchief to his visitor. As Strauss took it, his eyes were drawn to the old man's right hand. The flesh was horribly discolored and twisted into grotesque swirls and bulges: ancient burn scars. Leichman had never told Strauss exactly what had happened so many years ago, how his hand had been so badly disfigured. "An accident at the seminary" was the most he would ever say.

"I repeat: if what you say is true, and someone has found the talisman, it is already too late. They own it now. You know this!" Strauss said.

"Do you remember nothing?" Leichman admonished. "A person will not pair with the scepter until they willingly invoke its powers! Until then they can be killed like any ordinary person."

Victor gave Leichman yet another look of skepticism.

"Even if this usurper is paired already, we can use the gilded tomb to separate them from it," Leichman pointed out. "I know you rebuilt it years ago."

"Even if that was true, we don't know if it will work that way...we would need a pureblood Garade Gypsy."

"The tomb will work," the cleric insisted. "The Wallachian tomb suppressed its power for five hundred years, and for all we know, His Excellency the Count is still the rightful owner. Our tomb should work just as well."

Stuffing his hands into his pockets, frustrated, Strauss began to pace up and down the aisle. "The Count? Really? This is getting absurd. I won't risk my fortune on the tomb! And there are no more Garade!" He waved his hands in exasperation. "Every last pureblood was killed. They were purged, eradicated, devoured. The Nazis saw to that!" Strauss paused, then said, "I won't take that risk! Not based on your mystical theories."

"Yes, you are right." Leichman whispered. "After all, I am no magi. However, I am not the only one who believes it has been found."

Strauss turned on his heel and stared at the cleric, intrigued.

"There is an old hag ... she is a true mystic, a Gypsy witch who lives at the camp. She *also* believes that it has been discovered. Nevertheless, if you insist on playing it safe, then we'll just have to use a *Garade* Gypsy," Leichman replied. "We know that will work."

"Are you going deaf? There are no more Garade!"

"No, there is one left. He has been right under my nose for years."

"At the camp?"

"Yes, an orphan boy with the gift of intuition. And what is most interesting, I did not realize it until this evening ... the mystic has been keeping him safe, protecting him all these years."

"If that is true, she will continue to protect him," Strauss responded.

"Agreed. We must deal with her soon!"

Strauss stood up straighter at this news. He held his chin between his thumb and forefinger and slowly stroked it, his characteristic gesture when deep in thought. Leichman could tell he had finally convinced his old friend. "Do you have him in custody now?" Strauss asked with enthusiasm.

"I let him go."

"Why would you do such a thing?"

"Relax, my old friend... Throughout history, the Garade and the talisman always seem to find one another. If he's free to wander, he will lead us right to it."

"That is a huge risk, perhaps we need to put Operation Rubbish Removal into place, for added leverage," Strauss strategized thoughtfully, still stroking his chin.

"Agreed!" Leichman said approvingly. "Summon every man you can from your party. We have much to do. We must find the usurper, search for the artifact in case she does not have it, and best of all, clean out the Gypsy rat's nest."

IX

RUBBISH REMOVAL

"Two hundred? Come on! The parts cost more than that!" Mila exclaimed.

"It's not my fault you paid too much for the repairs," replied Ludwig, the heavyset junk dealer.

"What are you talking about? I bought most of the parts from you!" Mila reminded him.

"Hey, I'm a business man not a saint. Two hundred, not a penny more. Take it or leave it," Ludwig said.

This is going to be harder than I expected, Mila thought. He had been busy all morning and into the early afternoon. He had two tasks to accomplish. The first was to get the stolen iPhone back to Casey. The second was to sell his beloved motorcycle and donate the money to the camp, which was turning out to be the more difficult of the two.

Shortly after the *kris*, Mila came up with a plan. Using Casey's iPhone, he replied to one of Vivian's countless texts, pretending he was Casey. *"Hey Viv! Yeah, I'm still with Jack. We're heading back shortly. Can you remind me the name of the hotel we're staying at?"* Sure enough, a text came back from Vivian. *"Sometimes I wonder how you even pass any of your classes. You're so stupid Casey Richards. You know very well we are staying at the Bavarian Palace."*

Once Mila found out where Casey was staying, he waited until sunrise, then rode to the hotel before anyone at the camp awakened. Using his tourist costume, he approached the front desk of the posh hotel. The woman at the desk didn't seem very kind, but he was on a mission.

He approached her. "Hi, my name is Mi—I mean … Elijah. Yes, Elijah," he stammered, not wanting to give himself away. "Do you have a guest that is checking out today?"

The tired-eyed woman dressed in a blue blazer looked at him as if he had two heads. "Mr. Elijah, we have many guests checking out today, and checking in. Are you searching for anyone in particular? A name, perhaps?" she asked sarcastically.

"Yes, of course. Casey Richards. She's an American student traveling with her class."

"Ah yes, Ms. Richards. Are you from the hospital?" the woman asked.

"Hospital?" Mila responded confused.

"Yes, I received a call from the hospital, saying that someone will be picking up her things shortly and checking out for her. Is that not you?"

Mila wanted to ask if Casey was okay, but he also didn't want to get in any more trouble. Fearing that Jack might be arriving any moment to pick up Casey's things, he placed the phone on the desk in front of the woman.

"Can you give this to whoever comes to pick up her stuff? This is Ms. Richard's phone."

"Yes, of course," the woman said.

Mila then turned around and headed for the exit, but he couldn't resist knowing what happened to the beautiful girl. He stopped for a second and turned back to the woman.

"Ms. Richards ... she's okay, right?" he asked the woman.

She finally cracked a smile and said "Of course. Nothing serious. I believe it's just a sprained ankle."

Comforted, Mila left the hotel and headed straight for the scrapyard that was not a far walk from the camp, hoping to negotiate a sale with his friend Ludwig who managed the shop. Unfortunately, when Mila arrived, Ludwig was not there. He opted out to wait. After several painful hours, Ludwig finally arrived, and their haggling began.

"Come on, Ludwig, I need to sell it" Mila pleaded. "I'm in a whole lot of trouble."

"I don't get you, kid. You drove me crazy for months to get the parts for the damn thing, and now you want to get rid of it?"

"I made a lot of trouble for the camp. If you don't buy the bike, I'll be in even more trouble," Mila told him.

Ludwig glanced over Mila's shoulder at the glass door. "I think that trouble has already started," he said.

Mila turned to see what he was talking about. He saw a plume of smoke in the distance, mixing with the storm clouds. It looked almost like it was coming from the camp. At first, he assumed it came from the factories. Then, to his horror, he realized it was far darker than the factory smoke. Mila knew this was his cue to leave. He made a beeline across the street for his bike. A startled driver slammed his brakes, stopping just short of running into him. Mila jumped on his bike as the car's horn blared. As he raced down the road, he could see it clearly. The smoke was definitely rising from the Romani camp.

Pulling off at the nearest exit, Mila took the side road past Schmidt's to the camp. Men in hard hats and reflector vests blocked the road. They manned a set of barricades labeled Construction Zone, waving only work vehicles through. Mila skidded to a stop. He looked past the roadblock to Building A. The structure had been gutted. A wrecking ball was repeatedly smashing into the sides, reducing Mila's home to dust and rubble.

Beyond the demolition ball, he could see bulldozers plowing through the shacks and tents, pushing the debris into a series of bonfires. In the distance, near Building B, two crowds had gathered. One stood in tight, uniformed ranks: *police, of course,* Mila thought. Facing off with the police was a loose mob of ragged Rom: undoubtedly the residents of the ghetto.

Mila held on tight as he gunned his bike toward the camp. A construction worker darted out of the way as the bike blew past the roadblock. The motorcycle shook violently as he pulled off the road onto uneven ground.

This can't be happening! Mila thought. *Father Leichman protects us. He has a deal with the rubber factory. We're supposed to be safe.* With the word *safe,* Mila remembered the piles of eviction letters in Nasta's apartment.

"Oh no!" he cried out. *"No!"* as he sped up.

He crossed the football field, where a massive bonfire crackled and snapped, sending clouds of black smoke high into the air. The fumes stung Mila's eyes as he drew closer to his kin, who were gathered at Building B.

Up close, he noticed a loose organization to the mob. The women and children were pushed to the back, while the men had gathered at the front. From here Mila could see the *gadje* more clearly, too. They wore black, military-style uniforms with no police badges or other identifying marks. Each carried a baton and a riot shield. *Could they be private security?* Mila wondered. Lolo stood just a few feet from these men, shouting something. A violent confrontation was clearly imminent.

Mila pulled up to the women and children. He found Rosa right away. "Nasta and Petre are in there!" she cried, pointing to Building B. A second crane pulled toward the building. Mila's stomach began to churn as he watched the wrecking ball.

He jumped off the motorcycle and let it fall on its side. Passing dozens of his relatives with anguished faces, he pushed through the crowd of women and children to the front. Young girls sobbed while old women slapped their own faces hoping this was a bad dream and they could wake themselves up from it. Little ones clutched their mothers' hands and cried in panic and bewilderment. "We must take the children and run!" one woman shouted.

"They're destroying everything!" came the anguished voice of another.

"The church, we have to go to the church—it's the only safe place!" urged an older woman.

Mila made his way to the group of Romani men. He pushed his way to the front and found himself shoulder to shoulder with Stephan. The two exchanged glances, sharing a moment of fear, anger, and a sense of duty.

"There are people in there!" Lolo cried one last, desperate time.

A passing construction worker stopped, looking concerned, but a security guard shouted, "Ignore his Gypsy lies! It is empty. We checked."

Satisfied, the worker moved on as the Rom continued to shout with rage. The moment had reached its boiling point. Though well-armed, the contractors were outnumbered. The Rom knew they had a chance. The wrecking ball took its first swing. The ground shook as the heavy black sphere crashed into a concrete wall. At the same moment, someone threw a bottle at the security force's phalanx. That was all it took to set things off. The guards charged at the Rom, wildly swinging their clubs. A few of the Rom picked up bits of wood or stones, but most were unarmed. As the clubs swung back and forth, Romani bodies began to fall to the ground, writhing in pain.

A guard took a swing at Mila. He ducked just in time. While the man was distracted, Stephan went in for a tackle. He caught their attacker off guard and sent him toppling to the ground. They started to grapple with each other, creating a gap in the battle line.

"Go!" Stephan cried. "Get in there! Save them!"

Mila broke away from the melee and ran for Building B. The doors were chained shut. He leaped through one of the shattered windows and sprinted up the stairs to his great-aunt's apartment. The building shook as the wrecking ball crashed into it again.

At Nasta's place, the door was open as usual. There was even the lingering scent of cherry peppers in the air, the remnants of some unfinished meal. Tremors from the demolition had knocked cookware and dishes to the floor, which was now covered with pots, pans, and shards of ceramic. As Mila stepped inside, he heard a whimper from under the table. He lifted the old table-cloth and bent to find the source of the noise. Petre was huddled underneath, terrified.

"Petre, I'm gonna get you out of here," Mila said. "Where's Aunt Nasta?"

"The shrine," Petre whispered.

Of course! Mila thought. He ran to the closet and tore open its door. Nasta lay prone in front of her little altar. A bulky chunk of concrete had fallen on her leg, trapping her. Mila grabbed the piece of rubble and lifted with all his might. It was no use. The concrete wouldn't budge.

Nasta regained consciousness as Mila strained to free her. Weakly, she put her hands flat on the floor and pushed, raising her upper body slightly until she could see her great-nephew. Her ripped sleeve revealed to Mila for the first time a series of numbers tattooed on the underside of her arm. Mila stood looking down at her, his eyes wide with shock as he recognized the mark of the Nazi death camps.

"Mila, thank God," she said. She appeared close to fainting from the pain.

"I'll get you out. Just stay with me," Mila said. "Little man, get in here! I need some help!"

Petre crept out from under the table as if his cousin's courage had made him brave, too. He scampered into the room and wedged his hands under a corner of the concrete block. Nasta sat up as best she could to help them. The three managed to lift the rubble enough for the old lady to pull her leg free. Mila almost gagged at the sight of her mangled limb. But she managed to stand.

Mila gave her his arm, and she leaned heavily on it, keeping most of her weight on her uninjured leg. Petre ran to her other side and gave her his little arm to lean on. They both did their best to help her as she began to hobble to safety.

"Your dream is coming true," Nasta told Mila.

"Don't talk. Save your strength," Mila replied.

"Mila, you will listen to me," Nasta insisted.

The hallway shook and splintered as the wrecking ball struck again with a crash. They stumbled into the stairwell and began to descend at a snail's pace. Tripping now could spell disaster.

"The two *gadje* from the train station, where are they?" she asked.

"The hospital. The girl is injured, but I returned the phone," Mila said as they inched down one stair at a time.

"It's the work of the scepter."

135

"The scepter? What are you talking about?"

"The scepter from the painting," she explained. "Father Leichman knows this as well. The scepter is not just a flat object pictured on canvas. It exists. Here. Now. It is real. And it is a thing of great evil. I know what your visions have shown. I know what my divinations have shown. If this girl is suddenly sick, it is no coincidence. It is fate."

"What are you talking about? I don't understand!" Mila cried.

The wrecking ball struck again. Another wall crumbled. A portion of the ceiling collapsed, falling onto the stairway just above them. Nasta tripped and nearly fell, but Mila managed to grab the railing. They stumbled down the rest of the flight, coming to a stop on the third-floor landing. Nasta sank to the ground moaning in pain, her hurt leg now twisted beneath her at a crazy angle.

Without a moment's hesitation, Mila lifted Nasta into his strong arms and carried her down the stairs. Her frail body was heavier than he'd expected, but he managed to lift her and keep moving. Carefully but quickly, he went step-by-step to the first floor and then down the corridor.

Through the broken window where he'd entered he could see that outside the Rom had managed to push back the security forces. Lolo and Merikano stood on the other side. Mila rushed to the window and lifted his great-aunt across the sill and into her son's arms. Merikano added his arms for support, and they carried her to safety. Mila helped Petre out next, then leaped through the window just as the wrecking ball struck again.

The rear wall of Building B caved in. Then the entire structure began to fall in on itself. Piece by piece, crash after crash, their home crumbled to the ground as the Rom retreated to the field near the train tracks.

As entire families fled, the guards as well as the crowd of *gadje* onlookers jeered. "That's it, Gypsies! Run!" they yelled. "It's rubbish removal day—so get lost!"

The Rom ran for their lives. Mila pushed through the panicked crowd to find Nasta. She lay on the grass with Stephan, Rosa, Petre, and Korey by her side. As Stephan tore a blanket into strips for bandages, Rosa took them from him and did her best to set the old woman's injured leg. She groaned in pain; her leg was clearly shattered in several places.

"Mila, come closer," she moaned in a voice he could barely hear. He obeyed, kneeling next to her.

"Mila, you must find the scepter. You must bring it to me," she whispered weakly.

"There is no scepter," Mila insisted.

Rosa leaned over to Stephan. "What are they talking about?" she whispered. Stephan shrugged and continued tearing off bandages.

"There was a scepter. You did not realize it at the time. If the girl is dying, it is because of the scepter," Nasta insisted.

"Dying? What do you mean?"

"Yes, Mila. The girl is dying. The scepter is cursed, poisoned. That is why you must find it before *he* does. Only you can keep it from causing more harm." She reached into her apron pocket. Pulling out her tarot deck, she tried to flip through the cards. They scattered everywhere, yet she was able to find the Magician right away. She handed the card to Mila. He stared at it, puzzled.

"That is the scepter," she explained. "See?" she said, pointing to something the Magician held in his hand. "Do you remember the dead man in your dream? It was you! You're the Magician!"

Mila was amazed that Nasta knew he was the dead man in the dream. He was now realizing this was more than silly superstition. With that, he immediately thought of the girl.

"What about Casey, the American girl?" Mila asked.

"I told you: the girl is dying."

"But we have to help her!" Mila cried.

"No Mila, she must die. The scepter can heal her flesh but not save her life. Even if she does not die, she will be lost in the end. It would be kinder to let her go in peace. There's nothing we can do about that."

"What? That doesn't make sense!" Mila replied.

"There is no time to explain," Nasta said softly. She seemed to be losing strength. "Don't throw the card away as you did the *chukrayi*."

The admonition made Mila ashamed. *How does she know that?* He put the tarot card in his pocket as carefully as he could. Then he took Nasta's hand. It was cold and trembling. Mila swallowed hard, realizing how badly she was hurt.

"Don't worry about me," she said, reading his thoughts as she so often did. "Go now. Find this evil thing, but don't bring it to the church. This is your mission, Mila. This is why you are so strong, so special. This is why you are one of a kind."

X

~~\~\~\~\~~

THE POISON
SCEPTER

Mila gunned his motorcycle and sped down the
highway to Berlin. All this back and forth was
putting a real strain on him, and he was running low
on gas. He took the first exit for the city, leaning into
a tight turn. Shortly after the demolition, buses had arrived, courtesy of Father Leichman. They would take
the residents of the ghetto to the church and then to
some new refuge.

The rain still hadn't let up, and he had to take several detours. It seemed every other street was flooded.
As he rode through the city, he recalled his great-aunt's
grim warnings and the task she'd assigned to him. Mila
had always been on the fence about her mysticism. One
day, he'd find himself wondering about the meaning

of his dreams and worrying that a negative thought or word might bring bad luck. Another day, he'd think it was all nonsense and even laugh at her crazy ideas. But these recent events were too much to deny. The odds of what had taken place had to be in the billions, which could only mean that Casey was dying. A heavy sadness filled his heart. *We can't just let her die,* he thought.

He had to choose. Should he look for this scepter? Or would it just be a waste of time? The scepter might not even exist. *It could all be just an old legend of Nasta's,* he rationalized. Mila searched his feelings, struggling to make sense of everything. *Am I wasting my time looking for this artifact? Even if I'm not, how am I going to get down there alone?* It became clearer to him that he was yearning for just a bit more proof that Nasta's predictions could be true. *Maybe I'll head to the hospital and see if Casey is really sick. If not, I'll head back to the camp and put all of this silliness behind me. If she is, maybe the artifact really can save her, just as Nasta said. Maybe I could get this Jack guy to help me go back and get it. After all, it's his girlfriend in trouble. He should be doing this.* He felt both frustrated and jealous. *Who knows, with any luck, he may still have the scepter.*

Mila slammed on his brakes. His back tire drifted, and he spun in a full U-turn. The driver behind Mila's bike honked his horn at the reckless display. Ignoring it, Mila revved his engine and headed straight for the hospital. His thoughts raced as the bike sped through the city streets: *That spike Jack found—he called it an artifact. That's the scepter. It has to be.*

At the hospital, Mila locked up the motorcycle and headed for the visitors' entrance. Heads turned at the sight of the tall, dark fellow, strongly built and drenched head to toe. *What? You never saw a soaking wet Gypsy before?* he wanted to shout, striding confidently by as they gawked.

He scanned the waiting room, hoping to find one of the Americans. *Too many faces.* The place was packed. Nearest him was an older couple with bandages on their heads, probably from a car accident. A younger boy pushed past, his face covered in scratches and a bite mark on his arm: a dog attack, no doubt. There were dozens of patients in the waiting room but not the two Americans he sought.

A nurse carrying a chart scanned her ID and stepped through the double doors. Just before they swung shut, Mila glimpsed a sign pointing to the intensive care unit. *If she's dying, that's where she'll be. But how do I get back there? It's not like I can just ask to visit her.*

Before Mila could think of what to say, a nurse approached him. "May I help you?" she asked pointedly.

He thought fast. Spotting a child with a bad nosebleed, he suddenly knew what to do. "I'm here to give blood," he replied.

"Give blood?" she asked skeptically.

"Yes, because of the storm. There are so many people hurt," Mila explained, trying to play up the concern.

"You do understand, blood is donated for free," the nurse said patiently.

"Yes, of course!" Mila said, feigning outrage and shock. "I'm not trying to sell my blood. That's illegal!"

The nurse narrowed her eyes. She wasn't buying his pose. "Do you know your blood type?"

"AB negative," Mila blurted. He knew nothing about blood types, but he remembered this one from *Whistleblower.*

Her eyes widened. "Are you sure? That's an extremely rare blood type!"

"Well," Mila said with a grin, "I guess blood is like a box of chocolates. You never know what you're going to get."

The nurse gave him a quizzical look. Then she smiled. "All right, fine. Come with me."

Mila resisted the urge to pump his fist. *It worked!*

The nurse led him through the security doors and down a broad hallway brightly lit with harsh fluorescent bulbs. Her brisk pace put her a few steps ahead of Mila. That was his chance.

"We're going to have to run a quick test to confirm..." the nurse droned on as Mila silently slipped away.

He tiptoed down the hallway, slipping behind a pillar or around a corner now and then. The doctors and staff were all caught up in one thing or another. It wasn't hard to escape their attention. He checked the observation windows of various rooms. Some had the shades drawn; others had the blinds up and were visibly empty. He began to worry. *Where are the Americans? How will I ever find them?*

That's when he spotted Casey through the window of a room at the far edge of the ICU. She lay motionless in bed, her eyes closed. Medical monitors and equipment surrounded her. Attached to all the cords and tubes, her body seemed to have wasted away to nothing under the thin hospital coverlet. Above it, her face was gaunt; her cheeks were caved in and her bones showed sharply through her skin, which was deathly pale save for a few blue splotches. Her chest rose and fell so slightly that Mila could barely detect the gentle motion. *Can that really be the beautiful girl from the subway? My God—she looks dead already,* he thought as he pressed his shocked face against the glass.

"That's no mere sprained ankle," Mila whispered to himself as his heart pounded. "Nasta was right."

The room had one window to the outdoors. Standing in front of it was Deborah. She seemed to be shouting into a cell phone. On the other side of the room, seated in a thinly padded hospital armchair, was Jack, his army jacket was balled up into a makeshift headrest.

There isn't much time left. Throwing caution to the wind, Mila stepped up to the door of the hospital room and knocked hard. Jack answered, and Mila tried to put on a friendly face. "I need your help," Mila declared.

Jack seized him by the collar and pushed him across the hallway, slamming him into the wall. "You're not getting away so easy this time!" he cried defiantly.

He had the wind knocked out of him, but Mila tried to shove Jack away. The American grabbed his arms near the elbow and pinned him against the wall. Mila could only struggle uselessly as Jack held him back.

"Let me go! I'm here to help!" Mila insisted.

Jack turned his head and yelled down the hallway. *"Hey! Get security down here!"*

With Jack distracted, Mila moved as if Jack's head were nothing but a football. A fast head-butt to the jaw knocked Jack off balance and sent him stumbling across the hall. Deborah saw the scuffle and sprang into the hallway, her hands raised. She locked eyes with Mila. "Don't move!" she ordered.

"You've got to listen to me. Please!" Mila shouted. "Jack! That thing you found in the bunker. It made her sick!"

Two orderlies charged into the hallway and seized Mila by the arms. He struggled as they tried to drag him away. "Jack, she got cut, remember? That spike, that artifact—it must have been poisoned or something!"

The orderlies pulled Mila down the hall. He tried to crane his neck around the corner and keep eye contact with Jack. "We can save her!" Mila cried desperately.

Sensing that the orderlies were getting mad, Mila stopped struggling. They led him out of the ICU, then handed him off to a group of security guards. The guards were kind enough not to call the police. Instead, they tossed Mila out of the hospital and into the pouring rain.

Dejected, he leaned against the wall and slumped to the ground. Staring into the empty street, he watched the rainwater pour into the storm drain. *I tried,* he thought. *But I failed.*

Beside him, footsteps splashed through the puddles on the pavement. Mila didn't bother to turn his head.

"Do you really think we can save her?" a voice asked.

Eyes wide, Mila turned and saw Jack standing over him. Not knowing what to say, he simply nodded.

"Why did you steal her phone?" Jack asked.

"I can explain on the way," Mila stated.

Jack extended a hand. Mila took it, and the American pulled him to his feet.

"Do you still have it?" Mila asked. "That thing you found? You said you were keeping it."

Jack looked down at his shoes. "After all the confusion with the train...I left it in the bunker."

XI

~~~

THE ABYSS

"Lady Luck is on our side," said Jack.

"I don't know. I have a bad feeling about this," Mila replied.

The two boys moved quickly into the dark tunnel of Bundestag Station. Mila remembered Bundestag was much closer to the bunker than the main station at Hauptbahnhof. Apparently, the trains weren't running today. The flooding from the recent rains had caused some kind of technical issue, so they wouldn't have to worry about timing the trains. On the ride to Bundestag, Mila filled Jack in on the unusual turn of events, including what Nasta warned about. Unfortunately, Jack was not buying all of the superstitious mumbo jumbo. However, Jack did believe that the spike could have been infected with some kind of deadly poison, due to the fact that it was discovered in a military bunker.

Jack pulled out his cell phone. Mila spotted the motion and guessed what Jack was about to do. "Wait!" Mila said. "Let's get farther in before you turn a light on."

The tunnel was deep in shadow, and its air felt clammier than before. It was obvious that the rains had seeped through. Jack followed Mila deeper into the dark black tunnel, looking back at the train station again and again.

Suddenly, Mila realized exactly where it had to be. "There!" he shouted to Jack, pointing just ahead.

The boys jogged toward the spot. Jack flashed the light of his phone, then focused all his attention on finding the hole.

Mila stood at the edge of the pit and peered down into the darkness. Jack came closer and looked over his shoulder. The bunker was now flooded, the water dark and murky. The sound of dripping water echoed around them as they stared into the abyss that had once been the bunker.

"Oh shit, now what?" Mila asked.

"It should be right down there," Jack pointed to the center of the dark pool. "That thing was heavy as lead. It couldn't have floated off."

Using his lock, Mila secured one end of his bike chain to a nearby steel beam.

"Someone's got to stay up top to pull the other guy up. Which of us is going down?" Jack asked.

"I think you should."

"Why me?"

"No offense, but I think I'm a little stronger than you."

"Bullshit, I pinned you at the hospital!" Jack retorted.

"You caught me off guard. Look, it doesn't matter. You left it down there. You get it."

Jack couldn't argue with that. He cast his eyes heavenward and heaved a sigh. Then he looped one end of the bike chain into a makeshift harness.

Mila took hold of the slack and braced himself. Jack inched toward the hole. "Don't worry, I got you," Mila told him.

"You'd better," Jack snapped.

He set his phone carefully at the edge so the light shone down. Step by step, Jack edged down the side of the abyss. As he lowered himself into the darkness, Mila stepped forward. Jack hung above the bunker by both arms.

"Get ready!" he shouted, and with that, he let go. The chain gave for a second as Mila stumbled forward. Then he regained his footing.

"Whoa!" Jack's yell echoed up into the subway tunnel.

"Sorry!" Mila yelled back. "Got it now."

"OK, let it out a little..." Jack coached him. Then, "Gradually!"

Mila took a few careful steps toward the hole. Now Jack hung just a few inches above the water and looked around. *What a godforsaken place!* he thought.

The bunker must have been flooded to about four or five feet, he estimated. He knew he had to uncoil himself from the chain and plunge into the water. If his estimate was off and the water was over his head, his task would be much harder—and more disgusting.

He inhaled hard, then let go of the chain and dropped with a loud splash. The filthy water was chin high, and some of it managed to get into his mouth. He tasted motor oil, garbage, rotting leaves, and God knew what else. He spat it out, then began to swim to where he thought he'd left the artifact. He felt around the area with his feet.

No luck. He took a deep breath and submerged. But when he opened his eyes underwater, there was little to see. The water was too muddy, and the cell phone's dim glow couldn't penetrate the murky blackness. *Damn!* Jack cursed to himself. *Why the hell didn't we bring a flashlight?*

The filthy water stung so badly Jack had to shut his eyes. Squatting, he groped around blindly with both hands. *That thing was so heavy,* he thought. *It has to be lying on the floor somewhere.* After a few seconds, he had to come up for air. Over and over he emerged from the water, took a breath, and ducked back down. Each time he took the plunge he felt precious seconds passing.

Jack emerged again and yelled, "I can't find it!" Then he took one final plunge and gave one last sweep with his fingers for the mysterious object. His fingertips grazed something solid. He reached out and firmly closed his hand around whatever it was. He gave a strong kick and shot up out of the fetid pool. With his head clear of the water again, he wiped his face and opened his eyes to see what he'd found: a broken stapler.

"Damn it!" Jack gasped, his breath almost gone from the underwater search. He chucked the piece of junk across the bunker in disgust.

"Did you get it?" Mila yelled from above. "We're running out of time."

"I can't find it. It must have shifted," Jack said, still panting.

Mila bit his lip. *The cops are gonna come for me anytime now,* he thought. *And Casey's condition has to be getting worse. Jack said the thing was heavy. It's not gonna just float away.* "It has to be down there!" he shouted. "Don't give up so easy!"

"Dude, I felt all around. There's nothing on the floor!" Jack shouted, frustrated.

"I'm coming down," Mila responded tersely. He thought of his great-aunt and closed his eyes to do a quick meditation that Nasta would have called a moment of peace. "It's a way to clear all the...um...all the *universe* out of your mind," she would say delicately. "It can help you; it can do you good. You can use it to solve the dilemmas in life, little or big." He began to sense her presence, right there in the dark tunnel.

"Hey! Are you coming down or what?" Jack yelled.

But Mila was in a dream state, deep in the Middle Room, between the heavens and the universe. *"Dikh thele ando kalo pai, soamo tu si dikhas ki o kalfine,"* the voice in the Middle Room said. Then the voice quickly moved away.

Mila could almost feel the essence of the words leave his presence, like wind passing. He woke up with a sense of knowing what he must do. As the voice had directed, he looked back down into the hole, into the black waters. Left and right, deeper.

Suddenly, a spark glimmered for a quick second, then faded. The tiny light had shone out from right behind Jack, not far from where he was standing. Mila locked his eyes on that position. For a split second, more sparks shone out.

"There!" Mila pointed in the direction of the glimmer of light. "It's right behind you."

Without question, Jack followed Mila's pointing finger. He plunged in once again. Underwater, he used both hands to sweep the area Mila had indicated. His hand brushed a waterlogged piece of furniture. The desk the three of them had climbed on to escape? What else could it be? He moved his hands across the edge of the desk, and his fingers grazed something. All at once he knew for certain that there in the black abyss the scepter was within his grasp. He grabbed the object more firmly, gave a strong kick, and shot back up to the surface. Taking a deep breath, he yelled at the tops of his lungs, "I have it! Pull me up!"

Without either of them saying a word, as if instinct warned them not to, both of them realized they had just experienced something almost supernatural. Silently, Jack got back into the harness.

Mila began to pull the chain upward. Bracing himself, he walked backward down the subway tracks. He was strong for his age and size, but he found himself straining and struggling against the heavy pull of the water and the weight of the other boy. Finally, he saw Jack's hand emerge, a metal object in his clenched fist. Jack tossed it onto the floor and pulled himself up the rest of the way.

Both boys needed a moment to catch their breath. Then Jack picked up his phone and held it over the scepter. For the first time they could get a good look at it. The water had stripped away the layers of dirt and grime. Now, it was obvious that the object was made of pure gold, resembling a tent spike. One end was flat and inscribed with a swastika. The shaft had seven smooth sides that converged to its intimidating razor-sharp point; several of the sides had strange markings that resembled a Latin script. However, a few of the faces of the shaft seemed to have been filed off. One thing was certain: the artifact was beautiful.

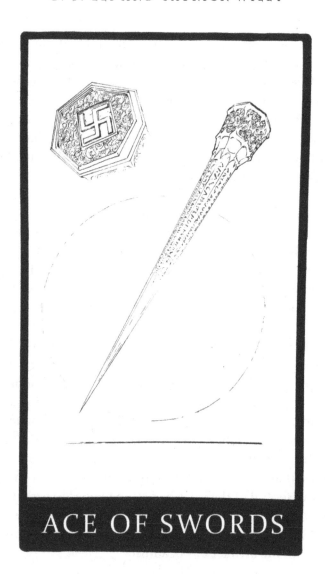

ACE OF SWORDS

"What *is* this? A weapon?" Jack asked with wonder.

"It's a nail."

"What are you talking about? This is no nail," Jack said in bewilderment.

"My great-aunt's spirit spoke to me. She said that only I could see it through the black waters," Mila explained, his tone becoming solemn.

"How's that possible?"

"Because my aunt just died," Mila replied. "I can feel it."

Jack didn't argue or ask how Mila knew, he put his logic aside for a moment and said, "I'm sorry, Mila."

Mila swallowed hard, avoiding Jack's eyes as he handed him the nail. Jack could tell he was holding back tears.

"Let's get back to the hospital," Jack said, trying to steer the conversation elsewhere. He turned and headed toward Bundestag Station.

The two boys ran back toward the station, but just before they got there, they noticed that barricades had been put up, and several metro police were blocking their exit. If they continued on, they would surely be noticed and questioned. Mila was starting to believe that the closing of the station had nothing to do with Lady Luck.

Having no choice, they turned back and headed toward the larger station in the hope that its tunnel wasn't also blockaded. They crept toward the platform, staying low. Fortunately, there were no police at this exit. The boys got up on the ledge and reached the platform. In the distance, they noticed two men with long blond hair, definitely not metro police, and a much older man, in his late seventies at least. He was dressed in a black trench coat and wore an armband matching those of the other men. The older man seemed to be in charge. He was deep in serious conversation with an official in a conductor's uniform.

Nobody was looking in Mila and Jack's direction, so the boys made use of the opportunity to creep a bit closer. Instinctively, Mila used the nearest pillar as cover. Jack followed suit. Once at the whisper corner. Mila peered around the side of the pillar. He spotted Stephan, Rosa, and Jolly, handcuffed and on their knees. Mila noticed Jolly had a black eye.

"Something is going on," Mila whispered. "Those are my cousins. They arrested my cousins."

"Who? Why?" Jack asked.

"Shhhh," Mila said as he pressed his ear to the whisper corner to hear what was going on.

"...it's not a matter of money. We can't keep this subway line closed any longer," the station official said. "I'm sorry, Mr. Strauss, but your team needs to be out in ten minutes."

With that, the conductor walked away, leaving the station through the main staircase. As he left, another man came in. Much to Mila's surprise, it was Father

Leichman. For a moment, Mila had the naive thought that he was going to negotiate for his cousins' release. As usual. Mila could tell the priest was angry. He could almost feel it, like the heat of a furnace.

As they approached, one of the guards began interrogating Stephan. He kicked Stephan over onto his back and pinned Stephan's hands beneath his boot-clad foot. With the boy pinned, the guard drew his baton and raised it threateningly, as if about to slam it down and shatter Stephan's fingers. Leichman's thin hand darted out like a claw and stopped him.

"My good man," the boys heard the priest say, "that is no way to get him to tell the truth. You can't use pain to persuade a Gypsy. They're used to pain."

Father Leichman turned away and snapped his fingers, summoning someone off in the distance. A guard with same arm band appeared, guiding Korey and Petre toward the priest.

"This is not good," Mila whispered to Jack.

"Family is everything to them," Leichman continued. "The safety of their family is far more important to any Gypsy than his own well-being." He turned to Stephan. "We are running out of time, Stephan! Now, for the last time, which tunnel did the Americans run into?"

"What Americans?" Stephan answered.

"Stephan, I've known you since you were a little boy, and I know it will take very strong motivation to get the truth out of you. This gives me an advantage. At this moment, we are holding your two brothers. Such beautiful boys, Korey and Petre. You know, I baptized both of them myself. Such a shame. Here is what we will do: you tell me which tunnel to search in, and in exchange, I will let you keep one of your kin."

Mila was puzzled at this offer. Its meaning didn't quite sink in. Going over the words in his mind, he placed his ear right against the pillar. Perhaps he hadn't heard Father Leichman correctly.

Bang!

A gunshot shattered the silence in the hall of the station and echoed off its high arched pillars. His ears nearly burst. All he could hear was a deafening ringing. Mila clenched his eyes shut instinctively. He heard Rosa scream, followed by sobbing coming from Stephan, Jolly, and Petre.

Jack whispered, "Oh my God ..." Although Mila was too terrified to open his eyes, he did so, praying that his assumption was not—

"No!" Mila screamed. *"No!"*

The horrible scene in the now-quiet corner of the huge structure came into view. The man in black held a smoking service pistol in his right hand. Korey's small body lay motionless at his feet, like a pile of rags, as still and silent in death as he had been beloved and animated in life. A red trail of blood oozed out of the child's head and dripped onto the stone floor.

Again, Mila screamed, *"No! No!"*

The priest looked straight at Mila, and their eyes locked for a split second. Then Mila felt a tug on his sleeve as Jack pulled him away from the horrific scene. They both began to run as Mila spotted Stephan and Jolly, still in handcuffs, lunge at the shooter, butting him with their shoulders and knocking him to the floor. Rosa picked her handcuffs, grabbed Korey, and ran to the opposite exit.

Soon, the two guards in the black suits were in hot pursuit. Luckily, thanks to Jolly and Stephan, Mila and Jack had a head start. They ran out of the station as fast as they could toward Bundestag, the guards about 20 feet behind and gaining fast. The rain had let up to a slight drizzle. Jack spotted a crowded street festival and pulled Mila into a large crowd of people holding umbrellas. In no time, the boys blended in to the thousands of covered shoppers. A few moments later, assuming the coast was clear, they ducked into an alley to catch their breaths.

"Should we go back for the motorcycle?" asked Jack, almost out of breath.

"It's too risky," Mila said, exhausted and bewildered. "Besides, the hospital is only a few blocks away." Then he sank to his knees on the pavement. The image of his dead cousin burned in his brain. He clutched his forehead, his hands covering his eyes, trying to stop the pain that flamed and flared inside his head. "Why ... why?" he cried in agony.

"It's not your fault, Mila," Jack told him.

Mila didn't want to hear a word. He turned his head away from the other boy as if nothing could comfort him. He just wanted the pain that now burned inside his whole body to stop.

"Hey, listen to me!" Jack said in a stronger voice. "It's not your fault," he repeated. He crouched next to his new friend and placed his hand on Mila's shoulder as the Gypsy boy fought back tears. "I can't believe what just happened. But I know you didn't make it happen," Jack said with conviction. "I had no idea what it's like for the Romani people. To tell you the truth, I didn't care."

Still fighting tears, Mila opened his eyes and silently looked at Jack.

"We can't let those bastards get away with this!" Jack said. He pulled the nail from the motorcycle bag and handed it to Mila.

Mila took hold of the object and began to examine it. The pain inside him shifted from grief to painful purpose.

"This is what they want. I don't know why," he told Jack. He looked back at the nail again. "What's so special about you?" he said, speaking to the nail itself as if it were alive and could answer him. "Why would a man of God kill an innocent little child for you?"

"What are we going to do?" Jack asked.

Just then Jack's cellphone began to beep again. He pulled it out of his pocket, and they both looked at the glowing screen. There were several missed calls from Mr. Garson and one text message that read only: Urgent - Deborah.

The boys looked back and forth from the phone to the nail. Then Mila stood up, fists clenched in defiance. "Let's find out what my cousin died for."

XII

~~~~~

THE MOSSAD

"What about Berlin Schönefeld? Can you land there?"

"Ms. Musef, they're rerouting every aircraft in a ten-mile radius. We're going to have to land in Munich. Have you tried a train—"

Deborah slammed down the clunky hospital phone before the private jet's pilot could finish. She missed the days when a simple phone call could get her anything from a medevac helicopter to a drone strike. With nothing left to do, she sighed and sat on a window ledge in Intensive Care Unit Three. The scent of alcohol and bleach filled the room. The gradually slowing beep of Casey's heart monitor was a constant reminder of yet another failed mission. As Deborah gazed out the window of the dreary hospital room, she watched the raindrops trickle down the window and thought of her father.

"All people have a duty to their beliefs, and they must live by their beliefs and ultimately fight for them," her father would often say. It was his credo. She loved her father deeply and wanted to make him proud. But this city and her connection to it only reminded Deborah of her family's struggles and achievements, which she could never live up to.

Her grandparents had emigrated from Germany to what was then Palestine: unlike many other victims of the Holocaust, they had survived to become pioneers in building the State of Israel. She wondered if her grandfather would be proud of her. How could he? A man who had helped to lay the foundations for the new Israeli homeland. A man who had assisted in the creation of the Israeli Secret Service: Mossad, the most advanced intelligence agency on earth. A man whose exploits aided in the capture of Nazi war criminal Adolf Eichmann. How could such a man be proud of her?

And what about her father? A military genius, he had fought in the Israeli Six-Day War and helped hunt down the conspirators and murderers of Black Friday. How could she even dare to compare herself to him? She couldn't live up to his accomplishments; she couldn't even remember his advice when it mattered most.

"Never mistake wishful thinking for instincts," she could hear him say. "Let your instincts help you when the facts give no clear answer. But don't use your instincts as an excuse to ignore the facts." Her father had told her all those things on the day she was made a field agent. But she had failed to follow—or even remember—his wise advice.

Her thoughts drifted to the last time she'd been in Berlin, what seemed like a lifetime ago. Rumors had circulated of a German industrialist funneling money to terror cells in Lebanon. Her team never found substantial evidence, but a kill order came through, nonetheless.

The assassination was a disastrous failure. Deborah would often play it over in her mind, wondering how it might have gone differently. *Who knows? That's no longer my life,* she thought. *I'm no longer a Mossad agent, and I no longer trust my instincts. They failed me in the job that I loved and with the man I loved.* Hopeless tears began to fill her eyes.

Suddenly, the door of the small room swung open. Deborah wiped the tears away as three men walked in. All wore scrubs, and medical masks covered their noses and mouths as if they were in an operating room about to begin surgery. The tallest of the three wore a white lab coat over his scrubs and a stethoscope around his neck. He had the air of someone not wearing his everyday, professional clothing, but rather a doctor's Halloween costume.

"These men are from the health department," said the tall man dressed like a doctor, his voice muffled by the mask. He gestured at the other two men.

Extending her hand to shake each of theirs in turn, she noticed the men wore gloves: not hospital-grade surgical gloves, but thin, cheap latex like one might buy at a pharmacy. She could see through the translucent material to an ornate tattoo on one man's right wrist. The unusual marking triggered her memory. She'd seen it before, she was sure of that. *But where?*

"They have some disturbing news about this young lady," the tall man said. "She has been exposed to a rare disease, and I'm afraid some hospital staff have been exposed as well."

The group now had Deborah's full attention. She shifted her gaze from one to the other. She couldn't see their expressions, only their eyes above the masks. But that was enough. For Deborah, the eyes were the most telling part of the face.

"What is the disease? And what about the other young people she's been in contact with?" Deborah asked, looking from one official to another and then to the tall man. "And who are you?"

"I'm a doctor," the man said shortly, not giving his name but instead moving on to respond to her earlier questions. "The disease displays the characteristic symptoms of the Ebola virus. That is the preliminary diagnosis. Of course, we are concerned about the other students. We contacted their teacher, Mr. Garson, but unfortunately, he and the group have already left the city. We reached him by cell phone on a train with the rest of the students en route to Vienna."

Deborah paused, processing the information quickly. *Ebola? How is that possible? There's no record of any Ebola cases in Germany right now. How could Casey have possibly been exposed to Ebola here?* Years of training kicked in, and she asked herself, *What would be the normal reaction?* She pasted a shocked, gullible look on her face.

"Oh, my, how awful!" she exclaimed. "Are you saying this poor girl may have Ebola? Well, thank goodness your city's wonderful hospital and health department are at the ready to deal with this crisis," she flattered the men.

The doctor's eyes narrowed above his mask. The other two men were strangely silent as they stood ominously at the other man's side. *Nothing feels right about this,* Deborah thought as she tried to keep suspicion from showing in her face.

"Ms. Musef, you've already been exposed to the disease just by being in this room. You must immediately scrub up and change into protective gear. The patient's nurse is just outside. She will assist you," the tall man said.

One of the other men spoke. "The girl has been in contact with Gypsies," he said. "They are carriers of this disease."

"It's a dangerous bug those people carry," the other added.

What health department official uses the word "bug" to describe a deadly virus? Deborah thought. And the way he said, "those people"—she couldn't miss the contempt in his choice of words and the tone of his voice.

The two health officials stood at attention, their eyes cold and empty. One of the two was completely still, while the other man steadily clenched and unclenched his fists. Deborah recognized his movements as nervous, even frightened behavior. The facts of the situation were ambiguous, but Deborah's instincts told her to get ready for trouble.

"If you'll please come with us," the doctor said.

"I'm sorry, Doctor, I'm not going to leave Ms. Richards. You see, I'm very close to her family back in the States. I feel I have to stay here with her, especially since her relatives' flights were canceled because of the storm," Deborah explained.

"Certainly, I understand. I can send the nurse in with the protective clothing. Now, if you will excuse me, I'll get her."

The doctor turned to leave. One of the other men reached out to open the door for him, and as he did so, his sleeve slipped back to reveal an intricate tattoo on his wrist: the same as his companion's. This time Deborah got a clear look at the design: a twisted red ribbon pierced by a sword. Her heart began to race, but true to many years of training, she appeared calm and relaxed, or as calm as someone would be who had just received the upsetting news about Casey's supposed infection with Ebola.

The man closed the door and returned to stand next to his companion. Deborah turned unobtrusively and moved closer to Casey's bedside. Uneasy, she glanced at the medical monitors, using the reflections in the screens to see what was happening behind her. A few moments passed, and the men did nothing but stand there. *Wrong again,* she thought. She relaxed a bit and her mind wandered off to Jack. *Where could he have gone?* she wondered. She took a quick look over at the monitor again. The reflection revealed that one of the men was now right behind her.

She knew by instinct that her neck would be his first target. He raised one hand and moved to hook it around for a choke hold. Deborah had only a split second to act. As his hand crossed her shoulder, she bent at the knees and seized her attacker's wrist with both hands. With her grip locked she stood up, snapping the man's arm over her shoulder as easily as breaking a twig. He cried out in pain and she pivoted, pulling his mangled arm behind him. She reached to his waist and found a pistol tucked in his waistband. In one swift motion, she drew the weapon while holding her attacker as a human shield.

The other man had drawn a pistol of his own. He struggled to aim properly. A million scenarios went through Deborah's mind. *Are they here for me?* she wondered. Could this be something from her past work? No, they were too sloppy, too clumsy. Only a fool would send such poorly trained men after an ex-Mossad field agent. Her focus remained on the armed man as she contemplated this.

Just then, the nurse entered with the scrubs. She screamed, dropping the garments at the sight of the guns. The man immediately grabbed her and pointed his weapon at her temple. Deborah never flinched. Her focus was still on the man's eyes.

"Let him go! And step away from the girl, or I'll shoot the nurse!" he ordered.

"Yes! Shoot her!" the other man yelled in agony from Deborah's grip on his broken arm.

Deborah realized she was not the target: they were there for Casey. She began to analyze the situation, still never losing her focus on his eyes, not even a blink. In a matter of seconds, she understood that if he wanted, the man could point his pistol at Casey and kill her, but he would die himself when Deborah returned fire. That told Deborah that this was not a suicide mission or a terrorist act. *These are hired men,* she concluded, *and not good ones, either.* This may well be their first hit.

"Release him and step away! Or I'll kill her at the count of three," he said tersely.

Deborah remained unmoved. Neither the man's threats nor the terrified look of the nurse had any effect on her. The man started his count.

"One...two..."

Bang!

The nurse screamed as the man holding her dropped to the ground, blood spraying from between his eyes. The terrified woman ran into the hallway leaving the door swinging behind her. Just before it could shut, a tan-skinned hand grabbed it and pulled it open. On the other side stood Mila, holding the door with Jack not far behind.

PAGE OF SWORDS

~~~☙☙☙~~~

XIII

THE COAL MINER'S SON

This was not supposed to happen, Siegfried thought as excruciating pain shot through his most certainly broken arm and wrist. *Who was this woman?* Her vice-like grip had never weakened a bit, even when she pulled the trigger to take out his partner.

"Jack, Mila, use the chair to jam the door," the woman called Ms. Musef shouted to the youths who had just entered the room. The boys immediately followed her instructions.

Without a second to think, Siegfried was turned around and placed in a chair next to Casey's bed. All the while the woman never loosened her grip on his injured arm. And now his own pistol was pointing directly at his forehead, cocked and ready to shoot.

"Don't shoot! Please don't shoot!" he shouted in terror.

The woman loosened her grip for a quick second, only to strike him on the side of his head with his own gun with a loud *thunk!* She then shoved him into a hospital chair. Dizzy from the blow, he knew he could die here like his partner. Desperately trying to keep his eyes open, he felt himself fading in and out of consciousness. *Stay awake!* he told himself. *It's your only chance to get out of here.*

He opened his eyes and looked at Musef, who was yelling something that he fought to understand through the ringing in his ears. Finally, it diminished, and he heard her more clearly.

"Why are you here?" Musef shouted in the tone of an aggressive interrogator.

Siegfried clenched his eyes shut, desperately trying to remember his mission. He tried to think back. The only thing he could remember was that his employer told him that these were just Gypsy-loving rats. But that's all he could recall amid the ringing and dizziness fading in and out of his head. He opened his eyes once again, but all he saw was darkness: he'd been blindfolded. Then he felt something like plastic wire squeeze against his good arm and tighten. He strained against it and realized he couldn't move. *She's zip tied me!* he thought.

Excruciating pain shot down his wounded arm and into his wrist again. The interrogation continued, but still all he heard was ringing and all he felt was the sharp stabs of pain from his injuries.

"We have to do something now! She looks terrible!" one of the boys said.

With that sentence, Siegfried remembered his mission. *The girl,* he thought. *I was sent here for the girl.* Despite the woman's tight grip still twisting his arm and wrist, he managed to force a few words through his lips.

"We were sent to kill her!" he panted in agony. There was a second's quiet pause, even a slight loosening of the vice-like hold on his arm. They seemed to be shocked by his answer. *What have I done? Did I say too much?* he wondered.

"Why? Who are you?" the American boy demanded.

"He's from the True Nationalist Coalition. They're a modern Nazi party," Musef answered. "I knew I recognized that tattoo."

Someone outside pounded on the locked door. *Bang! Bang!* "Ms. Musef! Are you OK? I have security here! The police are on their way!" a voice shouted from the other side.

Siegfried recognized the voice: it was the doctor who had introduced them to the woman in the first place. He'd assumed she was a teacher. Obviously, he was wrong.

"I'm going to ask you some questions, and you are going to answer them, unless you want to wind up like your friend on the floor here," Musef said.

Before he could answer her, the pain pierced his arm again. He heard the American say, "She's dying! What the hell are we going to do with this piece of metal?"

Musef ignored Jack's shouting. "Why would you want to hurt this innocent girl? What does your party want with her?"

The pain continued. He felt her hands rubbing and shifting his arm once more and heard cracking noises coming from his arm along with the unbearable pain he felt. *Oh my God, I'm being tortured,* Siegfried thought. *I'd rather just die.*

"We've gotta get this thing to the doctors so they can identify the poison," the American said.

"There is no poison," the other boy said, his accent revealing his Gypsy identity.

"Poison?" the woman broke in. "What are you talking about?"

As the boys argued, Deborah ignored them and turned back to her interrogation. He knew she had to get it out of him. He had to tell her what she needed to know, or she would continue her cruel torture.

Suddenly, Siegfried felt the sting of something cold and flat against his inner arm. He didn't know what would come next, but it couldn't be good.

"It has something to do with the golden scepter!" he shouted in terror.

Everyone went silent. the woman stopped what she was doing.

"We caught a little Gypsy boy. A priest, a friend of my boss, he got him to talk by promising to reunite him with his twin brother."

"Korey..." the Gypsy whispered.

"He told us how the girl got sick after running onto the subway tracks. The others searched the station. My partner and I were told to wait here. Then they called in and told us to kill the girl," Siegfried said desperately. Then the pain took over, and he began to choke with sobs.

"Who?" Musef asked. "Who ordered that?"

"The nail is bewitched!" the Gypsy boy yelled, still debating with the American. All the while, the banging from the hospital door never ceased. "Don't you get it? It has some kind of powers to heal her body! My great-aunt told me. That's why his boss wants it!" the Gypsy shouted.

"Are you completely insane?" the American asked.

Siegfried could feel the woman lean in close. "So, you Nazis are still searching for bewitched objects for your murderous crusades?" she whispered menacingly into his ear.

Tears began to soak Siegfried's blindfold. The pain had dulled a little; the emotional breakdown was probably distracting him. He tried to answer the question. Was it a bewitched item? "I was a young man when I heard of this object. No one really believed the stories," he said.

"Do *you* believe the stories?" she asked.

Shaking his head, weeping at the same time, he choked on his words. "No, no, I don't believe the stories. But I believe now that my superiors do. And they will kill for this object."

"Well, we know one person has died already," Musef said.

"Three people," the Gypsy said sadly. "Gypsies are people, too."

The room became quiet. The only thing Siegfried could hear now was the beeping of the heart monitors. The beeps got less frequent as time went on. The girl's heart was failing.

"I'm not interested in increasing that to four people, so maybe you can help me. In less than five minutes, there are going to be about fifty police on the other side of that door," Musef said to Siegfried. "Before they get here, you're going to tell me what I need to know."

He began to weep more pitifully. He put his head down. "I don't know much. I only know what Professor Hermann taught us years ago at Wewelsburg Castle. I was staying at the youth hostel nearby."

"*Wewelsburg Castle!*" she said, shocked. "This is getting better and better," she continued sarcastically.

"What castle?" the Gypsy asked.

"It was a temple that was intended to be the center of Nazi ideology. It's where the Thule Society gathered for their meetings. They believed they were descendants of Aryan gods, and the temple was going to be their Mecca," the woman explained. "Those psychopaths murdered millions of people... They needed to tell a lot of lies to accomplish that. First, they invented their own history. Then the next step was to invent their own religion. If Hitler had had his way, Christianity would have been abolished along with Judaism and every other religion except his own, the one they invented."

"How the hell do you know that?" the Gypsy questioned her.

"She's ex-Mossad, Israeli intelligence," the American said.

"You are NOT supposed to be repeating that," Musef snapped.

Siegfried now knew that the woman before him was not only a skilled agent, but someone of Jewish heritage, as well. *She must think my party is another pack of blood thirsty animals,* he worried as fear and shame overtook him. Siegfried hated being compared to the Nazis of the past. They believed in genocide and conquest, but that was not *his* belief.

Musef leaned in close again. "I see why you took the job," she hissed into his ear. "Your idols murdered millions. What would one more little girl matter to you?"

"I am not a murderer!" he declared. "I only believed in taking our country back. The SS were not the only people who paid the price for Hitler's war. The common people paid, as well—my family most of all. My family helped build this country. We mined coal for four generations, only to lose it all to the Communists. We lost everything! We still suffer to this day. I joined this party because I believe in purity, hard work, progress. Is it so wrong to want your people to have a country all their own?"

The woman pulled back. Siegfried sensed that he had somehow struck a nerve. "That kind of thinking always leads to bloodshed," she warned.

Bang! Bang! More pounding on the door. "This is the police! Open up at once!" an authoritative voice shouted.

"We have a hostage situation!" she shouted in return. "Pull your men back, *now!*"

Now Siegfried was even more frightened than before. The woman had just bought herself some time with the police. What's more, she was a convincing liar. *I'm the one that's being held captive. What if she kills me?* he thought in a panic. She could easily lie about that, too, and they'd probably believe her.

"Let me help you," he urged. "I know about this object. If the girl is sick and dying, then maybe there's some truth to the story."

From the darkness under his blindfold, he heard only silence.

"Please take off the blindfold," he pleaded. "Let me look at the object."

He could feel the covering over his eyes being untied, and there was light. It took a moment for his eyes to adjust. The first thing he noticed was the makeshift cast on his arm and wrist. It was primitive, but impressive. Confused, he looked up at Musef.

"I keep splinting materials in my first-aid kit. I managed to set your arm," she said matter-of-factly.

Siegfried stared at the cast a moment as Deborah drew out a penknife and cut him free of the zip tie. She raised the pistol slightly, just to remind him that she was in control.

"You didn't think I was really a torturer, did you?" she asked.

The sight of the cast brought a tear to his eye. The strange woman's act of grace humbled him deep inside and made him ashamed of his past. Siegfried decided he wanted to help them save the girl if it was at all possible.

The Gypsy boy brought the scepter closer. It perfectly matched the illustrations Siegfried had been shown at Wewelsburg Castle. He remembered how captivating those paintings were. The real thing was twice as entrancing. For a moment, he could only think of how beautiful the talisman was. He shook his head back and forth, trying to focus.

Then Siegfried closed his eyes, trying to remember what he'd been taught so long ago. "'He who speaks the incantation and invokes it will gain the power of vigor, and health, strength, and vitality will be theirs,'" he quoted, remembering the words he'd been told long ago. "Quick, look at the inscriptions. Do you see the word *vigoris,* written anywhere?"

The Gypsy boy turned the nail over, thoroughly examining the seven sides. It was clear to Siegfried that he was struggling to decipher the etched text on the nail. "Look. Here it is," he said, pointing to one of the seven sides. "Is this it?" He brought the nail to Siegfried's eyes and pointed to a word.

"No, that says *veritas,*" Siegfried explained, "Turn it over slowly."

The Gypsy began to turn the object clockwise. Passing through the texts, Siegfried noticed some sides had been completely filed off, as if to conceal something. As he rotated the nail, Siegfried could see the word *vigoris* clear as day. "That's it!" Siegfried shouted.

"Oh, great. How is Casey supposed to read the incantation and invoke it? She's out like a light," the Gypsy boy said in frustration.

"Give it here. Maybe we can open her eyes or something?" said the American boy called Jack.

The Gypsy boy reached across Casey's bed to hand over the nail to Jack. Suddenly, there was a crash of thunder. The lights flickered and went out for a moment. Everyone glanced up at the fluorescent ceiling lights as they came back on.

The Gypsy boy looked back at the nail, and his eyes went wide. He couldn't stop staring. "It changed," he said.

"What?" Jack said. "What are you talking about, Mila?"

"This side was in Latin before," Mila said. "I'm sure of it." He held it up for all to see. A series of raised dots had appeared on the scepter.

"It's braille," Jack marveled. He held out his hand to Mila, who seemed to understand. Mila handed him the nail, and Jack turned to Casey's bedside. He lifted her wrist and brought her fingertips toward the object, then paused to look at Mila. The Gypsy boy nodded. Jack began to slide Casey's fingers across the side of the nail. The tip of one finger reached the end.

A blinding flash of lightning angled in through the sheer curtains of the hospital window as if searching for someone inside the small room. Outside, a blast of thunder exploded with an earsplitting crash. The rain pounded violently down like a storm of falling rocks.

Everyone in the room shivered at the strength of the storm. They, including Siegfried, watched in amazement as Jack guided Casey's finger along the Braille text. *Can that thing really be … bewitched?* he wondered.

There came another flash of lightning and another crash of thunder. The room was bathed in white light for a fraction of a second. Everyone covered their eyes. They could hear the crackle of electricity as the heart monitor short-circuited. The smell of burned plastic and rubber filled the room.

Siegfried reluctantly opened his eyes, but before he could get a good look at the girl the door burst open. A squad of armed police rushed in and dragged him from the room and the dark sorcery that enveloped it.

XIV

~~~

BLAME THE GYPSY

Casey awoke with a gasp, sitting upright in a bed that was not her own. Her surroundings were new and strange. She raised her head from the hard pillows and took a quick look around. In the dark, she spotted the shape of a woman near her bed. The woman drew back the window shades, and the room was bathed in the golden light of the afternoon sun. The unseasonable rains had finally come to an end.

Squinting as she adjusted to the bright light, Casey tried to gather her thoughts after what she knew had been a long, deep slumber. It was clear she was in a hospital bed and the woman was a nurse, but why? She felt strong and aware of everything: not ill at all. The nurse was still fidgeting with the shades, revealing the large windows that looked out into a green, lush landscape at ground level.

On the other side of the bed, a medical monitor was attached to her arm. Asleep in a chair at the foot of the bed was a lumpy, blanket-clad figure with a face she recognized: Jack.

"Ahhh!" the nurse screamed, then covered her mouth with her hand, her face as white as the sheets on Casey's bed.

Jack sat up with a start. "What happened?" he and Casey shouted in unison.

The nurse uncovered her mouth. The color returned to her face as she grimaced with embarrassment. *"Die hunde,"* she said. "How do you say in English, 'stray dogs'? They've been outside the building all day! One was right outside the window, looking in, growling. They frightened me."

Casey sat up and peered out the window. Sure enough, a large, mangy dog was lurking outside. It stood still, and for a moment, it seemed to be directing its fierce, aggressive gaze right at them. Then the animal calmly wandered away.

"Never mind the dogs," the nurse said to Casey. "We're perfectly safe in here," she added, feeling more confident in her English. She stepped to Casey's bedside. She held a paper bag in one hand and gestured to her patient. "Your purse and clothing are here for you," she said.

She set the parcel down next to Casey and checked the IV stand. A blood bag that hung there was empty now. Pulling on some protective gloves, the nurse removed the bag and carefully placed it in a medical waste disposal container nearby. "You scared us a lot more than that dog did, Miss," the nurse said.

Casey wasn't sure if that was supposed to be funny. German humor was lost on her, and the nurse's accent didn't help.

"But it appears you have made full recovery," the nurse affirmed. "I will inform the doctor that you have finally stirred; he should be in to see you shortly." She then walked out the door.

Recovery? Casey thought. *From what?* She desperately tried to recall her supposed illness as she rubbed the sleep from her eyes.

Jack pushed aside his blanket, went to her bedside, and stood looking down at her. "Are you OK?" he asked. "How are you feeling?"

"I had a terrible dream," Casey answered. She extended her arms, stretching and flexing them as she sat up straighter against the firm hospital pillows. As she got the kinks out of her slender frame, she gave an enormous yawn. She was surprised by how strong she felt. Her muscles felt tighter and tougher. There was not a trace of soreness in her entire body.

"Yeah, I think I'm OK. Hand me my bag and turn around," she answered as she reached toward the nightstand. She found her glasses and put them on, a move that had become almost automatic for her. To her surprise, everything looked blurry. She pulled her glasses off and realized everything had been in focus all along, without the glasses. She gently touched her eyes and felt no contact lenses. *How is this possible?* she wondered.

"You OK?" Jack asked again.

Casey began to pull her glasses on and off, comparing the crystal-clear world she saw without them to the blurry one she now viewed from behind the lenses. She looked all around the room. Her vision was clearer than it had ever been before, even in childhood.

"What's going on?" she said. "Why am I in the hospital?"

"Mila thinks you were poisoned by the cursed nail," Jack said. "That thing I found in the bunker, it—I don't think you're supposed to remove that IV."

Casey ignored him as she closed her eyes and prepared for the pain of ripping the plastic tube out of her arm. To her surprise it barely hurt at all. She used the sleeve of her gown to stanch the bleeding, which stopped in seconds.

"Did you hear me? Turn around!" Casey demanded as she snatched the bag and rummaged through it for her clothes. *Was he joking? Did I hear that right? Nail?*

"It was like something out of a *Whistleblower* comic," Jack said, sounding on the edge of hysteria. "Two men tried to kill you ... there were corrupt police, neo-Nazis.

And they even murdered a little Roma boy at the train station."

"*Murdered?* What?" Casey cried. "Jack, *what* are you talking about?" she asked as she tore off the medical gown and pulled on her jeans and tank top.

"Casey, they tried to kill you," Jack revealed, going on to explain about the two hit-men who Deborah thwarted.

"Kill me?" Casey whispered to herself. "We've got to get out of here!" She said while tying her sneakers.

Jack turned back toward Casey to find she was fully dressed. "It was the nail, Casey," he said.

He told her what he knew about it, how the inscription in Latin had somehow changed to braille before their eyes, and how he had helped her touch the inscription.

"Then almost out of nowhere came a burst of bright light that filled the room. After that, the police stormed in and took Mila, Deborah, and me to separate rooms and began to interrogate us," Jack explained. "I told them all I knew, and then they brought me here to sit with you. That's when the doctor told me you recovered almost immediately after the burst of light. You see? It had to be the nail."

It all sounded too fantastic to believe.

"Can I see it?" she asked.

"See what?"

"The nail. Do you still have it?"

Jack pulled back his coat, revealing the golden nail. Casey stared at its gilded surface, her eyes tracing the enigmatic symbols unable to look away. It was as if the scepter had been pulled from the painting that had captivated her in the train station. In person, the allure was a thousand times stronger. Entranced by its power and beauty she felt compelled to hold it. Then she recalled the terrifying dream from which she had just awoken.

"This was in my dream, Jack," she said. "It called to me."

Suddenly, the door swung open. Jack quickly slid the lower half of the nail into his pocket and repositioned his coat to conceal the rest. In walked Deborah, the nurse, and an older gentleman with a shiny balding head and a gray goatee that matched the color of his suit. As the door shut, Casey caught a glimpse of two other officers outside. They firmly held another figure between them: Mila. She gasped. She knew better than to say anything. *Whatever you do, don't make things worse for Mila,* she told herself.

"*Nein, Nein!* Miss, you were not to remove that! Please, I put it back." said the nurse as she went over to Casey's bed to replace the IV. Casey pulled her arm away.

Then Deborah spoke. "Casey, this is Inspector Belz from the Berlin Police Department," she said.

Without any word of greeting, the officer pulled out a photo of Mila. "Do you know this *Zigeuner*?" he demanded.

"Yeah, he's...um...our friend, I guess," Jack replied. Casey was silent, still trying to get her head around the situation. Plus, she was still a little off from the horrible dream.

"Miss, if you please, it is very important. *Bitte*," he said, the German word for *please*, "look at the photo." Belz held the photo out to Casey. "Is this the man that poisoned you?"

"Poisoned me!" Casey cried. "What do you mean?"

Belz went to the door and opened it. He waved his hand, and the two officers rushed in, dragging Mila by his arms between them. Mila seemed to accept it. He didn't struggle or even try to argue.

"What the hell are you doing?" Casey demanded, taking an angry step toward the inspector.

The nurse instinctively rushed forward, trying to get Casey to hold still. *"Nein, nein...lie down, calm down,"* she urged, attempting to push Casey back into the bed. Casey pushed her away without even looking.

Jack was just as upset as Casey and he tried to approach Belz in protest. Deborah positioned herself between the two men, desperately trying to avoid more chaos.

"Enough of this!" Belz shouted as he ordered one of the policemen to position Mila in front of Casey, who was clearly distraught. "Is this the man who poisoned you in the train station?" Belz repeated. "Is he—"

"Poisoned?" Jack broke in. "This is insane. He's innocent! He helped us!" he shouted as Deborah continued to hold him back.

Belz raised his arms and spoke loudly in a clear, firm voice. "Will everyone please calm down!" he said. "Let me explain. Deborah – Ms. Musef – has given me your account of events. However, I find little evidence for the claims of a TNC conspiracy. The Nationalist Coalition is undoubtedly somewhat controversial. But they've always been completely supportive of the work of my department, as well as of the rule of law in this country."

Deborah's face betrayed nothing of what she felt. But Jack looked dumbfounded, and Casey was in total shock. She thought with amazement, *Something about this is not right.*

"Little evidence? Forgive me, inspector, but what about the two TNC men who came in here and tried to kill her?" Deborah demanded.

"After weighing the facts and examining the evidence, I am certain that those men were merely kidnappers taking advantage of Ms. Richards's condition, the cause of which was poisoning by that Gypsy," Belz said assertively. "Besides, I have evidence that this young man has been thieving wealthy Americans for the past few weeks. Not to mention, he almost killed me with his motorcycle while escaping arrest." He seemed very sure of his position—and his power.

"That Gypsy—" Jack stopped, hearing himself use what he now knew was a racist term for the Roma. "I mean, Mila—he didn't poison anyone!" He pointed at Mila, who still did not say a word in his own defense.

"No interruptions! You are not in charge here," Belz snapped. *"Nehmen sie ihn weg!"* he shouted to the officers to take him away. Each of the police tightened their grip on Mila's upper arms as they led the boy, still cuffed and silent, out the door and away. Belz shut it firmly behind him, then dusted his hands with finality.

"This is ludicrous," Deborah said breaking her calculated silence. "The boy's done nothing. Where are they taking him?"

Belz turned to her and scowled. "Ms. Musef, do not question my authority," he told her angrily. "Your part in all this is questionable. Don't forget that you killed someone. I could place you under investigation as well."

"Someone that was pointing a gun at an innocent nurse's head, inspector?"

He replied with, "Furthermore, I have the authority to revoke your passport."

Deborah crossed her arms and glared defiantly at him. Casey's chest tightened. She couldn't bring herself to speak. A seething rage began to build inside her as she realized the injustice of what had just taken place.

"Inspector Belz, we know Mila. He didn't do this," Jack insisted. "I know what happened to Casey, she got cut in the bunk—I mean the subway—"

"You Americans perhaps do not understand about our Gypsy problem here in Germany," Belz pompously declared, cutting Jack off. "Gypsies are vermin: a filthy, evil, criminal-minded race of animals. Crime is in their blood. They are skilled liars, with no regard for human life."

"You are so messed up," Casey heard Jack whisper under his breath.

Just then, Casey's ears began to ring, and the quarrelsome words of Jack, Deborah, and Belz began to melt away. As if from a distance, she saw Jack getting angrier and shouting, putting the inspector on edge. Deborah held Jack back and said something reassuring. All Casey heard was the ringing in her ears and the throbbing of her own heart.

Casey could not control the rage in her body that had escalated to pure hatred. Belz turned to face Casey and extended his arm, as if to put his hand on her shoulder. "I realize this must be hard to understand, perhaps upsetting—" he began.

Casey reached across her body and seized his outstretched arm. Without thought, she leaned over and bit down hard on his flesh through the cloth of his coat. Belz screamed in pain and shock as she sank her teeth further into his flesh. She tasted his blood in her mouth and saw the dark red liquid drip out at the wrist of his coat sleeve.

Jack and Deborah grabbed Belz, pulling him away from Casey's abnormal reaction. Belz began to frantically reach into his coat, no doubt searching for his weapon. Deborah moved like lightning to stop him, her bodyguard instincts kicking in.

As they pulled Belz away, Casey spotted the nurse in the doorway. The terrified woman crossed herself and ran away. Casey realized how monstrous she must have looked with blood running down her chin. What horrified her more was how the blood tasted. Instead of a bitter iron flavor, it was sweet. Disgusted by this realization, Casey spat out flesh and blood, nearly vomiting in the process. She slumped into the bed as Jack rushed over, protectively throwing his arms around her.

Deborah had pinned the inspector's arms behind his back. "Let me handle this!" he shouted to her. "Get me back up in here! Now!" he then yelled out to the hall.

"What's wrong with me?" Casey whimpered as she began to tremble in Jack's arms.

Her hand seemed to move of its own volition into Jack's pocket, instinctively seeking out the scepter. Her fingers brushed against the inscription. The strange Latin script was clear now. There was no sign of the braille Jack had mentioned before. She felt the grooves of the inscription. Obviously, she could not read Latin.

However, she could sound out the words, but their meaning was strange.

They can save you, she thought, not knowing who "they" were or even why she would think such a thing. *Invoke the power and they will save you. You don't have much time...*

"Whosoever utters this word shall possess the beasts: CALATIONIS" she whispered, not knowing where those words came from. *Were those the words spelled out on the surface of the nail?* she wondered.

"What?" Jack asked.

Suddenly, Belz released himself from Deborah's grip, and while struggling with the strong woman he managed to pull out his pistol and point it toward Casey's bedside. Casey could see the barrel of the gun that was about to directly fire at her.

"*Impete!*" she instinctively commanded.

They all heard a loud thud, accompanied by the crack of glass. Something had struck the window. Everyone turned to look, forgetting for a moment the chaos in the room. A long, ragged crack ran down the window. A German Shepherd rose from the ground, shook itself off, and trotted a few steps back. It lowered its haunches as if getting ready to run.

"Oh no..." Belz said.

The dog charged forward, leaped high into the air, and crashed through the window. Landing on the hospital bed, the beast began to snarl at Belz and Deborah, who retreated to the wall in disbelief. Jack pulled back from Casey a little. As he did, she let go of the nail. He looked at her, confused and frightened. Casey knew he was looking to her for answers, but she had none.

The other police and the doctor stormed into the room. The animal leaped for Belz's gun, biting his wrist in the process. Shots began to fire in the room. It wasn't clear if the police were firing at the dog or at Casey. "Run!" was all Casey could think to say.

Casey grabbed her purse, and leaped through the shattered window with Jack following close behind. As they fled, they heard more shots. Casey glanced back and saw Belz with his pistol drawn. The dog lay limp and motionless on the floor at his feet.

With no time to waste, Casey and Jack fled into the streets of Berlin.

XV

THE WOLF LEGION

The light of the sun broke through the waning storm clouds and shined across the narrow streets of Berlin, where it was reflected in the countless puddles the recent rains had left. The puddles glimmered in the sunlight like pools of gold as a lone dog charged through the streets. Splashing from puddle to puddle, the animal passed through an alley, then joined a pack of wild dogs that raced across the city like hellfire. There was fury in their eyes as they rushed headlong in a horrific stampede.

The pack of more than a dozen ravenous canines was not scavenging at random: they were racing through the streets with a purpose. Frightened pedestrians leaped aside as the dogs knocked every café table and anything else in their way to the ground. The bright summer day was transformed into a scene of confusion and fright as the dogs wreaked havoc.

A woman holding her little boy's hand spotted the pack racing toward her, growling and foaming at the mouths like rabid wolves, splashing through puddles, and jumping over curbs and benches. The dogs loomed closer. Terrified, she pulled the child into her arms and tried to flee. But she was no match for their pace. They charged past her. One crashed headlong into her knees, making her tumble to the wet sidewalk. The dog stopped a minute to growl at her as she lay prone and terrified, clutching her crying child. Then some unseen force drew the mutt's attention back to the pack, and he ran off to join the other mongrels on their strange quest.

The dogs continued on their course, raging through the tight streets, turning as one at the corner of Virchowweg Plaza just a few dozen yards from the Charité Medical Center. The pack headed straight toward the shattered, broken window of Casey's hospital room just as Jack and Casey fled. There, the pack split into two groups. One gathered before the window and blocked Deborah's path as she tried to follow Casey. The other went after Casey and Jack as they sprinted across the plaza.

Deborah hesitated at the sight of the snarling hounds. She moved left, trying to get around them. They shifted to block her. She moved slowly to the right, and they did the same. Each vicious dog assumed an attack position and Deborah wisely chose not to challenge them.

She looked down the road to see how far Casey and Jack had gone. She spotted them running toward the main entrance of the Charité Hospital, where a police van waited

As the other pack of dogs charged after Casey and Jack, it seemed as if they would overtake the two teens. But, instead, the dogs fell into step with Jack and Casey like some sort of mongrel escort.

"What the hell?" Jack exclaimed.

"Just keep running. Mila's in that van," Casey panted as they ran. "We've got to get him out."

Jack couldn't argue with that. They ran toward the police van, ignoring the barking of the dogs that surrounded them. The vehicle was pulling out. It didn't get far, for it almost immediately had to come to a stop at a traffic light.

"Come on!" Jack urged Casey. "This could be our only chance to catch it!" They bolted after the van with no idea of what they'd do once they caught up to it.

In the back of the police van, which was separated by a cage from the cab, sat Siegfried and Mila, handcuffed and bound. It was nearly empty back there except for

the hard plastic seats that didn't even offer the safety of seat belts. It had been quite a surprise to Siegfried when they brought Mila in. On top of that, he wondered why the Gypsy was so cool and collected. It made no sense. *Gypsies make no sense, period,* he thought. They were both being arrested, and surely they would be interrogated, booked, and thrown into a cell. Or they might just be summarily shot. He knew that was how things went sometimes, especially for Gypsies. So why did the Gypsy look so calm?

"They're going to kill us in police headquarters," Siegfried said, afraid.

"What? Why? Just relax," Mila said quietly. He tried to figure out what Siegfried was so afraid of. He glanced at the back of the driver's head: the police officer drove forward purposefully, in complete silence. Mila shook his head, hoping Siegfried would understand his gesture as a signal to be quiet.

"Professor Hermann! He was right! At zee castle. It's the nail of Christ. The one with the powers," Siegfried muttered with a heavy, German accent.

"Shhh," Mila responded.

But Siegfried was too panicked to care. "Can't you see...the political party, Victor, the priest! It's all clear to me now. They'll never let us be questioned!" he cried hysterically. He looked to the van's back window and spotted Jack and Casey chasing them down.

"What the hell!" Mila said as he followed Siegfried's gaze. Rising and moving closer to the window, Mila saw with amazement that Jack and Casey were chasing the van. A pack of feral dogs surrounded them.

Mila glanced at the driver. Was he looking in his rearview mirror? Had he noticed their pursuers? Mila couldn't tell. But Siegfried gasped with surprise, and the officer glanced in his driving mirror to see what was going on with his prisoners. Mila knew he must have seen the two human pursuers, and perhaps even the dogs, for the police officer accelerated, leaving all hope for rescue behind. Mila saw his friends fall farther and farther into the distance as the van sped away.

Distraught and shivering in fear, the other man was praying the Hail Mary. He reached the end and looked across at Mila. "Pray for me, Gypsy," Siegfried said fearfully.

"Me? Pray for you?" Mila answered, confused at the strange request.

"Don't you see, it's all true—it must be! *Die hunds!*" Siegfried responded, emphasizing the dogs.

But before Mila could ask what Siegfried was so afraid of or what he meant, something slammed into the front of the van, fast and hard. They were both tossed into the air, and as they tumbled to the floor, they caught a glimpse of the black SUV that had just slammed into the corner of the van's driver's side.

The force of the impact knocked the police vehicle onto two wheels. It careened over a curb, threatening to flip over before slamming back down on all four wheels. As it crazily careened about, Mila and Siegfried were tossed around, smashing repeatedly into the sides of the vehicle.

Mila was dazed and bruised from the crash. He tried to rise to his feet to see if he'd broken any bones. On his first attempt to stand, he felt a piercing pain in his right shoulder. It felt as if the limb had been nearly wrenched out of its socket. No doubt this was the consequence of suffering through the crash with his arms restrained. He cringed but managed to ignore the pain as he got to his feet. He couldn't stand up fully because of the van's low ceiling, but he could move around pretty easily.

Siegfried was on the floor groaning in pain. From the looks of it, he had hit his head. That's when Mila noticed the driver slumped against the wire cage that separated them. The driver was most likely dead. In the rearview mirror, Mila could see that his eyes were open but stared forward lifelessly, and his face was covered in blood from a deep gash.

Mila turned away from the violent scene, looking at the floor instead. That's when he noticed his keys. They must have fallen from his pocket in the crash. Mila immediately picked up the key fob and opened it, drawing out its lock picks. Using every bit of the agility that Gypsies were known for, he unlocked his own handcuffs.

Even he was surprised at how quickly he escaped them. Then he lifted Siegfried into a sitting position and unlocked the other man's cuffs as well.

"We're in here! Help!" Siegfried shouted in pain, trying desperately to rise to his feet. He lost his balance and collapsed onto one of the seats.

Someone opened the passenger-side door and climbed into the front cab of the van. From where Mila sat, he couldn't make out the face of the man who they believed had come to their rescue, only the back of his head, which seemed to be covered by some kind of knit cap. The stranger placed his finger on the neck of the driver, presumably to take his pulse.

"*Tot,*" the man announced, the German word for *dead*. Then he grabbed the van keys and slipped out of the cab. He slammed the door shut and headed around back.

Mila positioned himself near the doors so he could jump out once the good Samaritan opened it to rescue them. He watched through the window as the man unlocked the doors and then struggled to open them. They seemed to be jammed, no doubt from the crash. Siegfried was still trying to rise to his feet, but with no success.

"Don't move. You'll hurt yourself more," Mila said to Siegfried, who sank back on the seat to await their rescue. Sirens wailed in the distance: an ambulance was on its way. With one swift break, the van doors burst open.

"Thank God," Mila said. He could see two figures through the open doors of the van. Hopefully they were here to help. But then Mila noticed that the two men were wearing ski masks. These were no good Samaritans.

One of the men pulled a silenced pistol from his coat pocket and pointed it directly at Siegfried's temple.

Oh shit! Mila thought as he stepped backward. Siegfried raised his hand in front of his face in a feeble effort to protect himself.

Pop! Pop! Pop! Three shots came from the gun. The first bullet ripped right through Siegfried's hand and embedded itself in his temple. The other two shots were just insurance. As Siegfried died, the hitman aimed his pistol at Mila.

With nowhere to run, Mila covered his eyes with his hands. *Oh, man, this is gonna hurt,* he thought.

But instead of a gunshot, he heard a *thump,* then the snarling of a dog. Mila opened his eyes. The men were nowhere to be seen. Leaning out of the van, Mila spotted the gunman crouching low to the ground. Jack stood over him, raining down blows with his fists until he finally managed to tackle the assailant and knock his gun away. The other hitman was wrestling with a feral dog whose massive jaws were clamped tightly around his crowbar as he desperately held the mongrel back from sinking its teeth into his face. More dogs circled the crash scene, some of them barking while others howled like wolves.

"Are you OK?" Casey cried as she came into view.

"Yes, I'm fine! Get the gun!" Mila shouted.

Casey snatched the gun off the ground and aimed it at the fight. Mila quickly grabbed Jack's shoulders from behind and pulled him off the beaten and bloodied man. The thug began to rise to his feet but stopped when he saw the gun Casey was pointing in his direction. The dog stopped mauling the other hitman and shuffled backward. The entire pack became silent, and the beasts stared at Casey as sirens wailed.

"We've got to get out of here!" Mila said as he grabbed Casey's arm.

Casey was entranced by the power of the gun as she pointed it directly at the man's head. "They were going to kill you," she said.

There was something cold and empty in her voice that sent a shiver through Mila. "It's OK! We have to go! Come on, Casey, just turn around and let's go!" he pleaded.

But Casey just stood stock still, staring at the men, shivering. This was not the girl Mila knew. He looked around for Jack. Maybe he would know how to deal with this.

The masked man sat on the ground, unwilling to move. He knew the girl was not stable and could easily shoot him. Then Jack approached and gently placed his hand over Casey's grip. Whatever it was that Mila was sensing, Jack felt it as well. They both knew that she could, and would, pull the trigger. He coaxed her to open her hand, then slowly took the gun from her as she reluctantly released it. Jack pocketed the gun, and Casey shook her head hard, as a swimmer does upon leaving the water. Mila and Jack saw the Casey they knew slowly reappear as she emerged from the cold, trancelike state.

"Let's get out of here!" Mila said.

"Yeah," Casey answered. She reached for Mila's hand and grasped it tightly. Jack took her other hand and they, united in fear and speed, ran from the scene together. The pack of dogs took off behind them like predators.

The three teens had gone less than a block when Casey stopped. The boys slid to a halt beside her. She turned to face the dogs and commanded with uncanny authority, *"Go!"*

All the dogs in the pack began to whine and yelp in terror. The pack broke up into a motley assortment of scared, submissive animals with their tails between their legs. One by one they wandered off, dispersing into the streets and back alleys. But a single dog—a handsome, healthy-looking German shepherd—remained behind. It stood confidently in front of Casey and stared her down.

"You, too! Go! On your way. Shoo!" she ordered. But the dog just looked at her beseechingly. Then it sank to its knees, put its muzzle to the ground, and covered its face with its paws.

"Come on, Casey, or we're going to get caught," Jack reminded her.

Casey frowned. As they broke into a run, the shepherd rose to its feet and followed loyally alongside.

XVI

~~~~~~~~~

SYBIL'S GARDEN

Mila desperately tried to keep up the pace, but his strength was running out as the ache from his injuries increased. His shoulder throbbed with a piercing pain, and the ache in his left leg was brutal. As the three teens crossed the Spree River, Mila limped along behind. Then Mila exclaimed, "Wait! Tiergarten Park!"

"What park?" Jack panted, almost out of breath.

"It's about a ten-minute run from here. We can hide there," Mila said as he proceeded to take the lead, fighting through the pain.

Sure enough: about ten minutes later, sweating and panting, they arrived at ornate metal gates with the word *Tiergarten* rendered in wrought iron. The gates stood open, the bottom edges stuck in the grass as if they had been that way for decades. Once safely through the gates, Mila and his companions stopped to catch their breath. They would have liked to collapse into the green grass, but the cropped lawns were wet and muddy from the rain. The German shepherd still accompanied them, and he began to lap some water from a murky puddle with obvious enjoyment.

Mila gingerly massaged his injured shoulder, hoping to lessen the pain. "Are you OK?" Casey asked.

"I hurt my shoulder in the crash," he replied.

"Is there any swelling or tenderness?" Jack asked.

"No swelling," Mila replied. "I don't know about tenderness. Why?"

"My mom is a nurse and my friend broke his shoulder last year in our fencing competition," Jack said. "That can be very serious, Mila. We may have to get you to a doctor."

The nagging sound of sirens came again. They all froze in fear. Suddenly, a ringing sound issued from Jack's pocket, and their fear escalated to panic.

"What was that?" Casey cried out in a trembling voice.

"It's just my phone," Jack said. He pulled it out and saw a new text message. "'Mom calling,'" he read aloud.

"Don't answer it," Casey warned. "They can track it."

"She's right! Throw it in the bushes," Mila advised.

"What? It's a two-hundred-dollar phone," Jack objected. Casey ripped the phone from Jack's hand and tossed it into the nearby bushes.

"Hey, what'd you do that for?" yelled Jack. "I was going to ask my mother about Mila's shoulder!"

"They ... can ... track ... it ..." Casey said with authority.

Jack gave Casey a confused look, as if to say, "What the hell?"

"Come on," Mila said, interrupting the argument. "I know a place we can hide." He started off down a narrow path that was overgrown with huge rhododendrons.

The other two followed Mila down the path deeper into the park. The further in they went, the more trees there were, until it seemed as if they were in a forest that had sprung up right in the middle of Berlin. Soon, they heard the distinct sound of pigeons chirping in the distance. The chirps became louder as they approached a large statue.

STRENGTH

At first glance, the statue looked dark, even sinister. Made of bronze aged to pale-green verdigris, the massive sculpture rose perhaps as much as seven or eight meters into the air. The figure was a woman, dressed in a flowing robe that gracefully draped her body all the way to her feet. She was reclining on her side on an Egyptian sphinx, using its head as an armrest. A hood casting a shadow on her face, and in her lap sat a large book. She held the book open with one hand as though reading the text. While not a single bird sat directly on the statue, pigeons surrounded the entire sculpture, pedestal and all. As they moved closer to the impressive figure, Jack and Casey couldn't help but stare, enthralled by its dark beauty.

"Sybil Reading History," Mila blurted out.

Jack and Casey looked at him, impressed once again by his knowledge. Not only did he keep up with popular culture like *Whistleblower,* but he apparently knew European art as well.

"That's the name of the statute. Don't be so surprised! We need to know these things to help tourists. They're always asking stupid questions," Mila said matter-of-factly.

The teens crept even closer, frightening the birds who took flight as if on cue. However, only one bird remained, a pigeon in a hauntingly familiar shade of white.

The sight of the statue reminded Mila of the dream he had just three days ago: the woman that had guided him to the rooftop, and there, as if fate had commanded it, the white bird stood proudly on the structure. "You're the woman in the stairway," he whispered to himself.

"There were two. Correct? They will take you on a journey of darkness and power," he recalled Nasta saying when she interpreted his dream. He glanced over at Jack and Casey, and he realized that this was why Nasta had wanted him to ward off the dream.

"Shoo! Go away!" Casey commanded. The shepherd gave her another pitiful look and dropped one ear.

"I think he likes you," Jack said.

"He might even love you," Mila put in wryly.

"Shut up," Casey said, embarrassed.

"This way," Mila said.

He led them toward a dense patch of bushes and trees, and pulled back a branch to reveal a path cut into the shrubbery. Jack and Casey stepped inside, with the loyal dog close behind. They followed the short path, ducking their heads beneath the occasional branch, and soon found a small clearing. It was obviously a popular meeting place for teens: old beer bottles and cans were strewn about, and several buckets and milk crates were arranged in a circle for seating.

"We Gypsies hide here a lot. We can get away from police, store valuables, sometimes just hang out here for fun," Mila explained. "I think we should stay here and figure out a plan."

Jack and Casey nodded in agreement. Each of the three pulled up a milk crate and got as comfortable as possible. They sat without saying anything for what seemed like an eternity until Casey broke the silence. "Were you hurt badly, Mila? That crash was intense," she said.

She didn't really need to ask: she could tell he was hurt. The agony on his face when he rubbed his ribs gave that away. "I'll be all right," Mila said. Standing up, he started to pace around the clearing, rubbing his shoulder and stretching the injured arm.

"I don't think it's broken, Mila," Jack said reassuringly. "There's no discoloration."

"I'll be all right," Mila said yet again while nervously pacing. "We've got to figure out what to do."

"Guys, I think I should go back and look for my phone," Jack said. "I'll call my father. He and my uncle were stationed here in Germany years ago. I'm sure they'll have connections. And what about your bodyguard, Casey? Isn't she ex-Mossad?"

"Mossad?" Mila asked, confused.

"Yeah," said Jack. "Mossad, Israeli secret service. That's what they're called."

"What type of connections?" Casey asked with interest.

"I'm not sure. My uncle was special ops. Some of my family say he was even a spy. He was stationed at checkpoint Charlie for years. I can give him a call—"

Before Jack could say more, Mila interrupted. "And what are you going to say? That you witnessed a Gypsy boy being murdered while following another Gypsy into a cave? Or how about that you helped a fugitive break out of police custody while being an eyewitness to two cold-blooded murders?"

With that, Casey began to cry with her hands folded as if she were shivering. "I'm really afraid," she said.

Jack went over to Casey and put his arm around her to offer her comfort.

"I'm really afraid, Jack. My uncle back home, he's going to kill me," Casey said through tears.

"Calm down," said Jack, still hugging her. "It's going to be okay."

Mila stopped his pacing and stared at the beautiful girl hysterically crying as Jack held her. He realized how much trouble he had gotten them into, despite his best efforts to help them. He thought of Nasta and the dream, wishing she was alive so that he could tell her she was right about everything. Feeling a tear coming to his eye, he walked up next to the Americans.

"Jack, you're right," he said. "You guys are in enough trouble. You should go back, get your phone, and call your uncle. Blame it all on me. Officer Belz hates all us Rom. He'll believe you. And get Casey back home. I'll deal with the rest on my own. I have to find my cousins, anyways."

Casey wiped the tears from her eyes as she said, "But they'll kill you if we say it's all your fault."

"They'll try to kill me even if it's not my fault," Mila said. "You may as well tell them what they want to hear, so they can let you guys go. Otherwise, Jack might go to jail for trying to help me."

"He might be right," Jack said.

Casey pulled away from Jack and looked at him in disgust. "Are you kidding me? We can't just abandon Mila. He risked his life to save me. He's innocent!"

"It's all right, really," Mila assured her.

"No, it's not, and it won't even work," Casey exclaimed, struggling to keep her voice low. "It's not Belz we need to worry about. It's whoever's responsible for all the hitmen! I know how powerful people think. They won't let anyone get in their way. Not us, not our friends, not our families. They'll kill every last one of us, Gypsy or not, if that's what it takes to get what they want."

The sun began to set, and the shadows of the trees slowly lengthened around the three teens.

"It's the scepter they want, right?" Casey asked.

"It's a nail!" responded Mila.

"Why would they kill for this nail? What's so special about it?" Casey asked.

Jack pulled the golden spike out of his pocket for them to examine. "I mean, obviously there's things we've seen it do, or I think we've seen it do," he said.

"But how? Why? What exactly is this thing?" Casey asked.

"I think I might know," Mila said.

Mila grimaced, then sat down on a crate and paused for a moment. To Jack and Casey, this seemed as if it was for dramatic effect, but Mila was in fact considering if he should reveal more Romani lore to these *gadje*.

"Every Gypsy knows the legend of the nail," he began. "Most of us think of it as just a myth…a fairy tale."

"What's the myth?" Casey asked.

"Well, there are many versions …" Mila said slowly. His voice took on the hypnotic tone of a master storyteller, almost is if her were channeling Nasta. Jack and Casey listened intently. Even the dog seemed to be paying attention.

"… Some say the nail is a curse, others a blessing. Some say a Gypsy blacksmith made the nail; others say he just stole it. In one story, the nail chases Gypsies all over the world, always pursuing us, never letting us settle. Others say it gives us power, knowledge. Some even say it's a sign of God's permission for us to steal without it being a sin."

Mila noticed a judgmental look in Jack's and Casey's eyes.

"I think that one's bullshit," he quickly explained. "In all the stories, the nail comes from the crucifixion of Jesus. There were four nails made for the crucifixion, not three, as most people think. One nail was for his feet, and two were for his hands. The fourth was meant to enter his heart. A Gypsy stole the Fourth Nail from a Roman soldier. Now, some people will tell you that taking the nail prolonged Christ's suffering and that is why the nail is cursed, because a Gypsy made the Lord suffer worse. Then others will say that's why it's blessed, because without suffering, Christ couldn't have forgiven our sins. That much of the story, anyone can tell you. You could even find it on the Web if you just Google it."

By now, Casey and Jack were hanging on Mila's every word. Jack had stopped glancing at the scepter. Mila knew he had built up the story enough. It was time to reveal what he and his Gypsy cousins had been raised to believe: a truth they felt deep in their hearts.

"But what I'm telling you now is not found on any website or in any book," Mila continued. "It's what my great-aunt Nasta would tell me about the Fourth Nail when I was little. It's the one true story. It's true that the Romans hired a Gypsy to forge the nails for the crucifixion, and it's true that he forged four, one for each palm, one for both feet, and one for the heart..."

Gypsies were known for so many evil things throughout the world, and Mila knew that Casey and Jack were aware of this. It gave him no pleasure to let them know that his people would be responsible for such an evil deed. At that moment, they heard a rustling in the distance. The dog stood at attention, staring off toward the noise. Everyone went silent for a moment. Then they spotted a squirrel hopping through the bushes and gave a collective sigh of relief.

"So why was one nail made for the heart?" Casey whispered.

"Well, the story goes that the Fourth Nail was cursed, evil. If the nail would've entered his heart, it would've pierced his soul and thus halted the resurrection," Mila whispered in return. "Fortunately, God commanded the Gypsy to steal the Fourth Nail, hide it from the Roman soldiers, and flee Jerusalem."

"So, did the Gypsy get away? And what happened to the nail?" Casey asked.

"I'm pretty sure Jack's holding it," Mila said.

"Oh, right," Jack replied. He was so caught up in the story, he'd forgotten why Mila was telling it in the first place. Suddenly, it all dawned on Jack. He looked down at the item in his hand. "Wait—so this scepter I'm holding is actually a cursed, evil nail that was supposed to kill Jesus?" Jack said, trying to sound sarcastic but actually scared beyond belief.

"Pretty much," Mila replied.

"*Oh, shit!*" Jack shouted, impulsively throwing the nail away as hard as he could.

The nail spun in the air and landed point down, sticking straight up from the dirt. The dog trotted over to the nail, picked it up as if fetching a stick, and took it to Casey. Without thinking, she reached for the golden scepter. Rather than start a typical tug of war, the dog let go, walked to her heels, and sat by her protectively.

Casey examined the beautiful artifact again. As she ran her fingers across the cold metal surface, strange, foreign thoughts began to creep into her mind. *I need this nail,* she thought. *I've seen this before, but where?* She strained to remember. *Whatever happens, I can't let it out of my sight.* She slid the nail into her purse. "So, what now?" she asked. "What should we do?"

"Well, I'm trying to put the pieces together. My great-aunt was the only one who I think knew about this stuff, but she's gone," Mila said sadly.

Jack looked over at Casey as she scratched the dog's ears. She had tears in her eyes, and he could tell she was afraid and confused. *I must do something,* he thought. And then suddenly a memory came into his mind. "Siegfried!" he shouted.

"*Shhh!*" Casey and Mila said.

"Oh, sorry," he whispered. "Don't you remember? From the hospital? He said there was a professor at the castle who knew how the nail worked."

That reminded Mila not only of the hospital but also of the things Siegfried had said in the back of the police van. The man certainly knew something—something that terrified him. Mila wasn't sure he wanted to know what that was.

Overwhelmed, Casey tried to lighten the seriousness of the scene by playfully teasing the dog. The animal lovingly played along. Meanwhile, Jack gave Mila a serious look. "Let's see if the coast is clear," Jack said.

Mila didn't have to be a mind reader to guess that Jack wanted to talk to him alone. They asked Casey to wait before heading down the trail back to the statue. The sun had almost set. Its last few golden rays gleamed off the statue, giving it an almost angelic quality.

"Something is wrong with her," Jack said to Mila. "Did you see her with the gun? She was worse back at the hospital after you left. She...she...It's hard to explain..."

"Well, try!" Mila pleaded.

"*Impete*," Jack replied.

"What?"

"It means 'attack!' in Latin."

"What the hell are you talking about?"

"Like I said, it's hard to explain. Back at the hospital, the room was in chaos, and we were in definite danger, and then...and then..." Jack struggled to find the words, not quite comprehending it himself.

"And then what?" Mila demanded.

"Casey gave the order, and a wild dog burst through the window and attacked the inspector. Mila, I'm pretty sure Casey doesn't *speak* Latin."

The two boys fell silent. Jack whispered, "We've got to do something, right?"

Mila realized Jack was right. But should he try to help or just go meet up with his family and forget this whole crazy situation?

He glanced back toward the clearing. He saw Casey stepping out from the path with the dog following behind. She looked so playful and innocent. Their eyes met, and she gave Mila a soft look like the one she'd given him when their eyes met at the train station.

"Professor Hermann," he said, as if he'd made his decision to assist in this crazy crusade.

"Is that supposed to mean something to me?" Casey asked.

"When you were unconscious, the guy they sent after you, named Siegfried—he mentioned Professor Hermann," Mila explained.

And the castle. Deborah knew about the castle, too. They said some sort of Nazi cult met there," Jack said, trying to put the puzzle together.

"Wewelsburg Castle, that's the one they mentioned," Mila said.

"We've got to go there. Maybe we can find this Professor Hermann," Jack said.

"If there's someone there who can explain what this nail is doing to me, I want to go," Casey said.

"But we don't even know this guy," Jack pointed out.

"I hate to break it to you, but aside from him, we're on our own. Nobody is going to believe this supernatural shit, except maybe this Professor Hermann."

"Well ..." said Jack, mulling it over. "A long shot's better than no shot, that's what my dad always said. I'm in."

"You sure about that?" Mila asked. "We've got cops and Nazis chasing us. It ain't gonna be easy. Do you even have any money?"

Casey checked her purse. "I have ... six euros," she said, counting, "... and a Metro card. Oh wait—it's for New York, and it's expired. I've got a credit card, though."

"I'm sure the police are tracking it by now," Jack said.

Mila thought for a minute. "I've got it! Some of the shadier Roma meet here under this statue when it gets dark to divvy up their earnings. They should be here tonight, if they didn't leave for Romania yet. If I know these guys, they'll spend one more night ripping off tourists before skipping town. I can try to get some money and help from them. When they get here no one mention the nail. These guys are greedy as hell. If they hear we have golden treasure they might just turn on us."

Casey inched closer to Mila and stared into his eyes. Once again, Mila could sense her characteristic empathy and compassion.

"Mila, I just realized, you're the one who could run," she said. "Your people live all over Europe, right? You could just disappear, hide among them and let Jack and I worry about the rest of this."

"No way! Look, whatever's up with this nail, I need to find out," Mila declared. "I have to. I can't let them get away with this... They killed my little cousin right there in..." he stopped, choked with sadness. He caught his breath. "For all I know, they killed them all."

At that moment, Mila realized why he was doing this. He walked over to the edge of the statue, sat back, and waited. He hoped Simon showed up.

At least then I can get them to Wewelsburg, and maybe when this is all over, I can get vengeance for my family, no not vengeance...

"Justice," he whispered.

XVII

ESCAPE FROM
BERLIN

Simon Roarlock hustled the city of Berlin the entire day. The night had finally come, and it was safe now to go to the park and meet up with his cousins to barter the day's earnings. It was fun to barter. Sometimes you would steal a cell phone or a piece of jewelry, but instead of spending the next few days trying to resell it, you met up with your family or friends and barter it for something you wanted or needed.

He started to make his way to the park where he and his friends usually met up to barter. The rule was to trade only in the dark of night. That way you could avoid the police.

He began to feel strange walking alone. Normally, he would never do that to hustle the city: that was asking for trouble. You always needed a partner or an accomplice for obvious reasons. He'd lucked out and avoided trouble. The day's earnings were successful. That morning he'd snatched a purse from a woman who was tending to her child. It was full of money: almost two hundred euros. She also had the new iPhone and a heavy solid-gold bracelet. Then, later that afternoon in the train station, he had managed to strike up a conversation about football star David Beckham with a grungy-looking American teen boy en route to Vienna. He succeeded in slyly picking the boy's pocket while showing him the latest field moves. Unfortunately, all he got from the teen was a small bag of weed.

Oh well, he thought. *Maybe I can trade it tonight at the statue.* It was just a few short blocks from where he worked in the old quarter of the city. He didn't particularly like Berlin, but he would admit to himself and to his friends that the money was good there. After all, the tourists were just as rich as the ones in Paris and Rome. Best of all, in Berlin the number of Gypsies who stole for a living was much smaller than in other large European cities that were magnets for tourists. "So, the *gadje* aren't on their toes," he'd explain.

As Simon slipped through the iron gate of the park with only his thoughts to keep him company, his mind wandered to the events earlier that morning. Everyone at the camp had been too upset by the death of Nasta and the demolition of Buildings A and B to enforce the *kris*'s punishment. *These Berlin Gypsies have it too easy,* he thought. *No matter. Once they get to Romania, they'll realize how easy they had it here in Germany.*

Simon left the park's gravel path and headed into the grassy woods, still trying to avoid the police. His thoughts drifted to the past, to the night he fled Romania. He remembered the acrid scent of burning plastic from the garbage-bag roofs, the screams of Roma men, women, and children being burned, and the sight of his wife Layla clutching little Sophia, their skin chalk-white, dead from smoke inhalation. That night had left him with an unquenchable burning pain inside, a pain that screamed for justice that he could never seem to find.

At least the Berliners had the grace to warn the Rom of the eviction. They didn't burn the village down in the middle of the night when everyone was sleeping, he thought.

Resentful musings continued to ramble through his mind as he crossed the park. There in the dark woods, a sudden feeling of guilt fell on him. *Maybe I should've stayed and helped after the eviction, instead of being greedy and going out to hustle the city.*

"But I just couldn't," he mumbled to himself.

His words startled a young couple next to a tree, making out in the dark. Simon chuckled for a moment at their fearful reactions. Seeing them breaking from a passionate kiss in pure surprise put a smile on his face. For an instant, he forgot the pain in his heart.

"Sorry," he whispered as he passed them.

He was grateful for the couple's embarrassment: it had distracted him for a few moments.

Soon, he arrived at the massive old tree where he usually hid and waited, staking out the statue before he approached it. You never knew when the cops might be around. Always approach with caution: this is what you'd learn if you grew up like Simon.

Before he made his way toward the structure, he strategically peeked around the tree to get a better look. He could make out a shadowy figure next to the statue but couldn't be sure who it was. It could be Rom, tourists, police—anybody, so he paused for a signal of some sort.

He heard whispering near the base of the statue. Whoever it was, they were definitely not Gypsies. They spoke English, which also ruled out any German police. Then he heard the bark of a dog. The animal sounded vicious. He was not sure who these people were, but he didn't want to find out.

He stayed in his hiding place behind the tree, took a deep breath, and held it. He had to make a plan. He looked in the direction of the park exits and frantically calculated his route of escape. The dog's bark rang out again, loud and terrifying. Just as he was about to make a run for it, he heard a voice over the dog's bark.

"*Kon san?*" the voice said loudly. It was Romani for "Who are you?" Simon wasn't quite sure, but it sounded like Mila from Building A.

"It's me! Simon! Is that you, Mila?" Simon yelled back in Romani.

"Yes, it's me!" Mila called back, this time in English.

Strange, Simon thought. But after all, Mila was still his kin. He peered out from around the dark tree. He could recognize Mila now, but there were two other shadows with him, as well as a barking dog. One of the shadowy figures was near the animal, speaking softly to it as if trying to quiet it down.

"Come on, don't worry! They're my friends," Mila shouted.

Simon began to approach with caution. When he got closer, he realized that the shadowy figures were two young *gadje*. Things began to become clear to him. *These are the two Americans from the train station. But what were they doing here?*

As he approached, he could just barely hear the boy whisper, "Seriously, this guy again?"

"What have you got yourself into now, Mila?" Simon asked as he made his way over. "Aren't we in enough trouble with the elders already for getting involved with these Americans?" he added with a hint of arrogance.

However, when he met Mila face to face, his sense of superiority faded. There was a hopeless look in Mila's eyes. It was clear that there was more weighing on him than the eviction or the passing of one old lady.

"You were right not to listen to Father Leichman," Mila said with despair. And before Simon had the chance to blurt out a prideful "I knew it" or perhaps an exultant "I told you so," Mila tearfully added, "He killed Korey." Mila wiped away a tear with the sleeve of his shirt.

"What? How? When...?" Simon asked, his questions getting tangled up.

"It's true. I saw it," Jack put in, stepping out of the shadows.

"This is Gypsy business," Simon said with irritation. He gestured to Jack to stay out of the conversation, but Jack would not back down.

"Hey, I'm not the bad guy here! You're the one who got us into this mess! If you hadn't attacked us at—" he snapped back.

"I don't got to explain nothin' to you," Simon interrupted.

Before the argument got out of hand, the dog began to growl at them. They stopped fussing.

"Look, Simon, Leichman tried to kill me, too," Mila said. "Have you seen Stephan and Rosa? They were right there when Leichman killed Korey, and Petre should be with them."

"I think they're with the others. All of the families are heading back to Romania, and the priest is organizing their passage," Simon told Mila. "Most of the families are at the church. It's become like a shelter."

"They can't be there," Mila said. "They would have warned everyone. So, the families don't know about Korey? You must go back and warn them."

"Come with me. We'll tell them together. And then I'll kill Leichman myself!" Simon responded.

Simon watched Mila looking down sadly. He just told Simon the craziest story he'd ever heard, and that was saying something for a Gypsy pickpocket. If anyone besides Mila had told him such a story, Simon wouldn't have believed it. But if there was one thing Simon knew about Mila, it was that he had a lot of integrity. Simon knew that Mila would only lie if he had to. And if his story of hitmen, corrupt cops, evil priests and murder was a lie, the truth would have to be even worse.

After hearing about the day's crazy events, Simon was still not convinced that Mila should risk his life and go off on some crazy adventure with the Americans. He began to speak to Mila in their Gypsy language. "You can't trust non-Gypsies," he argued. "You know the *gadje* hate us. I can't assist you in helping them. I've seen too much suffering in our people to trust any *gadjo*. They're only good for their money."

"I have no choice," Mila replied. "I have to trust them."

Casey came closer to the boys, the faithful dog at her side. Her beauty mesmerized Simon. For a moment, he could see why Mila was so eager to help her. "That man tried to kill all of us," Casey added as she knelt to calm the dog again.

"This is nuts!" Simon blurted out. "OK, besides warning the family about Father Leichman, what do you want me to do?"

"We need some help to get out of Berlin. Leichman is searching for us, so we need to keep it quiet," Mila told him.

"I don't like where this is going," Simon replied with regret in his voice.

"We just need some cash, and maybe a cell phone," Mila said in desperation.

"I knew it!" Simon yelled. He turned away to head back to the church. "Look, I'll let the family know that Leichman is an asshole, but I'll be damned if it's going to cost me any money!" he shouted over his shoulder.

He began to make his way back toward the woods. Then he heard the girl shout back at him. "We can barter with you for the money!" she yelled.

That stopped Simon dead in his tracks. He slyly turned back and looked directly in her eyes. "Well, now, pretty lady, just what exactly do you have to barter with?" Simon asked menacingly.

Mila and Jack looked at Casey, confused. What did she have to barter with? They had nothing. Simon turned again and started to leave.

"How exactly were you going to kill Leichman? With your bare hands?" she asked cunningly.

Simon stopped and turned back again. "Maybe," he answered tersely.

"I think a handgun from one of Leichman's own bodyguards might do the trick," she said matter-of-factly.

Simon walked over to Casey. She pulled the gun from her purse. All four of them formed a circle around it.

"That's the real thing, isn't it?" Simon said to the others. Casey nodded.

"Damn, you know…I was kinda talking out my ass when I said I was gonna kill him," Simon admitted.

"Whatever. The thing's worth money, isn't it?" Casey asked.

Jack looked over her shoulder at the weapon. "That's a Glock 17," he said with assurance. "It's the most expensive gun they make, and who knows what the silencer's worth."

"*Bre*, this isn't America! You can't just sell a gun at the nearest pawn shop. I try to fence something that hot, I'll probably get burned."

"Here," said Casey offering her credit card, "it's got a $5,000 limit."

"I'm a thief, but I'm not stupid. If the cops are after you, they'll trace that," he exclaimed.

He looked Casey in the eyes, seeing desperation written all over her face. It reminded him of his own pain. *This is real,* he thought. *I have to help them, even if they are* gadje.

He took the gun and the card with a sigh and swiftly put them in his pocket. He took a seat on the ground, cross-legged, and reached into his other pockets to empty out his loot from the day. On the ground in front of him, he placed a wad of euros, a few American dollars, some jewelry, and the shiny new iPhone. The others stood over him, looking down at the merchandise.

"Well, come on, sit down," he urged.

Casey and the two boys formed a circle on the ground, sitting cross-legged like Simon. What would it take to escape from Berlin? They would need everything Simon had, and maybe more.

"All right, work with me here," said Simon. I can get five hundred euros out of that card before I have to chuck it, assuming it isn't canceled already. It don't matter how nice the gun is, I'll have to sell it cheap, or I'm a dead man. What else you got?"

Mila pulled something from his pocket and gently placed it in the circle. It was the BMW key.

"It's parked over at Bundestag Station. Ludwig offered me 200 for it."

"Deal!" Simon said as he snatched the key.

Just like that, the barter was over. Mila told Simon that he planned to head further west into Germany, toward Bielefeld. Simon gave them the impressive cell phone and the two hundred euros he'd snatched as well. Then he remembered something else that might help Mila. "Sabina!" Simon blurted out.

"Who?" Mila asked.

"Sabina, the fortune-teller. She used to live in the camps with us back in Romania. She's your aunt. Maybe you were too young to remember," Simon reminded Mila.

Mila shook his head.

Simon recalled quite well the sweet lady who used to practice divination and cook for the whole community. He reminded Mila that if he needed more money or perhaps a place to stay, she now made her home in the city called Paderborn, not far from where they were heading.

"How would we find her?" Mila asked.

"That's easy: just ask around town where the local fortune-teller is. That's a sure way to find her," Simon suggested.

"You think she would help?" Jack asked.

"It's been years since I've seen her, but I remember she was a kind of Gypsy mystic. She taught me some English—mostly how to swear," Simon recalled.

Their business finished, as if by silent agreement they all rose from the grass and shook hands.

"Don't buy your tickets all together," Simon advised. "They'll be looking for groups. And keep the cell phone turned off. Use it only when you really need it—I don't have the charger, and eventually the owner will try to trace it. You don't want to get busted for something I stole."

"Thanks, we'll keep that in mind," Mila assured him.

"One more thing. Do you think they killed Stephan... and the other twin—Petre?" Simon asked.

Mila paused for a moment as his eyes gazed off in the distance with a look reminiscent of the late Mystic, Nasta. "No... they're alive," Mila said with certainty. Jack and Casey wondered if that was just wishful thinking on his part.

"OK. Well...good luck, Mila," Simon told him. He turned away from his new friends and headed into the park's dark woods with the pistol and keys in his pocket. *I wonder if it's loaded,* he thought.

XVIII

~7I~

THE BEST WAY
TO TRAVEL

"The best way to see Germany," boasted the Deutsche Bahn Railway posters adorning German train stations. Unfortunately for Jack, Casey, and Mila, though, it wasn't the quickest way. Using the stolen iPhone, they checked the train schedules for early that morning. For them, the next train to Bielefeld didn't leave Berlin until 7:46 a.m. They spent the night in the park, where they hid in the clearing and tried their best to sleep on the cold, hard ground.

It was a three-hour train ride from Berlin to the city of Bielefeld. Once there, they would have to change trains and board a local to reach the small village of Wewelsburg. That would put them at the castle a few hours before closing time. With the cash Simon had so reluctantly traded away, they would be able to buy their tickets and even get some sandwiches for the trip.

As Simon had advised, they purchased their tickets separately to avoid being noticed. Jack got his ticket first; then Mila bought his. Casey waited a few moments before approaching the agent to buy a ticket for herself.

The agent noticed the dog, still at Casey's side as she approached the ticket window. Transferring his reading glasses from the bridge of his nose to the crown of his head, the agent inspected the animal from the safety of his ticket booth. *"Kann ich dir helfen?"* he asked.

"Sprechen sie English?" Casey asked in her best German accent.

"Of course I speak English," the teller said. "But I'm sorry, miss, live animals must be crated for transport."

"Oh, he's not traveling with us—I mean, me," she nervously responded.

The clerk gave her a puzzled glance and took another look at the animal, which was sitting right next to her. "Oh, I see," he said skeptically. Still, he gave her the ticket.

"Your train will be leaving in fifteen minutes from track four. So, you'll have time to figure out what to do with the animal that is not traveling with you," he said, an edge of dry humor in his voice. "The dog will not be permitted to board the train," the agent added in a kind tone.

Casey took her ticket and turned away. She looked down at the dog as she walked toward the track. As usual, he faithfully followed along.

"You're getting me in trouble," she scolded the animal that made a pitiful *arhmmm* sound, as if apologizing in dog language. Casey patted him, wondering what to do.

As they had planned, the boys boarded the train separately, leaving Casey to deal with the dog. She used some of her money to buy a hot dog, then removed the bun and fed it to the shepherd. Kneeling beside him, she petted the animal while he enjoyed the treat. "Look, I have to go...and you have to stay here," Casey said.

"Hey, Mom, look! That dog looks like a wolf," a small boy said as he and his mother passed by Casey and the dog.

"Wolfy," Casey decisively said. "That's your name."

She gave the dog a gentle pat on the head, stood up, and turned away, walking toward the track. Wolfy swallowed the last of the meat he was enjoying and continued to follow close. Just as Casey was about to board the train she looked back and saw the animal still tailing her.

She turned back to him and pointed her finger with authority. "No, Wolfy! Sit!"

He sat. "Stay!" she ordered, her finger pointed directly at his eyes.

Wolfy gave her a doleful look but didn't move a muscle. Casey was sad to leave him there all alone, but the last thing she needed was trouble from the conductor. She was surprised by how well Wolfy had followed her instructions. For a stray, he was certainly well-behaved.

Casey climbed the steps of the first car to board the train. Wolfy sat obediently on the platform and watched sadly as she reached the top of the steps. She glanced over her shoulder for one last look at him sitting there, obeying her commands to sit and stay. Then, regretfully, she turned away and proceeded into the car.

The German cross-country railway was different from the local lines—in fact, much nicer. The seats looked more comfortable, and at either end of the car were four seats arranged as if in a club car or a restaurant booth: two seats facing the other two, with a folding table between them. *That looks cozy,* Casey thought. *Maybe I can find the guys and we can all sit there.*

The train car held only a few scattered passengers: an older woman, a mother with two blond toddlers, and few others. Casey scanned the car in search of Mila or Jack. She spotted Jack first, sitting at a window and looking through the iPhone. Mila was a few seats in front of Jack at the end of the car, in the four-seater section. Across from him sat a voluptuous blonde woman talking on a cell phone.

Casey realized that the boys were not sitting together. Apparently, the plan to stay separate went for the train ride, too. She sighed, missing Wolfy already, feeling alone and a bit scared. She didn't want Jack or Mila to be completely out of sight, so she squeezed past an older lady settled in an aisle seat and took an empty place across the aisle from Jack.

None of them had gotten much sleep in the park, and this would be a good time to try to make up for that. Before settling in, she took a quick look over at Jack, who was still fiddling with the stolen iPhone. Then she peered over the seats in front of her to look for Mila. His seat had its back to the end of the car so he was facing the rest of the passengers. She could see him perfectly. He was already fast asleep.

Casey turned toward the window and watched as the train pulled out of the station. As the city of Berlin drifted by, she closed her eyes from pure exhaustion. But as soon as she closed them, she saw a vision from her nightmare in the hospital; she heard a mob screaming and gnashing their teeth, she felt burning heat, and worst of all, she saw impenetrable blackness.

"Ticket, Miss," the conductor requested.

She felt like only a minute or two had passed before he woke her, but the view from her window revealed it had been much longer. The glistening Berlin skyline had been replaced by the rolling green hills of the German countryside. All she could think of was her vision. Now she felt not just a little scared, but utterly frightened.

She handed her ticket to the conductor and looked over at Jack. He was now fast asleep with the iPhone lying in his lap. She looked toward the front of the car and found Mila, just in time to see the blonde woman leaving his section. *Should I go sit next to him?* she wondered. *There are plenty of other seats, and if I sit with him, he'll think I'm into him or something. Boys are so stupid...*

Her thoughts roamed for a minute; then she realized she was the one being stupid, jumping to ridiculous conclusions. The fact was she was too frightened to sit alone.

The conductor left and proceeded to collect the tickets from the other passengers, including Mila. He looked back at her, and as she returned his look, he nodded his head. Before she knew what was happening, she had risen from her seat and made her way toward Mila, passing a sleeping Jack and several other passengers. Instead of taking one of the two seats across from Mila, she opted for the seat next to his.

Mila was busy putting his empty lunch bag under the seat. He didn't notice Casey until she was right next to him. Her sudden appearance was a bit of a surprise. "I thought we were going to sit separately," he said.

"Well, aren't they looking for a group of three?" she retorted.

Mila looked over at Jack to see where he was. "He's sleeping," Casey said, knowing what he was looking for.

Mila gave her a "What are you up to?" look.

"Look, I'm afraid, OK?" she said.

Before he could ponder further, Casey grabbed the brown paper bag from between Mila's feet.

"What did you get for breakfast?" she asked while searching through the bag. "Anything left?"

"Um, egg and cheese, and there's still—"

Casey found an untouched apple. She held it up and gave Mila a doe-eyed look that could only mean "Can I have this?"

"Yeah, go ahead. I don't like apples," Mila said.

"Thanks. I gave my breakfast to Wolfy, so I'm starving now."

"Wolfy? You named a stray dog?"

Without answering, Casey began to shamelessly devour the apple.

"You've got a good appetite for someone so frightened," Mila joked.

She looked at him and took the final bite of the apple, leaving only its core. "Yeah … don't mind me. I guess I'm not myself these days," she said, slightly embarrassed.

"I don't know you," Mila said. She looked down at her lap, not knowing what to say. "So how would I know if you always eat apples that way?" he added jokingly, trying to break the awkward moment. Casey forced a fleeting smile.

"I'm always hungry when I get scared. I'm even afraid to fall asleep again," she confessed. "Back at the hospital when I was sleeping, I had a terrifying dream."

"Nightmare," he corrected. "They're only dreams when they're pleasant! Tell me what you saw."

"I don't know, I'm kind of afraid to talk about it ..." she told him, rubbing the wound she had suffered in the bunker. The gash was now nearly healed, and so was her ankle.

"It will help if you can tell me. The nightmare will lose its power over you if you talk about it."

She gazed out the window at the sprawling hills of the German countryside, abandoning the conversation for a moment. *He might be right,* she thought. She summoned her courage and began.

"Well, at first, it was a nice dream. I thought I was exploring Vienna or Berlin," she said. "From the looks of the section of the city, I figured that I must be in the Arab district. Most European cities have one, right? I was thinking that must be it." Mila shrugged his arms.

"Anyway, I was walking down a narrow cobblestone street packed with people, it was so crowded, I could even smell animals. But somehow in the dream the smells were stronger than I thought they should be.

"It must have been some kind of outside shopping mall. Everywhere I looked there were items for sale on stalls and merchants' tables. It was so hectic, dozens of people were arguing, bargaining, buying, and selling stuff. The people all wore flowing linen robes that seemed strange for a modern city. Everyone seemed to have some kind of head covering, from simple white cloths tied up around the forehead to beautiful shawls covered in elaborate designs. It was all so gorgeous, and so interesting.

"I tried to notice the locals and their faces as they passed, but for some reason they seemed distant and in a hurry. I didn't mind, I was enjoying myself and happy to be exploring the city and this beautiful market, sandy cobblestone streets and all."

"So, what was frightening?" Mila asked.

"I heard a mob off in the distance. They were gathered around this man..." she trailed off, a look of sheer terror on her beautiful face.

"And?" Mila encouraged her.

"They were throwing stones at him. I couldn't see his face ... when I moved closer, the man was on his knees, and in front of him stood a young soldier, he looked like a Roman soldier, he was handsome, but he had the cruelest blue eyes. He kept hitting the poor man again and again. Then a woman grabbed my hand and pulled me out of there. We were both running away from the crowd that was now chasing us. 'Don't look back,' the woman said. 'Run away, we need to run away. Faster! Faster! Run with me to the light!'"

"To the light?" Mila asked. "Did you recognize the woman?"

Casey tried to remember. "Yeah, the light! The woman, she was petite. Small, but strong. She kind of reminded me of you," she said. "We were running toward a bright, bright light. She kept telling me, 'Don't look back.' As we got closer to the light, I heard Jack's voice calling my name. I turned and looked back, and then the soldier threw a stone. It hit me in my eye. My eyes began to burn. I let go of the woman's hand and fell on the sand. Everything went blurry, and I thought of my mother. And I was afraid I was going blind, just like she did."

"Your mother is blind?"

"Yes," Casey admitted.

"You should tell me more about her. When there is something personal like that in a dream, it can change the meaning," Mila explained.

Casey took a deep breath, averting her eyes from Mila as she gathered her thoughts.

"My mom's been blind my whole life. I was always afraid that I would lose my sight, the same as she did. Of course, I hope and pray she'll get better. I wish for it every birthday, every shooting star, every time I throw a coin in a fountain. But there's a lot wrong with my mom."

Casey took a deep breath before she went on. Mila reached out and took her hand and she was grateful for it. "She went blind when I was little, probably from drugs. She got herself under control for a while, but when my aunt died it all went to hell. She's in a high-end assisted living facility now. My uncle John takes care of both of us."

Mila swallowed, and his grip on Casey's hand tightened. "What about your dad?" he asked.

"On her good days, Mom used to claim he was some sort of heroic doctor who disappeared, but who the hell knows if it's true," Casey replied sadly.

"You know, what you fear the most, you will not escape," Mila said thoughtfully.

"So, what does that mean? I'm going to be blind?" she demanded.

"It means fear is evil, and the more fear you have, the easier the evil will come to you. A wise woman told me that. And she used to teach me about my dreams..."

"Who was that woman—your mother?"

"So then what happened?" he said, changing the subject.

"When my sight came back Jack was there, sitting right next to me. He wanted me to read something—he said it would heal my eyes. The woman was calling back to me, and now she had reached the light. She was wearing a long chain of gold around her neck. She was yelling that there was evil and that the words are evil ..."

"Gold around her neck? Like a necklace made of coins?" Mila questioned her, then gave her a knowing look.

"What?"

"Nothing," he told her.

She looked at him skeptically, but continued.

"Jack said 'Read this.' He pointed to a short sentence on an ancient, yellowing piece of parchment. I said, 'What language is that? I don't understand a word of it,' and he said, 'You don't need to understand it, just read it. Trust me.' All the while the woman called to me from the light.

"I looked at the ancient scroll. I couldn't seem to focus on a line. Then Jack took my hand. 'Say it with me,' he said. And together we began to speak the words, as if we'd always known them," Casey paused and closed her eyes remembering the strange incantation, "*Kon godi phenel kako svato chi merel hai chi avel jevindi; Vigoris!*"

"That's Romani...You were speaking Romani," Mila observed.

"We began to chant in unison, and then a bright light appeared from the sky. It was as if the sun was moving closer to the earth, and the whole world was getting hotter by the second. The cobblestone streets were transformed into hot desert sands. I was suddenly struck by the blistering heat and fell flat on the ground. The heat covered my skin, and my insides started to boil.

"I closed my eyes and protected them with my hands. It was the only part of my body I wanted to protect. I began to scream. Just when it seemed like I couldn't bear it any longer, the pain and burning disappeared. I hesitated, then gently put my hands down. I opened my eyes and found myself at the hospital," she concluded.

They both paused for a moment. The green countryside passed by like a movie through the window beside them.

"What were the words that I said?" Casey asked, not really wanting to know.

"Basically, it means 'whoever says this will never die and never live.' That last word 'Vigoris' isn't Romani, it might be Latin," Mila explained. "It sounds like a spell or something."

"But what does that mean? Never die and never live? It makes no sense," Casey said growing increasingly distraught.

Casey looked at her wound again, and they both realized that the wound was completely gone. There was not even a scar.

"Oh my God, Mila. What's happening to me?" she asked tearfully.

She began to cry. Mila pulled her close. She rested her head on his white T-shirt and began to silently weep.

"What do you think the dream means?" Casey asked.

"It's funny, just a few days ago I believed that dreams meant nothing. I didn't care about their interpretations. But I know this dream and what it means. The woman you saw was my Aunt Nasta. She was trying to stop you from reading the braille. She told me when she was alive that the nail can heal your body," Mila responded.

"But why wouldn't she want me to read it if it can heal me?" Casey asked through her tears.

"I think she was trying to save all of our souls. I can feel her around me now."

"My mom believes in dreams," Casey said. "She says it's the only way she can see nowadays. My uncle says she throws money away on witch doctors and mystics. She paid all kinds of money to charlatans all over the world, trying to return her sight until my uncle put her away and cut off her allowance."

"You mentioned your uncle before. Is he like your guardian?" Mila asked, intrigued.

"It's complicated," Casey answered.

Mila looked down at her and raised an eyebrow. "I think we have moved past complicated, Casey."

"You're right. It's just so hard, Mila. My uncle, he's super paranoid. He's always worried I am going to be kidnapped. Or, worse for him, that I will do something to embarrass my late aunt's estate. He's been keeping me in a virtual prison for years and donated millions of dollars to Charlton Prep so they keep who I am a secret."

"Who are you?" Mila asked, even more intrigued.

"Me? I'm nobody. I've never told anybody before, not even Jack, but my aunt was Zoe Rich," Casey finally revealed.

"Wait a minute," Mila said, "*The* Zoe Rich?"

But Casey didn't answer. The swaying motion of the train had made her drift off to sleep.

XIX

~~~

GOD KNOWS
WHERE

"*Darf ich hier sitzen?*"

"Huh?" Jack responded, still half asleep.

He opened his eyes and looked up to see an old woman standing in the aisle.

"*Sprichst du Deutsch?*"

"Huh, what?"

"*Sprichst du Deutsch?*" she repeated with a deep accent.

"Um, no … English," he responded, stretching away his slumber.

"May I sit here?" she repeated in English.

The woman was asking about the aisle seat next to him. Finishing his huge stretch and wiping the sleep from his eyes, a sense of fear took over Jack. A knot formed in his stomach as he remembered the dire situation he was in. He was on the train to God knows where in search of God knows what. Doing his best to hide his dismay, Jack motioned to the lady to take the seat next to him. The old woman in the flowered sundress and matching oversize bag wearing a headscarf tied behind her hair pulled her flower-embroidered bag up in her lap and took her seat next to him. The lady smiled, and Jack forced a smile back. Somehow, it made him feel a little safer.

After watching the lady squeeze into her seat, his thoughts drifted back to the dream he was having. It was a wonderful dream about him and Casey back home at school, and soon it would be true, he mused. He and Casey were hitting it off amazingly, and he wanted it to continue back home, among his family and friends. A quick glance outside the window brought him back to reality, and the knot in his stomach returned. He glanced at the woman next to him; she politely smiled back. Unfortunately, her smile did not calm him like before. He grabbed the stolen iPhone and turned it back on.

When Jack first took his seat in Berlin, he used the stolen iPhone's Internet browser, realizing that he had a mini laptop in the palm of his hands, he did a quick Google search then switched the browser to English then typed in "Wewelsburg Castle," hoping to get some idea of what they could expect when they got there.

After a few minutes he was shocked to learn how much he didn't know about Nazis. There it all was, and the top hit on Google. He began to read: "Wewelsburg Castle was the center of the Nazi secret organization called the Thule Society."

"Interesting," he whispered to himself. He hit the related link on the Thule Society and continued:

"Thule Society: A secret organization who believed there was a pure Aryan race. This pure race originated from a lost landmass located between Greenland and Iceland. Thule mystics during the early twentieth century believed that this race was descended from Greek and Norse gods and they themselves had superhuman powers on Earth, resulting in their true name..."

"Nordic gods!" he shouted in shock, startling the woman next to him as well as the young couple that was sitting a few seats behind him. "Entschuldigung," he apologized in German. "This is nuts," he murmured to himself.

He left that page by hitting other related links, where he learned about the fascination the Nazis and Adolf Hitler had with all biblical artifacts:

"Nazi soldiers and SS Agents traveled the world over in search of anything related to Jesus' life and death," he read.

It was like something from a bat-shit crazy blogger's conspiracy site. But these stories cited U.S. Government Archives and Oxford historians. He read on, and his research revealed that the Nazis really did launch archeological expeditions in search of relics like the Holy Grail and the Ark of the Covenant, as well as the Spear of Destiny and a holy scepter that would create a new order king. Jack had always assumed that was something Hollywood dreamed up for the Indiana Jones movies.

SPEAR OF DESTINY

As he read on, he learned about the Nazis's famous symbol, the swastika. It was a symbol of peace that originated from the east, and some believed that it was part of a mystical order. However, the Germans inverted it to create a symbol of war and conquest. The Thule Society used this as a symbol of Aryan supremacy. Beneath the main tower of Wewelsburg castle, the Nazis had a giant swastika carved into the floor. In each quadrant was a small pit meant to house four artifacts. The function of these relics seemed to be a subject of debate. Some believed that these safeguards were the home of the biblical relics of Christ.

"This is completely insane!" he mumbled. He could not believe what he was reading. *Why isn't anyone speaking or teaching about this shit?* he wondered.

One name kept coming up in Jack's search about the Thule Society: Professor Solomon Hermann. Apparently, he was curator of the Wewelsburg Castle and one of the foremost experts on Nazi occult practices. He'd written several books on the subject.

"This is who we need!" he said loudly with a bit of relief, startling the woman and the couple again. He glanced back at them and repeated "sorry" in English. The couple nodded to him, then clutched each other tightly as if they were commuting next to a crazy person.

As he quietly returned to reading, what intrigued Jack was that among various academic honors the professor also had an illustrious fencing career. *Well, at least we have that in common*, he thought, trying to figure out a way to befriend the professor.

Jack pulled up a picture and a biography. According to the bio, Hermann was in his sixties, but he looked much younger. As he scrolled down the bio, it revealed many sites boasting that he was half Romani. That gave Jack some hope. He has to help us now, he figured. He'd seen how Rom stick together. Simon was willing to help Mila, even after everything that had happened in the subway station. Maybe Hermann would be the same way. *I'm sure there's some kind of Gypsy solidarity*, he assumed. *I've read enough. I've got to tell Casey and Mila about all this.*

He first glanced over to Casey across from him, then to Mila at the end of the train. Both were fast asleep. He knew they were tired, and he was, as well. It was at least two more hours before they would arrive at the castle. He noticed the ten percent battery charge on the iPhone and realized it would be dead soon. He decided to let everyone sleep before he revealed the crazy things he'd just learned. Besides, *I should preserve this battery power*, he figured. He turned off the phone and closed his eyes for a much-needed break. Just for a few moments, he promised himself.

When he awoke, he again turned on the iPhone and it booted itself back to life. He figured he must have been asleep for at least ten minutes. But, to his surprise, the iPhone revealed he had been sleeping for more than an hour and they were getting very close to their station. To make matters worse, the charge only read two percent. "What the hell?" he said, frustrated.

The old lady looked over to him. "Is there a problem, young man?" she asked with concern.

"No, ma'am. It's just this new iPhone, the battery power doesn't last long," he answered.

"Oh, well, I see how that can be a problem," she replied.

I better check how far the train station is from the castle before the phone dies, Jack thought.

Quickly Jack searched back through the browser, hoping to get detailed directions from the train station. As he flipped through the pages, he reached the page with the address. "Perfect," he said to himself. Scanning the text for the address, he noticed a hyperlink on the word Gypsies next to the description of professor Herman on the website.

Knowing he was running low on power, he debated if he should click the link or head straight to maps. Struggling through his worries, he clicked the link. Suddenly, a page appeared with all kinds of Gypsy sites and information on the culture. As he scrolled down to see if there was anything on the artifact or legend, he realized it was just a bunch of information on the Roma people with some random links to Gypsy cabs and moths. As he was about to leave, he noticed a small photo in one of the links of a girl that looked like Casey; it read "Kidnapped."

"Oh no!" Jack yelled.

He hit the link. It led to a video from British Voice News. He turned up the volume to watch, a feeling of great anticipation flowing through him. The iPhone now read 1%. Ignoring the low battery, he let the video play. "Casey Richards kidnapped by gang of Gypsies," the well-dressed British journalist said. "From this smashed window, they abducted Ms. Richards." He was reporting from outside the hospital room they had escaped from just yesterday.

"An American student was kidnapped yesterday from a hospital by a Romanian Gypsy gang," he said in his proper British accent. "It's been reported that Ms. Richards is being held for ransom. There is no word on what the kidnappers are demanding, but authorities say they're expecting the kidnappers to ask for a large sum, since it has been rumored that Ms. Richards is the sole heir to the late Zoe Rich."

"Holy shit!" Jack whispered to himself before returning to watch the video. It showed a video montage highlighting Zoe Rich's short life.

"Debbie Richards changed her name to Zoe Rich at the advice of a music producer she met at the age of 17. The singer went from country Western overalls to designer dresses that complemented her enchanting wide blue eyes. It has been reported that the producer loved the unique shade of blue in her eyes so much that she went through 3 color corrections to match the exact shade of violet that donned the cover of her first album, simply titled 'Zoe Gets Rich.' The album was released in the summer of 1983 and spawned an additional 8 albums, which sold over 150 million copies worldwide, including 13 number one hits, 8 films, 11 Grammys, and 2 Academy Awards. But all that success did not match the incredible success of the Zoe Rich makeup and perfume lines. The talented entertainer was worth an estimated $666 Million before a tragic car accident in Istanbul took her life while she was escaping paparazzi. There has been no word on the whereabouts of ..." At that, the phone's battery died.

"Shit, shit, shit," Jack said. "Zoe Rich," he whispered to himself still in shock. He placed the phone on the seat.

I better tell Casey and Mila what I found, Jack thought. He looked across the aisle to where Casey was previously sitting, but she was not there. *Where has she gone?* He began to worry that something had happened. He took a look back at the seats behind him. There were about a dozen or so passengers throughout the railcar, including the young couple, but no sign of Casey.

Jack's heart began to race. He stood up from his seat in order to get a better look. He scanned the train again, observing the passengers in front of him, toward the train's door. He saw Casey's foot sticking out into the aisle in the first seat. The sight calmed him, but he couldn't make out the rest of her. Jack noticed that she was now sitting next to Mila. She just moved over to the door to be more comfortable, or perhaps someone came and woke her. That's why she moved all the way over to that side, he desperately tried to convince himself.

He got up and politely asked the lady to make room so he could get into the aisle. The woman moved both her legs to the left so he could pass. He managed to squeeze through and into the aisle, leaving the iPhone behind. Even standing, he could only see Casey's right leg. He proceeded to walk toward the door.

The closer he got, the more of her he could see. Then he suddenly felt his heart drop deep into his stomach. Instead of fear, he now felt complete nausea. She was sleeping with her head on Mila's shoulder with Mila's head resting peacefully on top of hers. They looked like a pair of lovers on a romantic getaway.

Jack's mind was immediately overrun with images and thoughts of everything that might have happened while he was asleep. He stood there frozen in the aisle, pondering what to do next. *How could I be so stupid and naive?* he wondered.

His shame and self-pity were interrupted as the train came to its next stop and the conductor belted out via the loudspeaker: "Altenbeken ... Nächste Station, Paderborn."

The voice over the loudspeaker and the train's whistling woke Mila and Casey from their sleep. Casey saw Jack standing frozen in the aisle. Jack turned to return to his seat with his eyes still on Casey. He noticed she tried to get up, but Mila grabbed her hand and held her back. "Don't make a scene," Jack heard Mila say.

As he turned his head away—

Slam!

Jack bumped right into a man coming from the opposite end of the car. The impact knocked Jack backward and almost sent him toppling to the ground. The man grabbed the collar of Jack's army jacket with cat-like reflexes and pulled him forward, helping him regain his balance.

Once he was on sure footing, Jack gazed up at the man who had nearly knocked him over. He realized this was a very tall man: his black tie and square shoulders were right at Jack's eye level. Jack sensed something military about him. His posture was straight and suggested a life of discipline. As Jack scanned upward, he saw the harsh face of a man in his late thirties. Every line and crease in his pale skin made him all the more menacing. Long blond hair framed his rough face. Jack felt the knot in his stomach return as he stared into the man's cold blue eyes.

"Vere is the rush?" the man asked in a thick German accent.

"*Entschuldigung*," Jack stammered as he apologized in German.

"You should vatch vere you're going," the man warned.

Once he moved to the side, Jack pushed past. He looked over his shoulder and watched the stranger go. Turning to head down the aisle to his seat, he encountered another man just a few paces behind the first. He was wearing a black suit and tie that matched the other man's. Jack noticed that the similarities did not stop there. Their facial features were almost identical, except for the frightening scar that traveled from the second man's left eyebrow all the way down his neck and under his shirt collar. They must have gotten on at Altenbeken Station, he thought.

THE FOOLS

The scarred man stopped in the aisle near the old lady and pointed to the seat next to her. "Hier ist besetzt," she replied as she pointed toward Jack.

"Hündin," the scarred man replied.

Jack figured that the woman was telling him that the seat was taken, but judging by the appalled look on her face, he assumed that the word hündin could not be anything good. Frustrated, the scar-faced man took a seat across the aisle from her as his twin headed toward the front of the car, closer to Mila and Casey.

The train pulled away from the station. Jack turned back once again to check on his friends. Oddly, the blond man chose the same club seats as Mila and Casey, sitting directly across from them. He also noticed Mila pulling Casey even closer to him. It wasn't some playful act: Mila's face was dead serious.

The fear and nausea returned in the pit of Jack's stomach. His and Mila's eyes met, and Mila confirmed Jack's fear with the simple glance.

Jack came to a stop near his seat. Before sitting down, he desperately tried to assess the situation unfolding at the front of the train car. From his vantage point he could not fully determine whether or not there was any real danger. They're probably just commuters, he tried to convince himself.

The old lady pulled her legs aside to let him in, but he stayed standing in the aisle, ready for God knows what. *A signal from Mila would help*, he thought.

"Is everything OK, young man?" the lady asked.

"I don't know, Ma'am," he answered, never taking his eyes off his friends.

"Well, we seem to have some intimidating new passengers," she said, confirming Jack's suspicions. She waved her arm, signaling him to pass.

Jack still didn't move. He kept his eyes locked on his friends; he could feel that these were not normal passengers. There was no time for jealousy now. *We're in some kind of trouble*, he thought.

Confused by Jack's frozen position, the woman motioned with her hand once more.

"Sit down, Jack," a voice said from the seat across the aisle. It could only be the man with the scar.

Now Jack knew that his suspicions were correct. They were together, and he knew Jack's name. *I've got to do something*, he thought. Instinctively, he started to hurry toward his friends. The scarred man got up and followed close behind. As he approached Mila and Casey, Jack observed that the other blond man already had a gun pointed at them.

"Shit…" Jack whispered.

Suddenly, he felt something hard being pressed into his shoulder blade. The scarred man was so close Jack could feel his stale breath on the back of his neck. He had no doubt that the pressure he felt was the barrel of a gun, probably identical to the one the other man was holding on his friends.

"I said sit down," the scarred man ordered.

Jack took a seat next to the twin in the club seats across from Mila and Casey. The man with the scar took his seat across from Jack; his pistol was now tucked in between his body and his arm, discreetly pointing at Jack. The other man kept his gun aimed at Mila.

"Evee-vone jzzust be calm," the scarred man said. "Vhere is zee pitzel?"

"Pitzel?" Casey asked, confused.

"The pitzel you took from me at our last encounter," he replied with anger.

"I'm sorry. I don't know what a pitzel is," Casey insisted without fear.

"Zee pitzel, pitzel, you spoiled American!" the blond man argued.

"I am sorry, but I don't know what the hell you're talking about," she retorted.

"Casey!" Jack shouted, scolding her for her playful banter with the two thugs.

"He means the gun," Mila interpreted. "Wir haben keine," he assured the men in German.

Without another word, the blond man reached beneath Casey's seat and snatched her purse. His partner perked up, letting his gun show a little more clearly just in case anyone made a move. The blond man rummaged through Casey's purse, tossing aside makeup containers, drawing pencils, packets of tissues, and the small sketchbook. He found no pistol. Instead, he pulled the golden nail out of the purse.

"No," Casey gasped.

The blond man raised his pistol, warning them to stay back as he passed the nail across the aisle to his companion. The scarred man took the artifact and tucked it inside his suit jacket.

"My partner and I are going to get off at the next station, and you two are coming with us," the blond man said to Mila and Casey.

"Just them?" Jack asked with what he hoped sounded like the jealousy he had felt earlier.

The scarred twin nodded.

"That's just perfect," Jack sarcastically replied.

"Jack, this is no time to be jealous," Mila said.

Jack turned to Mila and started venting as if he had no regard for the dangerous situation the three of them were facing. "You're absolutely right, Mila," he said. "The time to be jealous was twenty minutes ago when I was sleeping. That's when you guys must have been going at it for real."

"What? You're crazy!" Casey snapped.

"Am I?" Jack retorted.

"Zhat vill be enough," the man with the scar demanded from across the aisle. He checked over the seats to see if anyone noticed the scene. It was clear that the old lady was glancing over with some interest. The scarred man pulled his pistol back, trying to keep it better hidden between his body and the seat.

"I hardly know him, Jack!" Casey argued.

"You hardly knew me, but that didn't stop you from throwing yourself all over me in Berlin," he argued back, wincing inside that he was trashing the fond memory of them together.

"Stop this at once!" the man guarding Mila and Casey insisted. "You're causing a scene!"

The scarred man took another look back at the passengers. Jack noticed Mila was scoping the situation. Mila's eye and natural instincts noticed a pencil that the man had thrown from Casey's purse had landed right next to her hand. The hitmen were already on edge; they kept checking the other passengers. Jack knew that Mila had a plan. He just hoped the goons weren't too keen to pick up on it.

"No sense lying now. You're right, Jack. She was all over me once you fell asleep, weren't you, Casey?" Mila said. "It was like in *Whistleblower,* issue one."

"What?" Casey shouted.

"I said quiet," the scarred man hissed.

Whistleblower? Jack thought. *What the hell is he talking about? Liza Carver doesn't hook up with anyone in issue one. The closest thing is ... oh ...*

He remembered the iconic comic panel of Liza disarming a distracted hitman by seducing him then stabbing him with a pencil. Jack locked eyes with Mila for a split second. Somehow that's all it took for them to realize they understood each other. Mila glanced at Casey, then down to the pencil by her hand. She gave him the same look of understanding.

"Come on, Casey, just admit it. Let's tell Jack what we did while he was sleeping," Mila insisted.

Casey started to play along. She put one arm behind her head and massaged the back of her neck while pushing her chest out a bit. Her gaze drifted past the armed man across from her, who was now even more on edge, then over to Jack. "I'm sorry, Jack, I just couldn't help it. You know how I get when I'm around guys," she said with a hint of seduction. "You know what? On second thought, let's show him what we did."

Mila put a hand on Casey's thigh and slowly slid it upward. *OK, you're taking this a little too far, guys,* Jack thought. He couldn't quite shake the jealousy, even though it was a front.

Casey seductively bit her bottom lip as Mila's hand got dangerously close to the hem of her shorts.

The blond man leaned forward, grabbed Mila's collar, and pulled him away. "Cut it out! Take your hand off her, you disgusting Gypsy!" he insisted in a threatening whisper.

"Come on, just give us five seconds," Mila begged.

At that same moment, Mila shot a glance at Jack, signaling to him that he was about to make a move. In a split second, the two of them leaped into action.

Mila grabbed the first man's gun and stood, forcing the weapon into the air. Jack did the same with the scarred man.

Casey grabbed the pencil and jammed it into the scarred man's wrist, forcing him to let go of the gun. As the alarmed passengers matched the scarred man's screams, Jack got a firm hold of the weapon. Unfortunately, it popped right out of his grip when the force from Mila and the other twin's struggling knocked him from behind. The gun slid down the aisle, heading toward the old lady. To Jack's surprise, the woman used her flowered bag to stop the weapon's advance. The other passengers moved away from the fight in great panic. As Jack sprinted toward the old lady, who now picked up the gun, he feared that she wouldn't return it, but to his surprise she simply handed it to him, then went on to hold her bag.

Mila and the blond man kept wrestling over the gun while the scarred man desperately applied pressure to his wrist to stop the blood that was gushing everywhere. Jack noticed spurts of blood splattering Casey's face. Some of it landed near her lips, and without thinking, she licked it clean. The scarred man dropped to the floor, and the entire train car flew into a greater panic as passengers screamed in terror and confusion at the near-deadly brawl in the midst of their morning commute. The front of the passenger car was turning into a bloodbath.

The scarred man was now weakened from shock and blood loss, allowing Jack to pin him against the wall. With their assailant immobilized, Casey reached into his suit pocket and seized the nail. Time seemed to slow as she drew it out and stared at its golden surface. She then stared down the scarred man with a fierce gaze. For a moment, Jack felt as if she was going to plunge the nail into her attacker's heart. She definitely was not acting like the sweet girl he thought he knew.

He snapped back to reality. Casey wiped clean some of the blood that stained the nail before slipping it into her belt like a sword. Jack was too busy holding their attacker against the wall to take notice. Channeling Deborah's actions from the hospital room, he pistol-whipped the man, striking him on the side of the head. Bam! The blow was so hard it knocked a tooth from the man's bloody mouth. Their foe was knocked senseless for the time being.

Casey's knees shook and buckled. The violence was obviously getting the best of her.

"Get her out of here!" Mila yelled as he struggled with the other man.

Jack grabbed a very distraught Casey and pulled her toward the other end of the car. The terrified passengers screamed and recoiled in fear at the sight of the gun in Jack's hand and blood trickling down Casey's face. The old woman was now gone from her seat to God knows where.

By now, the blond man was starting to overpower Mila. He pushed him into the aisle and then slammed him hard into the train's doorway. Mila was weakened from this maneuver, but he managed to keep his grip on the gun. Now he was in a more difficult position, being pinned up against the door of the railcar. The man realized his advantage. He started to bang him up against the door a few more times, and with every thud, Mila became weaker. The last slam against the door caused it to slide open behind them, causing the two of them to tumble into the open-air connecting section between the cars.

Mila was now on his back with the man on top of him. He managed to slam the man's hand into the safety railing. Mila repeated this move over and over. Finally, the blond man loosened his grip and the gun fell, lost to the German countryside. With the gun gone, the assailant flew into a beating frenzy, striking Mila repeatedly.

At that moment, Casey began to come to her senses. She looked back and saw Mila as he was struck again and again. "No!" she cried as she pulled away from Jack and sprinted over to help him.

"Wait!" Jack said. "Damn it!" he swore as he raced after her.

Casey jumped on top of the man as he beat Mila senseless. She grabbed him by the neck, trying to pull him off of her friend with a chokehold. Jack was right behind Casey, aiming the gun and waiting for an opportunity to get a clear shot, fearing he might hit her or Mila.

Mila could not free himself from under the blond man, and it was clear he had been beaten very badly. As Casey continued trying to choke him, the man rose to his knees and slammed her up against the railing, causing the nail, the key to their journey, to fall from the train and disappear into the thick brush.

The man spun around and threw a brutal hook, squarely punching Casey in the jaw. He drew his hand back, ready to strike again. Jack aimed the pistol and reluctantly placed pressure on the trigger. But before he could fire, a German shepherd unexpectedly leaped down from the roof of the train, landing on their attacker.

What the hell? Was he on the roof the entire time? Jack figured.

The dog tore into the blond man without mercy. The man and the dog fell off the train while it was still traveling at full throttle. Wolfy never stopped biting him; he sank his teeth into the man's throat even as they fell hard onto the side of the opposite tracks.

"Halt! Und lassen sie ihre eaffe!" someone yelled.

Jack peered over his shoulder to see a police constable with a pistol drawn. "Drop your weapon!" the man repeated in English.

Jack dropped the gun. "You are under arrest!" the officer shouted.

With his hands held in the air, Jack looked over at Mila and Casey, who were kneeling in exhaustion in-between the railcars. He slightly nodded his head a few times, gesturing for them to jump off the train.

With slow, careful steps, Jack walked back into the train car, toward the constable. Suddenly, a horrible shriek filled the train and the floor seemed to jolt violently beneath their feet. *What the hell?* Jack thought as he fell to the aisle floor. Someone had pulled the emergency brake.

The locomotive began to screech to a violent stop. The brakes screamed, and the force of the sudden stop sent the officer and a few passengers tumbling to the floor as well. Seizing this opportunity, Mila and Casey leaped off and disappeared from Jack's view.

Jack rose to his feet struggling to keep his balance as the train desperately tried to come to a full stop. The smell of burning brakes filled the car, and the whistle was ear-piercingly loud. Once on his feet, Jack ran back to the exit and only paused a moment to check if the constable was still in pursuit. Thankfully, the officer was still on his hands and knees, groping for his weapon, which had slid beneath a seat.

But wait ... was that? he wondered. And there she was, the old woman, grasping the emergency brake.

Using the chaos and confusion to his advantage, Jack jumped off the still-moving railcar and into the rolling hills of God-Knows-Where, Germany.

XX

⌒⌒⌒

THE HUNTED

The outskirts of Paderborn were covered in farm-
land more reminiscent of the wheat and cornfields
of Kansas than the European countryside. Mila and
Casey had landed in a dirty ditch close to one of the
many amber wheat fields that lay alongside the tracks.
They picked themselves up, climbed out of the ditch,
and began to run. Driven by pure instinct, they ran not
away from, but toward the train. It slowed silently a long
way down the tracks, with sparks still flying around the
wheels from the friction of its violent halt.

"There!" Mila yelled. He pointed, showing Casey
where Jack had just jumped off the train. They both impulsively picked up the pace, running along the sprawling wheat fields as fast as they could, desperate to reach
their friend, praying they could rescue him before the
officer could arrest him, or worse, one of the evil twins

attack him again. As they ran, they noticed that Wolfy was following alongside them. His snout was drenched in blood, and he firmly grasped the nail in his jaw, holding on to the treasure as if he had retrieved a bone.

Mila began to fall behind as Casey and Wolfy kept up the pace. With the excitement of the fight and their escape behind him, he became increasingly aware of his many injuries. His ribs ached from being slammed onto the floor of the train. He stumbled along as Casey and Wolfy continued running.

"Hurry, we have to get to Jack!" Casey yelled.

They could both see Jack on the ground in the distance, getting to his feet.

"Thank God!" Casey cried. "He looks OK."

Jack caught sight of them and began to run to meet them. Casey rushed right up to Jack as Mila slowly trailed behind. She threw her arms around him and pressed her head to his chest. Jack returned the embrace and leaned down to kiss the crown of her head. "Are you all right?" he asked her, "You're shaking."

"Yes! But I was so scared," she said.

They held on to each other for a few more seconds. Jack leaned back to examine her face for the severe damage he feared would be the result of the hitman's forceful punch. Amazingly, there wasn't a bruise or mark of any kind marring her beautiful face. "Casey, I saw that guy punch—" he started to say.

"She can't get hurt, Jack," Mila said.

"What?" Jack asked, shocked.

A low groan from Wolfy interrupted Jack's question. He held the nail up to Casey triumphantly. She knelt down, eyes glued to the mesmerizing talisman. "Good boy," she whispered in a sinister voice that was not her own as she gently took the treasure from the dog.

"Her ankle and all her other injuries are healed," Mila said.

"It's true," Casey replied.

In the distance, they heard voices from passengers and crew who were exiting the train.

"C'mon! C'mon! We gotta go!" Mila broke in as he clutched his right side and cradled his injured ribs. "C'mon! The train's right there, and the police aren't gonna stand around waiting for us to get away."

Wolfy took off running straight into the nearest field. The three teens followed the dog deep into the wheat as fast as they could, hoping for camouflage and protection amid the tall stalks. As the dog ran, the strong pads of his huge paws flattened an impressive amount of wheat, cutting a mini-trail. The plants became thicker as the runners dove farther in.

"You realize we are following a stray dog," Jack said.

"You got a better idea?" Mila hissed back.

In a whisper, Casey broke in. "As long as Wolfy's headed away from the train and those creepy twins, he's going the right way."

The animal kept a steady stride as if he knew exactly where he was going, but before Wolfy could continue leading them, Mila stopped, panting. All at once, he gasped and doubled over. He held his knee with one hand for balance and clutched his aching ribs with the other hand, trying desperately to catch his breath.

"Wait, Jack!" Casey called over to Jack as he began to head down the road.

"Sorry," Mila told her. "I must be hurt worse than I thought."

"Let me take a look," she told him gently. She examined his injuries and saw that the hitman had really done a number on him. He was sporting a bruised, badly swollen eye, and his nose was bleeding profusely. Was it broken? She couldn't tell. She put her fingertips on the edge of his black eye to see how bad the swelling was.

"Ow! Stop!" he pleaded.

"OK, OK," she said, pulling her hand back. "Let me see those ribs." She reached out and gently pulled his shirt up a few inches. She saw bruises of every color of the rainbow as well as what looked like a broken rib. "I'm no doctor, but I say we need to get you to one fast," she said.

Mila straightened up and wrapped his arms around his rib cage, trying to somehow ease the pain that racked his chest. Casey could see the excruciating way his face twisted each time he tried to take a breath.

"Mila, you're really hurt," she said, her voice a mixture of sympathy and fear.

By now, Jack had doubled back to them. Wolfy stood staring at Casey, wagging his tail slowly from side to side, eager for a cue from the girl to start them off on another run.

"Mila needs first aid," Casey told Jack.

Almost out of breath, Jack responded. "If we take him to a hospital, he'll be arrested for kidnapping you."

"What? What do you mean?" Casey asked.

Jack struggled through his heavy breathing to explain. "We're being hunted," he said. "It's all over the news. I saw it on the iPhone right before the twins got on the train. They think Mila and his friends kidnapped you for ransom. They said you were the niece of Zoe Rich, so there's an international manhunt for us."

"Wait, I thought nobody knew who your aunt was," Mila said to Casey.

"You told Mila, but you didn't tell me?" Jack said, jealously.

"Relax, I just found out," Mila said as he leaned over and spit out a wad of blood.

"Jack, never mind who I told first. We really have to get him some help," Casey said.

Jack paused for a second, acknowledging Mila's injuries. "Sabina!" he blurted out.

"Who?" Casey and Mila asked in unison.

"Sabina!" Jack repeated.

Mila and Casey looked at him as if he'd gone mad.

"Sabina!" Jack repeated. "Jeez, Mila, she's your relative. Don't you remember? The fortune-teller in Paderborn that Simon told us about. Look," he said, pointing to the road sign just ahead. "Paderborn: 2 Kilometers." Jack put his strong arm around Mila's shoulder for support. "Can you manage a slow jog?" he asked.

Mila shakily drew in his breath. "Sure," he said with bravado. "No problem."

"Great, let's stay in the wheat fields but follow the side of the road, that way we can stay out of sight," Jack said.

Wolfy set out in the direction of Paderborn as if he understood English.

Casey and Jack took turns helping Mila on their short journey. Jack began to fill Casey and Mila in on what the news story had revealed. In no time, they arrived in the city of Paderborn. After cleaning themselves the best they could in a nearby fountain and getting directions from some locals, they found a narrow cobblestone street named Warvenpatter Plaz just off the Rathaus Square. At first glance, the roadway resembled a small alley rather than a functioning street. It was a wonder that small cars could even fit through the tiny road, but despite this hardship, the street had a number of delightful shops. There was an old-fashioned shoemaker as well as a men's clothing merchant, its display window filled with elegant business suits. A small bakery provided the charming street a wonderful scent of baked goods, and just over the bakeshop was a bay window adorned by a carved wooden sign that simply read: "Sabina."

When they reached the stairs near the bakeshop, Mila sat down on the curb. It was getting late, and he noticed that the bakery was about to close. *There's no heading to the castle today,* he thought. It would have to be in the morning.

Casey, Jack, and Wolfy reached the door at the top of the stairs and began to ring the bell. After a few moments with no answer, Jack peered inside. "What do you see?" Mila asked.

"Just a living room. It looks like no one's home," Jack replied.

Suddenly, Casey began to pound hard on the rough old wooden door. Mila and Jack soon realized that she was getting upset. "Sabina!" she yelled, trying to make her voice heard through the solid wooden door. "Sabina! Let us in!"

Casey banged on the door so hard that Mila half expected her to dent it with her fists.

"Hey! Hey! *Wo ist das feuer?*" asked a heavyset woman wearing a white apron appeared from the bakeshop, holding a broom. Casey paused a moment, distracted. This gave Jack enough time to grab her hand, now bruised from pounding on the door, and to keep her from making any more noise. Casey pulled her wrist free but did not resume her mindless, trancelike assault on the door.

"Guten tag, frau," Jack said to the woman, conjuring up what little German he knew. "*Sprechen sie* English?"

"Yes, I do, young man, and I'll say it in English: where is the fire?" the woman demanded.

Mila had had enough of this and began to speak with the woman. He told her that Sabina was his aunt, he was in town from Romania, and he was looking for her.

"What's your name?" the woman asked in a thick German accent.

"Simon is my name," Mila answered.

"And who are these foreigners?" she asked, gazing at Casey and Jack.

"Oh, these are my classmates from the University of Bucharest. I wanted to have them meet my sweet old aunt. She would often play with all of us when we were children back in Romania and tell us fairy tales before she would put us to bed." Mila paused and then added, "You know—back in Romania."

"Fairy tales? Sweet old lady?" the woman questioned, with a shocked look on her face and a smirk on her lips.

"Yes, ma'am," Mila said, knowing that she was not buying his tale.

The woman looked over at the Americans and then back at Mila, giving them a once-over. She noticed that Mila appeared injured.

"Look, young man, I have a lot of work to do, and you look like you need a doctor. I don't know who this sweet loving lady is you are searching for, because the lady that lives here—" she pointed at the flat window "…is not sweet at all! And the only fairy tales she tells are the ones she gives her gullible clients during readings. You can find her at the Oasis Bar at the end of this street." With that, she returned to her bakeshop.

Casey, Jack, and Wolfy made their way down the stairs. They stopped next to Mila, who was still sitting on the curb. "We can go check it out and see if she's there. You can sit here and rest," Jack said to Mila.

Instead, Mila fought through the pain and got to his feet. "She'll never believe you. I have to go with you," he responded.

He trudged down the block with the others to the Oasis Bar. The tavern had a wooden motif. When they first entered, Mila noticed that the bar off to the right looked like it had been carved out of a single oak tree. There were dining tables throughout the rectangular space and a TV toward the back. It was obviously happy hour because the place was packed. There was a balding, middle-aged man tending the bar and a familiar-looking curly-haired waitress handling the tables. Jack and Casey trailed behind Mila. Casey tried to leave

Wolfy outside. She held the door open, gesturing to the animal to stay out, but no such luck. He followed her inside.

"*Sie können das Tier nicht Hierher bringen!*" the bartender yelled across the loud customers sitting at his bar.

Mila turned to Casey and explained that the bartender did not want Wolfy in the bar. Casey made one final attempt to get the dog to leave her, but to no avail. She agreed to wait outside while Jack and Mila scoped the place out for Sabina.

Mila and Jack walked further into the loud bar and looked around the place trying to find an old woman. "She must be at least sixty-five," Mila said.

There were a lot of people sitting at the large wooden bar. However, there was only one woman, and she was not sixty-five, more like a forty-year-old that drank too much and now could pass for sixty. They turned to look over at the tables, but unfortunately there was no sign of an old lady: just a few middle-aged couples in from work and about a dozen college-aged kids enjoying the football match on the TV.

"Come on, Jack," Mila said as he turned to walk out.

As Mila was turning to leave, Jack placed his hand on his shoulder to stop him. Mila noticed the expression on Jack's face. He appeared puzzled, so Mila turned to see what had caught his friend's attention.

Mila looked past the end of the bar into the corner next to the TV. A group of men were sitting at a table drinking a few pints. Two of them sat locked in a vigorous arm-wrestling match. One was an older biker type with a pointy long beard and leather vest. The other's back faced Jack and Mila. The stranger's hair was a mixture of gray and brown. Upon further examination of the patron's shoulders, Mila noticed that this grayish hair was in fact long, but it was tucked down into the arm wrestler's shirt. That was when Mila noticed that the stranger was wearing a pearl necklace. Mila spotted a pair of matching pearl earrings. Needless to say, it was awfully odd attire for a man.

Before Mila could put two and two together, the stranger slammed the biker's fist down to the table, stood up, and turned to the bar shaking both fists in a victory celebration. "*Ich gewinne!*" the winner shouted.

"Sabina?" Mila exclaimed.

Gypsies can recognize one another anywhere in the world. Some say their spirits speak to one another, but Sabina's choice of dress—a pair of overalls and a white T-shirt—really threw Mila off. Mila had to look in her eyes to know it was her. Even when she was reveling in victory, her eyes still carried the sadness he saw in every Rom.

The boys quickly made their way to Sabina's table. By the time they reached her seat, Sabina was sitting down counting her winnings. At first, she did not notice them, even though they were standing right next to her. She just sat there enjoying her win. Beside her, a tobacco pipe rested in an ashtray, a lazy trail of smoke rising from it. As she picked it up to take a puff, she noticed the two teens standing over her table.

"If you want to take your chances arm wrestling with me, you better show me your money first," Sabina said in German, taking a drag from her pipe.

"Bibío?" Mila said, using the Romani word for *aunt.*

Sabina sized up the boys for a second. Then she stared at Mila more intensely. *"Kon san?"* she asked.

"It's me, Mila, from Romania. Nasta raised me," he said. "We moved to Berlin when I was a boy." He paused for a moment to give her a chance to gather her thoughts. *"Ma Seades?"* he added. "Remember me?"

Sabina stood up and stared deep into Mila's eyes. They stared at each other a moment. Her shocked face softened, and then her cold eyes began to water. With that, Mila knew he was standing in front of his kin and that she knew him.

Sabina grabbed him in tight embrace. Her crushing hug sent pain shooting through his ribs. "Ow!" Mila groaned.

Sabina quickly pulled back and took another look at him, "You're hurt!" she exclaimed. "Come on, let's get you fixed up," she added, guiding them out the door.

As she led the boys out, pushing customers out of her way, she yelled over to the bartender and ordered him to put her drinks on the tab of the man she had just trounced at arm wrestling. "Who is this?" she asked Mila, referring to Jack.

"It's a long story," Mila answered.

"It always is," Sabina said, pushing the door open.

XXI

~~~~

THE HEALER

Sabina managed to set Mila's fractured rib back into place, then tightly wrapped up his chest with a white sheet. She slapped a thick cold steak on his eye and replaced the wads of napkin in his nose with clean cotton plugs. Mila was well taken care of, lying on the makeshift triage that was Sabina's kitchen table. Jack and Casey were in the sitting area of her small flat, drinking an unusual drink that Sabina had prepared for them by pouring tea over slices of fresh apples and oranges. It was sweet and very refreshing, just what they needed after the exhausting day they'd had. As always, Wolfy sat close to Casey, enjoying some scraps.

"I can help you, Sabina!" Casey yelled through the beaded curtain that separated the living room from the kitchen.

"No, that's perfectly fine. I have it all under control," Sabina replied.

She turned back to her Mila. It was the second time she'd refused Casey's help, and she could tell it was upsetting the girl. Sabina couldn't put her finger on why she didn't like Casey. The American boy was OK—good, in fact: a good soul, Sabina felt. But the girl—that was a different feeling. Sabina hadn't really used her true psychic powers in years, but the ability returned to her in the girl's presence. There was a peculiar gentle tingling sensation in the nerves of her spine when she first saw Casey sitting on the curb outside the Oasis Bar with that bizarre dog indicating that there was something dark about the beautiful girl. Ever since then she had kept her distance, even as she served her the traditional fruit tea.

"Now that you're all bandaged up, I'm going to give you something for the pain," Sabina said gently. She grabbed a pill from her cupboard, broke it in half, and handed it to Mila along with a cup of lemon water to wash it down.

"What's this?" he asked.

"I can't pronounce it. I take it for my migraines."

Mila shrugged and gulped down the pill. Sabina helped him up to his feet.

"There, all better now," she said as she led him over to the sofa next to Jack. Pulling up a chair in front of the three teens, she crossed her arms and smiled. Her posture mimicked that of a typical scolding parent. "So, how'd you kids get into so much trouble?"

The three of them began to weave a strange tale. They took turns in telling it. Jack frequently interrupted to correct them on one thing or another. It started off, as Sabina had expected, with Mila getting in trouble over some vandalism. Then things took a dark turn: neo-Nazis, legends of dark magic, the death of little Korey in the train station. But when Sabina heard that Nasta had passed, a single tear rolled down her cheek and dropped into her teacup. By the time the story was finished, Sabina's face was ashen and her smile had faded to nothing. Like most Romani Mystics, particularly fortune-tellers, Sabina could easily tell when someone was lying. That's what scared her now: these children believed every word of the story they'd just told. Her last fleeting hope was that they were all crazy.

"Do you have this object?" she asked.

Casey unwrapped Jack's balled up jacket revealing the golden spike. A chill ran down Sabina's spine as she stared at the object.

"I think it might be the Fourth Nail," Mila said, interrupting her stare. "The one from the stories."

Sabina stood up and shuffled into the kitchen. "I need to make some more tea," she muttered.

Drawing the curtain behind her, Sabina filled a kettle and set it to boil. As it heated up, she rifled through the kitchen drawers looking for something she hadn't used in years. Beneath a stack of dish towels, she found a ruby-red linen cloth. The sheet was what Rom call *vuzho*: spiritually clean. She gently pulled the cloth out and cradled it, remembering the person who had given it to her, remembering the last words she had said to her.

Nasta is dead, she thought. *My only sister's dead, and she was right all along. I told her she was crazy. I told her she ruined all our lives believing fairy tales. But they were real.*

More tears began to trickle down Sabina's cheeks and drip onto the cloth. She wiped her face with her sleeve and stifled her crying, then searched another drawer until she found a small red box labeled "Frankincense." She poured the grains of incense into the red cloth, then twisted it tightly.

The kettle began to whistle. With her composure restored, she made the tea, then shuffled back into the den with her best silver tea set on a tray and the cloth tucked under her arm. She put the tray on the table then without skipping a beat, snatched the nail from Casey's lap.

"Hey, what the hell!" the girl shouted.

Without answering, Sabina wrapped the nail in the red cloth and tied it tightly. Once the scepter was sufficiently covered, Sabina offered the object back to her. For a moment, Casey shot her a glare of pure hatred, then her expression returned to mere annoyance and confusion.

"What was that about?" she demanded.

Sabina took a seat and poured herself some tea. "The cloth is spiritually pure. It will hold back dark energy, and the frankincense will throw off your enemies," she explained.

"Sabina, we don't really know what we're dealing with here," Mila said. "Is there anything you can tell us?"

The old woman stirred her tea one last time and took a long sip. "Mila, this you know, but I will explain for the *gadje*," she began. "There were many Gypsy tribes, going back ages and ages, and each had its trades. The Kaldarash were known for metal-working, the Baschalde played music, the Lowara were great horse traders, and the Tshuara—well, they were kind of assholes."

The teenagers smirked at this.

"There was one tribe, however, which was secret," Sabina explained. She got distracted for a minute as she gazed out the window at her sign. The word *Sabina* was backward, since the sign was designed to be viewed from the outside. The setting sun gave the backward letters an orange glow.

"It's getting dark…" Sabina said.

"You were saying?" Jack asked.

"Ah, yes—the hidden tribe, the Garade. It was once the greatest crime to even mention them to a *gadje*, but I guess that doesn't matter now. Instead of a trade, the Garade had gifts…powerful gifts, and with those gifts a duty to be the guardians of evil."

"That sounds…bad," Jack said. "Like, they protected evil from being destroyed?"

"No, they protected evil from being used," Sabina explained. "How they did that, well, for the longest time no one knew, for it was a secret they kept even from other Rom."

"How come no one told me about this?" Mila demanded.

"I'm surprised Nasta didn't," Sabina replied. "Maybe she was protecting you."

"If the Garade were so secret, why are you telling us about them now?" Jack asked.

"There's no crime in saying it now, because the Garade are extinct, exterminated by the Nazis during the war." Sabina paused a moment and stared into her tea.

"Were you? I mean, were you ever—you know…" Jack couldn't quite finish the sentence.

"I never saw the camps," Sabina replied. "I was born in hiding, safe. After the war, we Rom all banded together. The survivors had all lost their families, so we would take them in. It is from them I learned of the greatest horrors of the war."

Everyone went silent for a moment.

"Destroying the hidden tribe was the Nazis' highest and most secret goal. They wanted to destroy those who could contain evil. Everything else came second," Sabina said.

"What about the Final Solution? Exterminating the Jews? Where does that fit in?" Jack asked.

Sabina took another sip of tea, then set her cup down.

"I don't know everything. Maybe the Jewish people were persecuted for all those reasons they teach you in your *gadje* school. Or perhaps Hitler knew that the Jews and the Rom had a holy bond. All I know is that there was a special unit dedicated exclusively to finding and executing the Garade Rom," Sabina said, bitterly. "The lead scientist for that unit was Josef Mengele—" *Pttt!* Upon mentioning the name, she paused and feigned spiting on her floor. "...that monster did every twisted manner of experiment he could on Rom. He would freeze people, give them drugs, cut off limbs and perform surgeries without any pain killers, there were rumors of forced breeding, and the blood—they say he had gallons of Gypsy blood. He was looking for a way to test who was Garade. Twins were his favorite; he preferred twin *Garades'* blood. It was rumored throughout the camps that he did most of his research on their blood. Whatever he was looking for he must have found it, because now the Garade are no more."

Once again, everyone fell into stunned silence.

"Why doesn't anyone talk about this?" Jack asked.

"Who would listen? No one cares about the Gypsies," Sabina replied.

Sabina noticed that Jack had a puzzled look on his face, or perhaps it was anger. "Forgive me, Sabina, but that's not true. People would care. It's like I just read on the Internet: The Allied armies were horrified by the camps. That's part of the reason Israel was founded. If more people knew about this—"

Sabina interrupted the boy because she knew he was going to go off on a tangent. This often happened when non-Gypsies first heard the tales about Gypsy suffering, and sometimes it brought a letter or two to a local politician. But it often led to nothing more than just angry words, and then they would fade away.

"Listen to me, young man. I understand that you believe that people would care about us Gypsies. This is because you're young and you're goodhearted. I can tell. But it's been sixty years since the end of the war, and the Gypsies burned right alongside Jewish people, burned and suffered, and no one cares. To this very day, we are persecuted and disregarded by the world. Our people..." She paused, then pointed over to Mila, "...have endured such hatred from mankind, such evil from human beings, it can only be supernatural."

Casey stared down at the nail, still bundled in the *vuzho* cloth. "What does any of this have to do with the nail?" she asked.

"You know, that's a good question," Sabina responded. She picked up the teapot that sat on the table and proceeded to refill Jack's cup, then Mila's. "How are you feeling, Mila?" she asked.

"Better," he said.

She returned to her seat and began to struggle with her thoughts, trying to find in her head a good place to start to tell her story or perhaps answer Casey's question. She turned her head left, then right. "I can't believe it," she said. "It must be true." She smiled, looking up to the clouds through the window and still turning her head back and forth. She then looked to Casey to answer her question. "If the legend is true, the nail has everything to do with it."

She turned back to Mila. "How did you find me?" she asked. "Did Nasta talk about me? Did she tell you to come look for me?"

Mila put his tea down. With a little bit of embarrassment, he explained, "Um, not exactly. Aunt Nasta never mentioned you. Simon from Romania told us you were here."

"Simon? Pedo's grandson? I used to teach him how to swear in English," she chuckled. "So long ago, so many memories."

Sabina began to tell Mila that she was Nasta's sister and that she and Nasta were both there at his birth back in Romania. She explained that Mila was born in her own home, which she shared with her brother, Jimmy; his wife, Persa; and their adopted daughter, Rachel.

That name struck Mila deep within his soul. "You knew my mother?" he eagerly asked.

"I helped raise your mother," she said proudly, crossing herself. "May she rest in peace." Then she took a deep breath. "You see, I lived with my brother and his family. I never married, but it was probably for the best." She turned to Casey and smiled. "I was never a pretty girl like this beautiful young woman."

Casey smiled back at her and blushed. "Thank you, but I'm sure you were very beautiful," she whispered.

"It's fine, sweetheart. God blessed me with other attributes," Sabina pointed out. She paused, realizing she'd lost her train of thought. "Where was I?"

"My mother," Mila reminded her.

"Oh yes. My father hid me away with a *gadje* family during the war. My siblings Jimmy and Nasta were much older than me. There were nine siblings altogether, but all perished in the camps except for Nasta and Jimmy. They found me later, and by then, I was older, too old to be married off by arrangement and too young to be an old maid. So, I spent most of my time with your mother, Mila. She was just a little thing when I came home. I was told that Jimmy and Persa had adopted her; they had no children of their own. Later, I found out that some mystic brought her to them when she was a baby."

Mila began to listen to the story more intensely. Sabina noticed that Jack and Casey were also moved by the tale. They shifted closer to Mila as he heard about his mother, possibly for the first time ever. Sabina could tell that these *gadje* cared about him. That made her more comfortable telling the story around the American teens.

"After Jimmy and Nasta found me, I moved in with Jimmy and Persa and young Rachel. We had a nice flat in the city, and with the Communist government we all had good jobs. Nasta and I worked in a factory side by side with the *gadje*. The Communists tolerated no racist segregation acts by the Romanians. It was a good life. We were finally happy, and we all were together. Your mother was just a little girl, and we were so close. I would come home from the factory early so I could pick her up from school—"

"Wait; my teacher said Gypsies don't go to school," Casey stated.

"Today they don't. In fact, for hundreds of years it was illegal to educate a Gypsy, but under the Communist rule all those racist laws were removed, and we Rom were allowed to attend school—required, actually. Even I'd have gone if I'd been a bit younger."

Mila smiled at this wonderful story of his family in better days. Casey made her way next to him and Jack. In a loving gesture, she warmly placed her hand on Mila's.

Jack was visibly hurt as he witnessed Casey's affection, but said nothing.

"Wow, back in the States we've always been taught that communism was a bad thing," Jack said.

"Well, for most people, it was," Sabina explained. "But if you're a Gypsy, it was a good thing because it forced the racist population to accept us."

"So, what happened?" Casey asked. "How did you guys wind up in Germany?"

Sabina turned to Mila and paused, fearing he did not know the full story of how his mother had died and who his father was. It took only a moment for Mila's keen sense of emotion to pick up on her misgivings.

"It's OK, Aunt Sabina. I want to know," Mila said as he tightly clutched Casey's hand.

Sabina gained her strength and proceeded with the story of what really happened to Mila's family. She took them back to the days of persecution.

"Communism fell," she said. "And with that, we were thrown out of our apartment and forced to live near the garbage dump." She began to rant. "Of course, I was upset by this, but my brother and his wife, along with Nasta and her family, couldn't be happier. To them, we were returning to our tradition. We were living like rats. We had the only decent house, if you want to call it that. It was a shack, really—two rooms—but the others had tents and houses they built from scrap metal they got from the city dump we lived on. I hated every minute of it.

"We were fired from the factories and jobs, and the government that took over hated us. We were back to living like animals. It was the last decade before the millennium, and we were living like it was the Middle Ages, horses and wagons and fires to keep us warm. It was pure insanity!" She shouted the last part.

Sabina nervously reached for her tea, and Casey rose and helped her retrieve it. Sabina took a sip and handed it to Casey to set down as she tried to continue.

"By this time, your mother was old enough to marry," she went on. "And I tried to forget our living conditions. I learned how to read the tarot cards and went off into the city every day to tell fortunes to help support the family. The thought of Rachel getting married was my only happiness. I wanted her to marry a nice Kaldarash boy from another camp, but Jimmy and Nasta wanted to wait for the right one.

"At first, I thought that they were just being overprotective, but then one day, a man appeared in our camp. Michel was his name. He told stories of how he and a few others overthrew the Communist government; what a mistake that was. It was a mistake for him, too, because police and the military were looking for him. He was much older than your mother, by at least ten years. So, naturally, when Jimmy and Nasta told me that Michel was to marry our Rachel, I was outraged. We had a big fight. But the whole family overruled me. And your mother seemed happy with him; I even believed she loved him," Sabina reminisced, finally with a smile. She paused because she noticed the wetness of Mila's eyes.

"Michel was my father's name?" Mila asked.

Sabina nodded.

"So, where is my father? And did my mother die when I was born like I was told?"

"No, Mila, she lived after your birth," Sabina explained. "She and your father lived with us for a while until he said that the new government police were looking for him and he feared his presence might bring us harm. So, he told us he must go. He left right before you were born. You came, and we watched over you. Jimmy was getting very old, and I was going out all the time to make money. By then, the Romanians in the villages constantly threatened us. The racism started up again. They would come in the night and warn us to leave our camps or die."

Sabina started to cry. Her tears caused Mila and Casey to cry along with her. Only Jack remained stoic. Sabina could tell he was holding back. Casey knelt next to her and took her hand. Sabina felt a warmth in her touch. *Perhaps I was wrong about her,* she thought, *or perhaps the cloth is blocking the evil I sensed...*

"We were in constant fear for our lives. And then hope arrived in a letter. The family that helped hide me during the war passed away and left me this flat here in Paderborn in their will. I was so happy, I told Rachel we could bring you, Mila," she said, reaching out to grab Mila's hand as she closed her eyes to remember, tears freely falling down her old face. "We were going to raise you here and educate you, but Jimmy and Nasta would not have it. So, I made a plan with your mother to run away with you and bring you here. We figured once we left they would follow, but the Romanians had a different plan."

She pointed to a tissue box on the nearby table so Casey could retrieve it for her. The girl grabbed it and handed it over, then grabbed a couple of tissues for herself.

"A week before we were to leave for Germany, I came back from doing readings and found my house and a few tents were burned by the Romanians. I tried to go inside, but it was too late. I was told everyone inside had died. I discovered later that your mother tossed you from a window. Someone caught you, I don't know who but God bless them, and you survived, but Jimmy and Persa and your mother died along with a few others. Soon after, I left angry with Nasta and the family, and I came here alone. Later, I heard that this priest who always hated me for fortune-telling brought the family to Berlin," she said, wiping her eyes.

"Leichman," Mila whispered with disdain.

Casey and Jack were shocked and saddened by this; Mila sat with his head down in despair. The room was silent. Sabina wiped her eyes one last time, and suddenly, she seemed content, as if telling this story took a great weight off her chest.

"OK, young lady," Sabina said, glancing over at Casey with a warm look on her face. "Would you like to help an old woman make a traditional Gypsy dinner?"

"Sure. I would love to," Casey replied.

XXII

THE LOST INSCRIPTIONS

Morton Alexander walked from his small kitchen into his darkly-lit living room holding two short crystal glasses half-filled with cognac. As he entered, he handed one of the glasses to a woman he had not seen in years.

"Hennessy?" Deborah asked.

"Of course," he replied.

Morton noticed Deborah's slight smile. He knew that she was pleased that he remembered her favorite drink. He also knew that she was not here to rekindle their romance, an affair both passionate and forbidden at the same time. He knew this because their passion had turned into much more and as a result compromised an important assassination mission. She was too stubborn to let a thing like that go. Besides, sappy emotional love reunions were not her style, and he knew they never would be. Still, some part of him was hoping she was there for just that. *Or maybe she just wants sex*, he thought. She looked so beautiful sitting next to the window; the strong June sunbeams highlighted the curves of her face.

"How are you?" he asked.

Deborah took a sip of Hennessy while she gazed out of the flat window to the bustling street that ran through downtown Berlin. "Do you have a cigarette?" she asked, ignoring his question.

Morton retrieved cigarettes and a lighter from a nearby drawer. He handed a cigarette to her and struck the flame from the lighter, igniting the cigarette while she took a drag.

"Morton, for the first time, I'm lost and...*confused*," she said.

A less observant man who was unfamiliar with Deborah might have found innuendo in that statement. Morton's instincts, however, were much keener than that. Now he knew this wasn't a social call. Matters of the heart never worried her. This was something infinitely more far-reaching.

"If you didn't need help you wouldn't be here," he said. "What's going on, Deborah?"

"I'm not sure. That's why I'm here," she said, then downed her drink in one shot and set the glass down on an end table.

"If this has anything to do with your previous employer and my current employer, you realize that my hands are tied and I can't tell you—"

"Cut the crap," Deborah interrupted. She took a drag from the cigarette. "Morton, I knew you kept investigating the new Nazi movement after I left. Hell, you were on the mission *way* before I ever arrived in Berlin."

Morton was not eager to be interrogated by his former partner, so he stood up and headed to the kitchen. "I'm not doing this," he said.

Deborah rose as well and followed him into the kitchen, not letting him avoid this line of questioning. "What if I told you I know why we were sent to kill Victor Strauss?" she asked.

Morton stopped dead in his tracks. She knew that this would get his attention. Nonetheless, he continued again to the kitchen, trying to avoid the discussion.

"What if I told you I know the real purpose of the True Nationalist Coalition?" she continued.

Morton did not say a word. He reached his small galley kitchen, returning to the bottle of Hennessy for another round. Deborah positioned herself closer to him, now taking short, nervous drags from her cigarette as she watched him refill his glass. She stared deep into his eyes. He knew she would never stop until she got the information she needed. She was relentless, driven, unstoppable, just like she always was. He glared back, and with a swift yet graceful move took her into his arms and passionately kissed her. After what seemed like forever, she pulled her mouth away and exhaled a puff of smoke, a drag she'd taken before the sudden kiss.

"I'm sorry. I had to," Morton said.

She pulled away from him but paused before letting go. She looked away, as if looking at him might be too much.

"Morton, a spy never apologizes for kissing a girl," she cunningly said, breaking the mood. She stepped back, leaned against a granite counter, and continued her pleading. "I need to put this puzzle together," she said desperately.

"Deborah, you know I can't tell you anything anymore," he said. He took a shot of Hennessy for himself and tried to figure out why she would ask about this. She never thought the TNC Party was a credible threat before. *What was it she'd always said?* he asked himself. *"We're on the wrong continent, baby-sitting a bunch of racists with an occult fetish when there are people on our borders with warehouses full of rockets and bombs."* Yeah, that's it, he thought, remembering Deborah's words as clearly as if they'd been spoken yesterday.

"Remember all those files we collected on the TNC's occult beliefs? What if I told you there's truth to those tales?" she asked.

Morton headed back into the living room, took a seat in an armchair, and looked out the window. Deborah sat across from him. "I never thought I would come back to Berlin again," she said. "A bizarre set of circumstances led me into the exact thing we were sent here years ago to investigate. I need your help."

"What bizarre circumstances?" he asked, knowing he was going to regret that question.

Deborah stood and then knelt down next to him, pulling out a cell phone with a cracked screen. "This phone belonged to Casey Richards, the girl I was assigned to protect. It's too complicated to explain right now, but to cut to the chase, I had to neutralize an imposter. Luckily, before his body was removed, I recovered this phone from his person, and thank God I did."

"Wait, I'm confused—why did he have it?"

"He and his comrade posed as health workers and confiscated it from the hotel her class was staying at. They said it needed to be quarantined."

"What would they want with this girl? Ransom? Blackmail?"

"That's just it, Morton. I don't think they even knew about Casey or all the money her late aunt left her. When I recovered the phone, the screen was opened to a bunch of selfies of her."

"Ah, I see. So, they were using her pictures to identify her."

"Exactly."

"These were just foot soldiers?" Morton understood now what Deborah was getting at.

"Remember all those records we lifted from European art galleries? The TNC was obsessed with finding paintings from Hitler's personal collection," Deborah reminded him.

He nodded in agreement and took the phone to get a closer look. Deborah assisted him and scrolled to the most recent photo reel. The image was of a large painting hanging in a train station. It had been severely vandalized. The painting seemed familiar, but he couldn't quite place where he might have seen it before. Thinking back while gazing deeper into the painting, it suddenly hit him.

"Stalingrad!" he announced. He looked at Deborah as she smiled back, realizing that they both had discovered something.

"Do you still have the files from our investigation?" she asked.

Morton looked at her suspiciously and pulled the glass to his lips, intending to take a quick sip. Instead, he downed the whole thing in a single shot, then set the empty crystal glass on the coffee table. "You're not going to shut up about this, are you?"

"I don't see how I can. The girl is in danger."

Morton got up with a sigh and walked to the other side of the living room where an oak table sat against the wall. The table had an old copper coffee pot and two silver candleholders on either end. A large mirror with an ornate frame hung above the table. With one swift motion, he pushed the table, causing it to slide along the wall in an unnatural way. The piece of furniture must have been on wheels or a track. Next, Morton tapped a seemingly random spot on the mirror's frame, causing it to slide down to where the table once sat. This exposed a large safe built into the wall.

Morton placed his thumb on the dial. After a few seconds, the safe beeped and a green light came on. He opened the safe, revealing stacks of European currency, gold coins, a few handguns, rifles disassembled for easy storage, and endless stacks of files. He grabbed all of the files and brought them over to the coffee table next to Deborah. She stepped out to grab the Hennessy from the kitchen, and they refilled their glasses before searching through the intel.

Deborah gazed at her past work: hundreds of documents filled with notes, reports, and photographs from the Cold War and prior to that. Within minutes, the small living room was covered with papers and files. Some read "Nazi Propaganda," some were marked with red marker reading "Decoded Intel from CIA," and a few were redacted, little more than scattered words blotted out by black ink. These had all come to light shortly after the fall of the Berlin Wall. The CIA had gotten their hands on all sorts of previously classified KGB documents, and they were willing to share. That's when

Morton and Deborah, young, rookie agents at the time, were sent in, and he found some unusual activity linked to the newly-formed Strauss Company, particularly the artistic tastes of owner and CEO, Victor Strauss.

Both of them examined the files. There were pictures of a young Strauss, along with records and receipts for hundreds of paintings. Under the Iron Curtain, he requisitioned them through a ministry he oversaw. After Germany reunited, he went to great lengths to purchase all those paintings for his private collection. Every one of them was once in Nazi possession, and many were in the personal collection of Adolf Hitler.

"What are we looking for, exactly?" Morton asked.

"I'll know when I see it," Deborah assured him as she shuffled through files and boxes.

"I believe it's important for you to know that the Mossad eighty-sixed the project years ago. Our official position is that this neo-Nazi party poses no credible threat to our national security. They're no longer concerned with this new political movement."

"Then why are you here?" Deborah asked.

"Nostalgia, I guess. Besides, I never bought that this Victor, his company, or his organization were clean. I keep an eye on them from time to time. It's not as if I'm a valuable enough agent for this to be considered a waste of manpower."

"Why doesn't the agency feel that this is a matter of national security any longer?"

"We launched one final investigation after you were sent back to Israel. With the help of the CIA, we tracked a series of rent payments being made by one of Strauss's holding companies," Morton explained. "They led us to an apartment in Munich. The place was filled with lost artwork stolen by the Nazis. There was an old man living there and breeding white pigeons out of the back window. Stoker was his name, if I recall," he thought back. "…Yes, that was it. Paul Stoker. He was part of the Hitler Youth years ago and a brilliant painter and artist, a hermit of some sort. He basically laid low for the past forty years living in that apartment like a prisoner with those birds as his only friends."

"Was Strauss ever charged for hoarding the paintings?" Deborah asked.

"Of course not. You remember; this guy was untouchable. He claimed the old man was a former employee and he didn't keep track of the thousands of people that worked for him, and that he had no idea he'd been in possession of illicit antiquities. He pulled a few strings, and the courts bought it. That worked out well for us because the old man agreed to be our informant."

Deborah sat up straight, listening more intently now.

"He confirmed all the rumors about their obsessions with the occult and the Thule Society, as well as their interest in stolen art. What surprised us was he insisted the party had no interest in interfering with the State of Israel. All our theories about them funneling funds

G. S. ELI AND PATRICK WILEY

to Hamas were refuted. Don't get me wrong—they're anti-Semites, but it's all talk. They have little to no active hostility toward the Jewish people. It's the Gypsies they target, very actively, and with considerable brutality. The man even claimed there was a secret Romani tribe they wanted to wipe out entirely, but then again, he was nuts. As soon as we submitted our report, Israel withdrew everyone but me from Berlin and put me on sleeper status."

"And so, Israel's official position on the TNC Party..."

"...is that it's no longer a threat to our national security," Morton finished.

"Well, what happened to Stoker?"

"I'm not sure. He was an eccentric old man, and he was obsessed with the idea that some priest was targeting his life force. That's why he kept the birds. He claimed they warded off the priest's spells and that if he drank little drops of their blood it would keep him from dying. He was a real whack job sitting on priceless works of art. The agency kept him for as long as we could, but legally, we couldn't get any charges to stick."

"Where is he now?"

"Not really sure. Istanbul, I would assume."

"Why Istanbul?"

"It's a guess, really. Our only clues to his whereabouts were several magazine clippings on his desk about pieces of the true cross of Christ discovered in Turkey."

Deborah was lost in her thoughts. Morton knew that she was putting a puzzle together in her head. "Those paintings they found in the apartment—did any have depictions of a spike or a nail, perhaps?" she asked.

"Wait a minute..." Morton began to think back. "He did. But why? What difference do the illustrations make?"

Deborah looked off into space, thinking.

"What did he say?" she asked.

"Who?" Morton asked.

"The man I got the phone from. He said... I can't remember. Something about lost text that can unleash more evil or something."

Deborah pulled a small cardboard box from the pile and placed it between them. "Strauss CO Files/Bio" was written on the front of it. She opened it like a magician unveiling a trick. Inside was a collection of old micro-film and a projector. She sorted through them with en-thusiasm. Deborah loaded up a reel and turned on the projector, using a manila folder as a makeshift screen. The first picture was an old black-and-white photo tak-en from a surveillance system in the eighties. It showed a much younger Victor Strauss bidding on a painting in an auction house.

"We knew all along that Victor had an obsession with art once held by the Nazis," Deborah began. She flipped through some similar images. "For a long time, we thought they were using them to funnel money to terror cells, but every lead we found refuted that."

"Right..." Morton replied, not following.

Deborah flipped to an older black-and-white war photo. It showed the ruins of Stalingrad. In the foreground was the wall of an otherwise demolished building. On the wall hung the *Proclamation* painting. Standing before it was a young man, blond-haired and fair-skinned, in a German chaplain's uniform. Beside him were two Hitler Youth, boys not much older than ten. All three stood giving the iconic Nazi salute.

"Do you remember finding these?" Deborah asked.

"Yes, it was in Victor's personal album," Morton replied. "We found it..." He trailed off as he realized the implication. Deborah finished for him.

"We found it and submitted it to our government the day before we got the order to take out Strauss," she recalled.

Morton ran his fingers through his hair and stared off into space, trying to get a grip on the situation.

"You were always a history buff. Let's talk about Stalingrad," Deborah said.

What is she getting at? Morton wondered as he raised an eyebrow. "What about it?"

"Why attack Stalingrad? Hitler could have gone straight for Moscow and taken the Kremlin. That would have guaranteed him victory on the Eastern Front," Deborah pointed out.

Morton's brow furrowed at this strange line of thought. "He wanted to humiliate Stalin by taking the city that bore his name," he stated. "Any history book will tell you that."

"Now, does that answer make sense to you? He sacrificed thousands of soldiers and let the war turn against him all because of the city's name?"

This elicited a shrug from Morton. "Hitler was nuts," he countered.

"Or maybe not. Hold this," Deborah said, passing Morton the microfilm projector. She rummaged through another file. This one was labeled Decrypted Nazi Communications. There were hundreds of papers all filed by year. She searched for what seemed like forever, and then finally she pulled out an old scrap of paper. It was stained yellow with age and bore the print of a military telegram. It was dated February 1st, 1943, the day before the Germans finally withdrew from Stalingrad. The message read: "Mission accomplished STOP Proclamation recovered STOP We are clear to withdraw all forces STOP."

"We thought 'Proclamation recovered' was a code phrase. That's why we overlooked it before," Deborah said, handing it over to Morton to examine. "It's no code. That painting is called *The Proclamation*."

"So, what are you saying, Deborah? That Adolf Hitler sent his army into certain death in Stalingrad to retrieve a magic painting?" he said sarcastically.

"I know this sounds crazy," she said, taking a drink from the last of the bottle.

Morton just stared at the telegram and shook his head.

"You remember my grandfather, don't you?" she asked.

"Of course! He was a hero of mine."

"He used to always tell me that World War II was a holy war, that Hitler was waging war against God himself."

"And you believe that now?"

"I don't know what to believe, but I know what I've seen." She flipped through the microfilm until she found one that zoomed in on the scepter in the hand of the Austrian queen.

"I've seen this scepter," Deborah said, "and I'm not talking about in another painting. I'm talking about the real thing."

There on the floor covered in mountains of files and old photographs, she told him the story of the hospital and Casey's healing. She explained how Casey got sick after falling into the Führer's bunker and how Jack and a Gypsy boy retrieved the scepter and brought it to the hospital. Morton tried to hide his skepticism when she explained how the nail seemed to save Casey from certain death. Deborah went on to explain how Casey was missing and being hunted at that very moment. She told him everything about their encounters with the TNC, even the bits that might incriminate her. She finished by saying, "All of this started because a reproduction of that painting hung in the train station."

"And don't tell me—you believe the paintings that were discovered in Munich have similar illustrations? Illustrations of this relic, right?" he asked. "Why horde them? What purpose does it serve?"

Deborah hesitated, and Morton could tell she didn't want to answer his question, no matter how valid it was. *She's going to have to answer me if she wants my help,* he thought. Then she pointed to the painting, drawing Morton's attention to an inscription on the shaft of the nail. He squinted trying to make it out, but the old microfilm shot was too grainy.

"I have a working theory right now," Deborah reluctantly said. "When I saw the scepter in the hospital, this section was blank. It looked like it had been filed off. I think this painting was made before that inscription was altered. I think what was inscribed on that face of the shaft of the relic before is valuable, or maybe it somehow makes the scepter more powerful. I don't know for sure. Look, Hitler was raping the nations of the world searching for paintings that have this inscription, and now the True Nationalist Coalition wants them, too. It can't be for nothing."

Morton shook his head. *She's really gone off the deep end,* he thought. This wouldn't be the first time he'd seen an agent descend into a world of ridiculous conspiracy theories. It was all too common when a person worked in an atmosphere of constant paranoia. On the other hand, he couldn't explain the outlandish story. The Mossad's psychological screenings were intense. Deborah couldn't just be crazy, and he knew she wasn't the type to take drugs, so that ruled out hallucinations.

"The relic is real. I've seen it with my own two eyes," Deborah insisted. "Look, if you can't believe in the power, can you at least accept that these people believe in it and that they'll kill for it?"

"Well, you've proven one thing to me: whatever this relic is, Victor wants it badly," Morton said. He stood up and paced about the room. He had a million conflicting feelings waging a war in his heart.

Deborah rose to her feet and crossed her arms. "What if I told you I know how to find it?" she asked.

Morton kept pacing as she waited for a response. Finally, he came to a stop and looked Deborah in the eyes without blinking.

"I want to make this clear," Morton said. "I'll help you, but I'm not doing this for you or us, or for your employer, and I'm certainly not doing it because I believe in this magic end-of-the-world nonsense."

"Not that I'm complaining, but why are you doing it?" Deborah asked with a smirk.

"Because I know Victor and this TNC party is up to something. I've been and I've always considered myself a good agent, and—"

He stopped mid-sentence, fearing he would go on a tangent. The frustration of the situation was getting to him, or maybe it was the drinking. He brushed his hand through his hair again, calming himself as he tried to get the right words out. "Look, this guy is up to something. My gut has been telling me that for years. But that son of a bitch always managed to outsmart me or outrun me, and I guess…" he stopped again for a moment. "I guess…I regret that we failed to put a stop to it all. I wish we'd killed him."

"It's not too late," Deborah said.

XXIII

༈

THE MAGI

ater that night, everyone slept soundly—all except for Mila, who tossed and turned, unable to get his mind off the stories Sabina had told earlier of his mother and father. Wonder turned into anger when his thoughts drifted to his aunt Nasta. *Why didn't she tell me?* he wondered. Lying there and struggling in-between the sheets and blankets of his made-up bed on the floor of Sabina's living room, he desperately tried to figure out the reasons why she had kept this from him. He hardly knew Sabina, yet she was the only one telling him the truth. She was honest, yet protective. She had even cooked them *sarme*, his favorite Romano dish.

Earlier over dinner, there had been a great deal of discussion of what to do next. They all had strong opinions on the matter. Mila listened while carefully chewing with his sore jaw.

"We have to go to the castle," Jack insisted. "That's the only place where there are answers. I found out about the curator on the phone. I'd show you but the battery is dead. Do you have a smartphone?"

"Yes, but I don't know how to use it," Sabina replied.

"We do," the teens said in unison.

Sabina got up from the table and went to her bedroom that was off to the side of the kitchen and retrieved her cell phone. It was an older flip model, but it had the Internet. Jack opened the Internet and surfed for a bit. Then he held out the phone. Casey grabbed it and flipped through his research. It was all pages about Professor Solomon Hermann. "Wow, he's written like six books," Casey said. "Is this him?" She pointed to a picture.

"Yeah," Jack said.

"How old is he?" Casey asked.

"Like sixty something," Jack said.

"Wow, he looks amazing for his age!" Casey exclaimed.

"I'm glad you think he's cute, but how do we know we can trust him?" Mila asked.

"I didn't say he was cute—"

"Whatever! That's not the point," Mila interrupted. "Siegfried said Hermann mentored all the TNC people. He might even work for them."

"He's a professor. He's taught all over the world. There's no way he works for the TNC. He's half Rom,"

Jack said. "He'd have to help us. I mean, as long as you're there. Right?"

The news of Hermann's Gypsy ancestry didn't stir much enthusiasm in Mila. "Half? It doesn't really work that way," he said.

"Why not?" Jack asked.

"Let me explain," Sabina said. "You see, children, what I share with your new friend and what makes us Gypsy isn't just our bloodline and our language, it's something more, something deeper. In Gypsy, we call it padimos; you would call it 'a burden.' We Gypsies carry a burden no other race can understand. To say it simply, it is a burden of centuries of oppression that Mila and I experience in our own lives. This Professor Hermann, although he may share some of our blood, although he may speak the language, he does not carry the padimos; he does not share the burden, and therefore he may not be loyal to us."

Jack and Casey looked over at Mila, and he looked back at them. He knew this knowledge changed how they saw him. Those few words told them more about who Mila was than all their adventures thus far.

"We Rom feel an obligation to one another because we share a common plight," Sabina went on. She held up the phone showing the man's picture and pointed to his eyes. "I can see from his eyes that he does not know our plight, and that means he is not a Rom."

Jack and Casey sat eating in silence for a moment.

"It's not wise to find this professor over at that castle. We must head back to Romania with this object," Sabina said. "I made some calls before dinner. I could not reach anyone in Berlin, so I called our family members in Romania."

"Is the family OK? Did they find Stephan, Rosa, or maybe Petre? Are they together?" Mila asked with excitement.

"No, Mila," Sabina said. "The only news is that the buses carrying the family did not arrive yet. Simon was seen being arrested. However, the police say they don't have him in custody."

"What about Korey's and Nasta's funerals? And Simon, he would have surely warned them not to get on the buses, of course! That's why they did not arrive yet," Mila said confidently.

"No, Mila, I'm sorry. I was told the buses will arrive in the morning. Our kin in Romania are awaiting their arrival. As I said, Simon was seen getting arrested and Stephan and Petre are missing, along with Rosa. They're not with the family. There are people we can stay with. We can hide there, be safe while we find out more about this—"

"Sabina, I am not going to run away and live in Romania! My uncle would kill me!" Casey said insistently.

Naturally, this started another argument. Jack was convinced the castle was still the answer. Mila could tell Jack was winning Casey over with his argument. Casey even noticed that Hermann lived on the grounds of the castle. Mila, on the other hand, found himself agreeing with his aunt insisting that they had to go back to Berlin and find Stephan, Rosa, and Petre. He never should have agreed to come out here. He began to argue that it was all a mistake and that the castle was the last place they should go. The discussion went on until they couldn't stand it anymore. In the end, they agreed to sleep on it. And that's exactly what Mila was trying to do now.

Maybe Jack is right, Mila thought. *Simon must have squealed to the police where we were going.* With that realization, he yawned and his eyes closed.

"The guardians of evil," he whispered as he drifted off to sleep.

Suddenly, Mila felt a hand grab his shoulder. He awoke in a fright and grabbed the hand, trying to push it away.

"Shhh, it's me, Sabina. Don't be afraid! Come into the kitchen, and don't wake the Americans," she whispered.

Sabina walked into the kitchen, stepping carefully over Jack. Mila stood and began to feel a little sore from his wounds. Fortunately, it was not as intense as before, but that might have been the painkiller.

Shifting the drapes to one side, Mila discovered the kitchen had been turned into some kind of séance room. The place was lit by half-melted candles scattered about the table. A single, unlit candle sat in the center of the table, surrounded by scattered pieces of gold jewelry flowing from velvet Crown Royal bags. There were a few earrings, a bracelet, and even a shot glass full of a brand of vodka that was filled with gold flakes.

What the hell? Mila thought. "Where is Casey?" he whispered.

"I put her in my room," she said, pointing to another door on the opposite end of the kitchen. "She's been sleeping for hours, and that damn dog won't leave her side."

Sabina waved to him to enter. Then she placed her finger across her lips reminding him to keep quiet. Mila stepped into the kitchen, looking back to peek over at Jack. Fortunately, he was sound asleep and the door where Casey slept was shut tight. Mila knew they wouldn't understand such unusual Gypsy customs.

"Why aren't you sleeping?" he asked.

"I've been here in the kitchen all night. Sit down," Sabina whispered as she pulled out a chair at the table and lit the center candle.

"Huh, I guess you and Nasta are true sisters; she used to keep all of her treasures in her leftover Crown Royal bags, too. But what's with all the old jewelry?"

"It traps evil. You should know this."

"You really are a Gypsy—thinking gold solves everything," Mila joked.

"Doesn't it, though?" Sabina joked back.

"Why are you using jewelry? And…is that vodka with bits of gold in it? Aren't you supposed to use nuggets or coins?"

"I had to sell a lot of stuff, OK?" Sabina admitted. "Telling fortunes ain't going so good, and arm wrestling doesn't exactly pay the bills. Now sit down so we can get this show on the road."

Mila sat and noticed a stack of tarot cards on the table surrounded by the candles. Sabina took a seat across from him. "We must finish the reading of the dark dream you had back in Berlin before all this started. Shuffle the cards," she instructed.

"How do you know about the dream and my reading?" Mila asked, puzzled.

"I was in the Middle Room, Mila. I saw Nasta there. I hope she appears to you some day. She wasn't as you knew her, but young and beautiful as she was when I knew her. We were in such a beautiful fortune-telling tent, the kind she always wanted…"

Sabina's face took on a far-off look for a moment. Then she snapped back to reality. "We're running out of time. Please shuffle the cards."

Mila shuffled the cards and handed them back to Sabina. She started to place them on the table. However, she laid them out differently than Nasta, placing them in the sign of the cross. "This is the Celtic cross spread," she explained. "It's more telling and the one Nasta should have used on you in Berlin."

After laying the cards out, Sabina began to examine them thoroughly. Mila, still tired and sore from the night, waited for her interpretation. He yawned, then rubbed his good eye in a desperate attempt to wake himself up. Sabina turned over the first card. Her tarot deck reminded Mila of his great-aunt's. The cards weren't the ordinary illustrations that could be found in any bookstore or mystic shop. They were more ornate, like ancient drawings from the Far East. The paper was tan with age. The first card was a heart pierced by swords.

"You're in love," she said.

"No," Mila retorted.

"You are, and she loves you," Sabina debated him. "But that's not the issue here."

She flipped another card, revealing a tower stretching toward the heavens. Lightening was striking the top of the tower, and people were plummeting from it to their doom.

"The one you love has been touched by evil. It has tainted her and is growing within her. All those around her are in grave danger," Sabina explained. "This is why Nasta gave you the *chukrayi* back in Berlin. She knew this evil was near, that it would cause great destruction and death."

Mila tried to hear Sabina's words. However, his thoughts kept drifting back to the phrase *"and she loves you."* As much as he tried, he couldn't focus on anything besides those words. Without thinking, he blurted out a question: "Does she love another?"

Sabina paused for a moment, then looked up at him from the tarot deck. "Really?" she said in a scolding manner. "That's what you want to know right now?"

"I have to know," Mila insisted.

Sabina sighed and turned over another card. This one was far less impressive. It just showed eight wooden sticks.

"It's difficult to tell. The cards are focused on your destiny and your truth," she said, clearly annoyed with Mila.

They both heard a noise from the front room. It sounded like something being dropped. Mila walked over to the curtain to see if anyone was listening. He saw Jack was still sound asleep, and he assumed it was nothing. He walked back and sat down. "It's nothing," he said.

Sabina ordered him to listen and pay attention. She pointed to the Magician card on the deck. "Do you know what this card means? Did anyone ever tell you why the tarot cards can predict someone's life?" she asked.

Mila looked at the card more closely.

"Well, when the Magician came up in Nasta's reading, she said it was a Gypsy. So, does it mean poor nomads or something?"

"Mila, don't be silly. This is serious."

"OK, what does it mean? Nobody told me," he said, frustrated.

"You are aware of Bible scripture, are you not?"

"A little—I mean, the main stuff, sure."

"The story of the power of the tarot begins about two thousand years ago, just before the birth of Christ," she explained. "The three wise men in the Bible story, they were from the east. They followed a star that led them to the city of Bethlehem. The Bible called them 'kings;' scholars called them 'astronomers.'"

Mila nodded.

"The word *wise* in ancient times often meant 'fore-teller,' not educated or a person of scholarly knowledge," Sabina went on. "They were certainly not astronomers because they didn't study the stars, but instead used them to predict the future, which would make them astrologers. The number of days that it took them to travel from the east into Bethlehem puts them in the region where the Gypsies originate from in northern India. The word *magician* originates from the Magi order, which are people that believe in spiritual power and used magic to combat evil. That is the Rom, Mila. The Magician card in the deck is our people."

"So, what does it have to do with the power to predict the future?"

"Look at the card closely," she instructed.

Mila peered closer, but he was not sure what he was looking for. He saw a man in a red robe holding a stick and making a sign with his other hand. *I've seen this a million times,* he thought. He noticed nothing out of the ordinary.

"This is no ordinary deck. Its illustrations are ancient. Only a few *drabarni* have a deck like this," Sabina explained.

"I don't see anything special. Can't you just tell me?" Mila asked.

Sabina sighed. "Kids these days. No patience," she said, shaking her head. "Nasta told me she gave you one of her cards before she died. Do you still have it?"

Mila's eyes widened. He reached into his pocket and pulled out the card. It was almost ruined. It had been soaked by rainwater. It was bent from miles of walking. Even drops of his blood had managed to get on it. The magician figure was faded, almost unrecognizable, but miraculously, one detail remained perfect. The golden scepter in the magician's hand was there clear as day. With the rest of the image faded, Mila could tell exactly what it was, but Sabina said it anyway: "The man in the illustration is holding the Fourth Nail of Christ."

It became clear to him that the nail had powers and even a depiction of it carried that power—just like the painting in the train station. That was why people were so intrigued or fascinated by paintings or illustrations of the nail.

"All Rom are kin to the Magi, but Garade are their direct descendants. There is something about true

G. S. ELI AND PATRICK WILEY

Garade blood that separates them from others," Sabina said. "Mila, I lied earlier, because this is knowledge the *gadje* should not know: the Garade tribe is not extinct."

"It's not?" Mila asked.

"No, Mila. *You* are Garade. Your mother and father were Garade. That is why he was hunted and she was in hiding with us. That is why she could only be married to him. You are the last of your kind, Mila—the last of the Magi."

This news left Mila stunned. Before he could organize his thoughts or ask any questions, they heard the sound of glass shattering. At that same moment, there was a pounding sound at the back door, which opened into the kitchen.

Sabina and Mila were startled at first, but they soon sprang into action, knowing someone was trying to break in. Mila took a knife off the counter and ran to the door that was just about to give way. He braced his shoulder against it, desperately trying to hold it in place. He heard a strange male voice shouting from the living room. The man must have come in through the shattered window. "Don't move! Hands on your head!" he ordered.

"Lemme go! Get the hell off me!" Jack cried from the other room.

The latch gave way and the door swung open, knocking Mila backward. A moment later, the barrel of a rifle peeked inside. Mila rushed forward again, slamming

342

the door back shut and pinning the rifle against the wall. Holding the door again, Mila turned to see the man advancing from the front through the living room. He was dressed in black assault gear and wore a ski mask. He moved toward Mila's terrified great-aunt, who was now curled up in the corner covering her head in fear. He aimed his pistol at her and yelled, "Let me see those hands!"

There was another hard blow to the door. The entire flimsy thing came off its hinges. Mila was knocked to the ground, and the door landed on top of him. The intruder planted a foot on the door, trapping him underneath. Sharp pains shot through Mila's injured ribs as he lay sprawled out on the hard tile floor with the door pressed against his chest. Not knowing what else to do, Mila flailed his arm, uselessly waving the kitchen knife. The other intruder, realizing Sabina was no threat, moved forward and planted a foot on Mila's arm, foiling his attempts to hack at their feet.

Now trapped with two guns trained on him, Mila was certain this was the end. Then one of the attackers pulled off their ski mask.

"Deborah?" Mila said.

"Mila?" Deborah replied.

Not taking any chances, she took the kitchen knife and tossed it out the back door. Then she removed her foot from the door and pulled it off of Mila. The other man helped the boy to his feet. The intruder removed his mask, revealing a fit middle-aged man with a goatee.

"I've got him," Deborah said to the man.

Mila had seen Deborah in action. He knew better than to make a move now. Besides, he could sense she had no malicious intent.

Everyone turned to see Sabina grab a rolling pin off the counter and hold it over her head, ready to swing it. Deborah and her friend tried not to laugh.

"It's OK, *bibío*; it's a misunderstanding," Mila said.

Sabina dropped the rolling pin, her arms shaking. "You're damn right it's a misunderstanding!" Sabina shouted. "Look at my house!"

"Sorry about the shock and awe, we couldn't take any risks, not with the TNC out looking for you," Deborah said.

The man stepped into the living room. He came back a moment later, leading a drowsy Jack along with him. His hands were bound behind his back by zip ties, but he was otherwise unharmed.

Sabina's hands were still shaking as her adrenaline wore off. Mila slowly walked over to his great-aunt and comforted her, letting her know everything was all right. She caught her breath as Deborah cut the riot cuffs from Jack's hands. In moments, Sabina was as calm as she could be, albeit annoyed. She raised a scolding finger to Deborah and her companion, saying,

"You owe me a new front window and a new kitchen door."

"Who the hell are you?" Jack asked the man as he rubbed his wrists.

"This is Morton," Deborah said. "He's a friend."

Jack looked Morton up and down for a second. "Is... is Morton...an old co-worker?" he asked delicately.

Deborah glared at Jack.

"Shhh...shut up!" Mila said through his teeth.

"How'd you find us?" Jack asked, ignoring Mila.

"The incident on the train caused a lot of radio chatter, and you don't have to have high-level security clearance to find the only Gypsy in Paderborn..." Deborah said. "Now, where's Casey?"

"What are you talking about? She's sleeping in Sabina's room," Mila said.

Morton shook his head. "There was no one in the bedroom."

Deborah shot Jack a questioning look.

"I don't know," Jack said. "Mila and I were in the living room."

Deborah did a quick re-check of the bedroom and found it empty. Meanwhile, Mila peered into the living room. "Wolfy's gone, too," he said.

"Wolfy?" Deborah asked.

"The dog," Mila explained. "It's a long story."

Mila could tell that Jack was getting worried and Deborah was getting angry. "Do you have any idea where Casey would have gone?" she asked.

"She must have—" Jack began.

"Quiet," Mila said, cutting him off. As far as he was concerned, these were authority figures. It was taboo for Rom to give sensitive information to the authorities.

Deborah stared at Mila. He could tell her eyes were tracing over his bruises. She extended a hand and gently touched his black eye. "Ow," he said.

"The same people who did this to you are now after Casey," Deborah pointed out. "They'll kill her if we don't—"

"Find her first!" Morton interrupted, then grabbed Mila, forcefully pulling him close by his T-shirt. "This is no joke," he warned.

"The castle," Sabina admitted. "She left hours ago for Wewelsburg Castle! Please, let him go!"

Morton released Mila into Sabina's embrace. She held him tight, then grabbed the tipped-over chair to sit on, exhausted from all the excitement. Once seated, she began to reveal to them where she believed Casey had traveled.

"Why do you think she went there?" Jack asked.

"After I set you boys down, I asked her to help with the dishes. Then she asked me if I would do her card reading," she said, embarrassed by her words. "The reading revealed she must seek out the hermit for help."

Sabina knew that Mila would be disappointed in her for lying about Casey sleeping in the bedroom.

"You knew she left and you let her go?" Mila asked.

"I had no choice, Mila. The reading revealed she was putting all of us in danger. I am sorry, but it was her choice. I left some money for her in an old Crown Royal bag on the kitchen table while I made a few more calls back to Romania to find out where Simon was being held. She was gone when I hung up."

"Is the hermit Professor Hermann?" Jack asked.

"I don't know. Casey seemed to think so," Sabina answered.

"Wewelsburg has been under TNC control for years now. Victor Strauss leases it through an NGO," Morton explained.

Deborah and Morton strategized quickly, keeping everything vague. Clearly, they didn't trust Mila, Sabina, or Jack to hear the details of their plan.

"It's my fault," Jack said. "Going to Wewelsburg was my idea. Let me come with you."

"Out of the question," Deborah replied.

"I can help—" Jack began.

"*No!*" Deborah snapped.

Jack looked offended and hurt. Deborah's gaze softened a little. It was the first time she'd shown any compassion, at least as far as Jack or Mila had seen.

"I know you care about her," Deborah said, looking at Jack. This made Mila's heart drop.

"Both of them do," Sabina pointed out as she stood and rummaged through a junk drawer looking for a screwdriver.

Jack gave Mila a confused look. Mila looked away, not wanting his expression to betray his true feelings. Before Jack had a chance to say anything, Deborah broke the moment with more orders.

"Jack, you need to get to the American Consulate. Your parents are worried sick," she said. "Mila...I guess you'll have to stay here."

"We need to get moving," Morton insisted.

Without another word, they slipped out of the apartment, leaving only shattered glass and a broken door. Everyone took a few minutes to settle down, then they set to work cleaning up. Mila held the back door in place while Jack screwed the hinges back on. Sabina fretted as she paced around the kitchen, putting away the candles and cards.

Mila stared out the kitchen window as he held the door. A layer of thick clouds shrouded the sky, dimming the light of the rising sun. He could just barely make out the streets of Paderborn at the end of a long back alley. No one was awake yet, except for a man at the end of the alley who leaned against the wall, casually smoking a cigarette.

"I'm missing an earring now," Sabina complained. "Must have fallen off the table. *Gadje* spies gotta barge in here..." she mumbled as she grabbed a dustpan and headed into the living room to sweep up the glass.

Jack was no less vocal about the situation. "This is bullshit," he declared. "The castle doesn't even open for hours. What's Casey going to do—camp out 'til they open?"

"Well, Hermann lives on the grounds of the castle, remember?" Mila reminded him.

"They could at least let us come along or something. How am I even supposed to get to the consulate?" Jack asked.

Sabina poked her head back into the kitchen. "After we clean up, you can call your parents back home," she said. "I'm sure they're worried sick, like the nice spies said. Then I'll drop you off at the consulate."

"How are you going to drop me?" Jack asked with a whine.

"With my car," she retorted. "What? You think I ride a broomstick?"

Mila chuckled at his great-aunt's sharp wit. "At least you get to go back to America. After this, I'll probably end up on the run or in jail," Mila said.

"You're going to stay with me!" Sabina yelled.

"Casey's got a powerful family. Maybe she can pull some strings or something," Jack assured him.

Mila knew that was not going to happen. He didn't understand how Jack could know so much yet be so na-ive. He kept talking, throwing out ideas about how Mila could avoid prison, but Mila stopped listening. He was distracted by an acrid scent that was slowly filling the room. It smelled like gas.

"What?" Jack asked.

Mila shuffled over and checked the stove. The knobs were all in the Off position. That couldn't be where the gas smell was coming from. "You smell that?" he asked.

This time, Jack didn't respond. Mila turned to see him staring out the kitchen window. A plume of smoke rose into the air, obstructing their view. Mila opened the window and leaned out. He saw flames coming from the bakeshop below.

Sabina barged in carrying her wooden sign, which was split in half. "The jerk broke my window sign, too," she lamented. Then she noticed the rising smoke.

The fire spread with amazing speed. Before they could react, the back stairs were ablaze. Smoke poured into the kitchen as the whole room took on an orange glow.

Everyone ran for the front. They threw aside the kitchen curtain and hustled into the living room. As they did, Mila turned back to see flames spreading to the back wall near the stove. It was only a matter of seconds before the gas lines...

Boom! A fireball burst from the stove. Mila and Jack dove to the ground just in time, but the flames hit Sabina and her dress caught fire. Jack grabbed a blanket from the couch and beat back the flames. Then he threw the blanket over her for protection.

Mila helped Sabina to her feet as they threw the front door open. To their horror, they discovered the front stairs were burning as well. Mila grabbed another blanket and tried to beat back the flames.

"That won't work!" Jack insisted.

Mila ignored him, forcing Jack to grab the now-burning blanket and rip it from Mila's hands. He turned to Jack, who yelled, "We have to jump!" and pointed to the front window.

The flames were spreading and the air was sweltering. The entire apartment was starting to feel like an oven. Jack grabbed the remaining quilts from their makeshift beds and threw them over himself and Mila. Jack, Mila, and Sabina stared out the front window, hesitating for a moment. Then they took a leap of faith.

The blankets shielded them from broken glass as they crashed through the broken bay window. The fall was a good twelve feet, so they fell pretty hard. Jack rolled across the pavement like a stunt man. Mila ended up sprawled on his back, which sent shock waves of pain through his injured ribs.

It took a minute for Mila to recover. Then he noticed Sabina lying on her side next to him, not moving. She was alive and conscious but clearly in a lot of pain from her burns.

"She needs a doctor," Mila said.

"I'll get help," Jack announced. He ran off to find an open business.

Mila kneeled by Sabina and held her hand.

"I'm OK," Sabina insisted. "I'll be fine."

Suddenly, someone held an oxygen mask to Mila's face. *Paramedics?* he thought at first. *How'd they get here so soon?*

Everything became fuzzy. The mask smelled like a mixture of glue and alcohol. He caught a glimpse of the arm of the "paramedic." It bore a red tattoo of a sword and a ribbon. Mila, dizzy and disoriented, looked down at Sabina, seeing a look of terror in her eyes. Then everything went dark.

XXIV

WEWELSBURG CASTLE

Dawn was breaking, and the sun began to paint the sky a beautiful reddish gold. Casey and her new best friend, Wolfy, began to walk up a steep road to where the taxi driver guided her. She began to feel helpless in her attempt to understand the mystery behind the golden nail, which seemed to attract danger at every turn. Pacing up the cobblestone road, she stopped for a moment to catch her breath. Casey pet Wolfy to calm her nerves, and she started to think back to her private reading with Sabina. Earlier that night in the kitchen, while Jack and Mila were sound asleep in the front room, Sabina gave Casey her very first tarot reading.

"You have now become the hunted. All those around you are in grave danger," she recalled Sabina saying.

The hermit card was the last card that Sabina had laid down. "What does it mean?" Casey asked.

"The last card reveals the solution to your dilemma.

"Should I run away and become a hermit?" Casey said, frightened about her impending fate.

"It's OK," Sabina said with compassion. "The Hermit card's meaning is someone who is alone or an outsider. Because it's the last card in the reading, it is telling you to seek out the hermit for your solution. Only he can help you and all others around you who are also in danger."

"But who is the hermit?"

Sabina motioned her head so as to say, "I don't know."

Casey came out of her thoughts, and she began to feel frightened. She started to shiver, not from the chill in the air but from fear. She wanted to rise and take a step toward the hill and the castle beyond, but her fear paralyzed her. She couldn't move at all. Unable to do anything else, she looked down at her companion.

"What am I doing, Wolfy?" she asked her furry escort.

She knelt down next to him and looked into his eyes. Wolfy looked back lovingly at her.

"I'm a wimp," she declared. "You don't have to say it. I know you're thinking it."

Casey continued speaking to the dog as if he could understand her. "I know what you're thinking: 'Just pretend you're Liza Carver in a *Whistleblower* comic,'" she said, trying to come up with something to shake off her fears. "Well, Carver never had to deal with the devil himself. Just some mercenaries and the occasional terrorist."

Wolfy tilted his head and gave a short bark: *rrrruff!* Casey looked down and saw he was pointing her to the Crown Royal bag with his snout, as if he knew what was inside.

"You're right," she said.

She looked down at the nail that was still wrapped in red. She stared at it a moment, then took hold of it. Her palm wrapped around it, feeling its shape through the soft cloth, and somehow, the fear was gone. She felt safe and strong. Her thoughts drifted back to her favorite comic book hero.

"Carver is always afraid when she has a mission," she recollected. "That's what makes that super-bitch so brave."

Casey stood up, placed the nail back in the purple bag, grabbed a hold of Wolfy's leash, and took her first step up the hill toward the beautiful sunrise.

THE TOWER

Just over the hill, the structure of a large stone building began to come into view. With every step, as the building appeared larger and larger, she somehow felt more confident in her decision to come alone. She began to think that perhaps within those stone walls lay the answers she needed to rid herself of this curse.

"I'm cursed," she said, realizing all that the word implied. She became frightened again. Her pace slowed, and her enthusiasm disappeared.

The ancient structure was now clearly in view. The beige stone building seemed more like a military fort rather than an elegant castle. It was laid out in a triangle shape, with three massive wings with peaked roofs that surrounded a central courtyard. At each corner where the wings met stood round towers. Two smaller ones topped with gray domes stood on either side of the south wing. A third much larger one with a flat roof loomed over the north corner.

Somehow the sight of the castle gave Casey a glimmer of hope. Maybe it was its imperial appearance, or perhaps there was some sort of strange energy about the place. Whatever it was, Casey's fear was once again replaced with confidence and purpose.

Maybe there's a way to control the nail, she thought. *Maybe I can be a superhero like Liza Carver—no, better than Liza Carver. Like if Liza and Superman had a daughter and then a family of rock stars raised her!*

Casey worked her way up a winding path and found herself at a bridge, which crossed the castle moat and led to a set of large iron gates. Crossing the bridge, Casey looked down to see not water below but a path running through gardens that surrounded the foundation. She spotted a sign written in both German and English that read, "Tours Start at 9:00 a.m." *I guess the taxi driver was right,* she thought.

She walked past the gate and looked for a bell or something, but found nothing. She placed her hands on the bars of the gate and pressed her face next to them. She felt the chill of the metal press on her face as she gazed around the courtyard. She tried to look into the narrow windows, then across the grounds for some kind of house. All she could see was a small rusted shack or toolshed off to the side of the huge castle. "A hermit could live there, right?" she said to Wolfy. *Maybe I should just wait,* she thought. Once again, she gazed back to the regal castle standing before her, mesmerized by its majesty and size. "Can you imagine what took place here through the years, Wolfy?" she asked.

She tried to remember what Jack had read about it over the Internet. She scanned along the wall to the main tower. Inside was the ritual room, or so Jack had told her.

"That's it," she said.

She felt a calling to that room, a pulling and a hunger. Her eyes became fixed on one of the tower's narrow windows. Forgetting about the chill in the air and the task at hand, all she could focus on was the inside of that room. As she gazed at the windows, she closed her eyes.

In the darkness in her head she began to hear the clicking sounds of many boots marching along a stone road. The sound was so loud in her head she felt as if people were marching right next to her. Surprised by the sounds, she opened her eyes, amazed.

Wolfy's sudden barking shook Casey out of her trance. An old man in tan coveralls was standing over them. *"Entschuldigen Sie, aber Hunde sind nicht erlaubt,"* he said.

Casey turned and almost jumped at the sight of the old man looming over her with a rake. He had wrinkled skin so pale she could see the veins in his face, as well as his sunken blue eyes that held wide open. Some thinning white hair clung to his scalp, giving him a face that reminded Casey of a skull. He wore tan coveralls and a denim shirt stained with bird dung on the right shoulder. On his belt, Casey noticed an odd-looking keychain with a large set of keys. Hanging from the chain was an old wooden spike about four inches long. The wood looked weak and frail. *That doesn't look safe,* she thought.

"I'm sorry, Sir, I don't speak German. But I was wondering if you could help me. I am looking for a Professor Hermann."

The groundskeeper stood silent for a moment, staring down at Casey and the dog.

"You are American," he finally said.

"Thank God you speak English! Do you know if Professor Hermann is working today?" Casey asked as quickly as she could. "I desperately need to speak with him. Please!"

"*Nein, nein.* You must leave at once! There are no dogs allowed on the premises."

Just then Wolfy began to viciously bark. Casey grabbed his leash to ensure he didn't attack the old man who was just doing his job.

"Wolfy, no!" she shouted, and he immediately calmed down.

"*Dame,* you must leave at once!" he demanded.

"Sir, you don't understand," Casey said desperately.

"*Nein!*" he said, pulling her away from the castle.

"Wait, please. I've come a long way," Casey cried as she was being pulled away.

The frail old man was slowly guiding Casey away from the castle as she continued to plead with him.

"Platzwart!" a man yelled from the distance. Casey turned and saw a man at the other side of the castle bridge. The man wore an elegant blue suit and had olive-toned skin. In his hand was a briefcase.

The groundskeeper halted at the sight of the man. The man started to shout in German to the groundskeeper as he came closer to them. The groundskeeper responded in German. Casey realized he must have been pleading his case because he kept pointing at Wolfy. As the man got closer, the conversation was definitely getting heated. Finally, the man approached and removed the groundskeeper's grip on Casey. He continued to yell at the groundskeeper in German. The only word Casey could understand was *hound*, so she could tell Wolfy was causing all the fuss. The man pointed away from the castle as he yelled, causing the groundskeeper to grab his rake in shame and slowly walk away back to his duties.

"*Fräulein, das Schloss öffnet nicht vor neun.*" the man said.

"I'm … I'm sorry, I don't speak German," Casey slurred in desperation. "I'm American. I am looking for Professor Hermann." she said pitifully.

"I'm Professor Hermann," the man said in English. "You said you are American?"

Casey covered her face and said, "Oh, thank God! Please professor, I need your help! I've come a long way. My name is Casey—"

"Casey?" he interrupted. "Casey Richards, the niece of Zoe Rich? My dear, you're all over the news."

"Yes, I know, Professor. Please, it's a long story, but I think you're the only person who can help," Casey said as she began to cry.

"Calm down, my dear. Calm down. Let me take you to my office, and we will figure something out." He put his arm around Casey and guided her toward the gate.

Finally, Casey felt safe. She wiped the tears from her eyes while the kind man guided her toward the castle.

"One more thing, Miss. We have to tie your dog up out here," he said charmingly. "We don't want to give the groundskeeper a nervous breakdown."

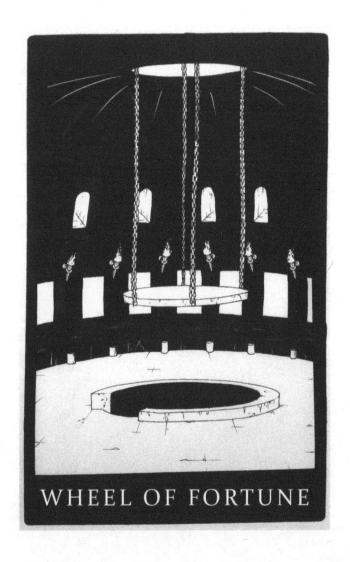

WHEEL OF FORTUNE

XXV

THE STEEL KNIGHT

The German Autobahn was empty at this hour, save for a pristine black convertible that cruised down the highway. Jack's knuckles turned white as he gripped the steering wheel. He realized he could go as fast as he wanted, so he put the pedal to the metal. The engine roared, and the quick acceleration of the car pressed him against his seat. He should have been on cloud nine driving a car like this, especially on a road with no speed limit. But he was too fixated on his destination to enjoy the ride. Further up the road storm clouds loomed, the rising sun staining them an ominous red. He knew that just beneath those clouds lay the castle, and hopefully, Mila and Casey.

Things had quickly gone even more to hell after the fire. He had run all the way to the Oasis Bar to call the fire department, only to find it closed. Further up the small road was a newsstand where a man was opening for the day. Fortunately for Jack, the man spoke English and he phoned for help. He had jogged back through the chilly morning air hearing the wail of sirens approaching. Emergency services arrived just as Jack did. Mila was nowhere to be found.

Where'd he go? Jack wondered. That's when he spotted Sabina being led into an ambulance on a gurney. She looked hysterical.

"Jack!" she shouted, "Jack, come quick!"

Jack rushed over to her, dodging the chaos of firefighters that were gearing up to fight the raging blaze that engulfed the bakery and Sabina's apartment. The paramedics were about to shut the doors as Jack reached Sabina. An EMT pushed him back and yelled, *"Sie können mit ihr nicht reiten, weil Sie keine Familie sind!"*

"No! He *is* family! Let him in!" she screamed. The EMT relented and let Jack get closer.

"Jack, someone took Mila. I saw it," Sabina sobbed.

"Who...where?" Jack asked.

"I don't know. He wore all black."

Jack noticed the burns on her body. He realized her leg was also swelling. She must have fallen on it hard when they jumped. It could be sprained, or worse. "It's OK. Calm down. You're really hurt. We need to let the paramedics help," Jack said.

"Listen to me, Jack, please! I don't trust those two," Sabina said. "The bodyguard...she's only interested in saving Casey. No one is looking after my Mila. Please, you must help him. You're his friend. They'll let him die!"

"OK, OK," Jack said, hoping that would calm her down.

Sabina lifted herself into a sitting position, pushing the paramedics away as they tried to get her to lie back down. She rummaged through her pockets, fighting her pain, and managed to pull out a set of keys. "Take my car," she insisted. "It's around back."

Jack took the keys as the EMT forced an oxygen mask on Sabina. "Vee sorry, vee sorry, vee must go now!" the paramedic said in broken English.

Jack stepped back and the ambulance doors shut. The firefighters were standing in formation around various hoses spraying down the burning apartment and hosing down adjacent buildings for good measure. Standing there, he considered what Sabina had just asked him to do. When Deborah and Morton were there, it was easy to try and tag along. The fire, however, reminded him of the seriousness of the situation.

This is life and death, Jack thought. *Deborah wouldn't abandon Mila ... would she?*

His thoughts drifted back to the many injustices he'd seen inflicted on the Rom during this trip. There was the murder of the young boy in the train station that no one cared about. Mila's entire home had been destroyed, and according to him, his great-aunt was mortally wounded in the process. No one seemed to care except for the other Rom. Jack also remembered how the police had so readily tried to frame Mila for the crimes of the TNC. And with that, he realized that Sabina was probably right. Mila was going to die. Deborah and her friend wouldn't help him. The neo-Nazis would kill him—and what's worse, nobody would care.

Jack slipped around the back of the building as the firefighters reduced the roaring flames to smoldering ash. He found a car parked on the street protected by a white cover. He pulled the cover back to reveal the gorgeous BMW convertible with the top down. It had an immaculate black paint job. It looked freshly waxed and had a vanity plate that read BROOM STICK.

"Whoa ..." Jack said.

Soon after, he found himself racing down the highway toward Wewelsburg Castle. He floored the gas pedal and watched the odometer as the trembling needle hovered just below 160 kph.

The stone palace soon came into view. An exit sign was conveniently marked with the words "Wewelsburg Castle." Jack violently swerved, nearly missing the exit, and skidded as he tried to slow down enough for the main road.

After a short drive, Jack found the access road for Wewelsburg. As he pulled toward the parking area, he noticed a roadblock. It read "Closed" in both German and English. *That's not a good sign,* Jack thought.

He parked just off the road and proceeded on foot. As he made his way up the path, he tried to reflect on what the hell he was doing. *What's the plan, exactly?* Jack asked himself. *Walk in there and say, "Hey, Mr. Nazis, I know you're heartless murderers and all, but could you please let my friends go?* He sighed. *I've got between here and the gate to come up with something better than that.*

Jack's thoughts were interrupted by the sound of frantic barking coming from up the path. *That's got to be Wolfy.* He followed the sound of the barking dog. He made his way along the main path and soon saw the German Shepherd tied to a bench a few yards from the moat bridge.

"Easy, boy, I got you," Jack said as he untied the leash.

Wolfy walked at Jack's heels as he crossed the bridge toward the gate. Suddenly, the dog stopped and his ears went back. The shepherd stood at attention and let out a low growl.

"What's the matter, boy?" Jack asked.

Suddenly, he sensed someone standing behind him. Then a stern voice said, "Halt!"

Jack turned and saw a man in a black uniform with an M-16 slung across his shoulder. *If this is museum security, it's overkill,* he thought.

"*Wir sind geschlossen, was machst du hier?*" the man shouted.

"I'm sorry...just walking my dog—my *hund*," Jack tried to communicate.

"You speak *only* English?" The guard asked. Then he shouted over his shoulder,

"*Fritz, kommen zie her!*"

The main gates opened, and a second guard came out dressed in an identical uniform. He rushed over while staring Jack down on approach. "You're trespassing," the other guard warned in slightly better English. "The museum is closed!"

Jack took a nervous step backward. He almost tripped into the moat as his heels pressed up against the edge of the bridge. Wolfy started to bark and growl at the two guards. The men took a step back as the dog strained against his leash, snarling like a wild animal. Jack struggled to calm him down.

"Wolfy, no! Sit!" Jack shouted frantically.

One of the guards unslung his rifle and got ready to fire on the dog.

"No!" Jack cried.

Pffft!

A puff of red mist sprayed from the man's head, and he dropped to the ground, lifeless. An instant later, there was another *pffft!* sound, and the second guard also fell dead. There was a moment of confusion before Jack realized the two men had been hit by sniper fire.

Jack ran for the open gate in total panic, keeping his head low. He raced inside, his heart pounding, and slammed the gate just as Wolfy slipped in after him. Once safe, he pressed his back to the wall and instinctively made the sign of the cross.

It took a moment for Jack to catch his breath and let his adrenaline subside. He closed his eyes, trying to remember the layout from the sketches he had seen on the Internet. With Wolfy by his side, Jack took his first tentative steps forward. He was in the central courtyard, which he didn't like one bit; it was too open, and there were windows overlooking it, giving him the constant fear that someone would see him. To make things worse, there was a van marked Berlin Museum with the back doors left ajar. Somebody would surely be coming soon.

With just seconds to spare, he spotted the door to the main entrance hall. *No way*, he thought. *That will be guarded for sure.*

He heard footsteps echoing across the courtyard. Searching for an escape, Jack spotted a door marked "Employees Only" and quickly darted inside.

Here the historic charm of the building disappeared, replaced by what looked like municipal offices. He passed a few small rooms with desks as he headed toward an unassuming stairway at the end of the hall. He snuck past a small file room where some castle employees seemed to be shredding papers. He reached the stairs without encountering any security. He tiptoed into the stairwell, knowing any noise would echo up and down the steps and alert anyone nearby. Jack and Wolfy got about halfway up the first flight before Jack heard someone coming toward them. There was nowhere to run and nowhere to hide. Jack got ready for anything.

"The museum is closed!" an olive-skinned older gentleman said to him. "And we don't allow animals inside which is why he was tied up near the entrance."

Jack immediately recognized the man's face. It was Professor Hermann.

"I'm sorry. I was looking for my girlfriend," Jack said. It was the best he could come up with.

"I see," the man replied. Jack could tell that Hermann did not care. "I'm going to have to escort you out."

Jack followed the professor, all the while strategizing how he was going to get away from him. There were corridors everywhere, but he didn't know the castle.

Hermann led him into a security room filled with monitors keeping watch over the entire castle. Four guards wearing the black uniforms and sword-emblazoned arm bands of the TNC were posted there, along with a maintenance man in a faded blue uniform fidgeting with the monitors. Jack took a quick look at each of the monitors, but they were flickering on and off.

Hermann and the security guards began to speak to one another in German. He picked up the words *wireless netzwerk*. Before Jack could figure out what was going on, Hermann stepped in front of him, blocking his view.

He began to speak to one of the guards while pointing at Jack. Jack could easily figure out that Hermann was ordering the guard to take him into custody. At that moment, Jack realized that Mila and Sabina were right. This man could never help them. As a matter of fact, Jack instinctively knew Hermann was not a friend.

Just then, another guard out in the hall shouted something in German.

"*Entschuldigen sie mich*, Professor Hermann," the guard said, excusing himself, then rushed out to see what the commotion was.

"There seems to be a situation unfolding on the bridge outside, which I'm sure you are perfectly aware of," Hermann said to Jack.

"You're Professor Hermann?" Jack asked, pretending he didn't already know.

"Yes, I am, young man, and I've been through this routine already once today with your girlfriend," he replied.

"Where is she?" Jack demanded.

"I'm afraid she's all tied up," replied Professor Hermann.

He glared at Jack, then glanced at the monitors behind him. He motioned for another one of the guards to follow him as he took Jack into another room. He obviously didn't want Jack seeing whatever was happening on those monitors.

Jack passively followed him into a small banquet room of sorts with Wolfy following calmly and obediently at his side. It had a long wooden table and chairs carved from rich mahogany. The walls were covered in ornate green wallpaper and decorated with various framed documents and letters. On either end of the room stood double doors flanked by suits of armor.

"We are going to stay right here until security gives us the 'all clear,'" Hermann declared. "Tie your dog up over by that suit of armor."

The guard stood by the door with his rifle at the ready. Jack knew he was no match for him, so he followed Hermann's instructions. Each suit of armor had a steel railing about a foot away, more a reminder not to touch them than to actually protect the artifacts. Jack tied up Wolfy to the railing. He tried to tie a loose knot that could be easily undone.

"Tie him properly," Hermann warned.

There's no getting anything past this guy, Jack thought as he fixed the knot. Then he pulled up a chair and took a seat. The adrenaline was still flowing as Jack racked his brain for ideas to get out of this mess. He began to look around the room at the ancient artifacts. Even in a crisis, he couldn't suppress his curiosity with everything historical. "What are all these?" Jack asked, genuinely wanting to know and hoping he could calm his nerves with some conversation.

"These are important documents associated with the castle," Hermann replied. "Now, stay quiet."

They sat a moment without saying anything. Then the intercom crackled, breaking the silence. *"Achtung, der Perimeter wurd beeinträchtigt! Alle Kräfte zurückhalten um das Ritual Raum zu verteidigen!"* a voice shouted.

"Tut mir leid, Professor, ich muss gehen," the guard stated as he rushed off.

Jack could only pick up a few words of German, but *Ritual Raum* was pretty clear. He and Hermann stared each other down for what seemed like forever, both of them waiting for something. Suddenly, they heard gunfire echoing in the distance, and both instinctively rose to their feet. The noise distracted the professor for a moment, causing him to look away. Seeing his chance, Jack reached for a sword slung about the waist of a suit of armor. The weapon slid free and, to Jack's surprise, appeared to be razor sharp. He menacingly pointed the sword at Hermann. Wolfy leaped to his feet, barking, snarling, and straining against the leash. The professor raised his hands and slowly backed away.

"Stop right there!" Jack ordered as he advanced closer.

But Hermann kept backing up, never letting his eyes off Jack. At first, Jack thought he was about to escape out the other door and warn the guards. Then he unexpectedly came to a stop next to the other suit of armor and drew a sword from its scabbard.

"Wrong move, young man," Hermann said.

Jack began to step backward as Hermann slowly advanced. Suddenly, the professor lunged forward, covering a seemingly impossible distance. Jack stumbled back, trying to parry as best he could. The tip of Hermann's sword came within an inch of Jack's face. Jack knocked it away with a frantic block. As the blades clashed, he knew Hermann was just toying with him. If he wanted, he could have speared Jack through the eye.

"I can tell you are little more than a beginner," Hermann mocked. He stepped back and returned to a fencing stance, then made a few feints, thrusting his sword toward Jack. The boy flinched every time. Then he struck Jack's blade, knocking it aside with a beat. The weapon was much heavier than the foil Jack was used to, and it took him a moment to raise it again to defend himself. Again, if Hermann had wanted, he could have gone in for the kill. Wolfy frantically barked and struggled to get closer, nearly choking himself on the leash.

"You should consider surrendering. I fenced in the Munich Olympics," Hermann bragged, "and I was undefeated at Oxford."

"That's cool," Jack replied, not knowing what to say. He bumped into the wall next to the suit of armor. There was nowhere to run. His adrenaline-fueled thrill had turned into pure fear.

Seeing this, Hermann dropped into a low fencing stance, conjuring Errol Flynn or Zorro. But instead of lunging at Jack and taking him out, he began to spin his blade in an arc, clearly showing off. Jack glanced over at Wolfy, who continued to bark frantically, looking like he wanted to tear Hermann apart.

"En garde!" the professor shouted.

"En garde ... really?" Jack asked, trying not to laugh.

Hermann didn't like that one bit. He scowled menacingly. "We'll see how funny you think it is when I split you in half!" he said.

Jack took one more step back. He glanced at the suit of armor that was just a sword's thrust away from him. He almost felt sorry for the old fool. "Yeah, good luck with that," he said.

Jack lifted his sword above his head, but instead of lunging at Hermann, he swung the blade straight down, severing Wolfy's leash. Hermann's eyes went wide, and he shrieked in terror as the dog lunged at him, clamping down on his arm. He dropped his sword and fell to the ground as he tried to pull away. He managed to wrench his arm free, only to have Wolfy bite down on his foot instead. He screamed in terror as Jack stepped forward and pulled the nearest suit of armor down on top of him, trapping him underneath.

Wolfy climbed on top of the armor and got face to face with Professor Hermann, growling. The helpless scholar whimpered at the site of the bloodthirsty dog.

"Wolfy! Come!" Jack ordered.

The dog looked at Jack, then continued to scowl at Hermann. "Come on, boy, we've got to find Mila and Casey," Jack insisted.

That got the dog's attention. He trotted off to join Jack in his search for the ritual room.

XXVI

~~~~~

TOGETHER AGAIN

Things felt far too familiar for Deborah as she placed her eye in the viewfinder of her sniper rifle. Unfortunately, there was no time for nostalgia. The flimsy roof of the abandoned barn creaked as she shifted her weight. It may have been a decrepit structure, but the vantage point was almost perfect. As she lay prone on the roof, she could see all the way from the south wing to the north tower, where she believed Casey was being held. She eyed the castle through the scope, swinging the lens of the powerful weapon along the various narrow windows of the tower.

As she zoomed her lens closer to the first-floor windows of the ritual room, she noticed that it was difficult to see inside due to the way the windows were constructed. All she could see was a brick shaft that slanted downward. The design let light in but made it impossible to see the room itself. From outside, Deborah couldn't even tell how deep down the chamber was, and the vague sketches they had retrieved from Morton's files didn't help much, either. *Maybe this vantage point isn't so perfect after all,* she thought. *No, the only way to get a clear view would be to climb up to that window and perch on the ledge.*

"That wouldn't be conspicuous," she muttered sarcastically.

She checked her watch; it was about eight o'clock. Morton should have finished hacking their network and would be back any minute. Her focus drifted back to the perimeter guards. One stood near the parking area, just in case someone ignored the roadblock. Another stood near the main gate underneath the shade of the archway. An additional pair of guards patrolled the grounds, walking through the moat garden and along the woods. As Deborah watched the perimeter patrol make their way to the far side of the castle, she noticed a large dog tied to a bench near the main door. *A guard dog?* She wondered. *Maybe it's that animal Jack was speaking of earlier. What was his name—Wolfy?* Deborah hoped that when Morton got back his intel would shed some light on the subject.

As if on cue, Morton approached. He announced his presence by imitating the sound of a bird. Deborah whistled back, giving him the "all clear" to approach.

Morton climbed to the top of the barn and crawled across the roof, staying low until he arrived next to her.

"Together again, eh?" he asked. Once in position, he pulled out his binoculars.

"What did you find out?" Deborah asked, ignoring the nostalgic comment.

Morton opened a laptop and switched it on. It showed a live feed of a hallway inside the castle. Several guards were on watch there with rifles in hand. He tapped the screen, flipping through the feeds of different surveillance cameras that showed both interior and exterior views.

"They've got cameras everywhere but the ritual room," Morton explained. "I was able to hack in. As you can see, it gives us a pretty good view inside."

"Any sign of Casey?"

"According to their transmissions, they'll be putting her in the vault. It's all part of some ritual, which means she's alive."

Deborah did not respond. She just stared through her scope at the castle.

"She's fine, I promise you," Morton assured her. "I set up the wireless jamming devices. We can blind them any time we want. They won't see us coming, not this time."

Deborah allowed herself to smirk ever so slightly. "Remember," she said, "we extract Casey first. We don't go after Victor until she's safe."

Morton nodded as Deborah put her eye back to the scope. He pulled out his binoculars and scanned the area, as well. They turned their attention to the security officer in the parking area. The man kept fidgeting, shifting his weight back and forth from one leg to the other. He seemed to be waiting for something. It soon became clear what he was waiting for. A white cargo van marked Berlin Museum pulled up to the roadblock. The guard pulled the wooden barricade aside and let the van through. Then he replaced the barricade and jogged off into the forest. No doubt he'd been waiting for the van to arrive before he could relieve himself. The van continued right up to the moat bridge and pulled slowly into the courtyard.

"Have you found a good point of entry?" Morton asked.

"It's either the window or the front door. The perimeter guard is pretty light."

"There are a lot more inside patrolling the major hallways. I count at least twenty," Morton informed her. "But the ritual room should only have a handful. I'm thinking one of us should approach from the forest and breach through the windows, and the other covers from here."

"That works. You cover," Deborah insisted.

"I was actually thinking I'd go in and you'd cover me."

"Morton, you've got too much at stake to go in there," Deborah warned. "My employer doesn't care what I do as long as I bring his niece back. He can buy me out of any trouble I might be in. I've got nothing to lose."

She surveyed the moat path, seeing if there were any other ways in. She noticed a small hatch behind some shrubs. It looked like a maintenance tunnel. *No*, she thought, *there's no telling where it leads.* She checked the path again to see if the guards had moved. "Oh crap!" she exclaimed.

"What?"

"Damn teenagers never listen!" she ranted.

Through her scope she could see Jack untying the dog. She followed the path down to the parking lot and trained the scope there just in time to see the guard emerge from the forest. *Don't see him, come on, don't see him,* Deborah prayed. No luck—the guard turned to his left and spotted Jack. Deborah watched as he approached the teen, who remained blissfully unaware.

"Come on, Jack, get out of there," she whispered.

Morton looked through his binoculars. The guard was just a few paces behind Jack as he stepped onto the bridge. Jack suddenly turned as the guard began to yell at him. The second watchman emerged from under the archway, trapping Jack on the bridge.

"Easy," Morton said. "Hopefully, they'll just eject him from the grounds. This could be the diversion we ne—"

Before he could finish, the dog took an aggressive stance, barking and growling viciously at one of the guards. In response, the guard drew his rifle, raised it to his shoulder, and looked down the sights at the dog.

Deborah had him in her crosshairs and could see his finger moving toward the trigger. *Pffft!* Her silenced rifle made little more than a squeak. The guard dropped to the ground. Without a second thought, she chambered another round and pulled the trigger. *Pffft!* The other man fell dead.

"What are you doing?" Morton demanded.

"Kill the surveillance," Deborah ordered.

"What?"

"Do it now!"

Morton hit a few keys on his tablet. The camera feeds all turned to static.

"He was about to fire. It would have put the whole place on alert," Deborah explained. She quickly scanned the castle grounds for the perimeter guards. They walked as casually as ever. No call had gone out. Not yet.

"Get your rifle out," Deborah commanded him. Morton knew better than to argue and got his rifle.

"I've got the one on the left," she said.

"The other one's in my sights," Morton replied.

Pffft! Pffft! They fired almost simultaneously, eliminating the guards. At times, Morton and Deborah worked perfectly in sync. It was a welcome change from their equally frequent dysfunction.

"How long will your jammers last?" she asked.

"Hours, but while they're active we're just as blind as they are," Morton replied.

Deborah racked her brain trying to come up with an answer. They didn't have long. Someone could spot the bodies of the slain guards at any moment. And Jack was in the courtyard—he could put the whole place on alert. Her gut told her to just move in, mount an all-out assault on the ritual room, and get Casey out before the TNC knew what hit them. That's what her instincts said. *Or is it just wishful thinking?* she wondered.

"What do we do? It's your call," Morton asked.

"We go in," Deborah said at last as she stowed the sniper rifle in a camouflage case. "You head in the front and secure the boy. I'll scale the side of the north tower and breach through the window and get Casey." She drew a submachine gun from the case and loaded a magazine. "Once you secure Jack, create a diversion for me."

"How the hell am I going to create a diversion?"

Deborah threw on a tactical vest. "I have no idea! Whatever you can do. Blow something up! Now move out."

XXVII

THE GILDED TOMB

The feel of the soft black robe reminded Victor Strauss of his youth. Even its musty smell took him back in time, and with that fleeting memory he looked upward to gaze on the brick dome of the crypt. The impressive round room gleamed with pale light from its elevated windows. Beneath those windows stood twelve short stone pedestals.

Strauss could almost see the SS guards standing on each pillar dressed in the vestments of the Thule Society chanting, *"Sieg Heil! Sieg Heil! Sieg Heil!"* He paused a moment more to admire the stone swastika seal that adorned the center of the floor and mirrored its counterpart in the ceiling. A set of chains that hung from openings at each quadrant of the upper swastika were anchored at four points on the seal. The chains fed into an antiquated motorized winch in the room above.

It had taken years and millions of euros from his shady foundations to return that stone tile-and-pulley system to its rightful place, to say nothing of what lay beneath.

The sight of the chains brought Strauss back to the last time he'd been in the tomb. He had been green with envy that day. It was the spring of 1944, and Strauss had just been informed that his peer, Paul—not he, himself—had been chosen to be the first of the *über-mensch*: the ultra-men, warriors of the new master race. Strauss remembered how the guards in their black robes had frightened him as a child. Their silence made him tremble. He only became more anxious as the Führer himself entered with Leichman to his left and Heinrich Himmler, the head of the SS, to his right.

"No!" Strauss whispered now, chasing the painful memories from his mind. *I can't indulge such memories,* he thought as he placed the morbid black robe over his head, feeling the velvety cloth brush his cheeks. *Those are weak memories. Paul was weak. That's why he left us. That's why he's dead now,* Strauss reminded himself as he slipped on the pointed cowl of the robe. Wearing the ceremonial vestments, he was the spitting image of the SS guards that terrified him as a child.

With his mind back in the present, Strauss looked down to a small ceremonial table. On the table between two candlesticks lay a golden box, and inside that lay the nail. *Nothing can stop me now,* he thought. *I won't just be an* übermensch. *I'll be their master, their king, their God.*

A groaning sound interrupted Strauss's fantasies. He glanced to his right where the American girl lay. She wasn't quite out cold—more dazed, weak perhaps, but not completely out. Castor, Father Leichman's loyal henchman, was hard at work binding her hands and feet behind her back. Strauss noted the bandages on Castor's arm and the bruising all over his face. However, the swollen lip and the missing tooth were the more unsightly new features. The man seemed unaffected by these wounds as he finished restraining the girl and dragged her into the center of the room, leaving her lying face down with the seal in front of her.

"Castor, are you sure the motor to raise the seal is in working order?" Father Leichman called from the chamber's only doorway. He entered, dressed in his usual priestly robes with Drago walking faithfully at his heels.

"Yes, Your Grace," Castor replied.

There was a hint of sadness in his voice, and Strauss could guess why. Pollux, Castor's twin brother, was dead, killed by the American girl's hound. Strauss watched Father Leichman approach his disciple and place a gentle hand on his shoulder. "I miss him, too, Castor," the father assured him as he took a seat on one of the pedestals. Once he was comfortable, he reached into his pocket and gave Drago a treat. "When this ritual is done, we may be able to bring him back. We don't know exactly what the nail is capable of."

389

"You can't imagine how badly I want to kill her right now," Castor said.

"I know, my son, but this is the only way," Father Leichman explained. "You could stab her a dozen times with the nail or a knife or a sword. You could shoot her in the head again and again. This will stun her for a time, but she will not die."

"What if I cut off her head and completely burned her?"

Father Leichman snickered at the thought. "Trust me, my son, that would work out very badly for you," he warned. "We know of only three ways to kill the master of the nail. The first is this chamber. The second is a pure *Garade* wielding the nail itself. Unfortunately, that option is lost to us."

Strauss's blood began to boil at the mention of this. "That option is lost because the Garade must be willing, and you had his little cousin murdered before his eyes! He will never trust us again!" he snapped.

"The boy would not have witnessed that if you'd hired some competent security," Father Leichman retorted. "Not that it matters. He's dead by now, isn't he?"

"Yes, that was a mistake, and I assure you that it will not be repeated. I've assembled the finest assault team to protect the castle." Strauss turned away to hide his smirk. "And, of course, he is dead. I sent my best arsonist," he said. "Not a trace left, just as you ordered." He quickly changed the subject. "We shouldn't be discussing this in front of Castor. You don't reveal your whole battle plan to a foot soldier."

The priest gave Strauss a scolding look. He ignored it as he strolled to the center of the room to examine the chains that hung from the ceiling and anchored in the lower seal.

"You worry too much. He has lost his twin brother to this cause. I think he's earned the right to know these things," Father Leichman replied.

Strauss's demeanor softened a little. He stepped over to Castor from the center of the room. "You should know that after tonight your loyalty will pay off. You will truly have all you desire. I will be in a position to give you all the riches of the world," Strauss said proudly.

"Ahh, be careful, my son. He who offers the riches of the world so quickly is only days away from losing it himself. Have you not read your Bible?" the priest cunningly interjected.

"Matthew, chapter four, verse nine," Castor replied with glee.

"Very good, my child," Father Leichman replied, beaming with pride.

Strauss gave them both an unhappy stare. Castor paced around the seal, analyzing it. "I still don't understand how this works," Castor said. "It's all so confusing."

"No, it's not. Let me explain," Father Leichman said.

This elicited a frown from Strauss. The priest wasn't listening to him. He began to wonder if Father Leichman knew who was really in charge here.

"Himmler was the first to realize it," Father Leichman went on. "We built this vault based on designs from a golden tomb in the mountains of Romania. At the time, the Führer was convinced that he could use this to give some of the nail's powers to his soldiers, turning them into unstoppable human weapons. He thought the project failed, but we knew better."

He gave Strauss a knowing glance. Strauss nodded back while stepping toward the ceremonial table. It was eerie how the priest's mind was on the very same memory that had troubled him just minutes ago.

"You see, he never realized how it worked. When the nail was sealed, Himmler noticed the Chancellor couldn't see. Do you understand?"

Castor pondered that for a moment. Then he announced, "Mustard gas! The Führer was blinded by mustard gas in the trenches during the First World War."

Father Leichman smiled. "And the nail healed him, but when the nail was placed in the chamber with a potential *übermensch*, his sight disappeared again." He sat up a bit straighter, rocked himself forward a couple of times, and then stood up. Once he was sure footed, he stepped closer to the seal and pointed down to it. "This tomb can separate the nail's power from its owner as completely as if they'd never had the nail to begin with."

"How do you know that for sure, master? Just because he lost his sight while the nail was in the tomb?" asked Castor.

"There was a Gypsy hag in Munich who the Führer captured and tortured. She was the one who informed the Führer of the nail's powers," responded Father Leichman. "She also revealed that if the owner of the nail seals the artifact in the tomb with an innocent human, that human will manifest evil powers."

"What powers, master?"

"Ahhh, super human strength, youth, and God knows what else. The important thing is that they would be loyal and obedient to the possessor of the nail."

"Wait a minute, if the nail gave him everlasting youth, then how did the Führer die?" Castor asked as that realization dawned on him. "You told me once he didn't really commit suicide, but you never explained what happened."

"You were always the clever one," Father Leichman said with a smile. "You're familiar with Operation Valkyrie, the assassination attempt on the Führer?"

"Of course," Castor said.

"Such a waste. We planned for so long and risked so much to retrieve the nail from the Führer. When the bomb went off, it knocked the nail from the Führer's grip and sent it flying out the window and into the streets of Berlin. Our plan was to recover it, but…"

Father Leichman looked down at the floor. Strauss knew that after all these years this failure still haunted him, filling the priest's mind with frustration and regret.

"The resistance caught wind of our plot and sent a Garade Gypsy to steal the nail. Once the Nazi high command realized that the nail was back in the hands of the guardians of evil, all hope was lost. Even I don't know exactly how the Gypsy did it—many of the extraordinary gifts of the Magi are still a mystery us—but once he had the nail, the Führer was a shadow of his former self. His powers grew weaker by the day, and the war went no better. We knew defeat was imminent. Himmler tried to surrender to the Allies, and the others either committed suicide or fled the country. And the Chancellor—well, he did not see the nail again until that Gypsy returned to the bunker and plunged it into his heart... Now go, my son. Place the candles along the top pillars and light them so we may proceed," Father Leichman ordered.

Castor looked more confused. However, he obeyed and retrieved twelve large candlesticks. He smirked as he noted a slight bend in one of them. He'd used it to knock the American girl out cold while the professor had her distracted. As he proceeded to place the candles on top of the pillars and light them, he posed another question for Father Leichman.

"I'm sorry, Your Grace, but I am still confused," Castor said. "How the hell did the Gypsy break into the

Führer's bunker? It was the most secure place in Berlin. And if the Führer was murdered, why did everyone think it was suicide?"

"Ahh, you are wise for asking such questions," Father Leichman said. "After all, you can't believe what they teach you in the history books. The guardians of evil can be quite clever. You see, the Gypsy did not break into anywhere. He walked right into the bunker. The Führer was planning to flee to his mountain strong-hold, the Eagle's Nest, but not before marrying his mistress, Eva Braun. He called for a priest, an old seminary friend of mine, to perform the ceremony. The Garade disguised himself as the priest's altar boy, smuggled the nail inside, and killed the Führer with it."

Strauss swallowed hard. As Father Leichman spoke, the memories of that day came rushing back to him. He could once again feel the terror he felt as the Gypsy killed their master. *I feared that Gypsy would kill me, too. Instead, he scampered off like the rat he was,* he thought.

"At that point, the bunker was in chaos," Father Leichman went on. "Everyone was scrambling to get out before the Soviets arrived. How exactly the Garade escaped, I don't know. Evidently, he never took the nail out of the bunker. He probably hid it, fearing what would happen if it fell into the hands of the Communists."

Castor finished lighting the last twelve candles. Father Leichman began to rant on, as old men are prone to do. "I had to help cover up the murder. I'd already sacrificed so much to keep the nail a secret. We burned the bodies, called it a suicide, and no one questioned it. The world was so happy knowing that a murderous dictator was dead they didn't bother to question his death—or his life, for that matter."

Strauss noticed Father Leichman catch his breath and was a bit angry as he proceeded on with his opinion of Hitler's reign. "The world is so naive that even the highest holy priest of the Vatican could not connect the dots," he said. "Only a man armed with the power of Lucifer himself can start from nothing and gain such absolute power over so many. Only the devil's charm can convince so many people to hate so much," Father Leichman droned on.

By then, Strauss's patience had worn out. He didn't care to hear this story again. He already knew it. He had lived it! "Enough!" Strauss shouted. He detected a bit of rage as the old priest stopped short and looked up at him. "Let's get this over with," he demanded.

"Just a moment," Father Leichman said. "We must wait for the painting."

He cast off his black outer robe. Underneath he wore his SS chaplain's uniform, complete with a service Luger and Hitler Youth knife.

Strauss was surprised and found something rather comical about seeing the frail priest in a uniform he hadn't worn since he was a young man. "What's this? Feeling nostalgic?"

"I wanted to salute you properly when you become our supreme leader," Leichman said as he bowed his head slightly.

Something about that didn't ring true to Strauss. Father Leichman almost sounded sarcastic. He suspected there was another meaning behind that pristine uniform, but before he got the chance to question further, his security banged on the door.

"We have a delivery from the Berlin Museum," a TNC operative said from the other side of the door.

Castor left his post, unlocked the door, and proceeded to let in two security guards. They carried a large painting covered in brown paper and an easel. They set everything up near the ceremonial table where Strauss was standing. Once the painting was placed on the easel, Father Leichman asked the guards to leave and to let no one in until he called for them. Strauss glared at the priest as his men stepped out into the long hallway. *Stop ordering my men around!* he thought.

Once the guards were gone, Castor locked the door from the inside.

"Castor, open the tomb," Father Leichman ordered.

Strauss proceeded to rip the paper off, revealing *The Proclamation*, the original painting, in all its glory. His eyes traced the contours of the painting, stopping on the scepter, where he could see the final inscription painted as clear as day. That inscription held the binding incantation, the one that had been filed off centuries ago. Even experts like Hermann and Father Leichman weren't exactly sure what the binding did, but their studies led them to believe that it permanently bound the nail to its master. They were convinced that once bound, the master would be invincible, safe even from the powers of the Magi's bloodline.

THE QUEEN
OF SWORDS

Strauss could not help himself, realizing that even he was becoming fascinated as he stared at the painting. He became so enthralled that he didn't notice Castor throwing a switch near the door. A grinding sound echoed through the chamber, and for a minute Strauss came out of his semi-trance, worried that the old machine would give out. The chains jerked and finally began to lift the marble disk into the air. At last, the gilded tomb was revealed. Beneath the seal was a solid-gold box about the size and shape of a casket. As the seal rose higher, it revealed an underside also made of gold. The air inside had a faint scent of frankincense and myrrh. For a moment, Strauss just stared into the glistening gold of the vault. He deeply inhaled to smell the sweet incense. Even that spectacular display couldn't keep his attention away from the painting for long. It seemed to call to him, and once again he gazed at *The Proclamation*.

"You know what to do," Father Leichman said to Castor.

Castor nodded. He picked up Casey with ease and roughly dropped her into the tomb. He sprinkled myrrh on top of her, then he retrieved some small grains of frankincense from a pouch within his pocket and placed them under her nose. The girl began to scream like a wild animal. Her cries were utterly inhuman as she struggled against her bonds.

Strauss covered his ears, turning away from the painting, his reverie broken. "Close it," he ordered. "I can't stand another second of that squealing!"

Castor threw the switch again, and the seal slowly began to lower. It descended toward Casey inch by inch as she screamed and struggled with pure rage. Her cries continued until the moment the stone slab closed over her, sealing her inside.

Father Leichman and Strauss both hesitated for a minute. They stood on either side of the ceremonial table, each a few paces away from the nail. There was tension in the air as they stared at each other. Then Strauss looked away. He had to steal one last glance at the painting. He gazed on it for a few moments, fighting its spellbinding power; at last, he forced himself to stop gawking.

When he turned back to the ceremonial table, he realized that Father Leichman had moved closer. But he still had some agility left in his old bones, unlike the priest. He rushed over as Father Leichman began to reach for the golden box that held the nail. They both snatched at the box and ended up knocking it onto the floor. The lid came open, and the nail fell out, rolling across the gray marble.

Strauss rushed for the nail, but it was too late. Drago casually trotted over to the scepter and picked it up in his mouth. The dog looked up at Strauss with his ears back and let out a low growl.

Click!

With a slow turn, Strauss faced Father Leichman again and was not surprised to see the priest had drawn his Luger and aimed it at him. As the two men stared each other down, Castor drew a pistol of his own and aimed it at Strauss for good measure. "Don't move!" Castor ordered.

"I'm not used to taking orders," Strauss answered. He moved toward Leichman. Castor forcefully raised his pistol, and the dog growled louder.

With no hope of overpowering two armed men, as well as a vicious German Shepherd, Strauss relented and stood very still. He stared daggers at Father Leichman as the old man whistled for Drago. The loyal dog trotted over to him. Father Leichman smiled down at the canine and collected the nail from his jaws.

"I'm warning you—put your hands up," Castor told Strauss.

"I knew you'd betray me, just like the Führer betrayed Paul," Strauss announced while lifting his hands to chest level.

"Then you're a fool," Father Leichman sneered back.

Strauss turned to Castor. *I need to stall,* he thought. *If I can just reach my coat pocket without them noticing ...*

"He'll do the same to you!" Strauss shouted to the scarred henchman. "I'm a very powerful man, Castor. You're making a very big mistake. Trust me—you don't want to betray me or the True Nationalist Coalition."

Castor just laughed at the threat.

"That won't work, Victor," Father Leichman said. "Castor is loyal to me, not your political party. I've taught him truths you still can't even fathom."

"What truths are those, old man?" Strauss scoffed.

"I'm not sure why you never understood it, Victor," Father Leichman began, his voice almost sympathetic. "Maybe it's the sort of thing a politician can't understand. Maybe you're too naive, or you didn't want to believe it. Or maybe you were just too stupid. This scepter was not just a supernatural means to an end for the Führer. The war was not about building some thousand-year utopia. All that nonsense about racial purity—you really believe in that, don't you, with your True Nationalist Party? Those were lies he told to ensnare the downtrodden people of Germany and convince them to commit atrocities unseen since the Middle Ages.

"The war was a holy war. The purpose of the Final Solution was to exterminate the descendants of Abraham, Isaac, and Jacob in defiance of their God. The same is true for the Magi and their kin the Gypsies. The Second World War was a war against Jehovah, waged to show that the beautiful one who reigns below is the rightful master of the earth." Father Leichman cast a reverent gaze to the floor and stayed silent a moment. "And now, that war will finally be won," he announced, gesturing to the painting. "I'll be bound to the nail, and nothing will stop me."

"You're out of your mind," Strauss snapped.

"You're a fool," Father Leichman countered, "and when I make you my slave, I'll remind you of that every day."

Father Leichman placed his finger on the sharp point of the nail, distracted for a moment. That was Strauss's chance. He slid his hand along the outside of his pocket, found the outline of his key fob, and pressed the button as discreetly as possible. The device would summon his guards. *It might be too late,* he thought.

Meanwhile, Father Leichman applied the slightest pressure, and the thorny spike pierced his frail skin. "I've waited so long for you, my Lord!" he cried.

Strauss watched as the old man closed his eyes, lips gently moving as he whispered the incantation. They all waited. Father Leichman shut his eyes tighter. A few drops of blood fell from his finger. Nothing seemed to be happening. Finally, Father Leichman opened his eyes with a look of confusion and disappointment.

"I don't think it worked," Strauss mocked him. "You don't look any stronger."

Father Leichman drew his Hitler Youth knife, scowling furiously at Strauss. "We'll just need to test it," the priest said as he took a menacing step toward him. "I'll try your blood first. If that doesn't work, I can surely use the profess—"

As Father Leichman closed within arm's reach, the doors burst open, and a TNC squad charged inside.

Strauss ducked out of the way as Father Leichman stood in stunned surprise. Castor barely had time to raise his pistol before a round struck him in the chest. He went down firing wildly. Drago, just as loyal as Castor, growled and leapt for the nearest guard, but he was immediately cut down by rifle fire.

Father Leichman dropped the knife and reached for his Luger again, but not before he was shot in the stomach. The armed neo-Nazi advanced and pointed a rifle at the priest's head.

"No!" Strauss shouted as he stepped closer. "Not yet."

He snatched the nail from Father Leichman and took his Luger as well. He leaned in a few inches from Leichman's face. "Who's the fool now, old man?" Strauss hissed. Then he stood to address his men.

"First squad, secure this room. Second squad, patrol the hallway," he ordered. He took out his walkie-talkie and held it to his mouth. "Bring me the Gypsy," Strauss commanded.

XXVIII

~~~

BATTLE FOR POWER

The ache in Mila's chest and face was worse than anything he'd ever felt. The painkiller had definitely worn off, and the irritating itch from the burlap bag over his head made him struggle for the use of his tied hands. His back was pressed against a rough, cold stone wall, and it was obvious to Mila that he was being held captive in some sort of dungeon.

He shuffled around it and found the space to be about six feet by four feet. He couldn't tell how high the ceiling was, but he'd felt a breeze blowing. The door felt different from the stony walls: smooth and heavy. *It must be made of thick wood or reinforced by metal*, he thought.

His thoughts drifted to where he could be or how long his captors would even keep him alive. When he finally accepted that his hands were bound too tightly and there was no way of releasing them, he tried to meditate, but he couldn't settle his mind. He kept thinking about how sorry he was for believing that being a Gypsy and living in the slums of Building A was so bad. He cursed the day that he had ignored Nasta and threw away the *chukrayi*. *You wouldn't be here in this godforsaken place if you had just done what she said. Maybe she would still be alive*, he thought. His stress had reached its high point.

At one point, he heard a dog barking, and he had hoped that it might be Wolfy. "Wolfy!" he shouted. "Over here, boy!"

He called again and the dog barked and barked, then suddenly stopped, leaving nothing but dead silence. Mila waited in that silence for awhile. He'd lost all sense of time. It could have been minutes or it could have been hours.

Suddenly, he heard the door swing open on its creaky metal hinges. Firm hands grabbed him and pulled him out. Mila flinched at first, worrying he'd be beaten again. Fortunately, his captors just rushed him into the hallway. They were in a great rush and practically dragged him along. He could hear the footsteps of at least three men, maybe more. There were far too many to try and break away.

As they rushed along, a woman's scream echoed through the hallway. "Check it out," one of the guards mumbled in German.

Mila heard some guards leave, but the others pushed him forward. They took him down a flight of stairs where he nearly tripped, then into another hallway. Finally, Mila heard the creak of two heavy doors opening, and a gust of warm air blew past him. He heard a man shouting, but he couldn't yet make out the voice. There was also a groaning sound, like someone in pain.

"A man like me doesn't get to where he is by taking unnecessary risks," the voice declared. "I've had your pet Garade in holding since early this morning."

"Ha! You're taking greater risks than you can imagine," another voice retorted. "There's no telling how many gifts have manifested within that boy."

"You think I'm scared of some Gypsy magic? That's nothing compared to the power of the nail. You'll see that soon enough," the first voice scoffed.

One of Mila's captors roughly pushed him from behind, causing him to fall hard to the marble floor. Once down, he heard a voice: it was raspy and weary, but he immediately recognized it. He had known that voice for years. It was the voice of a man he swore he would bring to justice.

"Why bother showing me anything?" Leichman demanded between labored breaths. "You seem to think you have all the answers, so what are you waiting for? Kill me and get it over with."

"All in good time, Father. Your connections to the Vatican might be useful to me. I'll use the nail to get what I want from you, then I'll kill you," the voice said as if making a simple business deal. "Get that bag off his head!" he ordered.

The sack was pulled free, and Mila could see for the first time in hours. It was not very bright in the chamber, but he still had to squint at first. Mila took in the room for a few seconds. He saw the scarred twin dead on the floor with an armed guard looming over his body. Then he noticed Father Leichman on the floor leaning against a stool. He was definitely wounded because he was clutching his stomach in an effort to stanch some bleeding. Mila's heart raced even faster, convinced he would die here. The sight of the wicked priest gave Mila a burst of energy. For a moment, Mila thought of trying to run clear across the room and fulfill his promise to himself by stomping the priest's face in. Unfortunately, he knew that wouldn't work. There were six TNC men inside, all with weapons at-the-ready. Mila also noticed the chains that fed into the dome of the ceiling. He wondered for a second what they were for.

"Open the tomb," Strauss ordered. "Bring her out."

His men complied. One of them pulled a few ancient switches that were alongside the brick wall. Slowly, the old rusted chains began to lift the tile in the center of the floor. One of the men carried Casey from the tomb and placed her on the floor, her hands still tied behind her back. She almost immediately locked eyes with Mila. Her gaze filled him with pity at first, but as he looked deeper into her beautiful blue eyes, he noticed anger and darkness. This wasn't the girl he'd come to know and care for. *What is the nail doing to you?* he thought as he held her angry stare with his gentle gaze.

Strauss stepped in front of Mila, cutting off his view of Casey. "You are going to kill her," he announced, "using this."

Strauss held out the nail, offering it to Mila while one of the guards cut his hands free. Mila lost his balance a moment and fell forward, sprawled on his hands and knees. He was filled with grief, more grief than he had ever felt in his life. He moved his head to gesture "no."

"I can't," Mila said. "I won't."

"Oh, but you will. You must," Strauss insisted, mocking him.

"That won't work!" Father Leichman shouted. He winced in pain and clutched his stomach tighter. "Remember: the Garade must be willing," he continued in wheezing gasps. "You can't force his hand, and he'd sooner die than help you."

Strauss swung his head around and gave Father Leichman a fierce scowl. "Luckily, you taught me exactly how to persuade Gypsies," he snapped. He slowly turned back to Mila and stared down at him with a cold, bitter gaze. He took the nail and began to graze Mila's cheeks with the tip. Mila tried to ignore the cold touch of the evil artifact as he stared forward in a defiant refusal to make eye contact with Strauss.

"I have your family, Mila. Most of them are on their way to my resettlement camp in Romania, but I kept a few close by here in Germany in case you were reluctant to help me."

Mila returned his stare with wonder.

"I will kill them, one by one...starting with Petre, then Stephan and Rosa, and then there's the loud-mouthed thief. My guards have become very fond of him. You know I could do it. You think it's the priest that was protecting your family all these years? Well, look at your priest now."

"You can't do that," Mila said in fear.

"Oh, but who will stop me? Furthermore, who will care? You think the world cares about Gypsies?" he reminded Mila. Strauss grabbed the back of Mila's hair and pulled it back hard so he could look directly at his face. "Ahhh!" Mila moaned in pain.

"Whose name was on that rubber factory? I let you and the other parasites dwell there in case some day you were of use to me."

Strauss took Mila's hand and placed the nail in it. He felt the cold metal with its smooth engravings. He stared down at the golden spike, and for the first time, he believed the words Nasta had told him. He was special, and in his hands was the proof. He knew right then it was his mission to take the nail away from here, to keep it away from Casey and these evil men. If only he could figure out how.

Aunt Nasta, I need your help now, Mila prayed. *I know you're with God now. Please ask Him to help me.*

He stood with his arms limp at his sides, not knowing what to do. He looked into Casey's eyes again, and this time he didn't see hate. Instead, she was her old innocent self, and her gaze was pleading with him.

"I can't!" Mila yelled, his words echoing across the dome.

Strauss looked over at Leichman, confused. "You're willing to let me murder your entire family?" he asked Mila.

"I love her," Mila whispered.

Casey stared back at Mila. A tear trickled down her cheek and dropped onto the marble. Weeping, she weakly whispered, "I'm sorry."

Strauss saw the affection the young teens shared and gritted his teeth with disgust. Leichman began to laugh, mocking his old friend. It made him hack and cough, but he couldn't stop laughing. *It's amazing he's still not dead from his wounds,* Mila thought.

This enraged Strauss. He took Mila's hand with the nail still in it and pushed him toward Casey, trying to force him to stab her. Two guards joined in and shoved Mila forward. He drew closer and closer to Casey, with Strauss forcing him to aim the nail at her heart. Mila resisted.

"Enough of this nonsense!" Strauss yelled. He grabbed the Luger that he had retrieved from Father Leichman and ordered the guards to release Mila, who fell to his knees. He kneeled there, looking at Casey, both of them helpless. He began to weep, for he knew that Strauss and his men were not going to stop. He felt the metal barrel of the Luger pressing against his temple.

"On the count of three, you either thrust that nail into her heart or you'll be shot!" Strauss yelled.

Mila looked at Casey once more. She whispered, "Kill me."

Strauss began to count.

"One! ... Two! ..."

Boom!

XXIX

BOMBSHELL

Morton and Deborah donned black facemasks and ran for the north tower like wild panthers locking on their prey. When they reached the moat bridge, they separated as Deborah had planned. She turned to the right, heading down a flight of steps and into the moat garden toward the outer wall of the north tower. Meanwhile, Morton crossed the bridge.

Once Morton reached the archway, he began to slowly walk through, pointing his powerful submachine gun ahead before entering the open area of the courtyard. His heart raced, for he knew he was vulnerable to anyone firing at him in the open space. Peeking through from the underpass, he saw the museum van heading toward him on its way out of the courtyard.

The driver, acting on instinct, slammed on the brakes and came to a stop right in front of Morton. The driver's eyes locked with his for a moment. He noticed the gun and put his foot on the gas, sending the van barreling forward in an attempt to run Morton over.

Pffft! Pffft! Pffft! Morton let out a burst of submachine gunfire as he dove out of the way. The rounds cut through both driver and passenger. The van veered to the right, hitting the inner section of the underpass and blocking any traffic or additional security from entering the courtyard.

Morton quickly slipped into the door to his left, fearing that he would be noticed. The door read "Employees Only." Once inside, he rapidly analyzed the place. There were offices to his left and a row of stairs to his right, and he heard guards heading down the stairs. He hid behind an ornate marble statue of a medieval nobleman and peered around to take a look at how many guards were coming. He counted four; they seemed to be escorting a hostage with a bag over his head. Though Morton couldn't figure out who it was, he could tell it wasn't one of the Americans. There was no time to worry about the captive's identity. The group advanced toward him, and he knew the statue wasn't enough cover.

To avoid detection, he slipped into an office. He glanced around to see what the layout was like. A table sat in the middle of the room covered in stacks of papers. He could hear the sound of a paper shredder coming from an alcove. *Someone's in here,* he thought.

Morton's eyes shot around the room looking for a place to hide. Too late—a tall, slender, blonde bombshell of a woman, her hair tied in a bun, emerged from the alcove. She dropped her papers and screamed, begging for Morton not to fire. *"Nicht schießen!"* she shouted.

Shit, Morton thought, ignoring the woman and aiming his submachine gun at the door.

A pair of guards entered with pistols drawn. *Pffft! Pffft! Pffft!* Morton fired, cutting down one of the guards. The other ducked back into the hallway. Morton aimed and emptied the gun's magazine at the plaster wall near the entrance, hoping he might wound the guard in the hallway. He then drew his sidearm and stepped to the wall near the door frame. He waited for the guard to come back. He peeked through to see the man's position but all he saw was the guard face down in a pool of blood.

Morton turned to the woman, who was now kneeling with her hands up. He began to interrogate her in German. He knew she would cooperate. It didn't look like she wanted to face the same fate the two guards had. Morton asked her where they were holding the young American girl. Without hesitation, she pointed toward a stairwell and directed him down a hallway.

Morton wiped the blood from his face and reloaded his submachine gun before heading down the stairs. He pressed his back against the door frame of the stairwell and pulled out a small mirror. He angled it around the corner and saw two guards down the hall guarding the doors. Looking up from the mirror, he spotted Jack coming from the opposite direction with that damn dog. *Does this kid have a death wish?* Morton wondered. If the two guards saw Jack pass, they would surely kill him. With no time to reconsider, he leapt across the corridor, firing a burst at the guards. His aim was perfect, and both dropped dead.

By then, Jack was within a few feet of the door. Morton grabbed him, causing Wolfy to bark with surprise. He pulled the boy into the stairwell and pushed him against the wall. Then Morton noticed Jack's odd choice of armament. "Why do you have a sword?" Morton demanded.

"Habit, I guess," Jack said.

They heard footsteps echoing down the stairs. *Reinforcements,* Morton thought. He pulled Jack into the cavernous stone hallway. The boy didn't resist as they rushed toward the doors. Wolfy ran straight ahead and began to scratch at the heavy wooden double doors in front of them.

"Casey's in there—Wolfy knows it," Jack said.

Jack pulled away from Morton and tried to open the doors, only to discover that they were locked. Morton took a look back at the end of the hall. A large team of guards in assault gear was heading their way.

"Did someone call for a party?" Morton said sarcastically.

He quickly removed a metal attachment from his belt and the silencer from his weapon, dropping it to the ground next to the fallen guards. He attached the metal tube to his submachine gun. Jack's eyes widened at the sight of the impressive weapon. "Is that a grenade launcher?" the boy asked.

"Yes, now get back!"

The humans pulled back to get a safe distance from the blast. Wolfy, with his supernatural instincts, also withdrew.

Well, Deborah, you did *say I could blow something up,* Morton thought. He pulled the trigger.

XXX

‚Äù‚ïê‚Äò

THE TEMPEST

R*iiiiiinng...*
The constant ringing vibration penetrating Casey's ears overtook all of her senses. There was a complete absence of any other sound.

She struggled to look around the room. At first, all she could see was a cloud of smoke and debris coming from the entrance. The acrid scent of sulfur and charred wood burned deep within her nostrils. *An explosion?* she wondered. A dull *rat-a-tat-tat* began and gradually built, overpowering the incessant ringing. Casey realized it was gunfire. She strained to see out the door, but the dust from the blast was too dense.

Squinting to protect her eyes from the dust, she saw a guard appearing from out of the haze, holding a rifle and heading straight for her. Her survival instincts returned, quick as lightning. She tried to move away from the guard, squirming back as far as her limited position would allow. She tightly closed her eyes and pushed back as hard as she could. When she opened her eyes, she only managed to get about two feet back. Fearing the certain attack from the approaching gunman, she closed her eyes in pure terror and began to scream. When no one came, she reopened her eyes. To her amazement, she saw Wolfy latch on to the guard's arm. He dropped his weapon. The dog kept his jaw clamped tightly around the gunman's arm, shaking his strong canine head from side to side and wrestling the intruder to the floor.

Casey swiftly took another look around, this time with a stronger sense of purpose. She knew Mila was somewhere in the room with her, so she scanned the area, searching for him. Before she could find him, two TNC guards came from behind, grabbed her, and dragged her across the floor away from the ruined doors.

As she uselessly struggled, she spotted Mila being pulled back by two other TNC men. He, too, was struggling with the guards, but in his weakened condition he stood no better a chance of escaping than her own. Overseeing the whole thing was the old man, Strauss. He frantically waved his hands. With her hearing still restricted she couldn't make out what he was saying, but her best guess was that he was gesturing to his guards to get them all away from the blasted doors.

Crash!

Shattered glass sprayed into the room from one of the overhead windows. *Boom! Boom!* Two more gunshots rang out in the chamber. Suddenly, she felt the guards' grip on her arms loosen and then the heavy weight of both men fell on her, crushing her. *"Oof!"* she cried.

She turned her face around to see a guard. His face was pressed against the stone floor just inches from hers. His blank eyes stared lifelessly into hers, and a trail of blood trickled from his mouth. *Is he dead?* she wondered.

Again, her terror gave her the strength she needed to keep moving. Writhing, still bound, she managed to pull herself from underneath both guards. She looked back and saw a bullet hole in the back of the other guard's head. With barely enough time to get over the shock of that sight, she turned toward the shattered window, only to find a masked figure, dressed all in black and decked out in combat gear, heading toward her. Casey tried to move away from the strange figure.

*Rat-a-tat-tat! Riiiiiinng...*was all she could hear.

The masked man fired toward Mila and the two guards struggling with him. Hit and bleeding, one of the guards immediately fell. His cowardice on full display, Strauss ducked behind the last of his TNC guards to protect himself. Mila took the opportunity to seize the barrel of the last guard's rifle, stopping him from returning fire at the black-suited figure. It took only a second for the guard to wrestle his weapon free and strike Mila on the side of his head with the butt of his rifle. Mila toppled to the ground, but before the guard could finish the deed, the masked vigilante let out a burst of fire. Bullets ran across the guard's chest with great force, pushing him back toward the wall. Strauss dropped to the ground along with his subordinate, but no one could tell if he'd been hit.

Before Casey could figure out if Strauss was shot or just faking, a masked face loomed over her, screaming, "Are you OK?"

Casey could finally hear words. *That voice sounds familiar,* she thought. *Is that—*

"Deborah, get over here now! I'm running out of ammo," a man shouted from beside the door.

Deborah pulled off her mask and ran toward the doorway. Seeing the face of her bodyguard gave Casey a sense of relief. Unfortunately, it only lasted a second. More TNC men were heading toward them from the hallway. Without enough time to even untie Casey, Deborah joined Jack and Morton outside the entrance. Deborah tossed an ammunition clip over to Morton. He reloaded, and together they opened fire on the approaching guards, holding off their advances and perhaps buying some time to escape.

She desperately looked around, trying to figure out how she could possibly get the hell out of this war zone.

She noticed an ornate knife lying on the floor next to the evil twin. "Score," she said to herself.

She started squirming toward it, but she noticed the evil priest, wounded, crawling across the floor heading toward the knife as well. She began to crawl quicker.

"Take cover!" Deborah yelled. Casey turned her attention toward the shootout in time to see Deborah throw something toward the advancing guards in the hall.

Boom!

Smoke filled the hallway and slowly wafted into the room. Casey turned back to the priest; however, there was no sign of him. He had disappeared from the room. Worse still, the knife was gone as well. Had he simply crawled out of view or escaped somehow? She noticed long trails of blood from where the priest had been slumped on the floor that led up to the stone wall.

"What the hell?" she whispered. "I needed that damn knife."

But with no time to further assess his disappearance, she began to scan the bodies around her. She saw the TNC men and the scarred thug from the train lying dead and their guns scattered about, but nothing that could cut her free. Desperate, she began to strain against her bindings, trying to pull them loose. Her captors hadn't done the best job of hog-tying her feet, and she managed to get one foot free by slipping her shoe off.

As she struggled with her other foot, she looked toward Mila. Her fear came back with full intensity at the sight of him, lying pale and motionless. To add to her horror, she noticed a pool of blood on the stone floor beneath his head.

"Mila!" she shouted. She twisted her hands, trying to get them loose. "Mila! Please wake up!" Seeing no response from him, she cried as the ropes burned her wrists.

Someone grabbed her from behind. She frantically turned, expecting another enemy, but instead saw Jack and Wolfy. The dog began licking her face as she tried to speak. *Is that a sword?* Casey thought.

"Are you—" Jack tried to ask.

"Mila!" she yelled. "Look, Jack!" She motioned her head toward their injured friend. "Help him!"

Jack dropped the sword and rushed over to Mila. Wolfy once again displayed unusual cunning by picking up the sword's hilt in his jaws and placing it in Casey's hands. With much difficulty, she managed to angle the blade against the ropes and began to work it back and forth slowly sawing through her bindings. All the while her eyes never left Jack and Mila.

Jack turned Mila over. He leaned in, listening for breathing, and then he looked back to her, his eyes filled with complete despair. Jack's reaction made her fear the worst. "Do something," she mouthed.

Jack bit his lip and returned his attention to Mila. He placed his fingers on his neck, checking for a pulse.

"I can't read a pulse, and he's not breathing!" Jack shouted.

He hunched over Mila and placed his hands in the center of his chest. He pushed down over and over, compressing Mila's chest, trying to get air into his lungs. Casey kept her eyes fixed on them as she kept working on cutting the ropes, praying for Jack to get a breath out of Mila.

"Cover me while I reload!" Deborah shouted from the doorway.

Casey turned her head to see what was happening at the door. Deborah ducked back behind the doorframe and pulled out a fresh magazine. Her friend leaned in to shoot, only to be struck in the chest with a shotgun blast, dropping him to the floor.

"*Morton!*" Deborah yelled as she grabbed him and dragged him out of the line of fire. She put one hand on his gaping wound, and with the other she began to fire down the hallway, fearless and enraged. Her livid state made her enemies back away for a few more precious seconds. Soon after, her weapon's magazine emptied, and she grabbed Morton's submachine gun, refusing to stop shooting. At that moment, Casey realized that time was running short.

"Come back, man! Please..." Jack begged.

The sincere pleading brought Casey's fears to reality. *He's gone*, she thought. *He's really gone* …

With no hope, and acting on pure desperation, Jack started to administer a few breaths by mouth. It was becoming clearer even to Jack that Mila was gone. Distraught, he resorted to slapping him across the face, trying to force some life back into him. Or maybe he was just angry with him for dying. Tired and saddened, he stopped slapping him.

"You can't die! You just can't…I know who you are now!" Jack confessed. He started pounding Mila's chest with more vigor than humanly possible. *"You're Garade!"* he announced.

With that word and the force of Jack's drive, a slight cough choked up from Mila's mouth. Casey and Jack both stared at him for a moment in utter disbelief.

"He's back!" Jack yelled to Casey. Their cumulative fear was lifted with those words.

Bang!

Casey's moment of jubilation was shattered as Wolfy fell dead in front of her.

"No!" she yelled.

She turned to see where the bullet had come from. Somehow, she knew who it was. To her complete horror she saw the evil old man Strauss standing over her, holding the smoking gun that just killed her loyal friend.

He aimed his gun at her, moving in closer, but then he kneeled to pick up something on the ground. Her gaze followed the man's arm down to what he was reaching for. It was the nail, lying just a few feet away.

No, she thought. *It's mine.*

In a show of sudden and unexplained strength, Casey strained against her bindings and burst the frayed ropes that held her hands. She leapt to her feet and rushing to grab the nail before Strauss's bony, wrinkly fingers could reach it, forgetting that her foot was still tangled in the line. As she tripped, she reached out for anything to steady her. Her hand seized a painting sitting on an easel, but she only succeeded in pulling it down with her. She glanced up to find the precious relic was now in Strauss's tight grip. She stared directly at him with fury, as he raised his hand taking aim at her head.

From the corner of her eye she caught a glimpse of the painting's image. She realized it was the nail that the queen was holding, not a scepter, as everyone believed. A closer glance of the shaft revealed an inscription.

"Tempestatis."

Once Casey comprehended the inscription, the text slowly scorched away leaving an ashen blot on the painting. She focused with razor-sharp intensity on Strauss as he held her nail. Her blood began to boil. An eerie howling sound started to build. A cold wind blew in through the shattered window, putting out the remaining torches that somehow refused to blow out before.

Strauss froze at the sight of this. He looked up in fear toward the windows. The room grew dark as storm clouds built outside. Suddenly, the room began to violently shake, setting off two separate cracks from the outer wall. The first fracture spread up toward the domed ceiling and landed in the center of the dome, breaking one of the chains that was attached to the stone cover plate. The disk began to wobble as it dangled from the ceiling. Soon after, the other crack finished its trail up to the top of the entire castle. The castle's fire alarms went off. Flashing lights shined and alarms wailed throughout the fortress.

The advancing guards forgot their task and looked around at the unnatural change in weather that had had such a dangerous impact on the ancient structure. Deborah took the opportunity to drag Morton further into the room, toward Casey and the others.

Suddenly, all of the windows blew in as hurricane-force winds and thunder ripped through the room, snapping the remaining chains holding the stone plate and sending it crashing down. It landed directly between Casey and Strauss, nearly hitting them both. In panic, Strauss leapt backwards. He fell hard on the stone floor causing him to drop the nail, which the wind swept even further from his grasp.

Some of the guards in the hall outside the chamber room ducked or took cover in whatever room they could find. A few made the mistake of advancing into the room, only to be thrown to the ground by another gust of wind, and alongside Strauss.

Casey instinctively realized this was the nail at work. It was responding to whatever she had read in that text, to her desire for destruction, and she dreaded that the doom was just beginning. But what was worse was that she did not believe that she could control it. The wind howled stronger. Gale-force gusts made it impossible to even stand, let alone hold a weapon. All she could feel was power, power rising within her.

Outside, storm clouds swirled about, turning into funnel shapes. The twisting wind that emerged headed toward the tower. As the swirling winds entered through the cracks and the broken windows, she began to feel herself rise up in midair, with the wind giving her lift, obeying her anger. She hovered upright a few feet off the ground as if gravity had no meaning. Her eyes then focused on the nail. It also began to levitate.

The structure groaned as more cracks expanded all over the hall. The chains that had held the seal before began to whip around dangerously.

Casey looked across the room to Jack and Mila. Jack was covering Mila and looked over at her, frightened. She stared deep into Jack's eyes. Her rage was too great to even get any words out. He stared back. Intuitively, she desperately tried to tell him, "Hold on, or get out of the way. I can't control this."

Jack seemed to get the message, in spite of the fact that she hadn't said a word. Straining against the wind, he made his way toward the center seal, dragging Mila along with him. He grabbed on to one of the chains and wrapped it around both of them. The force grew stronger as Jack waved to get Deborah's attention. "Hold on to something!" he shouted over the wind.

"What?" Deborah screamed back.

"Trust me! Grab hold of something *now!*" Jack yelled back, as if he knew what was about to take place.

The seal began to move, the wind slowly lifting it into the air as if it were a plastic frisbee. Still floating, Casey stepped onto the seal, letting it carry her higher. All the while, Jack clung desperately to Mila, tightening his grip on the chain. Deborah dragged Morton into the hallway and tucked him behind the door frame. She then clutched her fingers into an air vent on the floor, hoping it would be strong enough for whatever was about to come.

Casey looked up at the ceiling, focusing her attention on the swastika. The entire structure shook, and even more cracks expanded through the four sides of the design. The roof was torn clean off, along with half of the tower. Everyone watched in horror as the brick that was once the tower crumbled and lifted into the air, only to come crashing down into the moat. Chunks of stone and debris were tossed about in the storm. The wind whipped *The Proclamation* into the air and tore it to shreds.

Meanwhile, Casey rose higher into the air. She looked at the torn-up structure that was the east wing of the castle. Then she focused her attention on the remaining guards that were hiding in the hallway, holding on to anything secured. As Casey reflected on this, a tornado wind ripped through the wing, finding each guard and swallowing the men up one by one. This brought a smirk to her face.

She turned back to Strauss, who was tightly gripping one of the wall sconces that held the torches. The immense wind elevated him, and it was clear that the sconce would not hold out for long. He struggled in the forceful wind, raised his pistol, and opened fire. Round after round flew toward Casey, but a tempest swirled around her, deflecting each one.

Frustrated, Strauss tossed his weapon away and tried to run toward the floating nail. Fighting the wind, he snatched the nail and leapt toward Casey. The wind carried him upward and he ended up grasping the edge of the seal, hanging from it for dear life.

Casey reached down and grabbed the man's wrist. She easily lifted him into the air, as if he weighed nothing at all. She glared into his eyes for a moment with evil glee as they hovered three stories off the ground.

"It's mine!" Strauss shouted.

"You're wrong," she said, not knowing where those words came from.

She squeezed his wrist until she heard a cracking sound. Strauss cried in pain and opened his fist, releasing the nail. It hovered there as Casey held Strauss a moment, watching him squirm. His every pained expression only heightened her pleasure. Then she let go and he plummeted down, landing in the gilded tomb with a sickening *crunch!* Casey wasn't sure if his legs or back were broken, and she didn't much care.

She stared at the nail as it hovered in front of her. Then she quickly glanced downward, showing the nail where to go. The scepter turned until its point faced down, and then it shot toward Strauss, burying itself in his heart.

That was when she heard a voice calling to her over the din. "Casey! No more, please!" someone cried.

She looked down and saw Jack. The wind was so strong he was blown almost horizontal. He began to slide down the length of the chain, his grip on Mila growing ever weaker.

No, Casey thought. *I don't want this.* She grabbed her head with both hands.

"Stoooooop!" she cried, tightly squeezing her eyes closed.

Everything started to calm. The winds died down. Casey could feel the stone seal slowly lower itself as she stood atop it. It settled over the tomb, sealing it closed.

She fell to the floor, dropping to her knees on the swastika seal. Afraid to open her eyes, she began to tremble as she realized what had just taken place—or worse, what she had done. Then she heard a coughing sound. She opened her eyes and saw Jack kneeling next to Mila. He coughed again and his eyes shot open. He gasped for air, taking a few labored breaths. After a moment, he settled down, breathing normally and fully awake. *They're OK,* she thought as she fought back tears.

"Are you OK?" Jack asked.

"What happened?" Mila asked as he looked around at the crumbling, ruined castle.

Casey began to tremble again. Jack threw his arms around her, holding her tight.

"I killed those people. I killed them all," Casey whispered.

"You saved us, Casey," Jack said.

"If you did all this…" Mila said, "then you just saved me…and all my family in Romania, too."

She looked over at Mila, knowing he might be right. Just then, something seemed off. Mila was blurry, out of focus. At first, she thought it was dust or debris, but the air seemed clear.

"Mila, I can't see you," she said.

"Huh?" he replied.

Deborah emerged from behind the door frame, which had survived the disaster thanks to its sturdy construction. She came over and started to examine Casey.

"Deborah, I can't see," she said, seemingly relieved by this fact.

"OK, Casey, we'll get your glasses, but we have to get out of here. This structure is coming down."

"No, you don't understand!" Casey shouted. She then looked to the boys. "I need my glasses!" she repeated, beaming.

"The chamber is sealed with the nail inside," Mila said. "It's over."

"You need your glasses," Jack stated, happy as can be.

"I do," Casey said, just as joyfully. "Let's go home."

XXXI

CHILD OF MENGELE

"Professor Hermann, we need to evacuate the castle," a young secretary said on her way out of the building.

"All in good time," he replied.

The professor carefully placed the helmet back on the suit of armor that he'd wriggled out from underneath just minutes ago.

"There, all better. We will soon retrieve your sword, my old friend," he said to the armor as if it were a real person. He then turned to face the secretary. "You go on ahead, and please pull the fire alarm on your way out," he calmly suggested.

The young woman feared for her own safety, but she paused for a bit to study the professor's face. She was obviously puzzled as to why he was troubled about an old suit of armor and not the apparent danger at hand. She shrugged and hastened to one of the exits. The chaos that was taking place was very clear to the staff of the museum; the castle had suffered severe damage from some sort of earth tremor or explosion. A few staff members claimed some sort of terrorist attack was taking place in the chamber room.

Hermann stepped back from the ornate, regal armor and took a moment to admire its mesmerizing brilliance. Unfortunately, he was pulled out of his mediations by the sound of that horrid alarm and emergency lights.

As he looked around the beautifully restored room, he began to fear that it might all come crashing down. *Father Leichman has it all under control,* he thought desperately, trying to convince himself. *Every time I've ever doubted him, he's proved me wrong.*

Hermann thought back to when Leichman first promised him that he would be the curator of Wewelsburg Castle. He had doubted that promise. However, to his surprise, the gracious leader had pulled it off. All Hermann had to do in return was help reconstruct the chamber room and secret passages to Leichman's exact instructions. And with that comforting thought, his fears began to subside and he felt reassured that somehow his master would save his beloved fortress.

"He will save my castle," Hermann whispered, still trying to convince himself.

He turned from the suit of armor, exited the banquet room, and headed toward the main entrance. As he began to walk through the hall, he realized that the structure was breaking apart. Cracks appeared in the plaster walls, and stones and wooden beams came loose from the ceiling. He started to walk faster, trying to avoid the falling debris that was turning the historical site into a dangerous maze. He could hear violent winds howling just outside the stone walls.

As he reached the main hall, a large chunk of stone, seemingly from the dome of the ritual room, came crashing into the main foyer, leaving a gigantic gaping hole where the ceiling once stood. Gale-force winds swept in through the gap, knocking Hermann off his feet. He struggled to get out through the force of the maelstrom as it sent debris flying about the room. He slowly began to realize that there was little chance left of saving the castle.

Pushing himself through the strange wind, he emerged into the courtyard. He found some of the workers trying to remove a museum van, which blocked the moat bridge. As the workers pushed with all their might, Hermann slowly turned around to see his beloved castle in ruins.

"*No!*" he shouted in horror.

He looked back as the last of the staff pushed the truck through the archway. They ran over the bridge to the parking lot for safety. Hermann looked up at the north tower, holding his left hand over his mouth to avoid inhaling the clouds of dust kicked up by the mystical weather. He saw that a huge part of the structure had blown away. His thoughts drifted to the priest, for he knew he was in the chamber room, and with that realization, the wind suddenly stopped as if someone ordered it to do so. Before he had time to assess the damage, he heard a familiar voice calling him in the distance.

Could that be? he thought.

He turned toward the sound, and his eyes fell on a metal grate. Any layman would think the grate was little more than a storm drain, but Hermann knew better. He bent down to the grate and listened.

"Come, my son. I am wounded!" the voice cried.

"No!" Hermann cried.

There was no mistaking it. Father Leichman was down there. The professor tore the grate free. Sure enough, Father Leichman lay in the escape tunnel below. He must have crawled all the way from the ritual room. Hermann reached down and frantically pulled the priest out of the hole.

"Solomon..." Father Leichman gasped.

Hermann leaned in close, tears in his eyes. He supported the priest's head, cradling it in his hand. "You're alive!" he cried. "Thank the Beautiful One. Don't move. Please save your strength."

"I told you this passage would come in handy," Father Leichman said. He raised a feeble, trembling hand and placed it on Hermann's cheek. "You were always so loyal," he said. "Mengele was wise to have bred you. He knew you'd serve us well."

Hermann put his hand on Father Leichman's and looked lovingly into his eyes as tears ran down his cheeks. Despite the fact that Hermann was a grown man, he still felt like a small child whenever the father was in his presence. The priest has been the closest thing he'd ever had to a real father. He loved the priest immensely; after all, he'd kept him safe from exposure. If his true identity had ever come out, the entire planet would scrutinize his life forever. The father protected him from that horrible existence.

All these years, no one had ever found out that Professor Solomon Hermann was in fact one of Dr. Mengele's last experiments. Mengele was known for performing unspeakably horrific experiments on prisoners at Auschwitz. That was how he earned his nickname, Doctor Death. What no one knew was that among his most twisted projects was personally fathering a child with an unwilling *Garade* woman. The priest kept Solomon's birth at the concentration camp a secret. The generous man had even found him an Austrian family to raise him and provide for his expensive education.

Having the power to keep such a secret from the entire world was nothing short of a miracle.

"I'm going to get you out of here," Hermann said. "I'm going to save you!"

"Yes, Solomon, yes, you are," Father Leichman agreed in a strange tone.

He suddenly drove his knife into Hermann's neck. Blood poured from the wound, staining his suit. Confused and in shock, the professor began to shake and convulse.

"Shhhh ... shhh ..." Father Leichman said. "This is necessary. Garade blood is the most powerful medicine of all, even if it's only half Garade."

The professor began to feel disoriented and collapsed onto the ground, weakened to the point of paralysis. He saw Father Leichman place his mouth to his throat. Unable to move, he watched in horror as his beloved priest took away his life. He felt his blood rush out of his veins; he heard his heart beat louder and louder as it slowed until the very last thump.

XXXII

～✲～

THE ÜBERMENSCHE

Things were still a little fuzzy for Mila. The warm light of the sun streamed in through the missing half of the north tower. The blue skies and the sound of chirping birds were in stark contrast to the crumbling stone around them.

"We need to get out of here," Deborah insisted as she ran toward Morton, who lay on the floor, barely conscious. "Jack, get over here," she demanded.

Jack rushed over. He and Deborah stood on either side of Morton, placed their arms around him, and heaved him onto his feet. Casey took a hold of Mila. Pain once again shot through his ribs as they climbed to their feet.

They all made their way out of the crumbling chamber room and headed down the southeast corridor toward the main exit. They did their best to ignore the dead guards scattered about the halls.

As they made their way to the entrance hall, they couldn't help but notice the pure devastation the historic structure had suffered. The plaster walls were cracking, and dust covered the floors. Ornate statues were tipped over and broken. Even the grand staircase was battered and covered in chunks of stone.

Mila was badly hurt, but Morton was almost lifeless. His feet began to drag on the floor as Jack and Deborah struggled to move him forward.

"Put me down," Morton asked in a feeble plea.

Deborah ignored him, pushing forward toward the exit.

"Please, Deborah, I'm not going to make it out," he insisted.

Deborah kneeled down and placed Morton on the marble floor next to the regal staircase. Sad, but refusing to shed a tear, she obeyed the order. Casey didn't recognize the man, but he clearly meant something to Deborah.

"We met him in Paderborn. He was her partner or something," Mila whispered to Casey.

"We'll get you out. Just a few more steps," Deborah said to Morton.

With his last bit of strength, he reached into one of his cargo pockets and retrieved a small black device and handed it over to Deborah. She gently took it from his bloody hand and opened the black casing, revealing a small keypad and screen.

"Send a message home," Morton said. "Let them know we pulled it off after all these years."

The unusual request left the teens puzzled, but Deborah seemed to understand. Morton lovingly looked over to Deborah, trying to reassure her, and then he gently nodded his head.

She typed out a short message. It simply read: "Victor Strauss is dead. Agent 999 is KIA."

She held it out for Morton to see. He nodded with approval. "Send it," he said.

Deborah stared into Morton's eyes, her sorrow beginning to show through her stern expression.

"It's OK," Morton whispered with a weak smile. "Mission accomplished."

And there, on the base of the opulent staircase, in the once regal hall of Wewelsburg Castle, the loyal secret agent of the Mossad took his last breath. A single tear dropped from Deborah's cheek onto his lifeless body.

"Oh God, Deborah, I'm so sorry," Jack said. "He was your partner, wasn't he?"

"More than that..." Deborah whispered.

"You should not tear up, my dear. You'll be joining him soon," a sinister voice said.

A man walked through the main doors toward them. He had a pale handsome face, framed by golden blond hair, but his blue eyes were as cold as ice. The black Nazi chaplain's uniform gave him a ghostly appearance.

"My dream..." Casey whispered. "It's t-t-he soldier from my d-dream. H-He was beating the m-man in t-the square..." she said in a frenzied stutter.

As the man approached, Casey glanced at Deborah and saw the same look of recognition. "This is impossible," Deborah whispered.

"Who the hell are you?" Mila demanded.

The young man's face split into an evil grin.

"Really, Mila, you don't recognize the man who baptized you?" he asked.

Mila noticed the series of burn scars along the stranger's right hand. "Father..." he whispered in despair.

"Very good," Father Leichman said.

"How's this possible?" Casey asked.

"The chamber, of course," Father Leichman said. "I knew it worked when we sealed you in there. If only I'd gotten some blood before Victor interfered, we could have avoided this whole mess. No matter. Now I have the power of vigor, youth, strength, immortality—it's all mine."

Deborah stood up and stepped forward, blocking the path between her and the teens. Leichman didn't slow his advance. When he got near, she attempted to grab him, using one of her many well-trained maneuvers, but with one swift move he deflected her and threw her across the hallway, sending her crashing into a mural-painted wall. Deborah writhed on the ground, dizzy, with the wind knocked out of her. This struck fear deep into Casey's heart. She'd never seen anyone yet who could defeat Deborah in a fight, let alone someone who could throw her around like a rag doll.

The teens all started to take steps back up the collapsing staircase. Leichman turned toward them and took a step in their direction. "This is just the beginning," he declared. "I'll have all the powers soon."

With no hope of fighting, they fled all the way up to the top. Father Leichman followed at a relaxed, confident pace.

They arrived at the top of the stairs, only to find the upstairs hallway blocked by a collapsed ceiling, leaving them trapped. With nowhere to turn, both Mila and Jack blocked Casey like two guards protecting their queen.

"We don't have it anymore!" Jack yelled. "You're wasting your time."

"I know that, you foolish boy," Leichman said. "I'll retrieve the nail from the crypt—once she's dead, that is."

Acting on pure rage, Jack jumped from the top of the stairs and on top of Leichman, sending them both tumbling down the stairway. Casey and Mila ran down after them, neither having a better plan than Jack's desperate attack.

Holding on to each other, Jack and Leichman reached the bottom, slamming onto the marble floor. The rejuvenated priest easily pinned Jack down. Casey and Mila looked on in horror as he opened his mouth to reveal a row of razor-sharp teeth like those of a shark.

"I think you will make a fine soldier of darkness," Leichman seductively whispered in Jack's ear.

Jack struggled, fearing he had no chance of escape. He then closed his eyes and shouted the only thing that came to his lips. *"Jesus!"* Jack called.

Wham!

Everyone looked up to see Leichman clutching the back of his head. Behind him stood an old gardener with a shovel in his hand. The priest spun around, leaving Jack lying flat on the cold marble. He jumped up and seized the groundskeeper by the throat, staring deep into his eyes. The gardener dropped his key ring while he was lifted into the air.

Suddenly, there was a flutter of wings. As if in a dream, a white bird swooped into the room, retrieving the keys from the floor. The pigeon carried the keys toward Mila and dropped them at his feet.

The old man, almost out of breath, pointed to the key ring as the life was being squeezed out of him. Mila looked at the key ring, which had a very odd piece of decaying wood attached to it. Instantly, he knew this was the weapon that had appeared in his dream days earlier. It looked like a spike of some sort, about four inches long. But Mila saw more than just an old piece of wood; he saw purpose. He picked it up and held it like a switchblade. Casey watched as he fearlessly approached Leichman from behind, gripping the piece of wood tightly with his hand.

The priest let go of the old man, and he fell limp onto the floor. No one was sure if he was alive or dead.

Mila lunged forward, driving the dagger into Leichman's back and then pulling it out. Leichman howled in pain as if he'd been scalded with a hot iron. He turned to face Mila, grimacing in agony, and they both stared each other down for what felt like an eternity.

Mila felt powerful. For those few brief seconds, all the pain from his wounds mysteriously disappeared. He looked deep within Leichman's eyes with great intensity and no fear, and there within those pale-blue eyes he saw his ancestors before him, killing dark soldiers throughout history. The spilling of evil blood throughout the centuries went through him within mere seconds. Among the countless wicked people, he saw Hitler's terrified face in the bunker, a mustachioed warrior on horseback impaled with a spear, and an old man in a white tunic dying in a marble room. In that moment, it all became clear to him. He knew now that the person before him was pure evil. As he looked down at the wooden stake, he saw the wooden cross that held Jesus.

Instantly, he snapped out of his vision. Leichman stared back at Mila in desperation and fear, as if he had just met his judge and jury. Mila then took one step toward him with no apprehension.

"Forgive..." the priest pleaded in fear.

"This is for Korey," Mila replied, and he drove the wooden stake into Leichman's heart.

The priest gasped and went stiff as a board. Then he dropped to the ground, limp and lifeless.

Mila stared down at his former teacher like a hunter that had killed its prey. Casey and Jack watched in horror as Leichman's young body morphed, returning to its old, fragile state. Casey pressed against Jack's chest to cover her eyes from the horrid site.

Jack and Mila looked at each other. Jack, not knowing what to say, again uttered the first thing that came to his lips.

"It *is* you," Jack said. "You're the guardian."

The words felt right deep inside Mila. He heard those same words again. But this time they came from the gardener who was dying on floor. "G-guardian," he called.

Mila rushed over to the brave old man. Casey, Jack, and Deborah joined him. The man clutched Mila's hand. Blood dripped from his mouth. It was clear that he did not have long. He tried to speak again, but all he could manage was pitiful coughing.

"You need first aid," Deborah said.

But the old man waved his hand in refusal, struggling to get the words out. Finally, he managed to say, "Sa-sa-save me, Guardian."

"How?" Mila asked.

"Forgive me," he requested.

Mila wiped the dripping blood from the old man's cheeks and, without knowing where the words were coming from, he answered, "You are forgiven, Paul Stoker."

A single tear of joy fell from the man's eyes. Somehow Mila knew who this man was. It must have been the intuition Nasta had always spoken of. This was Paul Stoker, the man who had kept the paintings hidden from Strauss and Leichman. He had been at the castle all along, waiting for the guardian to release him.

Stoker then glanced at Casey and became afraid. He grabbed Mila even tighter. "Evil!" he shouted. "It's here."

"Be calm," Mila said. "You can go in peace. It's over. The nail is guarded," he assured him.

Stoker calmed at Mila's words and gently smiled at him, but pulled him closer so he could whisper into Mila's ear. "You must seek out the dead undead," Stoker whispered.

The words made no sense to him. But he knew the man was dying, so Mila nodded in agreement. And then Stoker closed his eyes as sirens began to wail in the distance.

Deborah checked for a pulse, then said, "He's gone."

"What did he say to you?" Casey asked Mila.

"Nothing that made sense," Mila answered.

"You better get out of here, Mila," Jack urged him. "The police will be here soon."

Mila paused, then looked at Deborah and Casey.

"Go on, get out of here," Deborah said. "They'll be fine. Casey's uncle is a powerful man. He'll be here soon to help."

Jack handed the keys from Sabina's car to Mila. "It's out back. Sabina is at the Paderborn hospital."

Mila turned and began to make his way out of the castle. Just as he was about to step out of the gaping hole in the wall that revealed the vigorous sunlight, Casey shouted to him, "Mila!"

Mila turned back. At first, he could not see her, for the glare of the sun was in his eyes. Squinting through the light, he spotted her blue eyes. He knew she was struggling to find the right words to say. He felt it deep within his soul.

"I'm sorry," she said.

He responded with a simple, "Me, too." Then he escaped from the crumbling castle.

EPILOGUE

The smog's not so bad up close, Mila thought as he surveyed the rubber factory. *I guess it used to just come straight up and then land on us.*

He sat in the driver's seat of Sabina's BMW. It was just before the break of dawn. The top was down, and he stared into the golden sky. He'd been parked right across the small road that entered the back gate of the factory all night, waiting for sunrise. It had been weeks since the events at the castle. From his hideout in Berlin, he kept tabs on what happened to Casey and Jack through the news headlines. The official word was that John Winthorp, chief financial officer of Christina Richards Inc., had graciously offered to fund the reconstruction of Wewelsburg Castle, which was devastated earlier that month by what meteorologists were calling a freak tornado. Winthorp had also made major contributions to the German Art Society. There were unsubstantiated rumors that two American teenagers were held in connection with the unexplained catastrophe at the castle but were later released.

Mila's own escape from Paderborn had been more difficult. He had to talk the doctors into letting Sabina out of the hospital early; he was honestly amazed when they released her. Once she was out, they bartered with the baker below Sabina's ruined apartment for some fast cash, agreeing to give her all the insurance money Sabina had coming, plus the deed to her burned-down flat. Then they headed to Berlin. The plan was to travel on to Romania to meet up with the rest of the family. But, before that, Mila had two things to take care of.

First, he tracked down his classic bike. Sure enough, it was for sale at Ludwig's shop. Second, he had to find Petre, Stephan, Rosa, and of course, Simon. When he received no information from the police or immigration, he realized that the authorities had never taken them in. Mila knew that Simon had been caught by some of Strauss's thugs and interrogated—how else would they have found them on the train so quickly? Realizing this, Mila's intuition told him there was only one place those neo-Nazi goons would have taken him: the rubber factory. And perhaps Petre, Stephan, and Rosa would be there.

He waited until just before the sunrise and headed to the back gate. He reached into the pocket of his black motorcycle jacket, a new acquisition thanks to the baker's cash advance. Mila usually wasn't a sucker for flash, but when Sabina saw this black leather jacket with red accents, she insisted "it's a magician's jacket!" He pulled out his favorite toy, the lock pick concealed within his keychain, and jimmied the lock with ease. Once on the other side, he walked right through the yard unnoticed. The back door was just a few feet away from him when he noticed the security keypad to enter the building.

Mila stared at the pad a moment, hesitating. *This code better be legit, or I'm screwed,* he thought. He'd obtained the pass code by bribing a factory worker at Schmidt's, using money he picked from the worker's own pocket. *That doesn't really count as stealing,* he rationalized.

He punched in the numbers—two, five, eight, zero, four, five, six—which formed the sign of the holy cross on the keypad. The lights blinked for a moment as the old system processed the code. Mila held his breath, then exhaled with relief as the electronic locks clicked open.

He knew from the worker that the factory had a security room, complete with a holding cell. The man also insisted they only kept one person on guard at night. Mila stepped into a hallway and came to a four-way intersection.

He closed his eyes, breathed deep, and let his instincts show him the way. Turning slowly to his right, he opened his eyes in time to see the guard stepping into a restroom, completely oblivious to his presence.

Perfect, Mila thought.

He slipped down the hallway and turned in the direction the guard had come from. It took him no time to find the security room. Inside, he found Simon sitting slumped in his holding cell.

The mischievous pickpocket leapt to his feet when he spotted Mila.

"*Bre*, what are you doing here?" Simon exclaimed.

"Getting you out! Where's Stephan and Rosa? They with you?"

"No, Petre and them got away when they caught me."

Where could they be? Mila wondered. Returning to the task at hand, he took hold of the gate.

"It's locked. The guard's got the key," Simon said.

"Please," Mila boasted as he drew out his multi-tool and opened its set of lock picks once again.

Wasting no time, Mila broke the cheap security lock, and Simon was free. "Come on, he'll be back any minute," Mila said as he led Simon out.

They headed back the way Mila had come from, but Simon stopped him. "This way's quicker," he said as he threw open the cafeteria door.

They hurried past the rows of tables and chairs into the kitchen. "There," Simon said, pointing to a door at the far side.

Just when freedom was within reach, they came face to face with a second guard as he emerged from the kitchen's walk-in pantry, with his arms loaded with snacks. *Damn it,* Mila thought, *the guy at Schmidt's must not have known what he was talking about.*

The guard dropped his food and reached for his baton. Mila prepared to run, but Simon had a different idea. He seized a butcher knife from a nearby table and swung it like a sword at the guard's head.

The man tried to dodge, but the blow sliced off the top of his ear. The guard dropped his weapon and crumpled to the ground, clutching his head and screaming in pain.

Mila seized Simon's wrist as he prepared to take another swing. He calmly pushed Simon aside and reached out toward the man. As he touched the wound, he felt a faint warmth in his fingertips. When he pulled his hand away, the injury was gone, the ear healed as if it had never been cut.

The guard put a hand up and gingerly felt the side of his own face, confused and stunned. Mila was no less shocked.

"What'd you do?" Simon demanded.

"I don't know!" Mila replied.

The voice of another guard shouted from the cafeteria, *"Halt!"*

Mila and Simon sprinted out of the factory. They hopped into Sabina's "BROOM STICK" before speeding away. Simon let out a sigh of relief as they raced down the highway. "What the hell just happened?" he shouted over the roar of the rushing wind.

"*Drabarimos,*" Mila replied. "Magic."

They rode for a moment, not speaking, listening to the sounds of the road. It didn't take long for Simon to realize where they were headed.

"I don't think we can stay in Berlin for long," Simon said.

"We won't. We're going to Romania. I've just gotta get a few things."

"*Yoi, dalé!* The hell if I'm going back to Romania!" Simon exclaimed. He continued his rant all the way down the road. "We could go to Italy! Or how about America? You speak good English. Or Austria! Beautiful mountains in Austria." He went on and on, suggesting every place they could go other than Romania.

Ignoring him, Mila pulled to a stop outside Ludwig's barter and junk shop. He parked the car and got out. "Did Stephan tell you where they were headed?" he asked Simon.

"No, they escaped while Strauss's thugs were interrogating me. I'm sorry, Mila."

"Stay here," Mila said. "Don't make any more trouble."

Mila headed into the shop as Simon yelled after him, "Hey, where you goin'?"

"Just gotta pick something up."

The door chimed as he stepped in. Ludwig sat behind the counter. He was reading a *Whistleblower* comic, not bothering to look up and see who had walked in.

"Can I help you?" he asked, never lifting his eyes from the comic.

"*Whistleblower*, huh? I didn't think you were the type," Mila said to the wheeler and dealer.

Ludwig looked up to see who was talking, surprised to see Mila. "Apparently, it's all the rage," he responded in shock. "Fancy seeing you here."

"Not really," Mila said. "You didn't think I'd come back for my property?"

"You see, that's the thing Mila, it's no longer your property."

"I'm sure we could come to some kind of arrangement," Mila said, approaching the greedy shop owner.

"I don't know about that. I kind of like the bike, and I had to add a few more details. You know, cost me a lot of money," Ludwig said sarcastically. "But I might part with it for a thousand. It's a classic, you know."

"It is classic. You gotta love classics," Mila said as he reached the counter. "Speaking of old things, you've been wheeling and dealing with Roma people for what, 20 years now?" Mila said, staring into Ludwig's eyes.

"Something like that. They're good negotiators, but not better than me," Ludwig replied with a smirk.

"That's true. You're the best. Let me ask you, though, in all that time did any of the Roma you dealt with carry any mystical gifts?" Mila asked.

"What, like a Gypsy spell? I don't believe in that crap," Ludwig said. "Look—one thousand, or get out!"

"I would, but the thing is, I'd hate to tell Officer Belz about all the stolen goods you get from the trucks that come from Romania," Mila said while staring into Ludwig's eyes.

"Wait, how do you know about that?" Ludwig asked, confused and a bit startled.

"Or I'd hate to have to tell your wife about the pretty blonde bartender you play around with when she is at home with the kids," Mila went on.

"Now hold on a minute, Mila!" Ludwig yelled.

"What's her name?" Mila asked as he gazed into the sky, conjuring Aunt Nasta. "Suzan, but you call her lemon drop. Pretty corny if you ask me."

"OK, OK. I don't know what you're doing or how you know this, but I think 200 is fair, and we keep all this to ourselves. What do you say, Mila? Friends?"

Mila put his hand in his pocket and pulled out a wad of euros. He placed 100 euros on the counter. on top of the *Whistleblower* comic, then slid it over. "I think this will be enough," he said. "You know, since we're friends."

Ludwig grabbed the notes, placed them in his pocket, then pulled out the motorbike's keychain. "It's out back," he said.

Mila grabbed his keychain and strode out the door.

As he headed out, he noticed a white pigeon outside, perched on the windowsill, looking in. It nodded its head, as if gesturing to something.

Mila looked down and saw a shelf full of newspapers by the door. His eyes were drawn to a stack of *The Times of Berlin*. He skimmed the headlines and spotted the words "Record-Breaking Sale: *The Dead Undead* Sold at Auction."

Mila picked up the newspaper and began to read.

"At Sotheby's Auction House today in London, John Winthorp, recently returned from Berlin, won the bidding on a rare draft of *The Dead Undead*. This unique manuscript of an early version of Bram Stoker's *Dracula* was only recently discovered in a literary archive and may be the earliest draft still in existence ..."

Mila skimmed down to a picture with the caption, "John Winthorp, husband to the late Zoe Richards, and his niece Casey Richards, heir to the Christina Richards estate." The photo showed a well-kempt middle-aged man in a stylish, white linen shirt, with a neatly trimmed beard, gelled black hair, and an unnaturally tan complexion. He held an auction paddle and receipt high in the air, obviously boasting. Next to him stood Casey, looking like she didn't really want to be there. In the corner of the photo, far in the background, Mila could just barely make out the lupine face of a German Shepherd.

Mila's stomach began to churn. A feeling came over him that he'd never experienced before. It could best be described as fear mixed with purpose. He stepped outside and secured the motorcycle's kickstand before hopping on and riding over to Simon.

"I got it! We'll go to France! *L'argent, s'il vous plaît?*" Simon whined.

Mila smiled. "How about London?"

THE END

CPSIA information can be obtained
at www.ICGtesting.com
Printed in the USA
BVHW082034091022
648875BV00003B/11